Ascend

THE BLAZE LEGACY
BOOK THREE

L.R. FRIEDMAN

Ascend

ISBN 979-8-9862079-5-7

Edited by The Editor & The Quill

Cover Design by Etheric Tales

Author's Note

The Blaze Legacy is an NA/Adult Dark Portal Romantasy that is full of magic, mythical creatures, delicious tension, and spice that builds through the series. It contains some explicit content best suited for readers over the age of 18.

For a list of content warnings, visit the back of the book.

To the broken ones fighting each day to become unbreakable—this is for you.

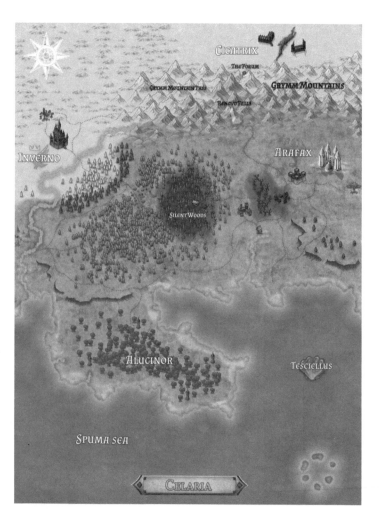

Prologue

DRU, AGE 5

"I heard she's beautiful and can grant wishes!"

My sister Fiona jumped on my bed, raven ringlets bouncing along with her. Brown eyes sparkling, she sprang toward me, gripping around my neck in a rough hug.

"Well, I heard she only casts spells on children and prefers little boys!" Imogen called over from the top bunk.

Fiona leapt off my bed, twirling around herself. I pulled the blanket up to my chin, clutching it, shivering against its warmth.

Imogen rolled over, putting her book down and lowering her tone, whispering across the room to us. "That's how she stays so pretty and young. She's actually hundreds of years old and has warts all over her face!"

"Ew!" Fiona screeched.

Our sister Enyd sat cross-legged on the bottom bunk, gaze stuck in her book. "That's gross, Gen."

"I wonder if it's true her wings can steal away your soul?" Imogen continued, laying back down in her bed and staring up at the ceiling.

Enyd's eyes shot up from behind her glasses to the top bunk, as if she could see her twin through the mattress. "That's not possible."

Our two older sisters were always fighting, total opposites in how they looked and acted. Imogen's cropped curls framed her face, while Enyd's straight hair fell down to her waist. Imogen loved spinning around in flowy dresses, braiding flowers into her hair, and telling our mother about all the gossip at school. Meanwhile, Enyd preferred ripped trousers, reading classic foreign books our father would bring her from the royal library, and practicing in the yard with her slingshot.

"She's magical! She could do anything." The front door creaked open, our father stepping into the house. Fiona waved at the doorway, the only light breaking up the darkness of our bedroom. "Couldn't she, Father?"

"Who?" he asked, slipping off his shoes by the front door before coming into our room.

"The Enchantress," said Enyd, her words stitched with annoyance.

"What about her?" He was still in his dark-red robes, golden flames lining the edges, matching the cord looped around his waist. We'd been waiting for him after begging our mother to let us stay up past our bedtime to say goodnight. As long as we were quiet enough and had the lights out, she usually didn't mind.

Our father had been working late the last few weeks, not getting home until after the dragons had done evening patrols. Prince Ciaran had him doing some research in addition to his usual duties for King Laisren, keeping the royal texts in order for Arafax's castle. Father often reminded us how powerful knowledge could be in the right or wrong hands.

That made his work pretty important to me.

"She can do anything, can't she?" Fiona asked, climbing up the ladder next to my head to get to her bed. She was a year older than me, so she got the top bunk. *Lucky.* Being the youngest of four, I'd always get last pick.

Mother stood in the doorway, smiling as she watched my father sit down and plant a kiss on Enyd's head before standing and doing the same for Imogen. "I suppose she can do a lot. No one really knows how she got her powers or where she came from, so it's hard to say."

"She's not even real, Gen," Enyd said, rolling her eyes and laying back on her pillow. "That's what Shailey said at school."

"What?"

"Yeah. She said the Enchantress is just a scary story our parents tell us so we stay out of the Silent Woods."

"Is that true, Father?" I asked, finally getting a word in. Not that it happened much. My sisters all loved to talk, and I didn't mind the quiet. "Is she made up?"

"Well, I've never seen her myself."

"See!" Enyd stuck her tongue out at Imogen, who couldn't see her twin, making Fiona and I giggle. "Told you so—"

Our eldest sister—by a whole two minutes—snapped her head to look at us, then glared down at her.

"Just because I haven't seen her, doesn't mean she isn't real. The disappearances in those woods are a very real thing," our father amended, shooting a stern look at Enyd.

My eyes went wide. "They are?"

"Yes. One of our friends actually traveled into the woods and never returned." He sighed, then pinched the bridge of his nose.

Mother came up behind him, wrapping her arms around his neck and pressing a kiss to his cheek. Everywhere she went she carried the scent of fresh-baked cookies and flour, a happy side-effect of baking in the castle kitchen all morning. "While the legend may not be true, the danger isn't any less real."

Fiona's small voice floated overhead, her bed creaking above me. "That's why we can't go into the woods?"

Father took a moment, meeting each of our gazes. "That's right, sugarplums."

3

"I'll never go into the woods," I said, puffing out my chest. "I'm a good listener."

"Yes, you are, Druce," my father agreed, giving me a kiss on the cheek before making his way to my sisters. He untied his robe as he left the room, hooking it on the coat rack in the hallway.

Imogen snorted at me. "How can you listen when your mind's always busy?"

She wasn't wrong. There was always so much spinning in my head, especially in the quiet. My teachers at school said they didn't think my mind ever rested. I'd been moved up a few levels already, now taking some lessons with my sisters.

I smiled at the miniature water-powered windmill I'd made from a scroll tube, a chip of wood, a cup, and some twine, along with the first-place dragon-shaped medallion beside it. I was always tinkering with different things I found around the house. Even Enyd's newest slingshot was one I'd built from a bunch of everwood sticks, held together by its hardened sap.

My mother went around tucking us all in. "Goodnight, little loves."

Coming over to me last, she brushed her fingers through my hair and whispered, her voice always able to calm my busy mind. "We can't wait to see how you change the world, our brilliant little boy."

20 years later

CHAPTER 1
Sloan

I t's the same thing day after day—hunting some sign that *she's* still there.

That she's still *mine*.

It'd been a month. The worst month of my life, if I could even call it that right now.

Nothing had changed. The Enchantress had taken Aislin, adding her to the coven of shadow wisps haunting the Silent Woods. Everyone tried to remind me that she was still alive. And I knew it was true. All previously champion-bonded pairs had suffered the same fate—when one died, the other soon followed.

Even still, their reassurances offered me little solace.

Mox's snout perched on the windowsill, inching forward, sniffing at the spectral silhouettes flitting a few feet away. They were huddled together, buzzing about something—no fucking clue what—*but they seemed anxious compared to the other times he'd been there.*

The Enchantress came into view, walking toward the windowsill. A crimson smile crept along her lips, canines glinting in the moonlight. She glided closer, the scent of wilted lavender clogging his nose.

I hated how strong his sense of smell was. My stomach gurgled, unsettled by the Enchantress's fragrant bouquet. Or maybe it was all the whiskey I drank last night...or maybe the whiskey from this morning.

It was hard to tell where the days began and ended at this point.

"Well, well, well. Back again, I see." She gave two quick claps, gripping the attention of her wisps before sending them away from the window and into one of the rooms past where he could see. Then it was just her, alone with Mox. Tapping her claws on the windowsill, her inky eyes narrowed in his direction. *"I know you're in there, Commander."*

My heart clenched in my chest, a growl vibrating through my ribs, coming from my familiar.

"No need to get fussy," the Enchantress crooned. *"I wouldn't dare hurt you or your sweet little fox."*

First of all, Mox was far from sweet nor little. I'd seen him shred apart full-grown men. Second of all, she'd already hurt me by taking away Aislin—a hurt that was as visceral now as it was the day our bond snapped out of my reach.

Our forever had only just begun.

And I still didn't understand how she had failed the deal. I'd seen her give the vial to the Enchantress—the only thing I could guess was that it wasn't Kyleigh's blood sloshing within it.

But if it wasn't hers, whose was it?

"I know you want her back. And I'm sure we could come to some sort of arrangement to make that possible." She bent down until she was eye level with Mox, their noses inches apart, divided only by whatever magical barrier contained the dark sorceress. The one that, thanks to Aislin's failure, still stood strong, imprisoning the evil bitch.

As tempting as any deal would be to me, Aislin had only one request before she'd been changed: not to come after the Enchantress alone. The military strategist in me knew that was the right call, but the broken woman...she was fighting against that promise.

I took another swig of whiskey, draining the glass and slamming it down, ready to feel numb again. "Another."

"She's here, you know," the Enchantress taunted.

Aislin.

Part of me wanted to believe the woman I loved was reachable, able to be fixed. The other part felt it was fruitless.

Clearly she wasn't.

How could she be? She might be alive, but she'd been morphed into something that simply existed, captive to her mistress's whims.

"Well of course you assume she's here as you've been watching. But I promise, I'm taking good care of her." The Enchantress *moved away from the windowsill, clapping her hands in two succinct beats. "Her magic was much stronger to take in. In fact, I think it's made her allure even more powerful than my other wisps. Maybe you'll see for yourself sometime. If you're willing to come visit, that is."*

A hoard of wisps flocked to her, their shadowy limbs reaching out and undoing the buttons lining the back of her lace dress.

"I still think we would all have so much fun together," she *called out, not making eye contact as she trailed her clawed fingers along the bodies of her dusky underlings. They nuzzled against her, worshiping her attention.*

One of those wisps could be Aislin, but I had no way of knowing which one. Obviously, she had no awareness of what she was doing. She'd never willingly lean into the Enchantress's touch.

Regardless, rage electrified my belly, striking through my chest.

Mox snarled, his agitation pulsing with my own. The Enchantress didn't even flinch at his threat. Instead, she moaned in response, while her wisps swirled along her naked body. A strange onyx film coated her arms, spreading its shimmer through her breasts and torso like she'd been dipped in glittery paint.

Did she always look like this?

The wisps clung to her, their wings trailing along her breasts, shadowed faces latching to her most private areas. "You're welcome to stay and watch," she panted, writhing against them. "Or better yet, come join in. I'm sure I could arrange for you and your beloved—"

Frigid water splashed over my face, and I wiped my eyes to find a blurry Neve glaring at me. Ox stood next to her, grimacing at my drenched state.

"Get up." Her tone was a firm command.

When I didn't move, Ox gripped under my arm, lifting me to stand. I could barely hold my own weight, leaning over slightly to the side while he braced me. If he let go, I was certain I'd crumple to the ground.

"You need to cut her off, Sweeney," Neve demanded, looking slightly clearer than before.

I needed to get back to Mox's sight. To *her*.

"Blazes!" Ox yelped as I curled over and threw up onto his boots. He sat me in a chair, then grabbed a towel from Sweeney before wiping off his shoes. Leigh must have come over because I heard her voice, seeing her flat brown shoes and crutch in the corner of my vision, a wet mop washing away the mess I'd left. She'd been awake three weeks now, and I'd moved into the inn to keep an eye on her.

It's what Aislin would have wanted, if she were here.

Which she fucking wasn't.

"She fucking wasn't what?" Ox asked, making me realize I'd said that last part aloud.

"She's not fucking here," I mumbled. "She's gone. I need to get back to her."

"Here, drink this first," Leigh said gently, handing me another glass of lavender whiskey. I was surprised she'd offered me one after Neve had said to cut me off, but Leigh always was the nice one. The glass wobbled in my hand, some whiskey spilling over the edge as I brought it to my lips and chugged it down, no longer feeling the burn of the fiery liquid.

Whiskey and I had become close friends.

I shut my eyes, ignoring the others, trying to re-establish the connection with Mox. His vision slowly returned, blotting out The Lavender, *a swirl of dark shadows moving around the cabin...*

Then everything around me became fuzzy, until it dissolved into black.

CHAPTER 2
Redmond

I t'd been a long day of meetings and strategizing—something I used to enjoy when Sloan was here—now a sore reminder that she wasn't. I'd stared at Celaria's map, going over next steps with my leaders until the lines of all the territories seemed to blend together.

Sipping my glass of whiskey, I headed to my blue velvet chair. The lukewarm liquor seeped down my throat, leaving a smoky aftertaste in its wake. I used to love Inverno's signature brew, aged in barrels I charred the walls of myself, a reminder of the phoenix fire that'd secured my kingdom's power within Celaria.

I'd been proud of the things I'd done.

Maybe that was the story I'd told myself so I could live with the ashes forged by my own hand. Because the lie I'd repeated all these years—that the accident that set off The Blaze was still wholly necessary to protect my people—well, it was a crock of shit.

Now, as I swallowed the amber liquid, forcing it down my throat in memory of the pain I'd caused, I had to live with the

12

consequences of how wrong I'd been. All the death I'd never rinse away.

So, I took another sip, choking myself on the magnitude of a decade of sins.

There was only one way forward. A path I'd chosen months ago when I'd proposed the alliance with Arafax—an enemy I'd never planned to be on the same side of a war with, but here we were.

There'd never be a way for me to balance the scales. All I could do was try to right as many wrongs as I could while I still drew breath. Despite praying for death to take away the pain, the guilt, I was also grateful to be alive.

Destruction might be my only legacy, but if the people I cared about could be safe, could really *live*—that would be enough for me.

I leaned back into the chair, my wings wrapping around myself, blotting out the world. Sometimes sitting in my own darkness was the best way for me to think. And I had a lot on my mind.

Slipping the glass through my feathers, I placed it on the end table, then brought my hands into my lap and closed my eyes to meditate. It was something I'd always done with my father as a child, a way of drowning out the world and collecting myself.

A king should always be collected to truly command obedience from his people.

I'd stopped over the years, not caring about decorum or what people thought of me. Keeping Inverno strong drove me, along with carrying on my father's legacy after he'd died. Even though the man was a frigid bastard, I still longed for his approval.

I'm not sure why I'd been so concerned with it after his death. I hadn't cared about what he wanted before then. He had all but explicitly forbid me from marrying Neve. I knew he wasn't happy with me choosing her, listing off other prospects within our kingdom along with a few noblewomen he knew of in Cicatrix, though they mainly kept to themselves. He'd offered to have Commander Syler escort us there to propose an alliance, uniting the northern territories.

I'd very politely told him to fuck off.

Looking back now, maybe I should have just done as he wished. We surely wouldn't be in this predicament otherwise. There would have never been retribution against Arafax.

And so much *death*.

Here, I was still Inverno's beloved king. People believed I set The Blaze on purpose. That I'd worked with my father on behalf of Inverno. That I'd been part of his plans.

But I knew nothing about them. And now he was dead. Neve had killed him, and I still didn't understand *why*. That plagued my thoughts most of all. There were pieces of that night I was missing and I desperately needed them for closure.

I needed to understand. To rationalize. To know how to move forward.

Neve killing him...it wasn't in her nature. Not that I truly knew her nature. She'd been one of Arafax's Revered right under my nose, in my bed, and I had no fucking clue. But I watched him die. Had rewatched him die, over and over, thanks to the Enchantress and her purple box of torment. The violence behind his death—Neve's aim wasn't simply to kill a threat. There was malice there.

What had he done?

Not that it mattered. Not that I could even ask her about it. I'd tried, and she'd shut me down.

Some explanations are better left alone, Redmond.

Since becoming king, I'd spent my days flying out to be among my people, mostly in my phoenix form as to not inter-rupt their daily lives. I thought by watching over them, as the rulers had before me, that I'd been helping them while spying on our enemy to ensure they stayed weak. But I'd been blind, and my own people had suffered in the process. Now I was trying to rectify things, not only with Arafax, but also with Inverno.

My people deserved a better life than the one I'd provided them since my rule.

They deserved to be connected to their familiars, living in harmony with the rest of Celaria. My people never left Inverno. I'd ensured they never needed to and that we could thrive from within.

But were we really thriving?

Blue flame ignited from my wrists within my onyx-feathered shelter as I inhaled and exhaled the way I'd been taught as a child. Thundering thoughts rolled through my mind, and I floated away...

A SEARING PAIN AT MY HIP PULLED ME FROM MY trance.

My body jolted, wings igniting before they retracted, hitting against the chair I'd been sitting in. I stood quickly, feathers folding in behind me, bringing my hands to my trousers and unbuttoning them as the familiar sting engraved my flesh.

Fuck.

My eyes clenched tight and I inhaled sharply. It was as if she'd taken the tip of one of her wretched copper claws and traced along the path of the mark, burning the sensitive skin.

Her summoning roiled through my gut. What once would have had me straining in my pants with dark carnal promise now just brought a sour, sickening feeling. I didn't want this. *Her.* I hadn't for a long time, if I looked at things honestly.

Had I ever really wanted her? Or merely wanted the distraction?

Sighing, I pushed my trousers off, letting them fall to the floor. There was no sense in losing another good pair of pants, and I was starting to run low ever since Sloan had left. Probably the thing I missed least about her in comparison to everything else her friendship had given me all these years.

I'd had a few pairs of pants brought in from the local seamstress in town but the fit of them—it wasn't the same.

Maybe *I* just wasn't the same.

But that didn't fucking matter because right now, I needed to be whoever the Enchantress wanted me to be in order to buy us more time. I needed Dru to translate that tome or find someone who could.

What if she'd realized I'd taken it?

What if *that* was why she was summoning me?

Her wrath, the wisps, the punishments, the purple box, the growing pile of husks beyond the windowsill... Weighing the options, I didn't quite know which was the best-case scenario for me.

But if I didn't show, the summoning would only worsen. And she'd know something was off.

There was still a deadly game here. One I had to play carefully.

Taking a deep breath, my wings splayed wide, igniting into my phoenix form. The wind whipped, and I used its momentum, heading in the direction of the Silent Woods.

CHAPTER 3
Redmond

"**D**id you miss me, darling?"

"Of course," I cleared my throat, quickly adding, "my dark queen."

The Enchantress's pointed claw grazed my shoulder, and I shuddered against her touch. It'd been a month since I was summoned here, after the last time I'd spoken to Neve. The night I'd left behind her ring, the one whose twin now sat tucked in my nightstand alongside a crumpled portrait of the two of us. I'd clenched the rendering tightly in my fist after finally acknowledging what she'd done—murdered my father right in front of me. We had appeared so happy when it was commissioned to celebrate our engagement. Knowing all the lies that had sat between us, ones I didn't even fully understand, could I really say that we were?

How real could love be when it was drenched in deception?

This train of thought was doing nothing for me or my charade for the Enchantress. When I looked over, she was frowning. "You seem distracted and you know how I feel about that."

My eyes immediately shot to the shelves, scanning among the jars for the purple box, but it wasn't there. Neither was the jar that contained neon-violet lightning bolts that would some-times shake when they hit against its glass walls.

"Don't be afraid, darling," she cooed, stroking her tongue against the shell of my ear and whispering low. "I didn't bring you here for punishment tonight. Though don't pretend you haven't begged for it in the past."

I swallowed hard. "That's true."

She wasn't wrong. And while I deserved punishment, prob-ably more than ever, I knew it wouldn't be enough to fix me or my guilty conscience. Plus, it wasn't her wrath I'd earned. It wasn't her wrath I wanted. But I'd take it in spades. I'd beg on my hands and knees if it meant giving us an edge against her. Celaria's future depended on it.

"Did you bring me here to beg?" I took my time roving over her body, feigning hunger while arching a brow. Beneath the surface, my phoenix boiled, working against me, like it knew I was putting us in danger.

"That won't be necessary." The Enchantress preened her wings at my attention, and they expanded outward. The tendrils shadowed the dimly lit cabin, making it even darker. Brushing her wings out to fluff them, they managed to take up even more space. "At least not tonight."

A lump caught in my throat and I willed that fucker down.

"Then why did you summon me?" I reached out to stroke a few of her tendrils, and she hummed, body vibrating with the touch. Wings were an erogenous zone, something I'd discovered myself, but when I met the Enchantress, I quickly learned that fact remained even when they were composed of shadow. I'd never heard of or seen wings like these before, not that many had wings outside of the faeries. I was one of the few—along with Arafax's Revered.

Not that I wanted to think about *them* right now.

I took a deep breath, attempting to dispel the heat flaring in my chest.

With two quick claps, the Enchantress's wisps surrounded her, swarming and running their gray spectral forms along her body.

When she shooed them away with a few more claps, she was bared to me with her wings spread. The glittering onyx that had only coated the lower half of her arms now snaked down her chest, her breasts almost blending into the background. Her pale skin started just above her belly button and her face still held its usual hue, the streaks of pitch stopping at the base of her throat.

"What's happening to you?" I asked, trailing my palm along the skin. It was scratchy, like a hundred jet-black diamonds had been crushed and painted onto her flesh. Whatever it was, it seemed unnatural. It took everything to resist the instinct to pull my hand away.

Sighing, she ignored my question before stepping closer. "Preparations are underway for our nuptials. One of the many reasons the gem you lost us would have been useful."

"How so?" I asked, wanting any semblance of a plan of what she intended to do once freed.

"That's no matter at this point," she said, brushing off my question. "Other arrangements have been made now."

Her eyes narrowed, lips turned down at my lack of interest as she stroked me. "Well, this is disappointing."

"Well, I can sense a barb when it's directed at me," I stated, knowing eventually I'd have to betray my heart and mind and use my own body against me. She wasn't naked right now without intention, I knew that much. What I didn't know was what she *really* wanted from me, aside from the temporary pleasure my body could provide her with.

My phoenix didn't like that idea one bit, clawing heat scraping my insides with every exchanged touch. Maybe it could sense whatever darkness was taking hold of her. Maybe I'd become more in tune with its magic since the gem had been restored.

"You usually love my barbs," she cooed, trailing her sharpened nail along my shaft. It pinched in a few spots, but I refused to flinch. Refused to react to the pain at all.

When I didn't respond, awaiting her answer, she acquiesced. "Unfortunately, I have found myself missing something that has put our plans on hold a bit." She continued to coax me unsuccessfully between her fingers. "It's made me a bit too distracted for our *meetings*, along with a few other recent developments" —*what developments?*—"and that wouldn't be fair to either of us."

"I understand, my dark queen," I said, not at all disappointed by her decision made in *fairness*. "I hate that anything would distract you from our plans together. What is missing?"

Changing tactics, I placed my hand within hers, trailing it downward and leaning in to press a kiss to her crimson lips, imagining they belonged to someone else. I tried to go through every action I should to ensure she bought it.

Linger. Drag a thumb across her collarbone. Stroke her canine with my tongue.

I just had to go through the motions enough times to keep her satisfied until I could strike.

Until we *could strike,* I reminded myself, absentmindedly brushing over the hardened coating along her skin with my other hand, wondering if she could feel any sensation when I thumbed her nipple. When she arched in response, I had my answer.

Every time I had to play along, my insides eroded. We were both horrible people, but I no longer desired my tarnished soul to be suffocated by her equally toxic poison. And while I may have destroyed lives in the past, I refused to be the cause of more loss. Maybe too much had happened for that to be possible, but I wanted to resemble the king I'd once aspired to be within Celaria.

And that wouldn't be possible with the Enchantress free.

"A rare tome was in my possession and I believe it was stolen."

Fuck. Did she call me here to punish me?

I focused on my breathing, trying not to allow any panic to show. My eyes shot to the windowsill, throat drying at the sight of the heap piled there. It didn't look any taller than the last time, which was a relief but not by much.

The Enchantress wrapped her tendrils around me, pulling me close so our chests were touching.

"Any idea who did it?" I asked, tilting my head inquisitively. Playing the fool had become natural to me. "What kind of tome?"

Her inky gaze raked up to mine. "A very rare and valuable one. And while there are a handful of people who visited me around its disappearance, I'm fairly certain I know who did it."

"I didn't realize you had that many visitors," I said, clearing my throat and training sternness into my expression, acting how the old Redmond would. "Should I be jealous?"

"Never. Passing amusements have always been fine between us." She lifted my hand to her lips and swirled her tongue around the pad of two fingers before pulling them into her mouth, giving them a long suck and dragging them down her front. They snagged in the spots that were no longer flesh. "You know what we have is irreplaceable, darling."

"No one could ever compare to you, my dark queen," I replied, willing down bile and continuing to stroke myself, grasping for any thought that would get me hard when her hand wrapped around mine. The abrasiveness of her touch was impossible to ignore but I tried anyway. "Any ideas who has the tome in their possession now?"

"I believe it was taken by Flynt during one of his deliveries to my cabin. And while I've utilized his services for years, I never thought he'd have the audacity to steal from me." She stepped away, and I was grateful for the distance between us, refusing to look too relieved about her accusation. "Too bad we can't ask a dead man where the relic is."

Too bad he's already dead because I'd love to have been the one to do it myself. But... "How do you know he's dead?"

She pointed to the scar slung low on my hip. "Our bond, of course."

Now that she'd admitted their relationship had existed, and they'd struck some bargain tethering him to her as much as I was, I had no doubts in my mind that she'd known where he'd been getting the blue dragon dust from. Did she know the truth about who was hidden beneath those scales that'd been hoarded away? Did Flynt's death have something to do with why the pile of ashen bodies wasn't growing? "I didn't realize you were *close.*"

"Being close with someone and finding them *useful* are two very different things."

True. But I was fairly certain they were the same when it came to the Enchantress.

"Of course. How lucky for me that I am both." I gave my best seductive smirk. "What is it you want from me?"

"There is something I need you to do. It's why I asked you here."

"And here I was thinking you just wanted me to fulfill some desire you'd recently conjured up."

"Well, I have missed that clever tongue," she said, tracing her nail along the edge of my lips, onyx gaze pinned to them.

"It would be hard not to with the things I do with it."

"That's true." She chuckled, licking her lips and giving me a look that told me she wasn't totally opposed to the idea. "I know Flynt had many dealings with King Morrow. Does Inverno still have ties with him or Queen Maren?"

"We've been established allies for decades, but I haven't seen or spoken with either of them since my father's death."

The Mer King was a pompous ass, from what I'd heard, whose main concern was appearances above all else. His people had been struggling, their population dwindling for decades. Many of their males had snuck off to the Otherworld where they could live as mortal men on two feet, only furthering the issue. Before his death, my father would visit their capital, Tesceillus, about three to four times a year, keeping up relations with their ruler.

I never had much of an interest in seeing what lay under the bubbling surface of the Spuma. My wings shivered at the thought of being submerged in the ocean's watery depths.

"Well, I need you to go to him and see if he somehow has possession of the tome. And while you're there, see where things stand with him in terms of an alliance. It never hurts to start building them now." *Didn't I know it.* "Even if they don't have it in their possession, perhaps they transported the tome via the waterway. Getting it back is of the utmost importance."

"Of course. But I'll have some things to situate for my people before I leave for a trip like that."

She'd get no hesitation from me. This would be the perfect way to see where King Morrow's loyalties were, hopefully securing the previously established alliance with him. Three out of six territories against the Enchantress, especially with theirs being the largest, would be a huge win. Possibly enough to sway the less inclined other three, which all tended to be wary of outsiders.

"Do what you must," she replied. "Just find me the tome."

"And if I come up empty-handed?"

"You'll be punished." Her tendrils extended out, wrapping around my thighs and ankles, pulling me to my knees. My phoenix thrashed, hot with anger, and it took everything in my power to stop my wings from igniting. From burning this cabin to the fucking ground.

She walked forward, and I kept my vision locked where the blackened coating stopped and her usual pallor began above her belly button. "Remember, darling, just because I'm condemned to the forest for now doesn't mean I don't have ways to get creative."

A coppery talon lifted my chin. "As a matter of fact, your former commander has been sending her oversized pet to check in on things...I'd hate to have to *deal* with them."

"You leave Sloan alone," I said through gritted teeth.

Just then, a wisp flitted out into the hallway, watching us.

The Enchantress's head shot back a moment before she clapped twice, sending the curious wisp retreating into the room she'd emerged from. Then the copper-clawed sorceress tapped the tip of her finger to my chin. "Interesting..."

"What is?"

"That you'd still want to protect her, knowing she's fallen for the assassin who tried to kill you. I figured you'd thank me for removing her distraction so you could have your commander back. Don't you want that?"

"Of course, but I don't want to see my friend hurting." She was right. Aislin had tried to kill me. But, while we had nothing remotely cordial going between us, Sloan saw something in her. Loved her. That was enough.

"Just as I don't want to see my fiancé killed." Her tendrils pulled me up to stand again but didn't release me, their grip only tightening. "You know she would kill you without a second thought if given another chance. She'd never forgive you for killing her family. For destroying Arafax. She would have found a way to do it eventually."

I didn't deserve Aislin's forgiveness. The ripples of my mistake would haunt me beyond when the breeze would finally carry me north.

My mind retraced its steps back to the Enchantress's words, snagging on what she said moments ago. "What do you mean you *removed the distraction*?"

She touched the base of my chin and lowered my gaze to

hers. "She won't ever be able to hurt you without my say so. As you just witnessed."

Shit. Heat rose in my chest, but I refused to let my wings ignite or display any sign of anger. *That wisp.* The Enchantress had stripped Aislin of her power, her essence, shaping her into another one of her dusky minions that flitted creepily around the cabin.

The fact that she'd done it and this is how I was learning about it...

Sloan really didn't see me as her friend anymore.

Lightning crackled against the Enchantress's fingertips, riding along the shimmering pitch of her skin, as if they were a conductor to Aislin's magic. She released me just before the violet bolts reached my face.

Had she discovered what other magic the assassin possessed?

No. If she had, she would have used it. And she wasn't descended from the bloodlines like Isla had explained to me after I'd discovered her daughter's secret—that she was both one of Arafax's Revered dragons and its heir to the throne.

However, was it that the Enchantress had taken over Aislin's power, had transferred it to herself, that had caused the quick shift in her body? Or was it because the tome was out of her reach?

Either way, it wasn't good.

We were running out of time to change the tide.

Once she was done with me, I'd hurry back to Inverno and prepare.

It was time to set another meeting.

CHAPTER 4

A Wisp

Clap, clap.

Our Queen ran the vial between onyx fingers.

Popping it open, she swirled it around, watching the ichor slosh within.

Her brows knit.

Something set her on edge.

Murmuring words in a language I didn't understand, she fumbled along the bookcase, searching.

Jars and books were disappearing off the shelves. The one that seemed to beat louder and louder each day, pounding its steady rhythm was gone.

I didn't know where it went, along with the one that glowed violet and sometimes bounced when I flitted near.

I liked its warmth.

But sometimes, I swore I could still feel its strands' familiar thrum.

Clap, clap.

She'd been sending the others away.

They left in shifts, carrying items.

Returning empty-handed.

When I asked where they went, they didn't recall.

None of us do.

Leftover leaves and dirt were brushed away by my coven's wings.

I must have been doing it as well.

Clap, clap.

The door was only open a crack. A few floorboards set askew.

Sitting on her bed, she held the purple box, bringing out the vial.

She popped open the lid and dabbed her finger in, and I flitted closer to watch.

She stared at the box, the rims of her eyes shining.

Then she dipped her finger into the vial again and clamped it shut before walking to the window.

I floated inside, but she didn't notice me.

Crimson smeared the wood, and she whispered to herself.

Sliding her hand along the ledge, she extended it out, her glittering onyx fingers reaching for the moon.

Clap, clap.

CHAPTER 5

Sloan

My head pounded and my stomach churned, the leftover liquor sloshing around my insides. I blinked a few times, opening my eyes to realize I'd been moved to Aislin's room, where I'd been staying since I came back to The Lavender.

Ox was standing over me, a cocky grin spread across his face. "Welcome back."

Pushing up to my elbows, I tried to ignore the urge to be sick. Though, I wouldn't feel too bad about throwing up on him again, considering. "You drugged me."

"Technically, I was the one that did that," Neve said, holding a tray of food in her hands. The bread looked decent. The meats, cheeses, and veggies touching it made me grimace.

"How long was I out?"

"About a day," Ox said, nabbing the tray from her and placing it in my lap. "We took turns staying with you to make sure you didn't throw up while you slept it off."

He grabbed the extra pillow on the bed, the one that still smelled like *her*, propping it behind my back so I could sit upright. I twisted—too quickly—toward the nightstand, my gut churning. Opening the middle drawer, I rummaged through it, seething when I didn't find what I was looking for. "Where the fuck is my flask?"

"You mean Aislin's flask," Ox corrected.

"You know what I mean," I scoffed, bending over to see if it had fallen on the floor before slapping my hand over my mouth. Neve stuck the wastebasket under my face, and I swallowed down the bile surging up the back of my throat. Heaving a deep breath, I stuffed down any whiskey that wanted to slither its way back up and turned to face my two wardens, eyes narrowing. "Where is it? It belongs here in her room."

Ox shrugged. "Don't worry about it. Sweeney is keeping it safe until Aislin's back."

Neve elbowed him in the gut, eliciting a stern glare from the giant knight. Guess he wasn't supposed to share who had the flask in their custody. I'd be making a visit to Sweeney as soon as they left me alone.

"Aislin wouldn't want to see you like this," Ox said, placing a hand on my shoulder.

I pushed his arm away, cocking my head to the side—regretting the angle when my vision didn't catch up with the perspective. "Like what?"

Neve held her hands on her hips, frustration washing across the glowing amber outlines of her eyes. "Wallowing."

"Well, she can't see me like this, can she? She's a wisp, for fuck's sake," I sneered, swinging my legs over the side of the bed and testing my weight on them before standing. Everything whirled a bit when I did, but I closed my eyes, taking a moment to steady myself before opening them again. "And yes, I know I could go make a deal to maybe get her back, but I promised Aislin I wouldn't do that. That I wouldn't go back there on my own until we had a way to handle the Enchantress. In the meantime, I can wallow however the fuck I want."

I wobbled a bit as I took a step toward the door, and Ox quickly braced his hand under my elbow. I lifted my gaze to see his brown eyes softening when they met mine. He lowered his voice to a whisper, which my hangover greatly appreciated. "Dru's been working hard to come up with a plan. A way to ensure if we take down the Enchantress that we won't harm the wisps."

"Isn't that what he's always doing?"

Ox and Neve's lips curled up at my remark. I missed my friends. I missed being able to laugh. But any living while Aislin was being held by the Enchantress felt wrong. Selfish.

"What am I supposed to do? Just sit around and watch her be ordered around by the Enchantress?"

"That's also why we wanted to talk to you," Neve said, eyes dropping a moment before she continued, "once you'd sobered up a bit, that is."

"Then talk." I gripped Ox's elbow, giving them both an imploring look. "Or better yet, make yourself useful and get me a glass of whiskey and then talk."

"It's five in the morning," Neve said with an exasperated sigh.

"Well, the numbing feeling I'm going for is an around-the-clock kind of thing, Neve."

"Every day you sit here wasting away, drinking, stuck in your head—Mox's head—you're letting Aislin down."

"You're her champion," Ox ground out, obviously irritated. "Act like it."

"What would you even know about it, Ox? I don't think you've ever been in love from what I gather. And you," I nodded to Neve, "all healed up from the actions of your beloved?"

She blanched, adjusting the collar of her tunic. Ox released my arm, and I crumpled to the ground.

"We're trying to help you," he murmured.

"Well you can't fucking help." I brought my knees to my chest as tears spilled down my cheeks. I wished I had more liquor to stop all this feeling they were forcing upon me.

Not going to happen.

The two of them lowered to the ground, flanking me with their presence. Neve combed back my unkempt strands, and Ox handed me a handkerchief, then put an arm around both Neve and I. Staring at the fabric, a lightweight cotton with golden embellishments along the edges, I let it anchor me, slowing my breath. "I felt our bond snap. Watched her wilt away into one of those possessed shadow creatures. If our bond is still there, I can't feel it. I can't fucking feel *her*."

Ox brought his other arm around, corralling us together as I cried into his chest, the stubble of his beard scraping against my forehead. "All I have is what I can see through Mox. And I've tried to see if he can sniff out the bond—any sign of her. He can't."

Ox gave us a squeeze. "We will figure it out."

I unleashed more sobs, a damp trail marking up his shirt. "She could be fucking the Enchantress right now and have no idea about it. Or be locked away somewhere in the cabin Mox can't see. I don't even know if she's okay. She could have ended up in the discarded pile of husks for all we know."

"Shhh. You can't think like that," Ox said.

"She's too valuable to the Enchantress to have been drained. From Dru's research, he believes the husks are made up of nulls." Neve broke out from our small circle, standing up slowly. "Redmond saw them hitting the Enchantress's barrier, so presumably there's a demolier from Cicatrix she's stolen some sort of reanimation magic from. Probably another wisp in her collection."

She said Redmond's name with complete detachment, and I didn't know whether to read that as she was over him or maintaining a façade to sound like she was. "If we can figure out how to free the wisps, we would have some powerful allies to help take down the Enchantress. Dru doesn't want to accidentally hurt or diminish the chance of saving the people she's transformed before we get rid of her."

I dabbed my eyes with the handkerchief, smears of makeup staining the white linen. "So he really thinks he can help Aislin?"

"He does," she said, eyes darting quickly to Ox, then back to me. "But he's still working on Isla. She's more concerned with getting rid of the Enchantress's threat to Arafax."

I pulled myself onto the bed, crossing my legs. "What's her great plan, then?"

"Well for one thing, we have the new magic folk that came back with Kyleigh through the portal. She's been trying to decipher where everyone belongs and what magic they wield, as they've all already agreed to join our cause." Ox gave an uneasy smile, then walked over to the desk and grabbed a glass, holding it out for Neve to fill.

"Oh great. A bunch of inexperienced wielders," I grumbled.

Neve waved a finger, a trail of glistening water droplets spiraling into the glass, filling it halfway. Then Ox handed it to me, giving a nod. "Remember, Kyleigh was an inexperienced wielder from the Otherworld and look at how much power she's brought with her."

"Is she really your great example?" I asked, taking a small sip. "I wouldn't call her power mastered. Not yet. These new folks could be just as dangerous as they could be powerful."

I took a longer sip, trying to wash away the thirst. When was the last time I drank water not in the form of ice in my whiskey? For someone who spent her days training and taking care of her body, the question made me wince.

Neve brought the plate of food back over, waiting until I took a piece of bread from it. "We'll just have to see what they can do."

"In the meantime," Ox said, planting himself in front of me. "Stop wallowing. Sober up. Then come help me train the recruits."

Neve handed me another piece of bread, waiting for me to put it in my mouth before she spoke. "Stop living in Mox's head and make changes with your own. Bring your familiar back here—"

"No," I cut in mid-chew. "I won't leave her there without back up, so you can fuck right off about that."

"Watching for her while you're in a drunken stupor isn't going to help the situation," Neve pleaded.

Assholes. The both of them.

"You could even give Dru information about what Mox has seen at the cabin. Who knows...it could help Aislin."

She did have a point about that. *Still an asshole, though.*

"Fine. I'll agree that maybe something he's seen could help. I'll go see Dru."

"And train the new folks?" Ox asked hopefully.

"I'm in no shape to train anyone right now. But I'll give the new idiots a quick inspection before I leave the fort," I said, finishing up the glass and handing it to Ox. "That's it."

"Fair enough," he agreed.

Neve opened the door, waving him toward her. "We will give you ten minutes and then we'll head out to the fort. And don't even think about scrounging up some liquor. We'll meet you downstairs."

"Fine."

I walked over to the armoire, taking one of Aislin's tunics and pulling it over my head, inhaling *her*. After tucking the oversized shirt into my pants, strapping on my holster, and brushing my teeth and hair, I still had about seven minutes to spare.

I closed my eyes, merging my vision with Mox's once again. He was skulking around the perimeter of the cabin, checking each window from afar. I cataloged everything I could in the room, noting that the Enchantress was nowhere in sight. Maybe she had moved into one of the back bedrooms? Unfortunately, not every space in the cabin was visible to him, but I'd take everything he saw to Dru.

The shadow wisps buzzed around the cabin, performing various tasks. One was dusting the bookshelves, working around each jar and tome. A few were pulling out vials and ingredients, setting them on the tree-trunk table in the center of the main room. A handful huddled together in the corner, as if gossiping. With a swift *clap, clap*, the entire bunch glided out the window and into the forest, pulling Mox's snout in their direction as he frolicked after them, chasing them through the trees.

CHAPTER 6

Kyleigh

"Tonight?" Dru kissed along my throat, thumb moving in tantalizing strokes up and down the center of my jeans, making me wriggle in his lap.

"Mm-hmm," I hummed, arching into him, savoring his touch.

He gripped my chin, pulling me in for a deep, lingering kiss. Ever since we'd reunited in Halston's library archives, he'd been anything but tentative. I glanced over at the desk he'd bent me over last night when I'd come to relieve him of his duties and considered trying to coax him into a repeat performance.

Knock-knock-knock.

Maybe not.

The door groaned open, Ox sticking his head in, not even reacting to me straddling Dru in his desk chair. Always the one for poor timing. "We were able to get Sloan here. Dru, she wants to talk to you about the cabin."

Everything had been a whirlwind since we'd returned to Arafax a month ago. Aislin had been taken by the Enchantress, leaving everyone on edge, teetering between wanting to rush in to rescue her and knowing better. When Dru told me about the

35

bargain she'd struck, I felt like an idiot for never realizing what she was dealing with. I'd been so focused on retrieving him from the Otherworld.

"I'll see you tonight," I whispered, climbing out of his lap. "Love you."

He caught my wrist as I started to walk away and pulled me back to him for one final kiss, then grazed my cheek with his nose, his breath warming the shell of my ear. "I love you too, and I look forward to showing you just how much tonight."

My thighs clenched a little, heat flooding my core.

You and me both.

I started out toward the hallway, thinking about our evening ahead. We were finally going to complete our champion ceremony. But this time, I wasn't wearing any fancy dress and there would be no special decorations or festivities. Just me and Dru. All we needed was each other. Besides, I didn't want to jinx anything after what'd happened last time.

Dru had been working tirelessly to find a solution to save Aislin, along with his sisters and the other wisps in the Enchantress's ghostly entourage. We couldn't move forward with taking her down until we'd exhausted every avenue.

We had to.

I couldn't imagine how Aislin was doing. Did she know what was happening to her? Would she remember it once she was back?

She'd sacrificed herself rather than give the Enchantress what she wanted. We didn't know how she'd broken her deal, but the blood in the vial Sloan had seen her give the sorceress couldn't have been mine. Whose had it been, though?

She'd protected all of us.

She'd protected me.

Dru was also now dealing with Vis's members who had recently come through the portal, researching the different regions of Celaria and their magics.

After landing in the castle's Great Hall, I'd shifted into my dragon form, taking everyone to the arena. Vis's masked gazelles, Savannah and Grace, had almost immediately sank to the dirt, black opalescent mer-tails curling around to replace their legs. They screamed, jaws expanding, making room for rows of razor-sharp teeth. And their eyes, once beautiful shades of moss and sky blue, faded until only cloudy white remained.

Ox had run off, coming back a few minutes later with a few other guards. They carted the two shell-shocked women in the direction of The Lavender, presumably to get them to the stream and in the care of their fellow mermaids.

The rest were all quickly escorted into the fort, Dru going in to help the Queen by taking down their names, information, and potential abilities.

I'd recognized most of the masked folks from my initiation. There was one who'd stood out, though, his penguin mask consisting of a series of sharp angles, like a piece of abstract art. It was slightly different than all the others and covered his entire face. He was the last to go in, following behind Daisy, the real name of the freaky bunny who'd been waiting in the grotto for me after I'd leapt off the quarry cliff, pledging myself to a secret society that only wanted to use me.

I was still leery of what their allegiance was actually worth. So far, though, they just seemed grateful to be in Celaria and for the lessons my mother and Dru were providing them at Arafax's fort.

Striding past the series of dragon statues lining the red carpet that ran through the main foyer, I exited the fort and headed toward the labyrinth, weaving through its stony corridors.

"Fuck!"

I froze. Looking for the source of the scream. Voices murmured along the breeze, sounding soft but urgent.

"No!"

I pivoted, going down a curved channel that led to nothing.

Following the loop, I came up to a wall of moss-covered stone. A dead end.

"Stop it!"

The shouts filtered through the stone, and I ran my hands over it, trying to spot where the noise could be coming from. In between the mortar, there was a rusty discoloration on one of the stones. Grabbing a small dagger from my pocket, one that Ox had given me, I pushed the tip into my finger, ignoring the sting. I touched the stained section of rock and whispered an unlocking enchantment I'd learned from Dru.

A moment later, the stone dissolved, leaving a long, carved narrow hallway in its place.

Along the rocky charcoal walls roman numerals were etched into the stone. There were no doors, windows, or bars but something about this place gave me the heebie-jeebies, reminding me all too much of my time in Inverno's dungeon.

Where the fuck am I?

"Let me out!" a voice shouted from behind III. I fumbled along the wall, looking for a knob or lever but none existed.

"What are you doing here?"

The familiar voice had my breath catching at the back of my throat, and I halted on the spot. I turned my head, finding my mother suddenly standing outside of room VI as if she appeared from nowhere. She was dressed in blue jeans and a red sweater, her chestnut hair pulled into a low messy bun. On her feet were a pair of red Chuck Taylors.

Warmth spread through my chest at the sight with a mix of unease.

Why was she dressed like the mom I remembered and not the queen she'd become?

CHAPTER 7

Kyleigh

"Why are you dressed like that?" I swallowed back the bittersweet emotions from seeing her in her old clothes. "What is this place?"

"You shouldn't be here."

"Stop trying to change the subject, Mother." I threw the final word like the sharpened blade it was. It was only fair. How often had she wielded it to her advantage as a shield to excuse her absence? There were no guards or servants around. No need to play pretend. "You keep claiming you want a relationship with me. That you care about me."

"I do."

"Then stop with the lies. I'm *so* tired of them." I pointed at the hallway of hidden doors. "Tell me what's going on. Who's in these rooms?"

"I don't know if you're ready for those answers."

"You haven't earned the right to decide what I'm ready for."

She hesitated a moment, then walked to the wall in front of me, pressing her hands to the III carving. The door disappeared, and we stepped over the threshold, finding a young man huddled in the corner of the room, a mop of black hair covering his face.

The room itself was nice, nothing like Inverno's dungeons. It was lush, like any of the guest rooms within the fort, only these were tucked away where no one would find them. There was even a full bar and refrigerator, like a tricked-out royal-looking dorm room.

He lifted his head, violet eyes piercing mine.

"How are you doing today, Jet?"

He blinked rapidly, then rubbed his eyes. "Are you real?"

"Yes, Jet," my mother replied, her tone still firm but a bit softer than before. "You're in your room right now. In Arafax's bunker. You're safe."

His eyes darted around, frantic. Confused.

"Where do you think you are?" I asked.

"The ceremonial chamber. There's fire." He scuttled on his knees, tucking deeper into the corner. "It's everywhere."

"It's okay. You're not there. That never happened. It's not real," my mother recited as if she'd repeated the phrase a million times. Maybe she had.

A knot twisted in my stomach. I hated thinking about that place. Somewhere I thought I'd finally get answers about my mother. Feel closer to her. And while that did happen, albeit not how I expected, that night still haunted me—despite the scars from the ordeal washed away by Renovo Falls' healing magic.

His breaths slowed, and after a few minutes he calmly peered up at us, like he hadn't just freaked out over being in a burning room.

"I'll be back soon, Jet. Why don't you take your sleeping potion and get some more rest?" She nodded toward the hallway for me to follow her while Jet got up and padded into the kitchenette.

"He's been down here this whole time?"

"Yes," she said, eyes downcast a moment before snapping up

to mine. "The weavers that came over had some unintended side effects. Unfortunately, we don't know enough about their magic, so I've been keeping them here, where they can't affect anyone else. Weaver abilities are beyond the scope of what I understand—and as a people, they steer clear of the rest of us."

"How many weavers came through the portal?"

"Two."

"The one that's in there," I said, indicating room VI. "What kind of weaver are they?"

"A memory weaver. Extremely dangerous."

"What makes them so dangerous?"

"They can make you relive anything that's happened in your past. They can spin the threads of your mind so you don't remember things correctly. They can erase memories with a thought. I'm sure there are other things, I just don't know what they are."

"That doesn't sound so bad." What I wouldn't give to be rid of some of my memories. I already relived some of the most terrible moments of my life—what could a memory weaver do to me that I couldn't already do to myself?

When I tried to walk past her, she placed a hand out in front of me, flames rising up from her palm in warning. "That's not a good idea."

"Why? If they came over here because of the deal I'd struck with Travis, I should at least know what we are dealing with."

"I understand your curiosity, but the use of their magic without proper training seems to wear at their minds. Like how our energy wanes after using our elements without rest. Their power comes with a mental cost, and until I can safely get them back to Alucinor, or find them help, this is the best place for them. If they were to touch you, they wouldn't be able to control what happened."

I reached out and smothered her flame with my hand. "I appreciate the warning. Now open up that door or I'll do it myself. Don't forget that your blood runs through my veins, so any magic you've cast, I can undo."

"Fine," she said. "But please, don't overreact."

Overreact?

She pressed her hand to the roman numerals carved into the last door, making it disappear.

"Oh my God," I shrieked, staring at the man laying in the bed. His eyes were glazed over, like he was lost in whatever he was staring off at. "Dad?"

He looked horrible. His wrists had angry rings around them, as if he'd been fighting against restraints of some sort. His hair was unkempt, along with the beard he'd started to grow, shades of gray peppering the black stubble. My legs shook, giving out as I crumpled to the floor, tears burning my eyes. "I don't understand. How—"

My mother's eyes filled with tears. "As soon as I saw him with the group and saw his eyes had shifted to violet, I pulled him aside. We both agreed it was the safest thing."

"You're the memory weaver?" I rasped, surprised I was even able to form words.

"Don't be mad at your mother, Ky." His voice strained, not carrying its usual warmth. "This was just as much my decision as it was hers, princess." His old childhood nickname for me suddenly made my throat go dry. "I wanted to get things under control before you saw me."

"Y-you knew. You knew who I was. Who she was..." My thoughts were spiraling, chaotic discs flying in every direction while I tried to figure out how this was possible. "How can you have powers? How can you even be here? You're from Dorset."

"That's true. But my family isn't," my dad said, glancing down a moment before meeting my mother's eyes. I sat there, completely confused, waiting for him to expand further. "My ancestors were some of the first ones who inhabited Dorset and established Halston University. We've lived there for generations. That world is all I've ever known but I'm not *from* there."

"What?" I felt like the punchline of a joke that everyone understood except for me.

"He was also part of Vis. Not a founder like I was, but a member as another descendant of Celaria."

Both of my parents were descended from here, a realm they'd never told me about. One they'd *pretended* didn't exist.

Both of my parents were in Vis, the secret society that had happily bled me out months ago to gain access to this world.

Both of my parents were fucking liars.

"How could you keep this from me?" My hands shook at my sides, sparks erupting from my palms and slithering up my arms. "I watched you mourn her. For *years*."

"I did mourn your mother," he said. "I mourned what we couldn't have all these years. The loss of it. But I also knew who she was—what might keep her from coming back to us. I always hoped she would, but when she didn't, I knew she was needed here."

I guess now it made sense why my dad didn't make a fuss when he packed up my room like Anna had mentioned.

My life had been a lie. Everything had been a lie.

My mother's hand stretched to reach for me, probably to calm the fiery power that was spilling out, but I stepped away from her grasp. "Why didn't we just come with you and have a life together here?"

"The deal with the Enchantress," my mother rasped. "We always agreed we would keep you away from Celaria until she was gone. We couldn't risk her finding out about you or taking your powers."

"Your mother and I stayed apart to keep you safe."

I took another step back from both of them. "I don't believe you."

43

"I know it's a lot to take in." My mother moved closer. "But we did this to protect you."

"Fuck you and your *protection*," I seethed, drawing a line of sparks in front of her. "You could have told me this whole time I've been here. When I found you."

I snapped my gaze to my dad. "And you. All these years, you let me believe she was gone. That she didn't care, or that she'd died. You watched me twist myself in knots wanting to be worthy of what she'd left behind. And you said *nothing*. You even encouraged me to follow in her footsteps."

I stood up, looking away from them both as I strode toward the stony exit, sparks still pulsing from my hands. "You fucking deserve each other."

"Kyleigh!" they called out to me, but I refused to even acknowledge them.

I needed to get away. To find someone that I could actually trust. Someone who had never lied to me and understood the damaging weight lies put on a relationship.

Storming past the guards at the front of the fort, I barged through the entrance, only allowing myself to focus on getting to my destination.

Frantically, I knocked on the door. As soon as it began to open, I pushed it in the rest of the way.

Neve's brows furrowed a moment, taking in the sparks still drifting along my arms.

"I need to get out of here. Come with me?"

She didn't question, she merely nodded.

I peeled off my clothes and sprinted toward the balcony. Scales ripped through me, heat coursing through my veins as I tore painfully into the sky. There might have been a million problems trying to pull me down right now, but sometimes when choosing between fight or flight, flight won out.

A moment later, Neve's brilliant blue dragon was at my back, only the sound of her wings *swooshing* along with the breeze. The wind whipped into me, and I lifted my snout, inhaling the fresh air. Then I twisted, barreling away from the fort.

Neve and I climbed higher, heading toward the mountains.

You okay? she asked through the link in our minds—something only possible to do with our fellow Revered ones and our champion.

No. But I will be.

A ray of sparks shot from my snout, raining down to the ground. I didn't have a destination, I just needed to escape. Twisting my head back, I caught Dru watching us from the fort. His eyes glittered in awe, and he lifted his hand off the leather-bound book strewn across his lap to wave. As he became a tiny speck in the study's window, I huffed to myself in satisfaction.

Tonight, he'd be mine.

But I needed to release some steam—or sparks, rather—before I combusted, and I refused to let this anger, or anything else for that matter, ruin our ceremony.

CHAPTER 8

Sloan

"A re you still watching her through Mox?" Dru asked, not bringing his head up from the paper. He'd been sketching out the cabin's layout for the third time, the other two attempts wadded up and strewn across his desk. There were a few rooms I couldn't fully relay since Mox's view was limited, so he'd shaded the unknown areas dark gray.

I hesitated, unsure if admitting that I had just been watching prior to arriving here was a good idea. Neve and Ox were adamant that I stop. They'd harped on it the entire walk over, talking about how it would only cause me more pain to see her like that. Like it would be easier for me to put her out of my head if I didn't have Mox keeping tabs.

The ghost of her haunted me wherever I went, whether I watched or not. She was stuck there with no recollection of who I was. There's no way she would have ignored Mox otherwise, and the few wisps who had shown him interest didn't do much more than visit quickly or leave him breadcrumbs on the windowsill.

"Of course you are," he said, brows furrowed, marking where the Enchantress's bookcase sat and jotting down a few items I'd remembered seeing there, along with ones Aislin had told him about before.

At least he seemed to understand. "Wouldn't you do the same if you could?"

"Of course. And thanks to you and Mox, we might be able to have an easier way to get to Aislin."

"What do you mean?"

"Do you think you could call him back and put something on him?"

"Like what?"

"I recently created a locator," he said, pointing to a scale with a sharpened tip sitting on the corner of the desk. "If you give me a little of your blood, then call Mox to the edge of the Silent Woods and attach a vial of it to him, I could use this locator to follow his path and figure out where exactly the Enchantress's cabin is since it's usually not discoverable by anyone she doesn't want visiting her."

"Let's do it," I said, rolling up my sleeve and offering him my arm without a second thought. "I can head there after I stop by to check on the new recruits for a few minutes—I promised Ox I would."

"That works. I have some time while Kyleigh and Neve are off... I saw them flying toward the mountains not too long ago, but they'll be back before tonight." He gave me a sheepish look. "We have our champion ceremony."

"Oh really?" I asked, a lump catching in the back of my throat. I forced it down, replacing it with a smile. "I'm happy for you guys. Truly."

My hesitation hadn't gone unnoticed, the sides of his lips flattening into a straight line.

"I'm sorry, Dru. I'm a shitty friend right now."

"No, you're not." He placed his hand on mine, the leather of his glove cool against my skin. "You're a grieving friend. I apologize for bringing it up, but I wanted to see if there was anything you could tell me about the ceremony and what to expect." He adjusted the collar of his button up. "The magic part, that is."

I barked out a laugh at his clarification. "And here I was wondering if you needed me to explain what to do with a woman."

"Kyleigh hasn't had any complaints so far," he mumbled.

My lips quirked up a moment, giving him a grin. "Well, that's because she doesn't know what she's missing."

"Let me grab a few things so we can get everything situated before you leave. You can give me some ceremony pointers while I collect your blood." He winked, squeezing my hand and laughing with me before walking out the door. I felt lighter than I had since Aislin had been taken. Maybe this is what it was like to have hope again. To have a friend to share it with.

Being a commander earned you respect if you did a good job, but it didn't earn you a lot of friends, especially when you were close with the king. Red had been my only friend for the longest time, but he'd been so focused on retribution for Neve and his father, we didn't do much laughing over the last decade. Lots of whiskey drinking, though. Maybe I was becoming more like my misguided friend than I cared to admit.

Since I'd come to Arafax, I'd been met with suspicion, which I couldn't blame them for, but I'd also gained friends, old and new. Having Neve back in my life was refreshing. Ox understood what it meant to serve someone other than yourself, but beyond that, he was incredibly kind.

I knew they both wanted what was best for me by barging into my room this morning, and I wanted to give them that. I wanted to be the Sloan from before, but I didn't know how to get there. How to be that warrior.

If I couldn't save Aislin, I might never be that person again.

We'd each been whole, but she'd become a key piece of me, our bond wrapping our entirety together into something beautiful, precious, and new. All I'd wanted was to explore what that meant for us, the future we'd build, but it'd been stolen away all too soon.

"Ready?" Dru asked. He was already back in his chair, pouring some cleansing elixir on a cloth.

"Of course." It tingled as he wiped the damp fabric across my forearm, and I quickly turned my head away, not wanting to watch the needle break skin. I hissed when it struck the vein, but kept my arm relaxed, glad to be doing something that would better our chances at rescuing Aislin.

"Okay, so tell me all about what to expect in the grove tonight," Dru said, still holding my hand as crimson filled the vial.

I smiled, renewed excitement coursing through me over getting to talk about it. I hadn't shared with anyone about the bond Aislin and I had forged into existence. The bond that had unraveled just as quickly.

"Well, Dru, you should expect one of the most incredible nights of your life."

Mox came trotting toward me, giving a satisfied grumble. I knelt, nuzzling my cheek to his snout. "I've missed you, Moxy."

I hated being separated from him. The snow fox had been my constant companion the last few decades since I'd solidified our familial connection at our bonding ceremony. Now, even that felt strained, and I couldn't tell if it was from the distance we'd had between us since arriving in Arafax, or if something had messed with it when I'd tied us both to Aislin and her bond was severed.

After all, a braid missing a strand was merely a pair of twisted-up threads.

I need your help.

He sat on his hind legs, cocking his head to the side in question.

Running my hands through his velvety fur, I hugged around him, reaching for the compartment on his harness. The tiny vial in my hands seemed too small to actually accomplish much, but Dru said it would work.

Mox's head snapped behind him, and I turned to find a single wisp flitting midair, watching us. Her wings hummed, but without any others from her coven, it seemed it wasn't enough to glamor me. I didn't feel any different, at least.

Strands of shadowy hair floated behind her, voluptuous curves making up the silhouette of her body. She still didn't move, hovering a few feet away as if curious.

"Aislin?" I asked, my voice breaking midway through her name. "Is that you?"

Mox growled at me as I extended an arm, keeping my palm turned upright to the spectral creature. When she started gliding closer, Mox moved between us, sniffing the air beneath it.

"It's okay, Mox," I said, not sure if it was but unwilling to pass up the opportunity that this could be her. Within my reach. Taking a step forward, I kept my hand out. An ashen limb extended toward me, fingers unfurling, trailing along my palm. The phantom of my lover closed the distance between us, caressing my skin, and sending a familiar electricity through my veins. Then she brushed back some of my silver strands.

A tear ran down my cheek, dropping onto the black tunic whose owner I stared back at.

"I love you," I whispered, knowing full well that she probably couldn't understand any of what I said, but needing to get it out all the same.

There was an emptiness in her eyes, one that didn't seem to

recall who I was to her. But behind it, there was maybe a glint of longing? I was most likely an alluring stranger in her mind, but I didn't care. This was her. I just knew it.

She curled against my body, and I pressed my cheek to the tingling sensation that came in response, her essence prickling against my skin. I could have sworn I felt the delicate bond in my chest trying to braid itself together, snagging against some unseen barrier.

Mox's ears pricked up, and she stilled. Turning out of my arms, the wisp began to fly through the trees.

"Don't go!" I called out to her.

Not again.

A warm snout nudged me. Mox. He had the vial attached to him. He could follow her back and get Dru the location about the cabin, but I couldn't let Aislin go again. Not when every thread of my being told me it was her.

Go, I thought, climbing onto his back.

And we were off.

Dashing after the tiny wisp, she became larger with each gallop he took to catch up with her. He sprinted through the trees, knowing better than to give up this chase.

We've found Aislin.

His elation purred between our chests, spurring him to run faster. We bolted between barren branches, threading through the Silent Woods in pursuit of her.

Time disappeared. There was only us and Aislin's essence within reach—a singular focus tugging me forward.

When the cabin came into view, fear suddenly struck, bubbling and acidic.

What if the Enchantress saw me?

I hadn't thought this through.

Slow up.

Mox pulled back his cadence, the cabin mere yards away. Aislin halted as soon as we stopped following. She'd come back here so quickly. Had she been summoned by her mistress? Could she break from her thrall enough to know I was here? I tapped Mox's rump with my boot, and he tentatively trotted toward her.

She held out a shadowy hand, and I took it in mine, rubbing my thumb against the strange vapor she was comprised of. It was flexible enough to move through when I touched it, but solid enough to slip between my fingers.

"Finally here to free your beloved?" a saccharine voice echoed through the canopy, jerking my attention to the Enchantress who was silhouetted by the light pouring through the cabin's window. "I'd hoped as much."

I shifted my weight, hand coming to the hilt of my throwing knife at my ankle. I was ready to find out what she wanted. How I could get Aislin back.

I'd do anything.

Mox growled, the force of it reverberating through me. He snapped at Aislin, jolting me backward before dashing with me in the opposite direction. Gripping his harness, I leaned down close to him.

Turn around, Mox. Turn the fuck around.

Ignoring me, he kept charging in the opposite direction of the cabin, as if shouting his unspoken response of *this is for your own good.*

His instincts had never led me astray. Even now. As badly as I wanted to get back to Aislin, to rescue her and find a way to return her to me, he was right. I'd promised her I wouldn't come back without help. If this was the final promise I gave to the woman I loved, I had to keep it.

Had it all been a trap? Had the Enchantress directed her wisp, my Revered, to lure me there?

I didn't want to think that way, but deep down...I knew.

Aislin wasn't doing anything she hadn't been instructed to.

CHAPTER 9
Kyleigh

Neve flew next to me, her blue snout tipped in my direction, only glancing ahead every few strokes of her wings. A naked patch of flesh covered her side, small jagged sapphire scales budding from their depths. It had taken a few months of healing, but they were finally coming in. She roared, nodding ahead just in time for me to dodge an ashen-colored hawk circling in the graying sky.

Shit. Diving quickly, I avoided killing the bird. With my luck, that was someone's beloved familiar.

Once I straightened out, I lined back up with Neve as she called out to me through our dragon magic. *Okay, Kyleigh. What's going on?*

Taking a deep breath, I released a stream of sparks into the air, making sure we were away from any fellow flying creatures. *My dad.*

Her body stiffened a moment, dipping midair a few inches before realigning. *Craig? What about him?*

He's here.

Spotting the woods between our territory and Inverno's, I descended, landing among the various sized rocks scattered throughout. I thought back to the night I'd spent here, when Aislin taught me about my powers. We were a bit too close to the Silent Woods for comfort—if my mother knew how near we were she would have a conniption—but at least there wasn't much here that I could burn.

Neve barely landed before stepping into her human form as smoothly as if she were simply removing a scarf. I watched her transition in awe. Would it ever be that smooth for me? Even when I could shift quickly, it was extremely painful.

My bones popped, body contorting back into place, wings retracting into their buds. Waving my hand around myself, my sparks floated into a makeshift dress, helping me feel somewhat less uncomfortable with the nudity that came with shifting. Following my lead, Neve used her hand to cover herself in a twisting blizzard, snowflakes flurrying around her curves.

"So, he's here in Celaria? How is that possible?"

"At Arafax's fort," I blurted out, swallowing down the bile edging its way up my throat. "Well, not in the fort itself but some hidden bunker I discovered in its maze."

She cocked her head, gaze penetrating. "What are you saying?"

"I'm saying that the weavers my mother mentioned sending off for everyone's safety weren't really sent off. They have been held in these weird living...quarters. And my dad is one of them."

Her throat bobbed a moment, eyes darting around before coming back to me. "I don't know what to say."

"Did you know?"

Were my parents the only ones lying to me about this?

Did they ever plan to tell me the truth?

Maybe they'd been waiting for the right time. But when would have been the right time to find out that the last decade we'd been separated my mother had been a queen in a magical world, and oh—guess what?—dad was magical too but didn't know much about it. Oh, and they were both in a secret society that tried to kill me.

There was never going to be a good time for that conversation.

I should have been thrilled my dad was here now, but I didn't know what to believe. Plus, according to my mother, it wasn't safe for me to go in and talk to him.

"I didn't know that Craig was here or that he had any abilities..." Neve's lips pressed into a thin line.

"But you knew he was from Celaria?" I clarified, reading between the words she refused to say. Heat radiated through my chest, igniting my veins. "That he was in the secret society my mom founded in the Otherworld. You two kept in touch. You knew."

Finally meeting my gaze, she blew some frost at me, dousing out the light emanating from my chest. "I did."

"Why didn't you say anything?"

"I didn't feel like it was my place," she said, taking a tentative step toward me. When I didn't retreat, she reached for my shoulder, placing an icy palm on it. "I tried to talk to Isla about it, but she was insistent." She shut her eyes a moment, taking a deep inhale like she was just as exasperated with my mother as I was. "It doesn't excuse keeping the truth from you, but I did believe you should know. I'm truly sorry."

Unlike my interactions with my mother, every time I'd talked to my godmother and asked her for the truth, she'd been honest. The fact that I felt closer to her, someone I'd only met months ago, compared to my own parents right now wasn't lost on me. Neve may have been able to put up icy barriers, but she never did around me, giving me more warmth than my fire-blessed mother.

"Are there any other secrets that I should be aware of?" I asked, needing the honesty my mother owed me to come from somewhere. Anywhere.

"If there are, they are ones I'm just as in the dark about."

"I don't know how I'm supposed to have a relationship with her—or my dad, for that matter." My body ached, the shifting and flying taking its toll. I walked over to a large gray slab and plopped down. "He can't even hug me because his memory weaving ability isn't in control. What if I get too close and he ends up forgetting who I am?"

Hot tears tracked down my cheeks, and I wiped them away, my hand trembling. "I already feel like I've lost one parent. I can't lose them both."

"You won't. We'll figure it out." Neve sat beside me, her tone calm and reassuring enough that I almost believed her.

Pulling my knees to my chest, I shivered, then wrapped some more sparks around myself to keep warm. "What do you know about weavers?"

"Honestly, not much," she replied, brow furrowing. "We were always told never to go into their territory." She scooted a few feet away, giving an apologetic look. I didn't understand at first, but then realized I felt warmer, forgetting that she'd wrapped herself in her own icy powers. Did she not feel the cold like everyone else did?

"Weavers use mind magic and can manipulate your thoughts, beliefs...ultimately your reality. It's dangerous magic, which is why your mother probably kept them hidden away where they couldn't cause too much damage."

"How do we help him, then?" I asked, thinking about how unstable my own powers were when I first arrived. I couldn't imagine being able to manipulate other people's minds and my own. "How do I get my dad back?"

"I'm not sure, but I'll think on it. Have you talked to Dru?"

"Not yet, but I will. Our champion ceremony is tonight, and I don't want to dampen the mood."

While I wouldn't risk making a big deal of our ceremony, I also couldn't have anything take away from a night that was meant to be special for the two of us. Dru already had so much on his mind right now. "Once we're bonded, I'll talk to him about it. Not that I'll be able to keep my emotions too hidden from him afterward."

"Yeah, that will be hard," she agreed, voice drifting off. Last time I'd asked her if she would ever take a champion, she hadn't seemed to want that level of commitment. It was probably a sore subject, considering everything that'd happened between her and Redmond. She shifted uncomfortably, hand poised at her chest.

"You okay?"

"Oh yeah," she said, clearing her throat, still distant. "Just was thinking about...Sloan. Wondering how she's doing after we finally convinced Sweeney and Leigh to cut off her whiskey supply."

"How's Leigh doing?"

"She's doing well. Grateful you were able to bring Dru back and for all his help when she woke. She's up and moving around. Needs a crutch for support sometimes, but that's about it."

"That's great to hear." Now it was my voice that was thinning. I hadn't seen Leigh since that night at the inn when she'd accidentally been hit by my blast meant for Flynt's men. She'd been unconscious for about two weeks, Dru making her a priority when we returned before turning his attention back to the Enchantress.

"You know, you should go see her," Neve said, a slight scold in her tone. I was being a coward, and while she wouldn't say it to my face, I knew that's what she was thinking.

"Yeah, it's just easier for Dru and I to be at the fort with all of his research, so I haven't been to the inn in a while." And I hated the looks everyone gave me at The Lavender. While some people seemed grateful to be rid of Flynt and his crew, many more local townsfolk who frequented the pub weren't happy with losing their trusted importer and inn proprietor.

"Understandable, considering everything he's working on." Neve nodded, standing up. "But I know she'd like to see you."

"I'll make it over there soon," I agreed, standing up to join her. She strode a handful of paces, scales rippling out from under her skin, her body and wings unfurling.

Closing my eyes, I pictured my coral and white opalescent dragon, feeling the shift beginning from my side where the scale markings climbed up, growing taller, snout jutting out from my face. I continued to let my bones adjust, fire coursing through the thick red veins spanning my wings. The holes were gone, left by the arrows from Flynt's crossbow, but long, jagged ridges of scars remained.

If I had healed them right away, gone back into human form, they probably wouldn't have become infected and left me with the permanent marks on my wings.

Dru had suggested going to the falls in my dragon form to rinse away any evidence of the attack, but I'd refused. Erasing the scars made it easier to pretend the wounds beneath didn't exist.

And I didn't want to forget.

Dru

Two hours.

Only two more hours left until I'd be meeting Kyleigh in Everwood Grove.

Tonight we'd opted for no celebrations, no special attire, nothing marking the occasion of our champion ceremony. Kyleigh had been adamant about not doing anything to jinx it— the events that had transpired last time we'd tried to bond too ingrained in her. But she knew better than to think I'd leave her now. While our bond hadn't been established, I was tethered to her in irreversible ways.

Pulling the box out of the drawer of my desk, I lifted the lid, removing the locket and holding it up by its chain. The heart at its scoop swung back and forth, golden filigree swirls billowing along its face, meeting at the seams, one lined by a set of clasps. I unlatched them, running my fingers over the smooth edges. It was empty for now. What would Kyleigh choose to carry inside of it?

Putting the box back in the drawer, I tucked the necklace into my pocket to give to her tonight. I was so curious what the bond would feel like. Would I always be able to sense her? How would our strengths blend together and manifest?

I could have asked Sloan more about it, but the connection worked differently for each dragon and their champion, according to the few things I'd learned. Besides, it was like rubbing salt in a wound when her very bond had been severed. I had to hope that it still existed in some way despite Aislin's transformation, but Sloan was too fragile right now to broach the subject. At least she'd been sober and willing enough to help me locate the Enchantress's cabin.

The paper with my hand-drawn map of the Silent Woods was pinned to the wall, and I traced along the paths Mox had taken in and out of the woods, staring at the large red circle around the spot he'd stopped for a period, lingering.

Now that I knew where the Enchantress was, I needed to find her weakness. Some way to free the wisps before we vanquished her.

The door swung open, the Queen entering and looking unsettled. Her eyes were bloodshot, arms crossed. "Any progress to report before you head out?"

"Finally nailed down where the cabin is, thanks to Sloan and Mox."

"Now we just need a way to kill the Enchantress."

I already knew when it came down to it, the Queen would readily sacrifice the wisps as long as the Enchantress was gone. What I didn't know was if I could live with myself if that was the only choice. So I refused to believe it was. I'd spend every waking hour finding a way to ensure the wisps could be saved, not just for my sisters anymore, but also for Aislin.

"My gut tells me that the tome King Redmond brought us from her cabin has the answers," I said, handing her the leather-bound text and flipping it open.

"Why do you say that?"

I continued to skim each page, pointing at the drawings as I flipped through them. "The pictures line up too much with the magics used to shield her cabin, and from what Sloan told me about her current appearance, it matches one in the book at the very back."

"Well, that's something."

"The only problem is, I have no clue how to read it. Everything is written in ancient faerie runes. You wouldn't happen to have some sort of book on how to translate it somewhere?" Her eyes flicked up from the text, shifting as if she were thinking about it. "I already asked Redmond, and Inverno apparently doesn't since they refused to ever get involved with the faeries."

"No. There wouldn't be any texts like that around."

My shoulders slunk down.

A smile peeled at the corner of the Queen's lips. "You know what this means, Dru?"

"What?" I had no idea what could have her perking up when I'd just been told I still wouldn't be able to decipher the text.

"The only ones who can read those ancient runes are the faeries. No books exist anywhere with a translation because they teach it to their young. It's passed down from one faerie generation to the next."

"So if only faeries can understand it and the Enchantress is using this book somehow, or has used it...then she must be a faerie herself?"

"Precisely."

I knew nothing about faeries, but even being able to put some label to the type of magic the Enchantress could be working with was more than I had before. Every small clue was another piece in the puzzle to figuring out how to deal with her. "I guess the wings make sense, then."

"Yes, though faeries don't usually have wings like hers."

I jerked upright, looking at her. "How do you know?"

"My older brother told me once." Her eyes softened a bit.

"He used to handle things for our father when it came to diplomatic affairs with the faeries."

"But no one knows where the faeries went."

"Yes, I'm not sure what happened once they were eradicated." She took the book, flipping through more pages.

"Eradicated?" No one ever talked about what happened to the faeries or where they went. Of course I'd been too little to know about it anyway, but considering my father had been a scholar, I'd think he'd know about a piece of history like that.

"Yes," the Queen continued. "According to my father, they were infesting the Evergleam."

It was hard for me to believe a population of people would be *infesting* somewhere they called home, even if that home was a large hollow tree. "You mean living in it?"

"It was a truly unfortunate situation," she said with a sigh. Shutting the tome, she set it on the table, then collapsed into the chair across from me. "Their king was a nasty piece of work. Wanted everyone else to cower to him, including Arafax since he held our power source. Even things like the champion ceremonies had to be approved by him. Can you imagine having to get permission for your ceremony tonight from someone who could fit in the palm of your hand?"

"I see." I sat down, bracing my elbows on my knees while I tried to figure out what to do with this information. My chest was tight, the whole exchange making me uneasy.

"I'll leave it to you to locate them and come up with a plan." She stood, pushing her chair to the table. "You can start on it tomorrow."

"Of course."

She reached for the door, turning to look at me before opening it. "Have you seen Kyleigh yet today?"

Curious... She hadn't brought Kyleigh up during our work together ever since she'd tried suggesting I convince her daughter to leave with me and return to the Otherworld. "Only briefly this morning."

"Oh. Okay."

I tilted my head. "Why?"

"No reason," she replied with a small smile. "Just curious."

Had she seen her? Tried to convince her not to bond with me? I knew my lack of power and influence didn't bother Kyleigh, that my strengths made me invaluable in different ways, but I didn't think her mother felt the same. While I shouldn't ask, while it wasn't my business nor my position to with her being my queen, I couldn't leave it unspoken. "I know you don't think I'm good enough for her. That you don't support this bonding."

She walked back over to me, and I stiffened, bracing myself for whatever she would say next. I had Kyleigh's love and I was devoted to her. It might not be enough for her mother, but it was enough for the two of us.

"I don't think anyone is good enough for my daughter." She chuckled, placing a hand on my shoulder and looking me in the eye. I held my breath. "But if anyone were to come remotely close, it would be you, Dru."

"Thanks." I exhaled, releasing the weight from my chest. "Have you ever thought about telling her that?"

All Kyleigh had wanted since her mother had left was to feel worthy of her. Even though she'd found her own way, I knew better than to assume that meant she didn't care about what her mother wished for her. She was her mother, after all. If my own were still alive, I'd want the same. "She may not ever admit it but your approval still means something to her."

"She doesn't deserve my approval," she replied, tone firm.

My body went still, fighting the urge to tell her off. "Exus—"

"She's above it."

I had not expected that response from her. "What do you mean?"

"I went to the Otherworld to live up to my parents' expectations for me. Thinking maybe that would be enough to secure my position within our family. It took me a while, but I realized that their approval wasn't what mattered." She shook her head, heading back toward the door.

"I don't understand."

"You will one day, if you are ever to rule by her side." The thought equally terrified and thrilled me for completely different reasons. "When you rule a kingdom, no one's approval matters but your own. Being a leader means *you* have to live with your decisions."

I didn't care about ruling. It wasn't something I ever saw for myself or my future. But I'd take any future alongside Kyleigh.

Starting tonight.

CHAPTER 11

Isla

W hen I'd told Dru I'd cover his lessons this afternoon, I didn't expect to be juggling the emotions of my daughter in the midst of it. Half distracted, I managed to instruct the new Celarians about the history of the six territories that made up our realm. That topic, of course, led to some uncomfortable questions about why the portal had remained closed to their people for so many decades, making me regret volunteering in the first place.

If they knew the real history about their founding, about the people who'd built Vindicatio Vis...they'd probably be shocked.

I still couldn't believe Kyleigh had been so naïve as to bring them through the portal, though many seemed harmless enough.

Except Travis Grymm.

That sapling didn't fall far from the tree. He was the spitting image of his father—handsome, arrogant, and deceptively dangerous. Luckily, Kyleigh had chosen to avoid him.

The memory of her finding Craig and I in the bunker made acid burn up my throat. I'd been trying so hard since she'd arrived, balancing on the blade's edge of wanting to have a relationship with my daughter and protecting her from those who would happily use her. To give her the things she wanted, even if I couldn't be the woman she wished for.

The fact was, neither of us was the same person we'd left behind in the Otherworld. But every time I looked at Kyleigh, I still saw my little girl.

That same little girl now glared at me with so much disdain, my heart felt like it ripped clear out of my chest.

Once upon a time, I was her world.

She used to think I hung the moon; that I could do no wrong.

Unfortunately, my duties as Arafax's Queen had pulled me away from her. I'd spent so many years wishing to be back in Celaria, then I'd returned to everything burned to ash. Never to see my family again.

Either of them.

I didn't have time to sulk, though. I couldn't. I had decisions to make, a kingdom to resurrect—to lift out of the rubble and rebuild. A decade later and the margin of change hadn't been steep enough for all it'd cost me.

For *who* it'd cost me.

I'd watched Kyleigh and Neve take to the sky, propelling themselves away from the fort. From Arafax. From me.

I should be grateful that she had Neve, her godmother—someone to look out for her that she didn't currently hate. But all I felt was envy watching them together, soaring above the clouds.

I'd fucked up, yet again, but no one wanted a queen that made mistakes. There was no room for that when you ruled.

Ruling meant making the tough decisions. It meant taking out personal desires and trivialities when leading. I hated it. Especially that it had kept me away from *them*. But there was no one else left here to lead. And the only person I would have trusted to take my place outside of the royal family had been imprisoned and stuck in her dragon form for the last decade.

Last in line for the austere red-tufted chair, I'd learned from my parents and elder siblings that being royal came with a cost.

Sacrifice.

They'd paid a steep price, and I refused to let Kyleigh suffer the same fate.

Whether she wanted to accept it or not, this would all be hers one day. I just needed to do my part to ensure what I left behind for her would be worth protecting and staying for.

Now that Craig was here too, we could finally have that life together as a family—once the dust settled and the Enchantress was no longer a threat. I hated that my burdens, my deal, now had become Kyleigh's problem.

My brother had helped lock the Enchantress and her corrosive magic away in the woods, keeping her poison from our people. He'd saved Arafax from the stifling hold the Faerie King had over our kingdom and our Revered. I didn't have to know the specifics to know that the realm had become safer without King Chadwick around.

I thought once the gem had been retrieved, placed back in the sacred hollow where it belonged, that I'd be the one to gain our bloodline's Revered magic. The strength of my ancestors, of our dragons and their champions, could assist me in destroying the evil sorceress and break that foolish deal I'd made with her all those years ago. Now that responsibility would fall on my daughter, Arafax's Princess.

Turning off into the hidden cove within the fort's labyrinth, I rounded the corner, activating the enchantment and entering the first room along the narrow hallway. It was empty aside from some clothes hanging in the closet and a few mementos on the desk. This place had become my hideaway over the years—a secret bunker to keep Arafax's royalty safe. If my family had been here, things could have been different.

My life could have been different with Kyleigh and Craig.

But that's not what the stars had in mind for me.

I slipped on the blue jeans, flannel shirt, and gray low-rise sneakers, then swept my hair back into a ponytail. It seemed to affect him less when I did these things.

When I was *her*.

Familiar.

Not the trounced-up queen I'd cultivated to protect my people all these years.

Reve—the dream weaver who'd given me aid against the Enchantress entering my dreams and protected Kyleigh's identity—had sent word to his people on my behalf, a request for aid with our new struggling weavers. He'd tried, unsuccessfully, to work with them in the meantime. When he finally heard back from Alucinor, their council had decided they would be unable to assist.

I'd just have to find another way.

"I DON'T THINK THIS IS A GOOD IDEA," CRAIG SAID wearily, hands clasped around mine.

I leaned back against the headboard, his head resting on my shoulder, thumb tapping an anxious rhythm on my knuckle. His brow was dripping sweat as he tried to hold back his magic.

"I know, but if this power works like our other wielders', it's the best way." I placed a hand over his to steady his nerves and stared up into the lilac pools of his eyes. They were still flecked with his blue hue, but now it scattered outward from his pupil like a firework—a trace of familiarity even with how much had shifted for both of us since we were both in the Otherworld together.

"You'll stop me if it gets to be too much?" he asked, uncertainty kindling his words.

"If it gets to be too much, I'll let you know." I brushed my fingers through the stray strands of his raven hair, somehow darker than I remembered—either from the time we spent apart or possibly from his weaver lineage coming through. "But we need to keep working at this, at least until I can get you more help."

"Last time..." The strained lines reaching from the corners of his eyes softened along their edges, his expression morphing into one full of apologies. "What if I hurt you again?"

I scoffed. "I assure you, it's nothing I can't handle." *Like he owes me any apologies after everything he's endured because of me. Because of who I am.* "Whatever you can dish out, I've dealt with worse."

His gaze drifted to the door before dropping to the ground. "Have you seen Ky since—"

"No." I shook my head, then shifted on the bed, moving in front of him. "She and Dru have their ceremony tonight."

"I need to talk to her," he said, resolve etched into his tone. "Help her understand."

"We both do. And we will. But not tonight." I rolled back my shoulders, guiding his hands to my temples. "Believe me, she's not ready to listen."

"I failed her."

"If anyone failed her, it's me. I won't allow you to take on any of that burden. You've carried enough for the both of us." I tapped the backs of his hands to begin their work, already starting to feel the thrum of his magic begging to pull from me. To consume despite Craig's attempts to keep his powers suppressed. It's why I couldn't let Kyleigh get too close earlier. That much charged emotion, it would have only spelled disaster for them both. "Now, let me carry some of yours."

"Are you sure?" His brows scrunched together to the point that it was painful to witness. "I don't want to bring up—"

Giving him a gentle smile, I urged him on. "You can't control what your magic does yet. Whatever happens, I won't hold it against you."

The worst part about this process was how real everything felt. While my mind actively knew anything I saw was the past, my heart never quite caught up.

I WATCHED THE STARS BLINK IN AND OUT OF VIEW against their blanket of pitch. Without that slight tinge of Celarian purple, the night sky was drab. Empty. There were no dragons flitting across the moon's backdrop. No comforting roar of their protection overhead.

It was quiet.

Too quiet.

I pressed my ear against the corium, giving a quick glance around the Quad to see if anyone was near. A few drunken students were stumbling back to their dorms together, not taking any notice of me.

"*Gar córan tar cloch*," I whispered to the stone before twisting my face and putting my cheek flush against it.

"Hello?" A gentle voice filtered over the swishing sounds connecting us through the stone, and I sighed with relief.

Things here had been so...tense. Unexpectedly so, even knowing our relations with Halston's Celarians would take time to repair.

That's why they'd sent me, after all. To appease them.

If we show them the Otherworld is good enough for one of our royals, they can't complain about being there, now can they?

My father's words rang through my head. Being the youngest, I'd been the easiest to discard. I'd only spoken to him once since I arrived here...and I wasn't planning on hearing from him again.

"Isla? You there?" Neve's comforting voice finally came out clearly against the wind obscuring our connection.

"Yes! I'm here!" Tears sprang to my eyes. "I've missed you. Tell me everything."

"Oh...where do I even begin?" She huffed out a chuckle, and I could almost imagine her smile, as if she were laying here on the stone next to me, talking like we always did late into the night when she'd come visit after her nightly patrols.

"How's...flying?" I asked, trying to use vague terms in case someone overheard. Of course, they would just think I'm crazy, talking to a rock.

"Incredible. I found a great quiet spot away from —everything."

Neve's family had been struggling since her grandfather had passed. Her grandmother had followed not long after. Arafax had mourned the loss of a Revered, but to Neve, to her parents, it was a huge hit to their family to lose them both. I was glad she had my sister, Nora, to give her guidance now and somewhere to escape to when things were too intense at home.

"Where?"

"Tucked away in the Grymm Mountains."

"Wow," I said, voice falling flat at the mention of that name. My pulse began to race as my gaze darted around the Quad one more time, in case any of his friends were following me again. Nestled in the corner, leaning against a dark-gray building, were a few guys, eyes flitting over to me before going back to their conversation.

Are they watching me?
Do they know who I am?

"Well, that sounds like an amazing spot, Neve." I forced a smile to my lips.

"Everything okay there?" she asked tentatively. She could always blot away any façade I tried to put up, a quality I loved and loathed about her. "You sound—"

"I'm fine!" I interjected before she could ask more, suddenly feeling like all eyes were pinned to me despite the near emptiness of the Quad. "But it's starting to get crowded here, so I better get going. Need to get some studying done before class tomorrow."

History. And considering I'd lived here for only a month, I was coming in with a severe disadvantage. I'd need a few golden goose lattes to get me through the all-nighter I'd need to pull.

"Love you, Neve," I whispered hastily. "Take care of yourself."

"Love you too." The smack of her lips throwing me a kiss echoed through the charcoal slab, and I returned the gesture. "Same time next week?"

"Of course."

Sitting upright, I swung my legs around and popped off the Sentry Stone. It was displayed like an inanimate fixture in the middle of campus—not the hub that could take me back to Celaria in a second. Something I desperately wanted.

Every day that passed tempted me more to disobey my family and go home.

Looping my arm through my backpack, I slung it over my shoulder. Footsteps mimicked mine, never closing the distance as I neared Halston's library. My chest pinched at the pair of reminders of whom I belong to.

Clutching my books to my chest, I ascended the staircase, eyes glancing over the illustrated history of my people. My home.

Not anymore.

I pushed the heavy doors open, letting them swing back, knowing they wouldn't slam shut behind me.

That *they'd* be there, following, smothering out the sound.

CHAPTER 12

Kyleigh

M y thoughts still spiraled over my parents' revelations this morning, but I refused to let it interfere with our champion ceremony. Their secrets had ruled enough of my life. I was doing this for me.

For *us*.

Last time I'd fretted so much about getting my dad's approval, unhappy with the fact he wouldn't know that I was committing myself eternally to Dru. I didn't even care now. He'd lied to me for at least half my life. He'd known my mother was alive, where she was, most likely what she was up to—at least to some degree that he never shared with me. That wasn't a person I needed to garner approval from when it came to choosing a family for myself.

And that's what Dru was for me.

My family. My hearth.

I'd always planned to go back to Vermont. Dru had said he would go with me after we'd defeated the Enchantress.

Now all those plans were up in the air.

We could do anything; go anywhere we wanted.

This life would be *ours*.

Starting tonight.

Slicing into my palm, I stood among the collection of stones sitting on the outskirts of Arafax's village, whispering the incantation to access Everwood Grove. Taking my palms together, I pulled them apart, the veiled entrance opening wider with my hands until it was large enough to walk through. Unlike a portal that took you to other locations, the Evergleam was always here, just shrouded by magic.

As if he could read my mind, Dru was already waiting for me at the edge of the grove.

"You're here." I released a sigh, instantly calmer by his presence. He held out his hand, and I slipped mine into his grasp.

"Of course I am. There was no way I would be late to this." My chest clenched, thinking back to the last time I'd been here, but before the sensation could settle, Dru dragged me to him and kissed me, his tongue exploring my mouth so expertly it reminded me of all the incredible things he knew how to do with it. The things he'd been showing me repeatedly during his very necessary *research breaks*.

He lifted me up, and I wrapped my legs around his waist, threading my arms around his neck. Heat was already building between us, and I was glad I'd expended so much of my power earlier with Neve so I wasn't worried about sparking any fires like I had done accidentally a few times since we'd returned. Luckily, Dru had grabbed the gloves he'd fashioned for Aislin and I for training that could stop our powers from emitting.

They had come in handy, just not in the way we'd originally planned.

It was strange to wear them, especially when everything else was disrobed, but it was worth it to keep Dru safe, at least until after we'd bonded. According to what we knew of Sloan and Aislin's ceremony, my power wouldn't be able to harm Dru after that.

My eyes dropped to the base of his harness, finding the coppery gloves not-so-subtly attached to it.

"I've been thinking about this all day," he said, the tips of our noses touching. His lips traced along mine, trailing kisses up my throat while he carried me through the rows of everwood trees. They were still lit, flickering every few steps he took.

"I guess it's a good thing we are powering up the Evergleam tonight." I raised an eyebrow at the twinkling grove.

"I'd say so," he agreed, gaze narrowing on the trees a moment before darting back to me. He watched hungrily as I took my time slipping my blouse over my head and dropping it before unhooking my bra.

He bounced me in his arms a moment, lifting me a bit higher to readjust our positioning and hiking my skirt up over my thighs. His head dipped down, his tongue swirling over my nipple, making me hiss. I wriggled my hips against him, my underwear growing damp in anticipation, wanting him inside me again. He continued, torturing the other sensitive bud in equal measure while he carried me toward the Evergleam.

I released a breathy laugh, my voice huskier than usual. "You're quite the multitasker."

"Oh this?" he teased, giving my nipple a playful graze with his teeth and sending a shiver down my spine. "This is nothing compared to the multitasking I have in store for you later."

A deep ache kindled in my belly. The bulge pressing into my center through his trousers told me he was just as eager.

"I can't wait, Ky."

My skin ignited, both at his words and his caresses, becoming a live wire that could only be stifled by the things his lips and stroke of his tongue promised.

"Then don't."

Every time we were together, I felt the depths of his darkest wants and the wonder of his reverence.

He made me feel revered.

And it had nothing to do with my rare dragon magic and everything to do with *me*.

It's why I loved him.

And why I had to have him as my champion.

He held out his gloved hand and I pressed the fifth stud, watching as the dagger fed out through the circle of faerie blood painted at its center. Taking it off his palm, I sliced my own for the second time tonight. He pressed a delicate kiss to my wrist, then nestled my back into the Evergleam, the bark surprisingly soft.

I dragged the dagger across his palm, a thin line of crimson bubbling up. Clasping our hands together, our blood coalesced, becoming the binding for the sacred enchantment. I dropped the blade to the ground and then Dru guided our hands to the bark, murmuring the incantation against my lips. "*Dilían cró derkomai bitháiach caur.*"

We repeated it together a few more times.

"*Dilían cró derkomai bitháiach caur.*"

Reaching between us, I undid the buttons of his trousers, pulling him out and stroking him a few times before teasing his swollen tip, making him jump in my palm. He groaned into my mouth. "Blazes, Ky."

He knelt, lowering me onto a heap of blankets and pillows at the base of the tree, then he looped his fingers around the fabric of my thong and pulled it to the side, parting my center. I lifted my hips, desperate for him. Desperate for the eternal connection that would ignite between us.

A few sparks fell from my fingertips, and we both inhaled sharply. Once they stopped and I made sure they hadn't caught anything on fire, I reached for the copper-lined gloves, the tightness in my chest easing up as I did. I wished I didn't need them right now, but we'd have plenty of time for that later, after we'd bonded. I refused to take any chances, my mind flitting over the memory of the pink scars scattered across Dru's deep bronze chest from when I'd first plummeted into Celaria.

So much had happened since then. And we'd gotten through it.

Together.

Stronger.

"I love you," I said, gripping his shoulders and clamping my legs around his waist.

"I love you too, Ky."

Shifting my hips so my entrance grazed his length, I let him feel how ready I was for this. "I need you. Now."

He pushed into me with decadently shallow thrusts, teasing me with his thick tip. Digging my nails into his shoulders, I squeezed my thighs around him, encouraging him further, anticipating the moment the bond would begin to form. How would it feel to have that connection with him inside of me? Would it heighten the sensations building deep in my belly? Without the need to stifle my magic, would I be able to give in more to the intensity of how incredible it was each time he drove into me?

"*Blazes*, you feel amazing."

I circled my hips, taking him deeper, making him curse again. God, he was sinfully sweet in all the best ways. My back arched against the blankets beneath me, pressure in my core building, demanding *more.*

The way he watched my body when he took me, like he was studying every reaction, may have been the sexiest thing I'd ever seen.

My chest heated, reaching out through my fingertips, feeding into the copper gloves. When he slipped a pillow under my hips without missing a beat, I was grateful I'd worn them. This grove would definitely be on fire otherwise.

Legs quivering and locked around him still, he curled his pelvis, angling himself so each thrust grazed along my clit. He drove deeper, his strokes pulling my body into knots, shaking uncontrollably as the pressure grew.

This was it.

He'd be mine and I'd be his.

Tethered for eternity.

He plunged into me, pace intensifying until my pleasure had no choice but to burst.

"Yes!" I moaned, anchoring my fingers into him. My body shifted past where the blankets were laid, my shoulders pressing into the Evergleam's roots, not caring about the scratch of them against my skin.

He grabbed my hand, removing the glove so the sliced palm was exposed. My chest stilled a beat, worried sparks might fly out, but as I came down from my orgasm, it seemed like most of my power had funneled out of me and into the glove already. Taking my hand with his and pressing them into the bark again, he whispered the incantation breathlessly a few more times slumped against my neck, and I joined him.

"Dilían cró derkomai bitháiach caur."

Burrowing himself deep, he came, filling me with his warmth. He held still there a moment, clutching the bark of the Evergleam, but instead of the calmness that usually followed, his eyes were pinned to the tree, jaw tensed.

Turning my head to look where his attention was focused, I watched as he peeled away the majestic tree's bark, the dark-brown wood flaky and limp, falling weakly to the ground. I grasped along the tree, rubbing some of the trunk between my fingers, feeling its texture as more came off onto my fingertips.

The fuck? This wasn't how I remembered it.

"Umm," I said awkwardly, bringing Dru's attention back to the fact that he was still inside me.

"Sorry." His voice was brittle as he slipped out of me and sat back on his heels. Running his hands roughly through his hair, he clasped them behind his head, the golden flecks in his eyes dulling with each passing second. "I think something's wrong with the Evergleam."

Tilting his head, his chin dipped down to look at his glove. He flicked on its flashlight and held it up to the tree's trunk before running it over the roots.

"Feel this," he said, touching a spot on a twisted root.

I placed a hand where he indicated, instantly jerking it back. "It's freezing."

"It's like the tree's sick. Diseased, maybe."

"Is that possible?" I asked, willing back the urge to cry that the ceremony hadn't worked. That this entire day was going to complete shit. There had to be some way to salvage it. "We could try again?"

"I don't think that will work..."

My heart sank.

"This has never happened before that I'm aware of, but I'll have to look into it," he said, shifting uncomfortably, lost in thought.

I reached out to him, and he finally seemed to notice me. "What is it, Dru?"

"I... I was worried your dragon was rejecting the bond."

"I don't understand."

"Your dragon, it's part of you, but it also is its own magic," he explained. "There have been cases where the dragon has rejected a potential bond. When the incantation didn't start working, I thought maybe it didn't like that I don't have magic, but I don't think that's the issue now."

"I definitely don't think that has anything to do with it," I said, wrapping my arms around him and pressing a kiss to his temple. "Look at the bark and how the grove was flickering before we even did the enchantment."

"I believe the Evergleam is broken." Concern laced his words, his gaze dropping down to the roots beneath us.

"How do we fix it?" My voice and body shook. *This was*

supposed to be our night. Now all I felt was disappointment and fear of what this could mean for Celaria's magic that had just recently been returned. I clenched my fists, hot specks popping frantically within my grip. I held them tight, the pain pricking my palms. While I knew I wouldn't burn from my fire anymore, it still stung.

"Without knowing the cause, I can't determine a solution." Dru picked up my discarded clothes and handed them to me, his face still sullen. "But it doesn't look like we'll be completing our ceremony until I find one."

CHAPTER 13

"Sweeney, my main man, pour me another," I shouted into the amplifier Dru had fashioned for me that hung from my neck. Tossing the empty thimble to him, the breezetender lifted a finger and caught it mid-flight, the makeshift copper cup slowly drifting down until it landed with a *plink* on the bar.

Not taking his eyes off the drink he was breezetending with his other hand, he called up to me, "Planning to come down from there at any point tonight?"

"Nah, I've got the best view in the house." I patted the wooden beam I was perched on, my legs dangling over its edge. My wings rested limply behind me, tired from flying back and forth from the fort for our training session with Arafax's Queen.

Now that I'd met the woman that'd rejected my father, it only confirmed my belief that she'd made the right choice. Kyleigh's mom was strong, determined, and a total MILF. I'd probably try my luck if I wasn't still holding out a sliver of hope that her daughter would come around to the idea of having an extra champion. Considering she was due to bond Dru soon, it wasn't looking likely. Perhaps once she got bored with Golden

81

Boy and his surely vanilla lovemaking, she'd be ready to get naughty with a little something on the side.

Maybe by then I'd figure out how to at least be the same size as everyone else around me. I was a social creature but having to avoid being stomped on or run into by people all the time made it hard to be. At least from up here, I could pretend I was enjoying tonight's debauchery alongside the other patrons.

Plus, the amors' tits looked spectacular from up here, watching them bounce playfully as they wandered through the tavern. It was tempting to swoop down and bury myself between them—experience that warmth up close and personal... I wondered if they'd even notice. My dick perked up at the thought.

A few coins the size of my head flew off the ledge, swirling until they landed in the register, and a moment later, the *clink* of the copper thimble dropped onto the beam next to me.

"Good man," I called into the amplifier from above the hubbub, leaning back and slurping down the amber ale, awaiting its buzz. It's not like it took much anymore. I was the definition of a lightweight in this form.

Faerie.

Some days I still didn't believe it.

Leigh had pulled out her old dollhouse from The Lavender's storage and placed it in the room I was supposed to be sharing with Jet. Each morning I woke up in my four-poster bed and pulled off the blanket, feeling completely normal despite sometimes crinkling my wings from sleeping on them in the night. For those few minutes, nothing had changed. I was still Vis's king, its savior that'd finally brought us home. Then I'd hear the shuffling of feet, the pounding of a fist against a door, the booming moan of an amor, and I'd remember—I was a freak. I still wasn't where I belonged.

Not even here.

Neither was Jet, apparently. He'd been quarantined from the rest of us, powerful beyond his control. An illusion weaver.

Lucky bastard.

How many times had I used faerie blood in rituals at Halston? If it was as potent of a substance as we believed, I had to have something within me. Some untapped power that would eclipse my Vis brethren.

The one thing we did know about the faeries was that they had affinities—strengths that they were naturally inclined to. I thought back to the things I'd excelled at in Dorset, and there were just so many. It was hard to narrow down what could be my affinity now. Plus, not being around any other faeries made it near impossible to understand how to tap into it. The Queen, Neve, and Dru had been trying with our training sessions, but I'd given up on participating, preferring to work on my own instead of being seen as a fool in front of my friends. I usually hung out and watched them fumble around with their powers for a few hours each day.

Two silver-haired amors walked by, arms linked with Athena. It was so strange seeing her without her owl mask on. We'd always worn them with pride at our meetings, I'd almost forgotten what everyone looked like without them.

"Hey!" I called to her. The trio's faces shot upward as I flitted to meet their eye level. Athena brushed back her brunette bob and stretched out her hand so I could land on her palm. She was apparently what they called a null, no magic having manifested upon arrival, perhaps making her the only one more disappointing than me. She'd always been desperate to take a ride on the Travis express, but as my second in command with Vis, I'd determined it was better not to fuck a colleague—something my father had been too stupid about when he'd allowed his thirst for pleasure to mix with founding Vindicatio Vis with Kyleigh's mom.

But that was then.

"Want some company?" I asked Athena, puffing up my chest and flashing a smile, the one that usually won women over.

Maybe my affinity was fucking. I excelled at it and I hadn't gotten a chance to try it out here—not yet, at least.

Her eyes drifted between the silvery amors before the three of them laughed. It hit me like a punch to the gut, but I brushed it off, trying to salvage my wounded pride. "You know what they say, it's not the size—"

"Unfortunately, I don't think that applies in this scenario," Athena said, shaking her head at me, not even in cruelty. In something worse.

Pity.

"Aw, he's so adorable though," the taller amor said to the other two women, her green eyes scanning over me before she brushed along my wing with her pointer finger. It sent a thrill through me, my trousers becoming tighter.

"An adorable waste," the amor with blue eyes replied.

I adjusted my waistband so they wouldn't notice the painful erection throbbing beneath. "No need to waste anything, ladies. There's plenty of me to go around."

"But is there?" The blue-eyed amor asked, continuing to laugh at my expense. Heat spread over my face, and I glared, mouth dipping into a frown. When she noticed, she stopped quickly. "I'm sorry, that was harsh."

"Goodnight, Travis," Athena inserted, obviously growing uncomfortable with the exchange. "Come find us when you've figured this out." She gestured to my small form, and I flitted off her palm before I had to feel any more ashamed than I already did.

I flew up the stairs, my buzz beginning to hit as I bumped into the railing a few times, watching people peel off into their rooms. Finally making my way to mine, I crawled under the door. The key was too heavy to haul with my wings.

When I got inside my house, I slammed the wooden door

shut and stomped my way up to the bedroom. Looking in the mirror, I inspected the iridescent patterns etched across my wings.

My stupid fucking wings.

Reaching over my shoulder, I gripped the root of one, giving it a tug as I twisted to watch in the mirror. Faeries were powerful. Their blood could carry the weight of the realm's most advanced enchantments, so there had to be more to me than *this*.

I gave one more tug, the sting tingling down my spine. Turning to face the mirror, I splayed my wings wide, knitting my brows together as I ripped off the scratchy doll clothes I'd worn —the only things that Leigh had found that fit me. They crumpled in a heap in the corner of the room.

I *was* more.

I'd grown up being told I didn't belong but that I would somewhere else. Now I was here and I still felt *other*.

But not for long.

Taking in my naked form, I ignored the wings behind my back, staring at the rest of me. I just needed to find where I truly belonged.

Tomorrow, when I headed to the fort, I would talk to Dru.

Nothing was going to stop me from finding the rest of the faeries and claiming the power that was rightfully mine.

CHAPTER 14
Redmond

"Our soldiers need to be ready to be called upon at a moment's notice, Commander."

A giant map of Celaria lay unfurled on the table, small phoenix figurines placed strategically along Inverno's borders leading toward the Grymm Mountain pass. I pointed to the area my people knew better than to ever go, tracing the outer boundary of Cicatrix. "We'll need another contingent stationed here."

"Really, Your Majesty?" Cormac asked, his throat bobbing. Just another reminder of how much I needed Sloan back. Her temporary stand-in was incompetent by comparison. I'd been spending my mornings training alongside my troops, finding it the best way to stay motivated since her departure and the loss of our daily training sessions. Watching Cormac's leadership up close only made it clear to me that he was not meant to command.

Sometimes the fiercest warriors, those who could slay anything that stood in their path, were the shittiest strategists and leaders. This was the case with Cormac. He was an unbeatable opponent, possibly better than Sloan in the arena, but he lacked what I needed in a military advisor and commander.

Unfortunately, Sloan was in no position to help me right now. She had enough on her plate with the loss of Aislin, but I had left her a note requesting a meeting along with a small token, hopefully one that said the things I hadn't been able to say aloud.

Cormac leaned down on his elbows, brows furrowed, eyes lining up with the tiny figurines on the table. "I don't think we need to cover that area. Cicatrix has never been a problem before."

"Just because they've never been a problem doesn't mean they won't be. Other than providing healers to the territories, we have no loyalty from their people."

Luckily, I'd taken time to learn about Cicatrix, more than probably any ruler prior. Their territory sat at the base of the mountains that blocked them from the rest of Celaria and nestled them against Inverno's northernmost border. Most of my fellow leaders were just grateful to have the healing assistance Cicatrix's people provided. It was their specialty. But the other half of their magic, cast by their demoliers, proved much more nefarious.

Unlike Alucinor and its weavers, where people usually left them alone and knew better, Cicatrix had been able to go centuries unnoticed, despite the dangerous arsenal of abilities at their disposal. "Until we can ensure the other regions are our allies, we need to treat them like they could become an enemy at any moment."

"Forgive me if I'm speaking out of turn, but I don't understand why we are doing all this," Cormac said, standing back up and pointing to the small defense I'd requested of him. "There's been no threat against us, Your Majesty. If anything, I'd say if we wanted to prepare to deal with an enemy, we could easily take Arafax. If we took out their dragons"—I clenched my fists under the table—"their population is so small, it could be ours. Then we'd have the largest combined territory in the realm...other than possibly the merpeople, but they aren't a threat by any means swimming beneath the Spuma."

It was my own fault that so much hatred had been accrued among my soldiers toward Arafax. I'd been proud of weakening them, even if unintentional at the time. Now all I wanted to do was undo the destruction I'd caused them. Myself. But that wouldn't fix itself overnight.

"You know what your problem is, Cormac? You think you know so much, but you really have no fucking clue how these territories operate. How rulers operate."

I couldn't allow anyone to know we were in alliance with Arafax. Not yet. Not while I was playing doting fiancé to the Enchantress. However, I also wouldn't continue to spew anymore hate toward a kingdom whose wrath I more than deserved.

"In fact, as of today, you're relieved of your temporary duties," I said, striding over to the hook, removing his uniform jacket and handing it to him. "Your skill set in training our officers is just too valuable. I'll be handling the strategy on my own until I can find a suitable replacement for Commander Sloan."

"But, Your Maj—"

"I appreciate your willingness to step up, Cormac." I put a firm hand on his shoulder and patted his chest with the other. "As a token of my appreciation, I'll have Oren from the stables drop off a few ponies for your daughters. Every young girl should have one. Remind me, how many daughters do you have?"

"Four, Your Majesty."

"Four it is," I said, giving him a gracious wave. "Thank you again, Cormac. Why don't you go ahead and get home to them? It's late. I'll have those ponies sent to your girls tomorrow."

I closed the door behind him, making sure to notify my

guards that I was done with visitors for the night. Walking back to the map, I traced my finger over our border. Picking up a blue marker, I drew a line along it—one I'd need to memorize for the next time I went flying.

Hopefully things wouldn't come to that last resort, but I couldn't leave for Tesceillus without knowing things were set in place, just in case.

I poured myself another glass of whiskey and sat at my desk, jotting down a few more instructions for my absence, ensuring I'd keep my people safe at all costs.

CHAPTER 15
Kyleigh

Heat shot through my veins, an inferno that used to be uncomfortable but I was getting more used to. My nose stretched into a long, scaled snout. My bones cracked and re-formed. Dru became smaller, swallowed up by the large arena as I expanded, wings splayed wide.

We were preparing to head to the Forum, a place that had been forged as a neutral spot for meetings and diplomacy to take place. The structure had been carved into the side of the Grymm Mountains, leagues above the ground and, according to Dru, it had a set of rules I had to follow. If the room sensed that you were going to hurt someone else, it would kick you out, dropping you off the side of its ledge. He had restated this more than once, making me think he was concerned about my impulse control—not that I could really blame him.

"Ready?" he asked, clutching my scales.

I gave him an approving huff and knelt so he could get onto my back. He hoisted himself onto the crook of my leg, then gripped another scale, climbing up until he settled behind my neck. Giving me a few gentle strokes, he pressed a kiss to my nape. I hummed contentedly in response, puffs of smoke with pink sparks flaring out from my maw.

I was still disappointed that we hadn't been able to bond. Sloan had gone with Dru to look at the Evergleam, noting the issues we'd found. They had come to the conclusion that it was definitely broken. It made me feel better that it wasn't something we'd done, but it was upsetting, nonetheless.

"I know you're angry with her, but should we wait for the Queen?" Dru asked tentatively, eyes darting over to the fort. My mother was supposedly making final preparations for the meeting today. I didn't have much interest in talking to her. What would I even say? My dad was still hidden away along with the other weaver, Jet, and I honestly didn't know what to say to either of them.

Besides, right now there were more important things to worry about—like the Enchantress.

I grumbled and took a deep breath, trotting forward before bending my hind legs and shooting into the sky.

"Woah!" Dru called out, startled by my hasty take off.

My wings pushed against the breeze, their span pumping hard to build momentum, lifting us higher into the clouds, the air skimming my body with its chill.

I soared over the lavender fields, inhaling their rich smell, one that'd become more comforting with each passing day.

Staring at the snow-tipped peaks ahead, I narrowed my silvery orbs to the spot Dru had pointed out to me on the map this morning. The Forum was hidden behind the mountain pass's pinnacle. I'd have to loop around to find it.

Ascending higher, stone pillars denoted the Forum in front of us. It was too small for me to fly into in this form, so I turned, gripping the mountainside ledge with my claws to let Dru off into the room. Neve stood at one of the open paneless windowsills, hands outstretched, freezing a large layer of ice to extend the ledge, building me a frosty landing strip.

Shrinking down, my body crackled, transitioning into my human form. I crawled across the frozen floor, shaking violently and slipping a few times. Finally, I made it into Dru's outstretched hands before he pulled me into the room.

I shivered in place, regretting that I'd insisted on flying instead of using portal stones. Neve raised a brow at me, as if to say *I told you so*.

Sloan, Ox, and King Redmond were already sitting at the crudely carved table situated at the Forum's center. Two chairs sat at either end with five lining its sides. Wind whipped into me, its chilling bite making me tighten my arms around myself, heat emanating from my palms.

A small pile of clothes erupted from the center of Dru's glove, and he handed them to me.

"You should have told me to pack a jacket," I whispered to him, throwing on a thin tank top over my bralette. Goosebumps skittered along my skin, covering my limbs.

He grimaced, hiding me behind a blanket he'd also stored in his glove so I had something to get dressed behind. After I threw on my leggings, he wrapped it around my shoulders, and I nestled into its warmth while he held me close.

"Figured you'd be arriving with the Queen, Your Highness," King Redmond said from one end of the table, making me still within Dru's arms. He slid the chair backward, the stone scraping against the rocky floor, the others following suit. He was shirtless, not even giving a single shiver, though he was wearing trousers, which was more than usual. The fellow shifter always seemed all too comfortable with his own nudity.

Bowing his head, I watched the others hesitate a moment before mimicking him, only instead of merely bowing their heads, they knelt, crossing a fist over their hearts.

Why is everyone being so weird?

Dru released me, dropping to do the same, making me feel all the more uncomfortable.

"Please stop," I said, waving for everyone to stand back up. "Save your formalities for the Queen."

The King's midnight eyes lifted, seemingly surprised.

As if on cue, the Queen *popped* into the room, appearing out of nowhere. She was dressed in a fitted red velvet jacket with matching pants and a set of golden heels. The King bowed again, and everyone else, including me, scrambled to the ground to kneel.

"Rise, all of you," she said, her silvery gaze pinning me from above. "Let's go over the plan."

I stood, wrapping the blanket tighter around me and moving toward the table. My mother chose the seat opposite Inverno's King, the farthest points along the corium table. Sloan sat perfectly between the rulers, reminding me that she must feel split between both kingdoms. She didn't have a formal role in Arafax, but she was champion to one of its Revered, even if her bonded was out of commission temporarily. Meanwhile, she was no longer Inverno's commander.

Ox and Neve took the seats on either side of her.

"Kyleigh," my mother said, patting the spot next to her at the table. Heading to where she'd indicated, I pulled out the chair next to it and sat down, eyes shooting to Dru, a silent plea for him to sit between us.

Dru shuffled over, tentatively sitting in the empty chair between us. My mother didn't react—that would be beneath her in this setting. Everyone else's eyes were lowered, pretending not to notice the slight.

Everyone except King Redmond. His gaze narrowed on me, cobalt sweeping through his irises. His chin dropped rapidly, and when he looked back up at the table, he seemed a bit perplexed, like he was trying to solve a riddle.

He blinked a few times before the shade disappeared into midnight, then he tilted his head, lips pursed, and turned his attention to my mother. "The Enchantress wants me to go look for the tome. She believes Flynt may have taken it to transport via the waterway. I'm to go to Tesceillus and see if they have it, as well as attempt to secure an alliance with King Morrow. My plan is to use it as an opportunity to see where they stand and if they will join our cause." He turned toward Dru. "This also should buy you more time to translate the text."

"How is your relationship with the merpeople?" my mother asked, tapping a scarlet nail on the corium.

"Well, my father had strong ties with them, though that was many years before he died."

"What about since his death?"

King Redmond clasped his hands on the table, leaning slightly back. "Nonexistent, but I know enough about King Morrow to know that he won't meet with anyone who's not a fellow royal."

"Yes. You will need to be the one to talk to him," she agreed, lips pressing into a thin line. "Especially since the Enchantress has asked you to go. However, getting to the King will be a process in itself and you'll need to have a good relationship with the merpeople to even visit Tesceillus." Her eyes scanned the table. "Sir Fergus should go with you."

Both men bristled, but she continued, ignoring their reaction. "He has a *personal* history with the mermaids, and they will be more willing to trust bringing you down to their capital with him there."

Ox rubbed his beard vigorously. "Your Majesty—"

"What if I go with Ox as the royal counterpart?" I volunteered. "After all, we both recently worked with the mermaids to retrieve Dru from the Otherworld."

I didn't want to get left out, sick of my mother's overprotectiveness. I could be useful, even if claiming my birthright wasn't something I was sure I wanted yet.

"No," she said, tone firm. "The Enchantress expects Redmond to go, so he shall."

"Of course, Your Majesty," I muttered. She might have a point, but there was no way I'd be staying in Arafax, sitting on my ass with my parents while everyone else ran off to secure alliances. The idea of being near either of them right now had rough knots coiling tightly in my stomach.

"Makes sense to me to go with Sir Fergus," King Redmond replied, as if trying to cool off the heat simmering between my mother and me. He gestured to Ox a few seats away, giving him a curt smile. "At least I know he can hold his own in a fight. Just try not to stab me with a scale again, okay?"

"I can't make any promises," Ox replied all too quickly.

Silence spilled over the table. Both Sloan and Neve looked uncomfortable with the pairing that would be diving into the Spuma to meet with the Mer King.

"Glad we've determined that," my mother said, her regal gaze drifting to Dru, who was pulling out a notebook and pen from his glove. He jotted down a few lines of notes, seemingly to keep track of where everyone was heading. "I'd like to propose sending a representative or two to visit the weavers."

"I'll go to the weavers," I cut in before she gave away all the duties and tried to keep me with her. She might enjoy the safety of hiding away in her palatial fort, but I had no interest in that.

"I think it'd be best for you to stay here."

I rolled my eyes. "We both know that won't be happening. Dru and I can go to Alucinor and discuss an alliance, along with securing a few weavers to come help with our new ones."

"You have new weavers? In Arafax?" King Redmond asked, concern threading his words. I'd have to ask Dru about the weavers and why everyone seemed so off-kilter at the mere mention of them.

She clenched her jaw. "Yes, when Kyleigh brought the Otherworlders here—"

"You mean Celarians who were not raised here," the King cut in, crossing his arms and leaning his elbows onto the table.

"Yes. A handful came through already displaying abilities. We have two weavers that are currently being quarantined in Arafax for everyone's safety."

"Two weavers? That's all you're going to say about them?" I seethed, my hands shaking a bit. The chair beneath me shook then dragged itself back a foot. Dru reached for my wrist, giving me a look that reminded me that I had to steady my emotions. This type of anger, or an outburst of my power seen as malevolent, could land me over the side of the Forum.

I took a deep breath, and my hands steadied, the chair sliding itself back into place. "What about the fact that one of them is my dad and you never said anything to me for the last month he's been here?"

She glared, obviously pissed I shared that information with present company. "All the more reason for you not to go there. You're too close to this."

"Interesting," the King said, tilting his head at my mother. "So, you married a weaver? And she's half weaver?"

I really hadn't thought about that at all. How did it work when two different magical people created a child? Would they possess magical attributes from both parents?

"She is," my mother said with some unease, then she redirected her attention to me. "However, I don't think it's a good idea for you to go alone to Alucinor."

But if I were part weaver, it made the most sense for me to go, especially if they could help my dad so he didn't need to be locked away.

Before I could say another word, my mother added, "Dru will be busy dealing with the faeries."

"The faeries?" I asked. "Like Travis?"

"Dru, why don't you share what we recently learned about the Enchantress thanks to the tome King Redmond retrieved?"

He cleared his throat, standing up as if he were giving a lecture. "The Enchantress is a faerie, as some of the rumors have said. The text is all in ancient faerie, which means only one of their own would know how to decipher it. The fact that King Redmond has also told the Queen she's looking for the tome suggests it's quite important to her. Therefore, once I figure out where the faeries are hiding, I will be heading there."

"But no one knows where the faeries are," King Redmond said, eyeing Dru curiously, his wings stiffening behind him.

"I do," Neve interjected, biting her lip when everyone's eyes snapped to her. "I can take Dru; however, they are wary of outsiders. Non-faerie folk are usually not allowed within their territory. They may take it as a threat."

"What if he brings Travis with him?" I suggested. "Travis is a faerie. If they are so protective of their own, they would let him in. Maybe there's some way you could help them in exchange for learning more about the tome and how to translate it."

"He did come see me and said he was curious about how to locate them," Dru agreed. "And I'm sure there's something I could do to help their people. I just won't know what that is until I'm there."

I hadn't dealt with Travis much since he'd arrived. He'd been hiding away, most likely sulking over finding out he wasn't a big force to be reckoned with. Maybe he could learn more about himself if he were with the rest of his people. Not that I cared much about helping the asshole, but taking him to the faeries also meant getting him out of my hair.

Neve cocked her head, as if she were testing the idea in her mind. "Hmm. I suppose that would work."

Dru put down the pen he'd been note-taking with and gripped my hand. "What about you, though? You can't go to Alucinor alone."

Sloan stood abruptly, bringing a hand over her heart. "I'll go with her."

Everyone's head snapped to the silver-haired warrior, shocked she was volunteering to do something more than consume whiskey at an alarming rate. "It's not like I have something better to do. Mox and I can keep her safe if danger should arise."

It would probably be good for her to leave Arafax. To have a purpose outside of worrying about Aislin. But I had my doubts if she was stable enough to be my escort with how she'd been spending her days drowning her sorrows at The Lavender. She didn't reek of liquor today, though, and that was a first since Aislin had been taken.

"You're actually willing to let Mox leave the Silent Woods?" Ox asked.

"Yes. It's time he's back with me." She sat down, wringing her hands together.

My mother released a long sigh, and I couldn't tell if she was glad I had the escort or was just resigned that I refused to hide away at the fort with her. "Well then, that's settled. Redmond and Sir Fergus will head to Tesceillus to meet with King Morrow. Neve and Dru will take Travis to the faeries, and Kyleigh and Sloan will head to Alucinor. Everyone will need to meet back here in one week's time. My gut tells me we can't afford much more than that. In the meantime, I'll be getting some securities in place at the fort and will continue training our new wielders for what's to come."

"What about Cicatrix?" Neve asked, mentioning the last territory of Celaria, one located beyond the mountains we were currently meeting in. Through the open columns that created the Forum's windows, a few tall gothic towers were visible, dark-green vines climbing along their spires. "And what will we do once we've all returned?"

"Cicatrix has never made an alliance with anyone. Ever. A trip there would be dangerous and look desperate on our part. Better to secure the other kingdoms," King Redmond said.

The Queen nodded in agreement, apparently in on some unspoken knowledge about the place where Celaria's healers hailed from. "Once we return, we will set up another meeting to regroup and discuss next steps. We can decide how to tackle the Enchantress, with or without the additional allies. We have one champion-bonded pair in working order at least. That gives us an edge. Kyleigh and Dru, you'll need to make some time to train your new skills before you leave and once you're back."

Heat spread through my chest, my face becoming flush. Dru's eyes shot to the ground. I never even thought to tell her the ceremony hadn't worked, considering I had no desire to be around her.

Everyone else around the table paused, either unaware or too uncomfortable to say anything.

"What is it?" my mother asked, breaking the silence I was completely fine basking in.

"We—er—weren't able to bond," Dru muttered, coming to my rescue. "The Evergleam is experiencing some sort of disturbance and wouldn't initiate the ritual."

A wrinkle formed between my mother's brows. "How's that even possible?"

"He's telling the truth," Sloan chimed in. "I went to look at it with him earlier and there's something wrong with it. Maybe it's because Aislin was taken after we bonded—if the Enchantress somehow warped the bond and, in turn, the tree when she changed her."

I'd never even thought about the effects of their bond being tampered with. Neve and Ox exchanged solemn glances behind her. We'd all been worried about Sloan this last month, but the two of them had been checking on her daily, trying to snap her out of her misery.

Was that even possible to do when the other half of your heart was snatched away right in front of you? All the whiskey in the world couldn't drown out pain like that.

"Erm," Ox began, but Neve sliced him with an icy gaze,

cutting him off, probably worried he'd say something that would upset Sloan back into another booze-infused stupor.

"I guess that could be the culprit," my mother said, eyes softening at the glint of tears threatening to spill from Sloan's eyes. If her broken bond was the cause of the Evergleam's sickness, I'm sure that only made her feel worse than she already did.

I wasn't used to seeing my mother as much more than Arafax's frigid queen, but maybe dealing with my father being here had brought back some compassion in her. I could only hope.

"As long as it's not impacting anyone's magic we should just move forward with the plans we've made. I'll try to see what I can find out while you all are away." The Queen turned her gaze back to me, regaining her regal demeanor. "Maybe by the time you're back it will be fixed for your ceremony."

I merely shrugged in response, not wanting to get my hopes up.

"What's involved in this bonding ceremony?" King Redmond asked.

"I'll tell you when you're older." Sloan smirked. It was enough to bring me a sliver of hope for her, but the sadness didn't leave her eyes.

"Let's go make preparations before you all set off," my mother said, standing from the table. Dru pressed the stud on his glove, and a handful of portal stones emerged. He passed them out as the Queen continued, "Even one more ally could make a huge difference going up against the Enchantress. We won't have much time to act once we are back, especially if she has deals already set with any of the other territories you'll be visiting, so try your best to be discreet."

With that, she placed her stone on the floor and stamped her foot on it, disappearing, signifying the meeting was officially over.

CHAPTER 16

Neve

K nock, knock, knock.
Giving myself one more glance in the mirror, I ran my thumb over the threading of my romper, plum lace cresting my hips and breasts, accentuating my curves.

I reached for the doorknob and an unfamiliar burst of acidic bubbles surged into my chest.

Anxiety?

Finally gathering the courage to twist the rusted metal, I opened up the door, stepping back to stay out of view of The Lavender's other patrons. He stepped inside, jaw tense, his anxiety boiling over. I was becoming more attuned to identifying his emotions. They crashed into me constantly, whether I wanted them to or not. It had only been a few weeks and there was so much I was still learning about what all of *this* entailed.

Fucking bond.

The acrid prickling sensation flooding the wire of our bond suddenly shifted, like it'd been drowned in honey, becoming thick and drenched. Feeling his desire pour through our connection had the lace between my thighs dampening with my own.

His eyes shot immediately to that spot, and I knew he could tell too—a grin spreading through his auburn beard.

He looked at me quizzically, making me wonder if he could sense my emotions right now, but I'd ensured he couldn't. I refused to let anything through to him that I didn't allow. He didn't need to know that, though. Being new to the bond and all it entailed meant he was still learning everything as much as I was, and I only shared things I deemed necessary.

He never blocked out his feelings, they constantly filtered into me. But why would he need to shield himself like that? Everything about him screamed openness.

Carefree abandon.

It was something I admired. One of the reasons I'd decided he would be my champion days before the words had slipped through my lips. Now, it was too much.

I envisioned melting the frozen knot in my chest, releasing its coil enough for desire to spread along the bond, adding in some lingering nostalgia from our previous nights together.

"You know why I'm here, and it's not for *that*," Ox growled, sounding almost angry.

"You sure?" I pressed a palm to his sternum, a few snowflakes drifting from my fingertips. He shivered against my touch but didn't pull away. "You seem pretty interested in *that,* even if you won't admit it." There was no hiding he wanted me between the heat rushing through the bond and the swelling steel in his trousers. I lingered my gaze there, some more of my own want flooding out to him.

"Stop," he demanded, eyes going a bit wide, the large bulge becoming more pronounced, like a tempting bullseye. The strand between us pulled taut a moment, reverberating through my chest at his intensity. "We need to talk about the Evergleam." He shook his head, cheeks flushed as his hand moved in front of his crotch, blocking my view. My gaze rose up to meet his. "What if we are the ones who broke it?"

"It seemed to work fine when we bonded," I replied with a shrug, the thin strap of my romper falling over my shoulder. I began to walk away from him. "Unless this constant feeling in my chest is some annoying variation of heartburn."

Gripping me by the shoulder, he whipped me around, bringing my chin up with the crook of his finger. "This isn't funny."

"I never said I was laughing."

"We need to tell them, *mó venéro*," he insisted, lowering his face until his lips were a breath away from mine.

"Tell them we bonded?" My heart ramped up its pace, a twinkling sensation pricking at my chest. My dragon's magic wanted this. This closeness. For me to reach up and bring my lips to his, like it had a mind of its own.

But *I* was in control, not my dragon's magic, or this bond.

Twisting my face away, I stalked toward the bed, sitting on its edge. "I don't see the point in anyone knowing yet. Do you really want to go on your mission, alone with Redmond, after sharing that with everyone?"

"Not particularly," he said, a chill streaking through my chest.

I didn't want Redmond to know yet either. Not that it bothered me if it hurt him, but I didn't feel like doing anything to jeopardize the already precarious relationship between Arafax and Inverno. The last thing I needed was to upset him and then have him reveal something stupid out of spite next time he was visiting his fiancée. "Isla is going to look into it while we are gone. It's not like Dru and Kyleigh can bond until we are back anyway."

Ox pursed his lips, then walked over to the chair at my desk, plopping into it, so massive it wobbled beneath him. Hands clasped, his knuckles were white as he wrung them together.

"The ceremony worked for us." It didn't make any sense that the Evergleam was broken, we'd had no issues with it when we were there. The strand connecting us tugged at me, needing reassurance, but I quickly froze the tether, pinching out any doubts I had. "I don't believe it's connected."

"You're really going to let Sloan think that her broken bond with Aislin is causing this?"

"Who says it isn't? Besides, Sloan will be busy helping Kyleigh in Alucinor." She'd have her hands full. The two of them were dealing with enough emotions to sate a nest full of weavers. I hated that they were going there, that I wouldn't be with them, but dealing with the faeries would be tricky enough for Dru, and he couldn't get to them without me. Plus, I had to make sure he and Travis didn't manage to kill each other. "I doubt she's sitting around worrying about a magical tree, if she's even sober at the moment."

He leaned forward, silver kissed brows knit together. "What happens if it's not fixed by the time we're back?"

My heart rattled against my rib cage, but I kept the walls around it frozen in place. "Then we'll figure it out."

He heaved an exasperated sigh.

"Now, stop wasting our last night together before we're territories apart."

Standing up, I peeled off the romper. Ox swallowed audibly, his eyes following the fabric as it clung to the edge of my hips. His pupils flooded out his irises, but he kept his hands laced together.

I melted some of the icy shards pinning the end of my bond, warmth flooding to him from within me, allowing the bond's magic to drive for a moment—nothing more. Reeling back control, I strode over to him, coming face-to-face with the handsome giant seated in front of me.

He released one of his hands, sliding it along my waist, caressing the delicate lace between his large fingers. My breath caught, a few scales popping out along my side, my eyes shifting into slits as my vision cleared, still not always in control between my forms. He stroked through the fabric, along the unruly scales and ridges of leftover scars, eyes locked with mine. "Will you at least tell me where you're heading? In case you run into trouble?"

I reached for the clasp of his chest harness, threading the leather through the buckle. "It's safer that you don't know. But I'm sure if anything becomes dire, the connection will tell you."

Pulling it off of him, I placed it on the table, then lifted his shirt over his head. My attention went immediately to the tattoos decorating his shoulder, wanting to trace them with my tongue again, to sink my teeth into their artistry as I came.

"If it's *dire*?" Ox groaned, snapping me from my mischievous thoughts. "You sure know how to comfort your champion."

I sighed, undoing the buttons of his trousers and patting his hip to lift a moment so I could peel them down until they fell around his ankles. "If you shut up, I'll show you how much I know about comforting my champion."

He raised a brow, body tense. Then his eyes softened a bit, along with the wiry thread between us. Giving my waist a firm squeeze, he whispered, voice deep and low, "Show me."

Turning away, I helped him pull the romper the rest of the way down. Heat thrummed between us and I slowly lowered myself, savoring him inch-by-inch until I sat flush against his lap. His hands drifted up my thighs, nudging them wider, my body stinging to accommodate the stretch of him. He stroked languidly along my sex with one hand, his teeth grazing the base of my neck. The other hand slid down to my wrist, tapping my finger. "Give me some of that beautiful frost."

I released some of my power, ice crawling over the pads and tips of his fingers.

Guiding them to my center, his other arm clamped around my waist, holding me in place as he skimmed my clit. I jolted at the sensation, body clenching around him simultaneously. Then

I wriggled against his touch, chills rippling through me. Releasing the knotted end of my bond a bit, still unwilling to untie it fully, I let him experience how much I was enjoying this.

"Stars above, you're tight," he growled, taking in a sharp breath before chuckling against the shell of my ear.

I'd always used my powers for protection, whether it was protecting Arafax as one of its Revered or protecting myself deep within Inverno's dungeon. The way Ox used my power on me, coaxing pleasure—there was a gentleness to how he wielded it.

Wielded me.

Sliding up and down his shaft, I absorbed the fullness of him, inch by indulgent inch. Hovering with his tip inside me, I swirled my hips, making him groan as he continued to stroke my clit. Every time the ice began to melt, he would channel my magic to refreeze it.

I sprinted toward my peak, feeling it closing in with each plummet of my body eliminating the gap between our hips.

Ox hissed from behind me, the thread between us tightening, drawing me to him. My body quaked as I rode his cock, shivering uncontrollably against him, but he kept going, the tension coiled deep in my belly billowing until it crashed out of me in waves.

He pressed slow kisses along my shoulder and I shattered around him. "I'm going to savor you now."

My body's energy spent, he magicked the ice around his fingers to melt, then slowly lifted me before inching me down his cock and spearing up into me with his hips.

He wanted slow, *gentle*, and now he was getting his wish, with my body exhausted, lazy with pleasure. He raised his hips, circling them in luscious patterns beneath me. When his hand slid between my thighs, I gripped his legs to steady myself for the onslaught of another cresting wave.

"Mó venéro," Ox murmured the name like an ancient

prayer, thumbing over my nipple, while his other hand stroked my clit.

Shaking in his lap, the bond between us twirled, another thread joining its delicate strand. I was too tired to fight it; to stop its weaving.

Jaw clenched tight at my shoulder, his hips plunged into me one last time, warmth spread along my insides and he released a slew of curses.

Still filling me, he scooped up some of our shared release. Heat flooded my chest, the frosty link between us thawing despite how my body quivered in his arms. Taking our wetness and swirling it around my clit again, he whispered against my shoulder, "Your champion's not done with you yet."

CHAPTER 17

I took another sip of ale, grimacing at the bitterness of the hops flitting across my tongue. Not really a fan of the stuff, I was more sipping it out of boredom than anything, using it as a tactic to avoid talking to Travis. When I set down the pint glass, he scurried across the bar top, plopping down in front of it and leaning back, propping himself upright with it. His hands wrapped around the copper thimble full of ale he chugged down before giving a satisfied smack of his lips and wiping his mouth on his arm.

This guy.

The pounding of boots descending the stairs pulled my attention from the annoying little faerie in front of me. Spotting Ox grumbling to himself while he adjusted the tilted collar of his shirt, I waved. He gave me a quick nod, then strode out the door, the handle of his pack twisted up in his giant fist.

"Ready?" asked Neve from behind me. She was in a mustard-colored tank top and black leggings. Her feet were bare.

"Yep." I patted the pack tucked at the base of my barstool, then nodded toward the exit where Ox had plodded off without a word. "Everything okay with him?"

"He's fine," she said, rolling her eyes before giving me a dismissive shrug. "Just annoyed about having to spend time with Redmond."

"Understandable." I wouldn't want to have to spend days with him either. I was still getting used to the idea of having him popping in and out of our lives, considering I'd spent years fearing the man and the incandescent blue phoenix he shifted into.

Travis let out a tiny burp, flying up to eye level. "We gonna keep chitchatting? Because if so, I could go jerk it or something."

"That hand been keeping you company?" Neve scoffed, causing the faerie to scowl. He clenched both his fists at his sides. "I heard you've been really trying to charm the ladies around here."

"They don't know what they're missing out on."

"I'm sure," I groaned, wondering why I should be surprised he was still full of himself despite being small enough to squish in my palm.

"Let's go," Neve said before Travis could respond with anything else idiotic. "I want to walk a bit before we take off so we don't stress out any of the patrons. They are still sensitive about seeing a dragon so close to the inn."

She glanced around us at the patrons scattered throughout the tavern before whispering, "I'll shift about halfway to the fort and we can fly from there."

"And you know where we are headed?"

"I do."

I equally admired her discretion and hated it.

"So, you've known where my people were this whole time?" Travis asked her.

"Your people?" He'd been mortified about being a faerie when he first arrived, spending most of his days drunk at The Lavender after giving up on lessons. His followers never spoke ill of him, but he definitely hadn't been earning their respect lately.

Every time I was here, he seemed to be picking fights, propositioning amors, or passed out.

I guess you could take the boy out of college, but you couldn't take the college out of the boy.

Neve's amber-rimmed eyes narrowed. "Yes. And you'll be glad I kept it quiet when the trust I've garnered with the faeries gets you access to them."

"Fair point," he said, giving her a smile that was all teeth. I got the impression he was afraid of our escort, which filled me with immense joy. After what he'd done to Kyleigh—to me—he didn't deserve any of my compassion, especially when he was still acting like a pompous ass.

I wondered how he would react to the faeries, and how they would react to him.

"The faeries are a very secretive bunch. Even more so since everything happened to force them out of their home." She led us toward the door, holding it open as we exited the pub. "They may not even allow you in. They are very wary of outsiders. I've never even gone inside their territory."

If they were as secretive as she was saying, I would need to ensure they would allow me to meet with their leader. That didn't sound like it would be an easy task.

"Then how are you able to get us there?"

"You'll see."

"Alright," I said, tapping the door of a small iron cage with a bench inside of it. "Time to get in."

"Is this really necessary?" Travis whined.

"Yes."

He stepped one foot in before his face shot up to mine. "You're enjoying this way too much."

"Can you blame me?" I chuckled, nudging him in farther with my finger. "It'll be safer for the ride."

"Unless, you're ready to really work those wings?" Neve

asked, arching a brow at him. "But I'm not slowing down for you to keep up."

"*Fuck*," he groaned, sitting down and pulling the buckle across himself. "Fine. But you'll never speak a word about this to anyone. Ever."

"You seem to think you're in charge here, Travis." I secured the cage to my chest strap. "How's it feel to be on the other side of it? Do we need to pack you a few more pairs of doll trousers for the trip?"

"Boys, if anyone is in charge here, it's me." Neve gave us a look that told me we were both being immature.

He started it.

"And if we are going to get the faeries to help our cause, to trust us enough to translate the tome, we're going to need to go in there united."

I scoffed at that.

"Or at least pretend to be," she added.

That was definitely a more realistic scenario for the two of us on this trip.

GRIPPING THE SCALES BETWEEN MY FINGERS, I thumbed over the rough sapphire, studying the swirls and patterns grooved into each one. Once we'd taken off from the ground, I'd realized I was getting much more comfortable dragon riding. I'd started sketching a prototype of a harness that could help someone stand upright to fight on a dragon's back, just in case it took longer than we'd like for the Evergleam to be fixed. Hopefully the Queen would figure out the cause of its disease before we returned, but if not, I'd start fashioning the harness before we took on the Enchantress.

We couldn't afford to keep putting it off. Eventually we'd be on the defensive if we waited too long, and my intuition told me that would be just about the worst place to be against the cunning sorceress.

"Let's see those dragon riding skills, champion," Travis crooned, his voice flitting up from the cage attached to my chest.

I unhooked it from the leather strap, holding him up to my face. "Shut up, Travis."

"Oh... Touchy subject?" He crossed his arms, looking smug. "Things not go as planned with our girl?"

Neve dipped quickly, making him slip out of the loosely done buckle, eyes going wide. Satisfaction curled like warm smoke in my chest, and I chuckled at his expense.

It was really hard to feel bad about it when he was always such a jerk.

"She's not *ours*," I groaned as he pulled himself back up to sit, strapping the small belt across his lap, tighter this time.

I'd hoped to avoid him finding out about our failed bonding. The last thing I wanted was for him to think it was his opportunity to swoop in. Not that I was worried about Kyleigh changing her mind. "Let me remind you that if Ky heard you say that, she'd only need a speck of her power to sizzle off that tiny dick you enjoy swinging around."

His chest puffed up and he glowered at me. "I'll have you know I'm *overly* endowed, despite my current size."

"Faerie females will be lining up at the chance," I replied, holding the cage up to my chest, about to reattach it.

"I'll be sure to save Kyleigh a spot," he said, delusional confidence wafting off him like bad cologne.

Rolling my eyes, I released the cage from my fingertips. It plummeted and bounced over a few scales before I caught it by the base.

"What the fuck?" Travis squeaked.

"Need another set of doll's trousers?" I asked with a chuckle, enjoying it far too much when his body went rigid and his eyes darted to his crotch. A second later he sighed in relief before shooting me a well-deserved glare.

I shrugged, snapping his enclosure back in place. "Apologies. Slippery glove."

WE LANDED ON A LEDGE JUTTING OUT FROM THE SIDE of the Grymm Mountains, fluorescent flora spilling from the edges of the cave's mouth in front of us. I instantly recognized where we were. There was no way I could forget the place Kyleigh had revealed her dragon to me and asked me to be her champion.

I tapped my glove and a sack of clothes bloomed from my palm, then I handed it to Neve, attention averted.

"*Damn beautiful!*" Travis's small, yet deep voice burst up from my chest, and I instinctively grabbed the cage, twisting my body so he couldn't peek at her any more than he already had.

"Thanks, but no thanks," she replied coolly from behind us. I stared out at the vastness of Celaria sprawled before us. Last time I'd been here, it'd been night, too dark to appreciate the view. Now I could see the rolling hills of lavender, the fort and village, small replicas poised in the distance. Hanging like a golden cloud ready to be plucked from the sky sat Arafax's castle.

Arriving there had been surreal when we'd returned from the Otherworld. It was so glum compared to how I remembered it as a child, dust littering every surface. I was grateful Kyleigh and Aislin had removed the remains left there. As much as I'd wanted to get Arafax's gleaming beacon glittering once again, bringing our people hope, I didn't think I could handle wondering which remains belonged to my parents.

The texts my father had been able to salvage after he'd gone back had been some of the most treasured things I'd had in my life. It was one of the reasons it meant so much to me when the Queen had taken me under her wing to help her, giving me full access to what was left of my father's legacy—the small collection of texts from Arafax's royal library.

"What's back there?" Travis asked, pointing beyond the stream that separated Arafax from the bowels of Celaria. Stone totems reached for the sky, and every so often glinting streaks would catch the light of the day's moon.

"Alucinor's peninsula." My lips pressed into a thin line, and I took a breath, stamping down my anxiety about Kyleigh going there. While having Sloan escorting her usually would have brought me some reassurance, I also knew she was hurting deeply right now. I'd watered down the whiskey in her flask, hoping it would help keep her sobered against any threats if she got the urge to pack it. They would both need to be fully alert to deal with the weavers.

"I'm sure they're fine," Neve said, as if reading my mind. "Besides, we need to discuss ground rules before we head inside."

I turned to face her and the cave's gaping mouth, unsure whether to view the illuminated pitch before us as inviting or ominous.

"You'll need to take me out of this cage," Travis called up, gripping the bars and poking his head through the slats.

"He's probably right." Neve gave him a cold glare. "Unfortunately."

"Fine." I undid the latch, and he flitted out. "But try not to be so...*you*. We need this alliance to work."

"Hey, I'm great with alliances." Travis flew up to perch on Neve's shoulder, making her roll her eyes at the tiny nuisance. "I was able to forge one with Kyleigh and get my people here. Maybe my charm is my affinity?"

"I wouldn't bet on it." Neve flicked him off her shoulder. He faltered, dropping a few inches in the air before I caught him in my gloved palm.

"You can sit right here until they let us in." My eyes snapped to Neve. "Wait, how will we even fit where they are? Aren't we too big?"

"A long time ago, faeries gifted tokens that would allow visitors in for an allotted amount of time, but I'm not sure if they do that anymore. I've never actually gone inside the cave before."

I didn't love the lack of intel we were going into this with, but the fact that we even had a location for the faeries when they were supposed to have vanished was worth something. Neve trusting me with that was a big deal. "So, what are these ground rules?"

"The only real rule I have is whatever they say goes." She glared at us both, making me bristle.

I do not like this one bit. "What kind of rule is that?"

"Well, I don't know what restrictions they have imposed now. So just be respectful of their customs and boundaries. They may not let any of us in. They may only let in Travis since he's their kind."

I sighed, exasperated, watching Travis puff up with pride. Like he needed any more of that. I was pretty sure he'd explode with another boost to his ego. "There's no way I'm relying on that asshole to secure this alliance and get us the tome's translation."

"Hey! *That asshole* is right here."

I glowered at him. "I said what I said."

He plopped down to sit with his legs crossed in my palm. "Let's just get inside. I'm ready to meet my people."

Neve ignored us, climbing over the wide lip of the cave's entrance, careful to avoid any of the glowing life boasting from its maw. It was chilly inside, but after a minute, my body began to adjust.

Moonflowers blossomed along the path, directing us toward a flurry of bursting lights that swirled around the darkness. Glowing streaks lined the walls that began to crowd in on us, the space becoming more enclosed as we moved deeper into the cave. Travis hopped off my palm, walking ahead of me, and I dropped down on all fours to crawl farther in. Pausing, I flipped on the flashlight attached to my glove, trying to get a better view and make sure I didn't accidentally squish Travis—not that the idea wasn't somewhat tempting.

My pulse raced with each step, the tunnel closing in around us, inhaling much too shallow to fully fill my lungs. Dizziness swept through me, along with the sensations of floating in the dark confines of a box.

Steadying my breaths and trying to drown out the engrained sounds of pounding my fists against the crate's interior, I continued forward in a daze, focusing on the swirling neon lights ahead. When high-pitched shrieks echoed off the cavern walls, snapping my attention, I halted.

"Turn it off," Neve commanded over her shoulder.

My gaze dropped to my glove, tapping off the light emanating from it. When I looked back up, hundreds of glowing eyes stared in my direction.

The faeries beat their fluorescent wings midair, watching us encroach on their dark, hidden oasis. Most stayed still aside from the flutter of their wings, seemingly too stunned to do anything. A few moved quickly, parting like an illuminated rippling stream, making room for someone whose bootsteps echoed through the small expanse.

A single red neon wing protruded from his back, the other had been shredded, with only a few pieces hanging limp behind him. He was dressed in black leathers, his jacket designed with openings for the wings to feed through. His skin was a rich brown, dark against the red eyes that scanned over us like tiny lasers, taking in Neve, Travis, and then finally me.

My chest clenched, half ready to bring up my glove in case they attacked. He looked at my hand, then arched a white brow matching the unkempt hair atop his head, assessing the strangers now in his territory.

"I wondered when you'd find us."

CHAPTER 18

Redmond

"So, you have a personal history with the mermaids?" I asked Sir Fergus when we met up by the stream behind The Lavender Leigh Inn & Pub. I'd never actually been to the establishment, only visiting the castle in my official capacity as prince and then flying above it during my years of watching Arafax after I'd become king. "I didn't realize they gave land dwellers much notice."

Sir Fergus carried over two packs, throwing one at me, along with a pair of pants. "Well, you wouldn't, being all high and mighty stuck up in Inverno." He pointed to the stream that would take us out toward the water that ran parallel to Arafax's border. "They will come up to the surface here every so often, especially during mating season, looking for company."

I quirked a brow at him. "*Oh.*"

Sir Fergus muttered something under his breath, pulling out a canteen from his pack and taking a swig from it. I'd heard from Sloan that the giant was fun and good natured, but understandably that hospitality didn't extend to me.

This was going to be a long excursion.

"Have you ever been to Tesceillus's castle before?"

"No," he said, walking out toward the stream, then kneeling down to roll up the bottom of his trousers. He peered back up at me from over his shoulder. "Have you?"

"No. I've heard amazing things about the kingdom, though. My father never took me with him on his quarterly visits beneath the Spuma, and I avoided flying that far south after he died."

Sir Fergus bristled, voice lowering as he stood up to face me, which wasn't really possible since he claimed a full foot over me in stature. "You mean after you burned my kingdom to ash?"

"Yes," I said, keeping my tone even, not wanting to escalate the tension that already existed in spades between us. "After that."

I looked up at him, meeting his gaze. "I doubt it means much at this point, but I do regret what happened."

"You're right." His eyes were slits above his nose, glaring down at me. "It doesn't mean much."

He peeled off his shirt, puffing out his muscular chest with pride, easily twice the size of mine. "Lucky for you, I am more concerned with Arafax's future than its past."

Thank fuck. At least that gave me something to work with.

"Besides, stabbing you with Neve's scale was very cathartic."

"I bet," I deadpanned, a phantom pain slicing through my healed shoulder blade.

"Do you think we'll be able to secure an alliance with their king?"

"No clue." Once we got to Tesceillus, I wasn't sure what the protocol would be other than requesting an audience with their ruler. "I've never met King Morrow, but from what I do know, he's very into pomp."

"I'll make sure to bow and kiss his fins properly, then."

"You and I both," I replied, stealing a glimpse of a smirk from the large knight.

Striding down the dirt path leading toward the stream, Sir

Fergus stepped off the ledge and plopped into the water, splashing me. "By the way, how are your wings going to handle our trek underwater?"

Shaking off my feathers, I stretched them out into the moon's light. I hated that I wouldn't be able to ignite my phoenix fire while they were wet, instantly making me more vulnerable. "Not well, I'm guessing. Not that I have much choice in the matter."

Swiping the droplets away from my eyes, I sighed, then knelt down to roll up my trousers. It seemed silly to wear them in the water, but I followed Sir Fergus's lead.

"Once Opal and Aurelia take us down to the capital, it shouldn't matter much. It's enchanted, so land dwellers can walk and breathe normally. It'll just be getting down there that'll be the hassle. Hope you're okay with swimming."

Great.

"You don't know how to swim, do you?"

"I mean, I know how to." I held out one foot and dipped it into the water. Its wet icy grasp sent me recoiling. *This is going to be miserable.* "I just haven't swam since my wings came in."

"I was wondering...do any other people have wings or shifting abilities? Why don't you have a familiar but your people do?"

Finally braving the water, I hopped off the platform, shivering once I landed. Taking a few steps back and forth in the shallow water, I could feel my body acclimating to the frigid temperature. I still had no desire to submerge my wings so I kept them held stiffly above the surface. "The wings will appear on the next in line to the throne when they turn magic age. It isn't necessarily the oldest, though. I was the only child so there were no other options. Our rulers have never had familiars, just our phoenixes, for whatever reason."

"So when you have children—"

"*If.*"

"*If* you have children, one of them would get the wings and would be next to lead Inverno."

"Yes. Though I have no plans to procreate."

Years ago, it would have been a different story, but I didn't want to have an heir just to have one. And love wasn't something in the cards for me. Not anymore. I wasn't the man I once was. And there was no fucking way I'd reproduce with the Enchantress if I somehow ended up forced to follow through on our marriage. A harrowing prospect. The only thing more harrowing than that was the thought of her as a mother.

"Who would take the throne then?" Sir Fergus asked, some of the previous vitriol leaving his voice, replaced with genuine curiosity.

"I don't know. There's always been at least one heir." I shrugged. It seemed like a minimal issue compared to everything else right now. "Guess we'll find out when it happens."

I glanced around at the stream, unsure how to get a mermaid's attention. "How does this work?"

Were we just going to wait for one to swim by? The very idea made me shiver.

Without a word, Sir Fergus bent down into the water, whispering against its current. Standing up, he wiped a hand across his beard.

Before I could say anything, two mermaids peered out of the water, only their white, seemingly vacant eyes and bright sapphire-and-amethyst streaked hair peeking above the surface.

"Long time since I've seen you beauties," Sir Fergus said, walking farther into the water to greet them. They gave me another tentative glance, eyes snagging over my wings, probably the peculiarity of them. Then they rose up out of the water, glued to Sir Fergus's sides.

They were completely naked from above their onyx-scaled tails, their nipples poking between the strands of vibrant hair. Smiling up at Sir Fergus, rows of sharp teeth made up their maw.

I gulped back my surprise. Father had definitely left that part out when describing the mermaids' unparalleled beauty.

"Do you, by any chance, have more blood on you from that rarity?" the pale one asked Sir Fergus, making me wonder what blood she was talking about.

"Oh, I'm sorry. I don't today," he said. "How did it go with the vials we gave you?"

"Splendidly!" the other mermaid with a dark complexion answered, clapping her hands together. "We recently settled down with a wonderful male. Just in time for mating season. Figured maybe we could pass some along to our friends who are still on the hunt. They're all so jealous."

"As they should be," Sir Fergus said with a smile. "Congratulations to you both! I look forward to meeting the lucky merman."

"Your friend looks interesting, Fergie." I stifled a laugh at the nickname. "Think he would be willing to help our friends out?"

"Look at those wings," the other one swooned.

"I'm sure King Redmond of Inverno would be happy to help." His eyes locked on mine, as if daring me to say otherwise. "He's also got rare blood that is sure to impress some males for your friends."

Bet it was hard for him to choke that compliment out with a straight face.

"This is Opal," he said, eyes roving to the pale mermaid, then he turned his head to the other. "And this is Aurelia."

"Wonderful to meet you, Opal and Aurelia. And sure, I will help your friends with some blood." *Though I have no idea what it's for.* I'd have to ask Sir Fergus about it later, privately. The last thing I wanted to do was offend them with my lack of knowledge about their customs. "That is, if you're willing to help us."

"What are you needing, Your Majesty?" Aurelia asked, cocking her head to the side. Despite already being mated to some male beneath the surface, she seemed very interested in the men above it, and I didn't know how I felt about that.

"We need an audience with King Morrow," I stated, not wanting to mince words. We only had a week until we had to be back. Ideally, I'd return to Inverno sooner. Not being able to easily get to my people because I'd be leagues below the Spuma's froth-coated surface had my wings flaring bright blue.

"Oh, he's adorable, Fergie," Opal said, giving me a sharpened grin, which I returned on terrified instinct. *Yeah, I'm fucking precious.* "Unfortunately, meeting with the King won't be that simple. He is incredibly busy, especially during mating season. You would need to come with us to Tesceillus and then we would vouch for you through the appropriate channels."

"Of course." I took a few more steps forward into the deeper part of the water, holding my wings behind me, still avoiding getting them wet. "Completely understandable."

"Could we at least get a ride with you and get that word put in?" Sir Fergus asked, the mermaids swishing out of his grasp as they swam toward me.

"We would, of course, help your friends in exchange." I truly hoped giving them my blood didn't involve being bitten by those teeth they were smiling at me with.

"I suppose that would work," Opal said, looking to Aurelia for approval. They traded an odd expression I couldn't quite pinpoint before turning back to us. "You'll have to find other lodging, though. Our male wouldn't approve of you staying with us. There are a few places that should have some rooms available."

"Not a problem," Sir Fergus agreed.

Aurelia beckoned me forward with a crook of her finger, and I descended into the water, gripping the silty floor with my toes. I lowered my wings until they were partially submerged, hissing as my feathers became saturated. Wading closer, she gripped my face in her hands bringing her mouth toward mine.

"What are you—"

"Pucker up, Your Majesty," Sir Fergus chuckled, enjoying my discomfort way too much.

Aurelia still hovered mere inches from me. Eyes glued to my lips. I gulped, pushing down any fear. This couldn't be worse than the pretending I had to do with the Enchantress.

"You're lucky I'm not in the mood to tell Jasper how eager you were to kiss a stranger today," Opal teased, splashing her friend before gliding over to Sir Fergus. She sniffed him a few times, wrinkling her nose.

Odd.

Aurelia gripped my chin and pressed her lips to mine. It was brief but sent a chill through me, like kissing a sheet of ice. When she pulled away, I traced my lips with my thumb, wondering what she'd done to me.

"Now you should be able to safely swim down to Tesceillus without worrying about holding your breath," she told me, and I nodded in thanks, still dreading the trip to her kingdom.

"You taste funny," Opal said, drawing my attention to her and Sir Fergus. She grimaced, smacking her lips a few times as if she'd eaten something rotten. Meanwhile, the giant's mouth had turned a navy color, making me suspect my lips had done the same.

"Sorry, must be the onion and barley soup I had earlier," he said with a shrug, pink staining his cheeks.

Opal tilted her head at him before dipping down and rinsing her mouth in the stream. When she came back up, she spit the water out in a large arc that landed a few feet away. "Maybe?"

"Shall we?" he asked me, and I nodded.

"Just leave your packs. Our friends will transport them for you." Opal and Aurelia dove beneath the surface. Sir Fergus waited for me to submerge myself before he followed. I took a deep breath and closed my eyes. Bending my knees, I pushed off my feet and into the current.

It was jarring to be underwater but not needing to hold my breath or head back to the surface. I took an inhale, expecting to choke on the water surrounding me, but whatever had activated with the mermaid's kiss let me swim and breathe freely.

The water fought against my wings when I used them, so instead I pulled them behind me, trying to keep them as rigid as possible. My body did not enjoy being completely covered in water. It hadn't since I'd developed my wings. It was why I always showered, avoiding baths and large pools of water.

I pursed my waxen lips. I'd heard of the mermaid's kiss but more in bedtime stories and ballads, never thinking much about it. What else would I discover on this mission? If I wanted to gain King Morrow's trust and alliance, I would need to learn as much as I could. They were the third largest territory in Celaria. Garnering their support would give us an advantage, especially if the other territories sided with the Enchantress or refused to get involved.

Using my arms to push through the murky water, I kicked my legs, diving after the mermaids, using their hair's bright hues as my compass.

With each stroke toward Tesceillus, new life vibrated through the water, keeping my attention on the unfamiliar world around me and distracting from the exhaustion I'd feel later. I knew we had reached the sea when a family of Spuma turtles floated alongside me, their white shells glistening with tiny rainbows of color against a bubbling lilac backdrop. They followed us a while, Sir Fergus swimming up to keep pace with me, smiling at them. He reached out a massive hand, stroking one of the turtles' backs, and it flipped over, doing a backstroke so the giant rubbed its stomach.

I extended my hand out to the inverted turtle, wondering if it'd feel as smooth as its body looked. As my fingers neared, it snapped at them, making Sir Fergus garble out what I knew to be a laugh.

Ass.

The deeper we swam, the darker the water became, going from shades of lilac to rich violet that neared black.

A hand grabbed mine, and I startled, preparing to fight off whoever it was until I saw it was Opal. She pointed to a massive illuminated clamshell below us sitting on the ocean floor. Tesceillus. The current, other fish, and ocean flora all seemed to flow around it, like a stream rippling around a rock. Some sort of protective magic veiled the territory.

Shielding it.

Magic that was eerily familiar to me.

Even as we drew nearer, I couldn't see anything within its walls. Opal and Aurelia pressed their lips to the bubble hiding Tesceillus and a moment later the shell split down its barely visible seam, revealing the mer-capital like a treasured pearl. I thumbed along the barrier as we slipped past, the thin but effective protection keeping this world well hidden from outsiders. I peered down at the village, waves of vibrantly colored houses capped with coral reefs. Men walked around on two legs among the throngs of merpeople flitting about.

Land dwellers.

How is that possible?

"The castle's over there," Aurelia said, pointing to the spires reaching up ahead of us. A line of bubbles rose from her lips.

"Wow." I released my own stream of bubbles, startling myself. Whatever enchantments they had cast here made it so that I could speak and breathe without the water choking me, though my voice came out deeper and slower than usual. It was as if the water still flowed for the mermaids but was breathable to its visitors.

The castle was magnificent, its highest pinnacle reaching the top of Tesceillus's protective edge. Bits of broken shells created beautiful mosaicked waves and swirls cascading along the castle walls and lining the large arched windows. Giant coral reefs decorated the villages that framed either side of the castle, brilliant jades, crimsons, oranges, and marigolds giving pops of color. The homes were all constructed with shells and mortar, like the castle, only much smaller. Tiny fish jetted in and out above each house's rooftop coral reef, leaving bubbles in their wake.

Opal swam in front of us, her tail whipping some bubbles into my face. "Let's get you situated with a place to stay. Your bags will be delivered in a few hours."

I nodded in agreement, excited to explore the kingdom but also wanting to get some food and tend to my wings first. Looking back at them, the feathers were glossy, pinned against their frame. Hopefully there'd be enough space to stretch them out in my room.

Then we'd need to secure an invitation to Tesceillus's opulent castle.

CHAPTER 19

"You knew we'd be coming?" I asked in surprise.

Could his affinity be some sort of psychic ability?

"No, just figured you'd be curious," the white-haired stranger said in a steady tone. "We've been hidden for decades now, and you're the first ones to wander into our territory, though we've seen her before..." He squinted a bit, his neon-red eyes darting toward the thin sliver of light coming from the cave's exit, "in both her forms."

I took a few shallow breaths before I could finally manage a deep one, clenching my gloved fist tight to tether myself.

I'm okay.

The walls aren't closing in.

I'm just in a cave—not in that casket floating to the Otherworld.

"Neve!" A silvery voice chimed from behind the red-winged leader. A pair of delicate gossamer wings gently pushed through the crowd of faeries that had come closer to see their visitors. She had pink-kissed cheeks and cropped blonde hair sprinkled with gemstones that glinted in a prism of colors as she passed the neon flutter around her. "It's so good to see you again. Been too long."

The leader bristled at her familiarity with Neve, pulling his single wing tight behind his back. "Wynnie, how do you know this outsider's name?"

"Oh hush, Harkin," she said, running a hand along the edge of his wing. He visibly relaxed into her touch. "I met Neve many moons ago, after I first arrived here."

"It was purely a chance meeting," Neve interjected with a warm smile. "The ledge beyond your territory is one of my favorite spots for escaping."

"It is a nice secluded spot." He pressed a kiss to Wynnie's head before looking out at his congregation of faerie folk. "Part of the reason we chose to settle here. To be left *alone*. Our people have endured enough."

Sweat beaded across my brow, dripping into pools outside of their glowing cavern metropolis. If I didn't get this exchange moving along, I didn't think I'd ever leave this cave. "We're here because we need your help."

"And why would we help an outsider?" His eyes locked with Neve, and she pursed her lips.

"Not all of us are outsiders," I offered, nudging my faerie foe closer. Travis gave a wide smile and a head nod to *his people* in front of them. "He arrived here from the Otherworld and found out he is a faerie. Doesn't he deserve to better understand his roots?"

"I suppose a sapling's roots shape them even if they've been transplanted elsewhere." Harkin gave Travis a seemingly disapproving look, which I didn't mind in the least.

Travis bowed his head. "I want to understand. To learn my affinity. My history."

I rasped for air, drawing everyone's attention to me. "Our people are *all* in trouble. That's why we are here. We need your help. The woman called the Enchantr—"

Audible gasps echoed against the partially illuminated walls. The hundreds of glowing eyes wide and pinned to me.

Harkin lifted his hand, waiting a moment for the faeries around him to relax from their heightened state of shock. As I worked to calm my racing heart and the panic clawing up my throat, he turned his attention back to me. "I know you don't understand our customs, but we don't believe in calling her by that false name."

"I apologize," I heaved. "I'm not a fan of tight spaces and obviously have much to learn as well. Would you be willing to allow us passage into your territory so we could discuss this further?"

"All of you?" His eyes drifted behind me to Neve. "Including the Revered one?"

"If it would make your people feel more comfortable, I will go stretch my wings for a bit and then come back and wait for them outside," Neve offered, pointing toward the cave's exit.

Shit. I really didn't want to do this without her, especially since she seemed to already have some established relationship with Wynnie. "Wait—"

"That would be best," Harkin replied before I could finish explaining my very logical reason for Neve to stay. One that would reassure the faeries around us. I didn't really have a reason, but I'm sure I could have had one pop up with a few more seconds to catch my breath.

"Thank you for your understanding, Neve." Wynnie tilted her head toward her old acquaintance. "It would be for the best, especially with your...unique abilities."

I guess a human that could shift into a ginormous ice-blasting dragon wasn't an ideal first visitor for the faeries of... whatever this place was called.

Wynnie pulled out a coppery coin, holding it out to Harkin. "Look, sugarplum, I was able to find a few of these stashed away with my old things."

He took it from her, showing it to me. "This token will give you twenty-four hours of access. If you do not remove yourself by that time, it will spit you back out in Arafax. You understand?"

I remained silent, still catching my breath, but nodded.

"I'll be back for you soon," Neve said to us before backing out along the path of moonflowers exiting the cave.

Harkin placed the token against the back of my hand, whispering an incantation. There was a slight jolt as it adhered itself to my skin. A wave of dizziness crashed into me, and I gripped my knees to stabilize myself. When I was able to stand again, I found myself in the same spot, only the room had expanded. My lungs finally drew deep breaths, so I took a few deliberate inhales and exhales, grateful not to feel the suffocating pressure that had claimed me since we'd arrived.

Spinning my timer on my glove, I set it for twenty-three and a half hours from now.

"Shall we?" Wynnie asked, waving us to follow her toward the glowing metropolis ahead. "Welcome to Renegade Trench."

CHAPTER 20

Neve

E xpanding my energy outward, my scales rippled to the surface, body reshaping to accommodate my dragon's form. While a small part of me felt guilty leaving Dru and Travis to fend for themselves with the faeries, I also understood their wariness around me. Dragons may be Revered by Arafax's people, but they were feared by the rest of Celaria.

And with good reason.

This ledge where I'd come to for years had been my safe haven when I was younger. A place I could run off to when the expectations others had sidled me with became too big a burden to carry—even for a dragon.

Coming back here after returning to my human form was one of the few comforts I had from my past, but looking out at the current view soured any previous sentimentality.

The rubble-filled village where the heart of Arafax used to be.

The empty, yet sullen-looking castle looming in the clouds.

The soldiers with blue capes standing ready with their familiars and weapons in the distance.

This was not the world I remembered prior to my capture.

My family was gone. My friends as well, aside from Isla, who'd managed to distance herself from everyone. Redmond was still here, but we were very different people now. Maybe we always were, but we'd been too young and too enamored with each other to see clearly.

The love we shared had been real. As real as the snowflakes puffing into the sky from my scaled maw. As real as the steep drop from this ledge that somehow used to ground me. As real as the thread tacked deep in my chest, tethering me to another man.

But the love we shared had also been a manipulation. External masters pulling our strings.

Arafax and Inverno's royalty were so supportive of our engagement when we'd finally had the courage to announce it publicly. They'd been eager to hold our wedding, to shower us with events and lavish praise for bringing our kingdoms closer. I was so blinded by happiness I didn't notice both rulers were busy looping strings around their stubby fingers, dangling us from their own agendas.

You know what you have to do.

The familiar voice and the dreaded memory attached to it knocked at the door of my mind, wanting re-entry, but I twisted the lock with a *click*, sealing it away again.

I'd had a lot of time to think about that day, replaying the memory and the hours that followed from behind the iron bars of Inverno's dungeon. The decisions that had led to my imprisonment. It didn't take long to come to a very solid conclusion.

We'd been idiots.

So naïve to what games were being played. Redmond especially. And he had been for the last decade as well because he *still* didn't know the truth. The full truth. That was partially my own fault but, honestly, I still wasn't sure it was worth telling him.

It wouldn't change the fact that I'd buried hundreds of icy spears into his father's chest right in front of him.

It wouldn't change the fact that Redmond and his blue phoenix fire destroyed Arafax, or that he held me captive for a decade.

I could see that he was trying—truly trying—to make amends. To atone. I wouldn't ruffle that with any unnecessary confessions.

And forgiveness, while he'd never ask for it, didn't feel like such a foreign concept anymore.

Not like it had once upon a time.

CHAPTER 21
Redmond

"We'd like to get two rooms for a few nights," I said to the mermaid behind the desk at Snatch of the Day. Her hair was emerald with pink tips floating around her chin, leaving her bared from the waist up. Mermaids sat along the edges of the brothel, inside oversized clamshells, waving at the various patrons that came in.

The land dwellers definitely seemed entranced by how exposed the mermaids were, their breasts always on display since their hair flowed around them in bright, bold colors, but nudity didn't do much for me. Not in the general sense. Being a shifter, it was as natural as breathing. But with the trousers I'd thrown on earlier glued to my body, the mermaids ogled me with nothing left to the imagination. I couldn't wait to get to my room and have some privacy.

"Unfortunately, there is only one room available," she said with a shrug. "Don't let that discourage you, though, we have many private coves to enjoy."

She winked at me, nodding to the mermaids spread throughout the lobby.

"You can't be serious." I had no interest in finding a private cove and had even less in sharing a room with Sir Fergus.

"Look, it's mating season, which means many mermaids are bringing land dwellers to stay in the capital."

"I don't understand," I said, not wanting to bring up the fact that I was a king, considering it might not be the best way to secure a meeting with King Morrow. "Can't these land dwellers stay with the mermaid that was kind enough to extend an invitation to them to come mate?"

"Well, that would be disrespectful to their males," the mermaid said, crossing her arms over her chest and giving me a stern look. "Territorial lot, they are. Besides, don't be so coy, isn't that why you've been brought here? I'm sure Jasper would be thrilled to host you while you breed with his wives."

"I beg your pardon!"

"The look on your face is making this all the more enjoyable," Sir Fergus cut in, a roguish grin spanning his beard.

I shook my head, ready to get this over with. "We'll just take the key to the room, Lady—"

"Madame Jade," she said, staring up at me through hooded eyes before swishing out from behind the desk and circling me. She grazed a hand over my wings, and I quivered, morphing my grimace into a charming smile. She swam ahead, leading us through various channels until she came to a door labeled with the silhouette of ten tiny guppies. "Hope you enjoy your stay. Wishing you and your slippery swimmers a successful mating season."

As soon as she'd glided down the hall and was out of sight, I shut the door, spinning around to face the giant who was already kicking off his shoes. "What the fuck is going on around here?"

"Well, there are exponentially more lady merfolk than males. So, to keep the race growing and avoid inbreeding, they tend to borrow land-dwelling males during mating season." He lay back, propping his legs up on the bed, only it was too short. Rolling to face me, he bent his knees to keep his ankles from dangling over the edge. "Why else do you think they'd have enchantments making it so easy for us to wander around?"

Fair point. Though that didn't lessen my unease. "Opal and Aurelia aren't planning to mate with us, right?"

"Probably not," he said, rubbing his beard, bushy brows knitting together.

"Probably?"

"We didn't promise them any of that, just some of your blood to help their friends out for mating season."

Thank fuck. Slice my arm and leave my *slippery swimmers* alone.

"Of course, if you decide to do more than that while we are here, I wouldn't judge," he said, waggling his brows. "Though I'm sure the Enchantress isn't much for sharing."

"You'd be wrong about that," I grumbled. Trying not to think about the Enchantress. I wasn't looking forward to our next visit, much less if I had to marry her. The very idea made me shudder. I couldn't believe I'd been so foolish as to get involved with her in the first place.

"When they said only one room, I didn't realize that meant only one bed," I groaned, staring at Sir Fergus taking up more than half of the mattress.

"Well, we are in a brothel," he replied, patting the empty space. "Haven't you ever been in one?"

"Can't say I have."

Ox's brows lifted into the ridges of his forehead. "I would think a king would have ample access to company."

"Having access to company doesn't mean I frequent brothels."

"Ah yes, they could just come visit your bedchambers at the castle."

"Something like that." I had no interest in using people for sex, even if they were getting compensated for it. I'd rather just give them the coin they sought. It was hard enough pretending with the Enchantress.

Plopping down on the edge of the bed, I swung my semi-dry legs over the blanket, wishing once again that I was alone right now and not in soaked trousers.

Hopefully our visit would go well and we'd be back on land soon.

"You hungry?" Sir Fergus asked about fifteen minutes after we'd sat awkwardly in silence.

"Starved." I was grateful to do anything to get out of this room, this bed, and pass time before our stuff arrived. "Let's get some food in the tavern."

"Good evening," said our server. She had cropped purple hair and silver bars pierced through her nipples.

"Good evening to you," Sir Fergus replied, shifting on his stool and keeping his gaze strategically pinned to her face. "Things seem busy."

"Yes, mating season always has everyone in a bit of a tizzy." She leaned forward, jutting out her chest. "Have you partaken?"

"No, not yet," Sir Fergus said hastily before I could reply. He pointed over to the bar. "We'd both love a shot of your house rum."

I raised a finger at the mermaid before she swam off. "Make mine a double."

A merman jetted in, a beautiful female on his arm with bright-yellow hair. She stroked his side, arm looped through his. The amors in the clamshells began to primp and pose in earnest, trying to garner their attention. The couple stopped in front of a shell where a mermaid with blue cropped hair lay back, whipping her tail side to side, beckoning them closer. When they moved to her, she flicked her tail up their scales, eliciting a heavy sigh from the female. The male swam toward the row of coves set behind the front desk, the two females following him.

Moans echoed along the walls, coming from the private area they'd disappeared to, easily marking it as a place I wanted to avoid.

"Hmm...interesting," our server said, leaning over not-so-subtly to place her breasts in front of us as she set down our drinks. "I know you're off limits," she said, frowning at Sir Fergus, "but is your friend at least available?"

My throat went dry.

"I'm flattered, but I won't be taking on any companionship during our visit," I bit out as kindly as I could. "Don't let me stop you, though, Sir Fergus. I have heard many a tale of your... escapades. You don't need to abstain because of me."

Perhaps if he found a private cove, I'd get the room to myself for the night.

The mermaid bristled, seemingly offended by my rejection. "I may be interested in cock and coin," she said with a glare, "but even I'm not desperate enough to interfere with his newly formed bond."

Sir Fergus paled, ice rimming the edge of the table where his fingers gripped it, tiny trails of snowflakes streaking toward me. His eyes dropped to the frost before he quickly picked his hands up, shaking them as he dropped them in his lap.

A lump caught in my throat, my voice barely above a rasp, gaze pinned to the frost between us.

"Newly formed what?"

$\mathcal{N}$eve

Tiny flecks of snow floated up into the air from my mouth, the lavender whiskey rolling along my tongue and warming my insides. Handing the flask over to Ox, he took a swig, watching me undo the top three buttons of my lace blouse, revealing peeks of my black-lace bralette before pulling it over my head, letting the fabric flutter to the ground.

I'd come back and get it later, on the way to go check on Sloan. We couldn't leave her alone for too long.

After finding her draped across the window seat, staring off at nothing, we'd instructed Sweeney to cut her off for the night. I hoped he listened. He was a push over, though, especially when it came to nursing a broken heart. According to him, he had only been marginally better when Pierce disappeared after The Blaze but only because he'd had Aislin to care for.

Ox took another swig, then handed the half-full flask back to me. His eyes skated over my breasts, the dark lace caressing them. Arching a brow, he reached his hand out and caught my wrist before I took another sip. "You sure you want to do this?"

"Yes," I said, shaking off his gentle grasp. "Don't tell me you're about to wuss out on me."

I bent forward, rolling my pants down my hips until they pooled around my ankles. The trees glowed from above, a halo of illumination spilling Ox's massive shadow over me. I could feel his attention frozen to me, thickening the air between us.

I stepped out from the fabric, tucking the flask into it, then continued my stride toward the Evergleam. Running my fingers along my side, I fumbled over the scarred remains of my time in Inverno. They scraped against the pads, and I clenched my fist tight as I brought it down by my side.

"I'm just making sure you know what you're doing," he called out tentatively from behind me, and I turned, coming to a halt.

"You haven't had any complaints so far." It'd become a nightly occurrence over the last few weeks, escaping with each other in secret. The perfect concoction of feeling everything and nothing all at once. Filling my body with pleasure and emptying my mind of the war that'd taken root there over the last decade. Something we both seemed to desperately need.

And no strings attached.

At least not until now.

"That was different." His face began to redden as he stumbled over the words. "This is—"

"Giving us an advantage over the Enchantress." It didn't need to be anything more complicated than that. A power up; a tether to a friend—the fact that he could make me come was a bonus.

Catching up to me, he lay a hand on my shoulder. He was barely touching it, but it was still enough to send a chill down my spine, my toes curling against the cool ground. "Yes, I get that, Neve."

He was always so gentle, and I always had to remind him not to be. There was nothing delicate about me. Not anymore. The jagged pieces leftover from the last decade ensured that.

His gaze narrowed. "But don't you think this is a bit

drastic?"

Ice shot through my veins, steeling my resolve. "You want to take her down?"

"Of course." He ran his hand through his beard, looking at the glowing tree ahead of us.

"That's what I want, too. And I intend to be successful. With or without you."

His throat bobbed in the majestic light of the Evergleam, standing before us, illuminated in all its glory.

I remembered the first time I'd come here, when the champions and ceremony had been explained to me. The ceremony itself sparked the bond, but the dragon still had to accept the champion, and the pair would then strengthen their tether over time, nurturing it. The blending of their powers was almost instantaneous, while the boost to Celaria spread at a slower rate, usually starting in the heart of the grove and then crawling outward to the farthest territories of the realm.

"This isn't drastic," I reiterated, gripping the top button of his tunic and undoing it before running my palms down his chest, my nails grazing the firm panes of muscle. He was still staring over my shoulder at the Evergleam's massive trunk. It burst into branches tipped with crystalline leaves, one of which we would infuse with our bonding tonight. Pressing my nail into his collarbone finally brought his attention back to me, and I raised a brow at him. "It's necessary."

"I don't want there to be any regrets later," he replied, lifting his hand to stop me from continuing my work. His irises, the color of rich cocoa, softened.

"Look, I'm doing this. If you've gotten cold feet—"

"Don't even finish that sentence, Neve. I'm in. I just..." He cradled my chin, not letting me look away, searching my eyes for...something.

Whatever he was looking for, he wouldn't find it here.

"Think of the Fergus name," I said, lacing my fingers

through his wrapped around my jaw and guiding it to my breast, helping him free me from my bralette. "The legacy you'll leave behind." His pupils dilated, and he released a heavy sigh as he began to torment me with his palm. Leaving his hand there, I traced along his waistband, unthreading the clasp of his belt and pulling it through the loops. "Champion to a Revered one. Slayer of the Enchantress."

"I mean, that does have a nice sound." He gave his usual roguish grin, kneading my breast. With his free hand, he slid the strap of my bralette down, exposing me fully, then stepped back, gaze skating over me with desire. "Stars above, you're gorgeous."

He watched me as if he'd never seen anything more captivating, an expression he'd perfected after years of being the village rake.

"Stop," I said, cutting him off.

The last thing I wanted was to be treated as something fragile. To be looked at with anything beyond pure want and temporary claim because there could never be more than that for me. Not with him. Not with anyone. If I could champion myself to better my chances against the Enchantress, I'd be in this grove alone, with only my hand as company. But that wasn't possible.

I didn't love Ox, but I trusted him. I knew him enough to know he'd do anything to protect Arafax. Especially wrestling with his guilt over what'd happened to the royal family the night of The Blaze. So, if he was going to be here, if he was going to be the one to share this dragon bond and whatever it meant for my magic, I wanted to be out of my mind, body numb with pleasure, unable to utter intelligible words.

Love was out of the cards for me. Fate may have tried to deal me some romance once upon a time, but my life was no fairy tale and I wasn't a princess to be rescued.

When Ox and I had each moved into the rooms on either side of Sloan's, trying to keep an eye on her as she dealt with Aislin's ghost, we'd found comfort in each other. Grief sometimes did that to you, I supposed, and I was tired of grieving. I'd spent the last ten years grieving the life that'd been taken from me. The happily ever after I thought I'd deserved.

That'd been my first naïve mistake.

Life didn't give us what we deserved.

But that didn't mean I wouldn't find a way to rebuild and find happiness on my own terms. Starting with taking control of this champion business.

Trailing my fingers along his abs, I lowered my knees to the ground, my eyes trained to his. Pulling off his final layer, he bobbed free, so deliciously thick, the scent of apple pie and a hint of whiskey wafting off the giant above me.

"This all mine?" I asked coyly. Licking my lips, I glided them along his shaft, wrapping my fingers around most of the base. He bucked against them, and I huffed out a sigh. I had him right where I wanted him. Before long he'd be gripping my curls and shoving himself deep into my throat. He couldn't resist it, and I loved watching the moment when that tether of warrior-level control snapped. When the man I'd heard stories about came out to play.

"Blazes," he said, hips pressing into me as I wrapped my lips around him once again, running my tongue along his skin before licking the slit on the tip of his cock. That move always made him jerk, and I lapped up the salty zing of his precum.

"What's got your laces tangled, Ox?" I frowned at him, lazily tracing along his length and staring at him through hooded eyes. If his nerves needed some playful coaxing to follow through tonight, I'd happily oblige. "Don't wanna be my champion?"

"Of course I want to. It's a huge honor," he hissed, and I could tell he was fighting the urge to push his cock between my lips. "But this is permanent."

"I know," I said, giving him a few long twists, feeling him grow harder against my palm. "And you'll be helping me out. Knight in shining armor, damsel in distress and all that."

I smirked up at him, batting my lashes.

"You're far from a damsel, and if anyone's in distress right now, it's me," he said with a frustrated growl, combing his fingers through my curls, keeping my face an inch too far away to lap up the precum building at the swollen tip of his cock.

I sighed in frustration, staring at the shimmering bead. "You are overthinking this."

Feeling his restraint release, I took him between my lips and swallowed him down, the head of his cock stamping the back of my throat. The grip in my hair became tighter, and I peered up at him through my lashes, tears blurring my eyes. I knew I must look like a mess. I'd seen my reflection after our nights together, black streaked down my cheeks and teeth marks along my thighs.

"Yes," he gritted out, jaw clenched as he rocked into me, "but—"

I replaced my mouth with my hand, twisting it. "I need this power boost so we can face the Enchantress. So we can try to get Aislin back. Sloan promised her she wouldn't go after her without help. That's us now, Ox. *We* are her help." I quickened my pace. "We do this. Kyleigh and Dru will be doing their ceremony any day now—that's two bonded pairs against her."

"You're right," he said, putting out a hand to stop me.

"Look at you." I smiled, leaning over to grab the dagger from his holster. "Already learning a key phrase to making this bond between us work."

"So, what do I need to do?" he asked, collecting his breath and trying to concentrate.

"We need to do the incantation, then seal it." I twisted the tip of the blade into my palm and handed him the knife.

"That's it?" he asked, arching a brow, then slid the blade across his own palm.

"Well, I plan to make it a little less straightforward and more enjoyable."

"I can get on board with that."

We clasped our hands together, our blood mingling before placing our palms on the base of the trunk. I said the incantation first and he joined in the last few times until we had said it in unison.

"Dilían cró derkomai bitháiach caur."

He gave me a roguish grin, leaning forward, his lips so close that when I released a frosty exhale, tiny flecks of white peppered his beard. His eyes fell to my mouth a moment before shooting back up. "Now what?"

Before he moved closer, I slid a finger in front of his lips, then stepped back and pointed that finger at the Evergleam. "Now you fuck me until we forget why we're here."

Holding out my palms, I released thick flurries of snow, spraying the uneven roots. Ox came up behind me, a calloused hand gliding over my hip, reaching for my center. Slipping his fingers through my folds, he pushed into me with one before having a second join, driving in and out of me with slow, curling motions. While I covered the ground in a blanket of fresh snow, I rubbed myself against him, the pleasure building, the force of it making the snow jet out in a blizzard until there was a heap large enough for us to lay on.

Ox shivered. "Not sure that is going to be much better."

"No more talking unless it's something dirty," I said, shooting a few flakes at his balls, causing him to wince.

He hissed as his ass met the snow-covered roots. "Get over here and warm my tongue."

Laying back next to the tree, he patted the top of his chest, but when I knelt down, he grabbed my waist and flipped me like I weighed nothing, facing me toward his legs. Wasting no time, he licked me clear up my center, making me arch like a cat. I released a breath as he ran his hands along my sides, skimming over the scars there, then gripping me in place before I could wriggle away.

"This," he whispered, humming against my clit. He lapped

at my center again, making me shudder. "It's all mine now, mó venéro."

The ancient meaning rolled through me, taking me by surprise, though I didn't allow it to show. His beard grazed the tips of my thighs, mouth working its magic. He ate me greedily, like he was starved and I was his last chance at dessert. Gripping his knees for support, I jerked against him with abandon, taking my pleasure without shame. There was never any of that between us. Not even now as he held my scars, thumbing along their ridges.

The pressure below my belly grew, and he speared his tongue into me.

He left one hand along my markings, taking the other and replacing his tongue, curling his fingers inside of me as he sucked my clit between his teeth, the perfect balance of pain and pleasure.

I cried out, my legs more and more unsteady with every flick, every stroke, every nip.

"I'm going to come," I whimpered, snowflakes floating out from my lips, ascending the Evergleam's branches. The tree itself had started to glow, brilliant blue light flickering over the markings along its bark, growing brighter as my body convulsed.

"Oh no you're not," Ox said, gripping my hips. "You'll finish on your champion's cock."

He lifted me up barely a moment, then shifted me lower on his body, dragging me down his length. I screamed out at the overwhelmingly blissful intrusion. He was so thick, I had to remind myself I could take him deeply. It wasn't hard with how worked up he always seemed to get me.

"Atta girl," he huffed out, voice gravelly. I rolled my hips, riding him as he bucked, closing the gap between us with each thrust. He could pierce right through me and I wouldn't even care.

I wanted more.

I wanted it all.

Deepening my strides along his shaft, I gripped the bark with one hand and his leg with the other, noticing his toes beginning to curl.

My eyes locked on the small bead of red that floated up from where we'd placed the enchantment, coursing along the branches until it dripped into a clear crystal, turning it a rich crimson.

"Come," I demanded, pressing into the spot I knew would be his undoing, pinning my core to the base of his shaft and rolling my hips vigorously against him.

He roared, hips punching as warmth painted my insides, followed by a burst of cold. I jolted up an inch, but Ox gripped me, pulling me back down.

"Did you do that?" I asked, peering at him from over my shoulder, his ice-cold length numbing me from the inside. It had startled me, but it felt good after riding him, considering his size and my *enthusiasm*.

"It worked," I said, smiling with giddy abandon. Feeling somehow lighter.

"Were there any doubts it would?" Ox's charming confidence billowed over the words as he puffed out his chest a bit.

"Now we can go after the Enchantress." I breathed out with relief, making a move to get up.

Ox's hand splay across my lower belly, stopping me.

"There'll be plenty of time for that." He sat up and nuzzled his beard against my cheek, bringing his hand over the snow on the ground and making it spiral in his palm. "But first, I'd like to play with you and this new magic of *ours*."

I shrieked as his thumb skated over my clit, drawing icy circles that had me clenching around him. My body begged to move again, so I slid up his shaft, making him groan.

"Let's see if you can keep up, champion."

CHAPTER 23
Redmond

"Newly formed what?" I choked out, repeating the words I couldn't grasp.

Sir Fergus said nothing, but his cheeks turned a deep shade of crimson beneath his auburn beard. My eyes kept dropping to the power he was releasing, which had now drawn the attention of some of the other mermaids in the brothel.

"This one's scent is intertwined with one I know better than to fuck with. No doubt a powerful woman you're bedding," the mermaid said, giving Ox a mischievous grin and swiping her finger through the frosted tabletop before swishing off.

Growing up, watching them soar across the sky, I'd always assumed the bonds were similar to our familiar ones. I didn't know exactly how it worked, but my previous assumptions about the Revered and their bonded champions were quickly shifting. Definitely not the same kind of connection Inverno's citizens had with our familiars. And the *ice* coating the table's ledge was making my throat constrict.

I'll tell you when you're older.

The look on Sloan's face.

Oh...

"Tell me it isn't true," I croaked. My heart thudded, ramping up its pace. My entire body began to heat, feathers sizzling with the desire to ignite, stifled by the enchanted waters of our surroundings. Instead, inky droplets of ash sizzled away from them. "Tell me you didn't."

"I—"

I held up my hand for him to stop, unable to hear him say the words. If he did, that would make it true, and I desperately wanted to believe anything else. Standing up from my stool, I picked up the conch shell filled with my double shot of rum, downing it in one gulp. Dropping it to the table, I staggered back, right into our server who was talking up a potential customer. The pair glared at me, annoyed by the interruption.

"S-sorry," I stuttered, taking a few coins out of my pocket and handing them to her before whipping around and striding down one of the corridors.

I couldn't go back to the room. *Our* room.

As I wove through the seemingly empty corridor, pleasured moans and grunts filtered into the hallway. I'd chosen the wrong place to escape to. In one of the coves, a mermaid was inverted, held up by a land dweller as she took him in her mouth, his face buried into the onyx scales where her sex was hidden...if that's how it worked. I really wasn't sure, though *Sir Fergus* would know.

He probably knew a lot of things if the rumors surrounding his reputation were true.

No doubt a powerful woman you're bedding.

Bedding!

Fuck. It was as if I couldn't breathe, tears stinging the back of my eyes. Continuing to stumble forward, I ignored the bodies on either side of me in various states of pleasure. There were only two people I couldn't get out of my head, imagining them contorted in all manner of positions.

I didn't deserve Neve. I didn't deserve anybody. And I

wanted her to find happiness. It was something I'd hoped she'd have after everything she'd gone through. But I wasn't ready for how crushing it would feel. The reality of it. Maybe if I'd known they were together before finding out they'd bonded... A bond like that was eternal, until death—at least from what I gathered.

Spinning on my heels, I cleared my throat and headed back toward the tavern. The table was now empty, aside from the glasses and a few coins left behind. I threw an extra handful down and strode against the invisible current, moving as swiftly as I could to our room, blinking away the hot tears obscuring my vision.

I could do this. I could talk to him rationally.

The door was unlocked, as if he knew I'd be coming for him.

Sir Fergus sat in the corner, hands clasped, elbows glued to his knees.

"You—and—Neve," I heaved, the toll of my body working against the enchanted waters finally kicking in.

"Yes," he said slowly, his palm motioning to the bed. "Why don't you sit down?"

"I don't want to." I wanted to ignite, to feel the comforting flame of my phoenix fire, but there was nothing, merely soot floating away from my wings.

He arched a brow, studying the mirk surrounding me. "You sure about that?"

"Fine." I padded over to the bed and plopped onto the edge of it. Everything was cold, and I folded my arms over each other, trying to quench my distress. The urge to fly away and hide within the incandescent protection of my phoenix clawed at me. It was struggling with how to cope in this situation.

I was born to burn. To soar.

Beneath the Spuma, I could do neither.

And as much as I wanted to leave, I couldn't. There was a king to sway and an alliance to secure.

Closing my eyes, I tried to slow my breathing. To center

myself like I did in meditation. My body wasn't listening, though, my heart beating rapidly, every breath shaky and shallow.

She's moved on.

I wanted that for her, didn't I?

She didn't belong with me. But the finality of this choice—her choice—smothered the single ember of hope that existed within me.

Bile stung the back of my throat. "Do you love her?"

Sir Fergus stilled, face turning bright crimson. "Erm, I-I—"

"Look, we've moved past the point of being shy." *We both know you're sleeping with my ex-fiancée.* More than sleeping with. This wasn't a casual fling or a distraction. They were *bonded*.

"Do you love her?" I repeated.

"I'm pretty sure..."

"Pretty sure?" I cocked my head at him, acid bubbling in my chest, threatening to erupt. There was nowhere for this chaotic energy to go, and I didn't know if that was a good or bad thing. "You do realize that's not a very compelling answer when I'm fighting off the urge to torch your ass right now."

"I'd like to see you try." He smirked, scratching along his beard before flicking some ice at me. Working so seamlessly, like he'd had time to play with her power.

"You're enjoying this way too much." I sighed, exasperated, a small chuckle escaping me somehow.

"I'll admit, I am taking some enjoyment from watching you squirm."

His cockiness was both admirable and vexing.

"Is that why you two did this? Some form of revenge?"

I could take her wanting to be with someone else. I could handle it being Sir Fergus as long as he did right by her. What I wouldn't take was being the driving force of something else that would hurt Neve.

"No. I can confidently say that it had nothing to do with sticking it to you."

Well, that's something, at least.

"What's with all the secrecy?" I could understand keeping it from me, I was still in a precarious position with Arafax, but obviously they hadn't told anyone else that'd been at the Forum.

"We didn't want to make a big deal of things, especially with Sloan going through everything she is," Sir Fergus said, clasping his hands together.

"But you let Sloan think it was her fault when you knew that the magic was perfectly fine for your...ceremony."

"I feel bad about that, but Neve made me promise to wait to tell anyone."

"Then why do it? Why not wait?" My voice cracked as my mind tried to make sense of their seemingly spontaneous decision.

"Neve insisted we move forward with the bonding." His eyes darted to the floor a moment. "She has her reasons, but I really think that's a conversation for you two to have."

That was probably true, *if* she was willing to ever have that conversation with me.

"So, the Evergleam being broken," I said, genuinely curious about what could be going on with Celaria's power source, "that's your doing?"

"I really don't know," he replied with a shrug. "Everything seemed to work when we—"

I put my hand up, stopping him. A vision of Neve's lithe form bent in front of Sir Fergus as he drove greedily into her flashed through my mind.

I shivered, shaking off the image.

"Letting that imagination run away, aren't you?" Ox asked, cracking a smile.

"Fuck off." I shot him a glare before bringing my gaze down

to my hands white-knuckling my knees. "Don't act like you wouldn't do the same."

"Of course I would." He chuckled, leaning toward me. "But whatever you're imagining right now probably doesn't do the real thing justice."

Heat flared through me, a numbing burn spreading through my wings, but still nothing more than ash floated from them. I knew if we were not stuck under the sea they'd be fully ignited, protecting me instinctively.

Standing up and crossing the room, I drew back my elbow, not giving a fuck about the slowed trajectory with the viscosity of our surroundings. Before I could even deliver the blow, Ox's massive hand lifted, clutching around my entire fist.

How the fuck was he so massive?

"Put those fists down." His eyes dropped to my free hand that wasn't currently imprisoned. Raising his brow, he waited, keeping us pinned in place until I began to slow my breathing. "We both know the one you want to hurt isn't me."

"Fuck," I ground out, pulling my fist out of his grasp and shaking it out. It stung, but I was glad he stopped me. The last thing I needed to do was punch Neve's champion—not that I'd be able to get one in on him down here.

I hated this place already.

"I'm sorry you had to find out like this," he said, placing a hand on my shoulder, the gesture nothing less than genuine. He held my gaze, even though I was sure this situation made him uncomfortable too, just in a different way. "Probably would have been better to come from her."

I shook my head. "To be honest, it's probably best it didn't." I stepped backward a few paces until the backs of my legs hit the edge of the bed, then sat down on its edge. My eyes drew up from the ground, capturing Sir Fergus's attention. "Look, if this is what she wants, then I'm happy for her. But if you do anything to fuck this up after what she's been through—"

"Because of you."

Ouch.

"Yes, because of me," I growled, not needing the obvious restated right now—the knife was already dug in far enough. "But hurt her and I won't waste a moment once we're on land to show you the full force of my wrath."

"That won't be necessary," he said, his casual confidence only irking me further. "But I'll make sure to note your future threat."

"Thank you."

My breathing continued to slow. I hated knowing that the pent-up magic in me had no real way to release. I'd learned how to control my abilities, not letting my emotions drive them, but that was harder to do when they were cloistered like they were now.

When I was a young idiot, I had a big enough ego to think I could smother them down. That my emotions wouldn't impact my magic like everyone else around me. My father rarely showed emotion. I'd never seen his magic go beyond his control. As Inverno's prince, the same should've gone for me, right?

The Blaze was a horrible way to learn how wrong I was. But that shameful moment had taught me that I needed to release my power in small increments, not allow the emotions to fester within and lead to an outburst.

And now I was stuck with no outlet for them until we left.

Sir Fergus cleared his throat, breaking the awkward silence that sat like a third person in this tiny room. He crossed over to the bed, making it sink. "If it means anything, I don't think Neve hates you as much as she lets on."

"I highly doubt that," I shrugged, annoyed. That statement alone made him the better man between us, "but thanks anyway."

I scooched back, bringing my hands behind my head, resting

my wings against the headboard. Sir Fergus lay back, avoiding the wing that'd taken up some of his side of the bed.

The one fucking bed.

I cursed up at the stars that were obviously watching and laughing despite the foam-covered surface obscuring their view.

I'd have to set my feelings aside, deal with them later. We had a realm to save and a kingdom to recruit to our cause. "Let's just get some rest before we go see your friends."

And with that, I closed my eyes, tucked my wings around myself, and prayed I could fall asleep.

CHAPTER 24

Travis

Moving farther back into Renegade Trench, I could see that what I thought was just a desolate cave full of weird flowers was actually more of a bustling city. Carved buildings reached four-to-six stories tall lining the path toward Renegade Trench's center. Glowing flower petals were pressed into their walls, creating intricate patterns of light. It was like the Atlantic City of Celaria.

I already fucking loved it here.

Shops took up the foundation of the tall structures, top levels housing faeries whose wings glowed in a variety of neon shades through the windows. I tried to take in everything all at once. There was a market with many different foods I'd never seen before, all looking like various plants with things sprouting from them. *Meh*.

It made sense. If they didn't leave the cave, how did they hunt? Guess I'd be going vegetarian, at least temporarily.

Next to the market sat a beauty parlor with paintings of hair swept in an array of bold styles and colors, all neon of course, followed by a healer's shop and an adult entertainment club called Fluoressence.

I bet these faeries could get freaky.

Maybe I'd fit in after all.

Harkin pointed over to a series of ornate glowing thrones carved from what I assumed to be the stone of the caverns' walls. They were set at the corners of a large pool of water. "This is where our council meets."

"So, you don't have a king—"

"Or queen," Dru added hastily.

"There hasn't been a faerie king or queen in decades," Wynnie replied. "King Chadwick was the last before his death, and he was a horrible leader. Many of our people died trying to escape his rule."

The edges of the pool had been smoothed, I'd guessed from the water lapping over it at times as it wasn't very deep. Overhead, a series of small holes exposed a few strands of the day's moonlight that reflected into the water.

"Here in Renegade Trench, we believe our strength comes from all our people. With faeries, that is certainly true since our essence—our blood—is undiluted power." Harkin's wing flared out in pride, making me wonder what happened to the other one. "Our council is comprised of four leaders from within the community and one of those is chosen among ourselves to be the Overseer, the face of the group."

He strode over to the right corner and sat down, indicating for us to sit on the edge of the pool in front of him. The bottoms of my wings hit the water, quickly retracting. I shook them off before curling them around my body to keep them dry.

"The council will be convening here shortly to discuss your request." Harkin's single wing fanned back and forth like a giant red flag. I still didn't know if I trusted this guy or not, but he was my ticket to understanding myself and my power, so I'd suck it up and bide my time. It was better than the alternative of waiting around in Arafax, jerking off in a dollhouse, hoping The

Lavender's patrons didn't accidentally squish me every time they set down their drinks.

Harkin tilted his head, as if trying to make up his mind about me as well. Then he turned to face Dru. "I know your time here is limited, so what kind of help are you after?"

It annoyed me that the only reason I'd been brought here was because Kyleigh's boyfriend needed help with something. Neve had known this whole time where the faeries were and was willing to share that information all of a sudden, when I'd been stuck as a faerie a full fucking month with no way to come into my full power. To find my place.

Here they had been hidden away in the middle of the Grymm Mountains.

My mountains.

That couldn't just be a coincidence, could it?

Destiny had brought me to Celaria and now finally to the people I'd descended from. It was only a matter of time before I learned the truth and the full strength of the blood that flowed inside of me.

Undiluted power.

I liked the sound of that.

Dru straightened up in his usual golden-boy way. Like he was about to run another lesson at the fort and not desperately ask for help. "I recently came into possession of an ancient tome I believe is in your native tongue. While I know you normally reserve teaching that to your own people, is there any way you would consider sharing that knowledge with me?"

Harkin's brows lifted in what seemed like surprise. "And this helps you with Deirdre how?"

"Deirdre?" I asked.

Dru's eyes narrowed, looking as perplexed as I felt. "That's her name?"

"It was, yes."

Not very formidable sounding considering how frightened

everyone seemed to be of the Enchantress. Not that she scared me at all. There were worse monsters out there in search of power. In fact, I'd been spawned from one. Luckily, he was still far away while I sorted myself out. Next time I reported to him, it would be to share my triumphs in his fortunate absence.

Dru leaned forward, curiosity piqued at any opportunity to learn more. *Nerd*. "Did you know her?"

Harkin shook his head. "No. I've never met her myself. I was born here in The Trench. But I've heard about her from others... at least about the faerie she was prior to The Great Betrayal."

"What great betrayal?" Now my curiosity was piqued.

"Deirdre struck some deal with Arafax's royalty. One night, red smoke filled Faerie Hollow, knocking most of our people there unconscious. When they awoke, the kingdom was gone. Disappeared. Those that still were alive after the fighting that broke out escaped here. Up until that point, we'd been gradually smuggling faeries out of The Pitch, bringing them here to live a better life. We haven't left the cave since."

His eyes darted over to Wynnie, who'd perched herself opposite us on the pool's edge, listening intently. "No one is really supposed to."

She smiled up at him, and he shook his head back at her in half-hearted chiding. Her wings didn't glow, like mine. Intricate patterns detailed them instead. She looked like an angel, and I wondered what it would be like to have her show me heaven.

Fuck. Was I just really horny because I hadn't gotten laid since I arrived in Celaria, or was this a faerie thing?

"Why were they looking for a better life?" Dru asked, bringing me out of my lust-filled haze. "What is The Pitch?"

"The Pitch was the outermost rung of Faerie Hollow's hierarchy. Where that faerie blood you outsiders love to use comes from. King Chadwick bled his own people to maintain his stronghold within Celaria." Out of the corner of my eye I could see more faeries gathering around, whispering to each other as they watched us. "As you can imagine, donating the blood needed to supply the demands of Celaria's power-hungry territories took its toll on the faeries cast aside there. For years, a discreet contingent of brave rebels helped get those in need out of Faerie Hollow and brought them here."

I turned to Harkin, finally realizing something that'd been nagging at me since I'd seen the crowd of faeries lighting up the edge of Renegade Trench. "How come everyone here seems to have glowing wings, aside from a few who are more like me? Like her." I pointed to Wynnie. Her eyes finally met mine, and I flashed her a charming smile.

Harkin cleared his throat, reminding me to face him so he didn't kick my ass for smiling at his girl. "Our fluorescence was actually evolved to survive The Pitch's darkness. It made it easier for us to become acclimated when we came here. Then those born also had it, like myself. Those, like you, without glowing wings and irises, have been born to the light. *Leuxers*."

Losers? My wings stiffened. "What the—"

"That's from your ancient tongue, isn't it?" Dru cut in before I could pick a fight with a faerie that, despite having a damaged wing, looked like he could easily kick my ass.

"It is."

"What does it mean?"

"Light drinkers." Harkin waved Wynnie to him. She stood up slowly, the bodice of her strapless navy minidress hugging every unattainable curve. Striding toward him in her bare feet, the material climbed dangerously close to exposing her ass, making my cock perk up uncomfortably in the confines of my toy trousers. That shit wasn't designed to accommodate the erection that was threatening to get me kicked out of Renegade Trench quicker than the time I was blackout drunk sophomore year at Spanky's Pub and gave an impromptu bar top striptease.

My father hadn't been too happy with me after that.

Dru was still asking questions but only had half my attention, my gaze drinking in every shift of Wynnie's hips as she pressed up against Harkin, perched in his lap.

"Did they teach you nothing of your own history?" he asked, wing pulled taut at his back.

I lifted my chest. The last thing I wanted was my people thinking I'd *chosen* to not learn about them. They wouldn't be eager to teach an ignorant ass who didn't take initiative. I understood the importance of history. I'd spent years learning about Halston's; about all of us who had been cast out to the Otherworld. "To be fair, I've only been in Celaria about a month."

"I apologize," the golden boy interrupted before I could defend myself further. "I'm sure there may have been texts on it in our royal library, but most of the things we had were lost in The Blaze."

"Not this tome, though?" Harkin asked, a new layer of interest seeming to grasp at Dru's words.

"No. It was in *her* possession."

"And now it's in yours?"

"Yes."

"Did you bring it?"

"I have access to it if you are willing to translate."

"Someone's intelligent with their bargaining," Harkin said, tone approving.

"I hear you have to be with faeries." Dru's eyes narrowed but he held his ground, probably one of the first times I actually had some respect for the guy. I had to admit, Harkin's interest in the tome had my attention.

"You heard right on that," Harkin said. Wynnie's hand drifted down his thigh, giving it a squeeze.

Could that be her affinity? I still didn't understand much about them, but they were supposed to be natural, not taking much effort for faeries to express. Maybe they'd explain it to me better once Dru left and there were no more outsiders here.

Harkin frowned. "Well, if you're not going to show me this tome yet, can you describe it to me at least?"

"It's black leather with faerie blood painted in ancient symbols along the spine."

"That narrows it down a bit but not enough," Harkin said, fingers stroking along his chin. "Sure you don't want to show me it?"

"Not until I have your word that you'll help."

Get it, Golden Boy. I knew I was supposed to still hate the bastard for thwarting my plans with Kyleigh, but I couldn't help but be impressed with how he didn't shy away from this powerful leader, especially considering his null status.

"Anything else you can tell me about it?" Harkin continued to push. "You said you think it has something to do with Deirdre's powers. How so?"

"I have heard that she has glittering onyx coating her skin" —*sounds hot*—"and it is continuing to worsen, now at a quicker pace. But I'm unsure if it's from the tome being out of her possession or the gem being returned and power being stronger in Celaria."

"And what do we get if we help you?"

I was wondering when Harkin would bring that up. Why would the faeries do that when they hated outsiders? They had been burned by their own people and were now happy to stay tucked away, living on their own terms. Free.

"Vengeance for The Great Betrayal, for one thing," Dru offered.

Damn. I didn't see that coming from him.

Vengeance never seemed like Golden Boy's cup of tea, but I guess desperate times and all.

Harkin's fists were clutched around the edges of his throne, digging into the rock, but he didn't say anything. Obviously weighing his options. How much was vengeance worth to this man?

"I can also help make things better for you here, that is, if you extend my timeline—if that's possible."

Dru pointed up to the holes in the ceiling. "I see you've notched those into place, wanting to let in water from the rains, but the angle is off. In fact, it should be coming from the western wall to increase the amount of water procured. There is water running along the veins you can almost make out if you cast enough light there." He lifted his glove, turning on its flashlight and pointing it in the direction of the wall. Thin, barely visible streaks were lifted just off the stone's surface.

"That would be helpful," chimed in a faerie with lime-green irises and matching wings splayed out from him. He took one of the other thrones as an aqua and yellow faerie filled the other two.

"There are loads of other things I could probably help with," Dru added, a confident smile peeling across his face. "Even help you fly again, if that was something you'd be interested in."

Harkin stiffened. "Impossible."

"If I may?" I raised my hand, pulling everyone's gaze to me. "If he says he can do something, I wouldn't doubt it."

Dru's eyes shot to mine, and he gave a small nod in thanks. Hopefully he'd remember that next time he considered throwing me off a dragon's back mid-flight.

The four council members exchanged glances, silence filling the expanse of the cave, somehow making me feel smaller than ever. I needed this to work. Not because I cared about Dru's fate, but because I needed his outsider ass to leave so I could learn all the real faerie secrets.

"We will extend your visit by an additional twenty-four hours. You fix what you can by this time tomorrow, and we will assist with your translation." He waved Dru over to him. Whispering low, he took the corner of his sharpened incisor and tapped the pad of his finger, then he touched the token attached to Dru's hand. "In return, we want assurances that the tome will be destroyed, if it's the one I believe it to be."

Dru hissed, grabbing his hand before shaking it. "I promise."

The council stood, moving to talk to a few faeries that seemed to have questions about our presence.

Harkin came over, his arm draped around Wynnie. She beamed up at him, then smiled at us both. "Looks like you'll get what you came for."

Dru bowed his head appreciatively, and I followed suit.

Though I was far from getting what I came for, I knew I would get it here in Renegade Trench.

CHAPTER 25

Redmond

After a night of no sleep thanks to Sir Fergus's inescapable snoring, I headed downstairs to grab breakfast at Snatch of the Day. About an hour later, introducing himself with a loud yawn, Sir Fergus emerged, dressed and ready to visit Opal and Aurelia. I was grateful to be on the go, not wanting to have to broach the subject that hung over us like a frosty blanket.

"What are you two doing here?" Opal murmured, barely cracking the door open to their coral-topped villa. Swirls of yellow and peach shell bits covered its aqua exterior, and a school of tiny guppies swam around us, a few overly curious fish jetting between my feathers. Retracting my wings against the invisible current, I tried to shake them off, finding it futile. The glossy black feathers were slicked to their bones.

"We came to find out about next steps with our request to meet with King Morrow." Sir Fergus leaned against the doorway, giving a charming grin. He was working her, and despite still wanting to punch him, I couldn't blame him for trying any tactic he could.

She winced. "Unfortunately, we ran into a bit of a hiccup arranging a meeting with him."

166

"What kind of hiccup?" I asked.

She opened the door fully, revealing Aurelia draped over a very disgruntled-looking male, stroking his chest. Markings wrapped around his upper arm, a band of waves and bubbles meeting at a large hoofprint stamped at the base of his shoulder. Spuma's sigil. The tattoo indicated that he was part of their army, from what I remembered from my tutors growing up. He was not someone we wanted to cross if we wanted to meet with King Morrow.

"Jasper saw us swimming in with you yesterday and was less than pleased. He thinks you've come here to mate with us," Opal said.

"This is all a misunderstanding." I bowed my head to Jasper, taking a step into their villa. "I'm King Redmond of Inverno, and I have no intention of mating with anyone while I'm here. I just need to meet with your King about diplomatic matters. Ruler to ruler."

"And what about *him*?" Jasper brayed, the sound carrying something guttural with it, a familiar pitch that I couldn't quite determine. "I can already tell he's marked them before."

"To be fair, he's probably done more than mark them," I teased, regretting it immediately when that only seemed to turn the male's face a deeper shade of purple. "But he's already mated to another. Bonded, in fact, so you have nothing to worry about."

He swam closer, sniffing around Sir Fergus, his onyx tail swishing back and forth. Wrinkling his nose, he scanned up the length of the giant who'd formally bedded his mates, then turned to me. "Fine. I believe that he won't interrupt our mating season. But how do I know you won't change your mind?"

"I suppose you can't be certain." Jasper frowned, but I continued before he could reply. "That doesn't change the fact that I am royalty and have requested the presence of your king.

The quicker that happens, the faster we will be gone from Tesceillus. So how can we make this meeting happen?"

"Please, Jas," Opal pleaded, swishing her tail to curl around his before pressing a kiss to his cheek. "He's promised to provide lure for our friends to find mates."

He cocked his head at us, eyes narrowing. "Is this true?"

"It is," Sir Fergus chimed in.

I flashed my most charming smile, keeping my tone pleasant despite not being thrilled about lending out my blood as *lure*. But doing this, bleeding for my people, was a much easier sacrifice than the ones I made every time I visited the Enchantress. "I'm happy to help."

Jasper glanced at his two mates, puffing out his chest a bit. "I think I have a way I can get you in to see the King without much notice."

"We knew you could make it happen, Jas," Aurelia squealed, joining her mates and giving him a kiss. He beamed, pleased with the effect his sudden heroics was having on his females.

"What did you have in mind?" Sir Fergus asked.

The mermaids' tails were tangled together, like the throuple was ready to be wrapped in each other. "The King is hosting the Frenzy tonight at Equis Castle."

"Frenzy?" I asked.

Opal ripped her mouth away from Jasper's neck, a few bloody bruises blooming along his throat. "It's a way for unmated merfolk to meet each other. The King has been trying to secure a mate for his daughter for a few seasons now, to no avail."

"Why hasn't she secured a mate? Wouldn't many be interested in aligning themselves with the royal family?"

Maybe this was another area where things were different between our cultures, but usually securing a match with anyone of royalty was fortuitous. Men and women alike would vie for a spot at the side of a prince or princess. I'd spent years ignoring the affections of ambitious families looking to gain their place within Inverno or build an alliance with our kingdom. It was one of the things that had first drawn me to Neve. Her disinterest. The fact that she didn't fall at my feet.

In fact, if anyone fell, it was me at hers.

She was older than I was, though, and I'm sure her father would have rather her taken up with one of Arafax's princes or princesses. For whatever reason, I'd won her heart.

Then I'd fucked it all up.

Now it belonged to Sir Fergus, whether he was ready to acknowledge it or not.

I rinsed the memories away, reality washing over me. More than anything, I needed to make this fucking alliance work with King Morrow.

"Oh, there has been interest, but every suitor has darted out of that castle after meeting her. Apparently, she's...*difficult*."

"Well, I'm not going to mate her if that is where this proposition is headed. I'm already promised to someone."

Someone I'm currently trying to destroy.

"Oh no, I was thinking you could offer to help with her lure for the Frenzy. Royal blood would be very hard to resist," Jasper replied.

The thought sent ripples of nausea through me but, hey, if they wanted to be covered in blood by choice, who was I to judge? This was their custom and I'd respect it.

"It would be of great intrigue to the males for sure. You are so brilliant, Jas," Opal cooed, giving me a quick wink.

Aurelia, trailed her hand along Jasper's waist, where the top of his onyx scales met flesh, dipping low a few inches below his belly button. "You should have seen how quickly this male flipped his fin for us when we used the lure from that coral-haired woman—whatever she was."

"Just thinking about that day has me wanting to reenact it," the merman growled, nipping at Aurelia's ear and stroking below Opal's breast with his thumb.

"Well, don't let us stop you," I said, more than happy to get out of their orbit. Taking a few steps back, I nodded toward the door, looking at Sir Fergus. "Wouldn't want to interrupt mating season."

The giant cleared his throat, making the threesome pause their fondling. "When should we meet you to go to the castle?"

"Be here in three hours' time," Opal said, hand moving dangerously low over Jasper. Though I still wasn't sure how it all worked for their *activities*, I wasn't interested in witnessing it firsthand. She gave me a pleasant smile, but didn't stop her caresses, coaxing a contented groan from her mate. "That way we can get our friends their lure before we head to the Frenzy. Once the King sees them, he'll desperately want some for Princess Moray."

"Sounds good," Sir Fergus agreed, exchanging a glance with me that said he was just as ready as I was to leave their villa. "We will return then."

Aurelia detached herself from her mates, following us toward the door. "The Princess will be mated in no time with your help, I'm sure of it," she said, before shutting it quickly behind us.

CHAPTER 26

Sloan

We'd left a day later than everyone else, making sure to set up safe passage for Mox to meet us in Alucinor. Nearing four hulking totems, we finally had the weavers' territory in sight. White carvings crisscrossed their panes, each one marking a point to create a large rectangle around the lush forest from my bird's-eye view. Delicate, iridescent strands swayed in the wind beneath us—only noticeable when the moonlight hit them just right—threading through each other where they connected, creating jagged designs with no discernible pattern.

Following a glittering strand, it twisted around a few others before ending at another large tree-trunk spire.

"Who made this?" I asked Kyleigh, patting a patch of her opal scales and getting merely a huff in response. They were so shiny, like they'd each been polished by hand, my face reflecting back in them. Large ashen semicircles lined my eyes, their irises a sallow shade of their former hue. My lips were pale, blending in with the rest of my face, and I bit them, feeling how dry and cracked they were. "Let's make sure to stay away from whatever it is."

Kyleigh nodded in agreement with her oversized peach

snout, then tilted us eastward, dipping down and preparing to land. She picked a strip of ground that seemed deserted, part of the rest of the peninsula that was still Alucinor's territory but remained unmarked by the strange net-covered canopy. I jolted as the coral dragon met the ground, but it was much smoother than the last time I'd rode on her. The ghost of Aislin sat in front of me, my body pressed to hers, feeling like a distant memory, though it hadn't even been a few months.

That night, I'd seen the fear in her eyes when she realized I'd witnessed her kill Flynt, but I'd never been more in awe of her. One night of witnessing what that man had been capable of, it was hard to imagine what Aislin had been through all those years after he and his crew had overtaken the inn. She'd been taking care of herself since she was sixteen and, looking back, I couldn't blame her for being untrusting of me.

Of anyone, for that matter.

But she'd let me in, and for those fleeting moments, I was happier than I ever imagined I could be. I'd never been in love, but it'd struck me hard with her. Now Dru believed we could save her and still bring down the Enchantress. It was the only thing driving me forward, stopping my hand from reaching for the flask buried within my satchel.

Hope haunted me, fear gripped me by the throat, but I'd rather die trying to get her back than continue to watch her suffer.

"Where'd you go?" Kyleigh asked, threading her head through a white shoulderless blouse. She was wearing black leggings and a matching corset I'd constructed for her that had leather buckles securing various vials of elixirs, burn repair, and healing balms to her torso. Her faerie blood gloves were attached to the belt loop slung low on her hips. I could tell she was uncomfortable wearing red still, so I hadn't put anything in her bag in Arafax's color, except for a few items I'd tucked at the bottom in case we needed to break out the royal regalia.

"Just thinking about if I packed enough," I said, which was partially true. I'd made sure to have some light armor on and packed outfits for any sort of situation we could encounter, with backups. One of the many ways shrinking enchantments came in handy.

Mox would be meeting us soon, thanks to Kyleigh securing a ride for him with the mermaids, and I split my vision a moment so I could see what he was up to.

THE LARGE PLANK OF WOOD WOBBLED BENEATH HIM, *water spraying up onto his furry coat as he crossed the stream, ferried over by six mermaids. A merman with lime-green and orange streaks chuckled, and Mox growled at him.*

"Thank the stars we will be done before tonight's Frenzy."

"Yes, and now I have this lure!" A mermaid with a bright-rainbow mane beamed at the others, pleased with whatever the lure was she spoke of. She held up a small vial with crimson sloshing around in it.

I don't even want to know.

Cedar and the musk of damp grass flooded Mox's nostrils, making him scrunch his snout. He sneezed, large paws sliding against the wet wood, nearly taking him out with the current. A mermaid with plum and maroon hair stabilized him on the makeshift raft once again. She smiled and stroked his fur, her sharp maw making Mox still a moment before nuzzling in for the affection.

Water sprayed into his eyes, and as he blinked it away, I filtered out his vision.

"He should be here soon."

The logistics to get Mox to Alucinor were not the easiest, but I figured a quick ferry across the stream would be more doable than trying to fly him on Kyleigh's back. She had no interest in getting a ride across the stream. When I mentioned the idea to her, she clenched her fists at her sides and started muttering something about a watery coffin.

"What do you know about Alucinor and its weavers?" Kyleigh asked, pulling her satchel over her shoulder.

"Not a lot. From what Redmond has told me, they usually keep to themselves and he prefers it that way. Inverno avoided dealing with them at all. I don't even think King Reynard visited for diplomatic purposes. If so, my father would have gone with him, and he would have mentioned something like that to me."

"Yeah. Dru said something similar about them not being much for dealing with other Celarians. I've only ever seen the few at The Lavender, but they all quickly disappeared after a night or two."

I was slightly worried about how they would react to Kyleigh if they recognized her, but I wouldn't dare bring it up. Had they seen her shift into dragon form? Did they report that back to Alucinor's leadership?

Either way, I needed to be ready to protect her.

"But they all have mind magic. That has to be interesting," she said, shrugging.

"Freaky if you ask me."

Kyleigh merely replied with a shiver, looking more distant than I probably did when slipping into Mox's sight.

"So...you didn't know your father was a weaver?"

"None of us did. My parents met in the Otherworld—no

abilities over there."

"Ah." I didn't think about the fact that none of the new folks Ox and Neve had wanted me to train even knew fully what their lineage consisted of. Only that they were Celarian. "Makes sense."

Kyleigh had brought over about ten wielders, just as out of control as herself, though none of them would have the dragon magic running through them like she did.

Like Aislin did.

I reached out for the cord that once connected us, tugging it for any response on the other side, feeling nothing more than a floppy string severed from its other end. My chest ached constantly, only dulled slightly by the whiskey I'd promised to give up for the time being.

"What kind of weaver is he?"

"A memory weaver."

From what I understood, memory weavers could manipulate your recollection of the past, erasing, altering, or even inserting experiences into someone's mind that they couldn't differentiate from their real ones. "So, what's wrong with him?"

Kyleigh tucked some coral waves behind her ear. "He's never been trained with his powers. Every time he comes in contact with someone, he can't help but pull forth their memories, sometimes erasing them or distorting his own in the process."

"That sounds awful."

"It is," she said softly, gaze dropping to the ground as we continued to walk toward the spire ahead of us, veering closer to the stream to meet Mox.

"So, you're part weaver?"

"I am."

"And you wanted to come here to learn more for him or yourself?"

"More for him," she said before finally meeting my eyes. Her irises shone like moons, glistening with the beginnings of tears.

"Though I'll admit, I'm curious about them. I don't have any abilities that I know of, but I'm still a quarter weaver. Even if the magic doesn't present itself through me, it could down the road in my children, so I should understand it."

Pink stained her cheeks, and she quickly added. "I mean we are still very young. Not ready for any of that stuff yet. But Dru and I want a family. One day—when it's safe."

When. Not if.

I wish I was that certain we'd get to that point. But I'd been in combat. I'd seen enough battles to know even the victorious route was one paved in blood. No one escaped the violent price demanded—on either side—and the stars would collect.

"Will you go back to the Otherworld once this is all over?"

Kyleigh still hadn't claimed her title as Arafax's Princess and heir to its throne, but I'd treat her as such. While I had a split allegiance between Inverno and Arafax, both senses of duty would have me lay my life on the line for hers. Even if she refused to claim it.

"I think so... Maybe?" She shrugged, then threw up her hands. "Fuck. I really don't know."

Mox trotted toward us, pausing a moment to shake out the water from his snowy fur, spraying us. We looked over and waved to the mermaids who all smiled back at us with their fierce jaws before they dove under the surface.

Wiping her face with the sleeve of her shirt, Kyleigh continued, "Now that my dad is here and I know he's from Celaria, is there really a reason for me to ever go back?"

She bent down, petting Mox like he was a dog and not a snow fox as large as she was. He hummed into her palm appreciatively, turning his nose up at me. "But on the other hand, is there really a reason to stay?"

"Being a princess not good enough for you?" I teased with a small laugh, the feeling almost foreign to me, filling my empty chest with warmth.

"Honestly…" She breathed out a deep sigh, tension claiming her shoulders a moment before they slumped down. "I spent so much time trying to figure out what my mother would have wanted for me in the Otherworld. If I do decide to claim my place as Arafax's Princess, I want it to be because *I* want to, not because of anything she's influenced. Her legacy has hovered over enough of my life."

"I can understand that." I patted my thigh and Mox skulked over from his new favorite person, standing next to me. His snout hit in line with my sternum, and I reached a hand out, grazing the small patch of subtle light gray marking his forehead. It'd been more pronounced when he was a kit, but now it blended into the white, nearly faded away. "My father was Red's commander and military advisor. It's all I ever knew. All I ever wanted to do was live up to what he was. I never really thought about what I wanted for myself."

"Do you think you would have chosen a different path?"

"I don't know," I replied, continuing to walk between her and Mox. "I don't think so. I loved serving. The purpose it gave me. How strong it made me feel."

"Made. Not makes?" she asked, cocking her head at me. "Are you going to go back to Inverno or will you stay in Arafax once we get Aislin back?"

"We never had a chance to talk about that far into the future."

She was taken before we could.

"We'll get her back, Sloan."

I wanted to believe her words—that we'd be able to save her —but I knew if it came down to it, Aislin would want me to take down the Enchantress no matter the cost.

A life still claimed by her through the bond mark wasn't a life to Aislin.

I'd make sure she'd be free when I got her back.

I owed that much to my Revered.

CHAPTER 27

Sloan

It looked like the woods were empty, but we knew better. There had to be at least a few hundred weavers living within the shelter of Alucinor's glittering canopy. I stared up again at the iridescent threads. It wasn't the same as looking at the netting from above, but I felt no less like prey.

I peered over at Kyleigh, the three of us stood on the outskirts of the marked territory with two pillars on either side of us spanning the width of the peninsula. "Why don't we have Mox scout it out for us so we know what we are getting ourselves into?"

"Okay."

Go on, boy.

Our vision merged as he sauntered through the invisible line between the two spires, completely disappearing from view.

A HANDFUL OF COZY IDENTICAL CABINS LINED THE streets, more strands of iridescent thread connecting between them. There were no people out, though, and no movement through the windows of the houses. It was like a ghost town.

"Where'd he go?" Kyleigh's voice filtered through to me.

"It's weird," I responded, not tearing my attention away from what Mox was seeing. "I can sense through him that there are people there, but he can't see any of them."

Suddenly the world warped, folding in on itself, then expanded again. Now, Mox stood in the middle of the woods. A dark figure loomed ahead in the distance. Plaited brunette hair with peeks of purple caught the light, jolting his attention.

Aislin.

"Come here," she said, giving him a smirk that streaked hot through my chest. Mox trotted to her and nuzzled into her palm. She pressed a kiss to his forehead, on the gray patch missed by many.

"It's her."

BEFORE I KNEW WHAT I WAS DOING, I'D RUN THROUGH the barrier, sprinting for her. My feet pounded against the dirt but it was like I was gliding on a cloud, the tether of our broken bond somehow lifting from the depths of my chest.

Running into her arms, I looked up into her emerald eyes, brushing back the waves of her hair. "It's you."

"Not quite," she said, giving me a gentle but sad look.

"Sloan!" a voice shrieked from behind me. "That's not who you think it is."

Not-quite Aislin released me, stepping back, clutching the prismatic gem hanging from the chain around her neck.

My hands shook, chest throbbing, twisting in knots.

Of course it wasn't Aislin.

Aislin was in the Silent Woods. A wisp.

"Who are you?" I asked, stepping back.

The figure pulled out a handkerchief and wiped at the gem, and the illusion vanished, returning to the series of empty cabins lining the path ahead.

Aislin's faux twin now had thick black hair that was shaved on one side, wavy locks draped over the other. Both of her hands were wrapped in onyx bandaging that climbed up her wrist, disappearing under a shimmering black coat that hit above her knees. A ruffled white shirt sat half buttoned against her voluptuous chest, and a pair of violet eyes narrowed their gaze at me.

She looked down and ran a palm over her talisman. The curves that had been there prior disappeared, jaw squaring, and the previously long hair became wavy and cropped. "I am Ever. All. Eternally whoever I wish to be."

Then with another swipe to the talisman, the hair and jaw returned to how they'd been a moment prior, the curves discarded.

I sat there, stunned. "But how did you know what she looked like?"

Ever stared past me. "I have to admit, I did have some help."

Two more weavers stepped into view. One had white hair that fell to her hips, a single braid framing one side of her face. The other, a tall, lanky raven-haired weaver, wore a white button-down with a pair of beige suspenders and black corduroy trousers.

"We truly meant no harm," Ever continued, flicking a small speck of glitter from their hair and shrugging. "People tend to have their hackles raised when we're around."

"Well, you're fucking with our minds. Can you blame us?"

"Don't blame you at all," they said with a small smile. "Just was curious about you. Can you blame us when you're the first to wander onto Alucinor's peninsula in decades?"

It was apparent to me that they really had no clue how much seeing Aislin knocked me off my axis. I guess it made sense they didn't often have visitors here—who would willingly let their mind be toyed with? Isla had brought in a dream weaver who'd been staying at the inn to help her with her nightmares, to keep the Enchantress out of them, but other than that, it was rare anyone chose to deal with the weavers.

"Oh, and this one...Kyleigh..." Ever said, ignoring my commentary. Scanning her up and down, their brows lifted briefly. "Intriguing."

They all placed two fingers to their temple, like an odd lingering salute. "As you may already know, my specialty is illusion. This is Rue. His is memory."

I nodded to Rue, bringing my hand across my chest to show them some respect since they didn't seem to be threatening me, though my palm shook against my collarbone. Ever shifted their gaze to the weaver with white hair. "And that's Volett. She's euphoric."

"How did you know my name?" Kyleigh asked, taking a shaky step back.

"I saw it in her mind," Volett said, dropping the salute to point at me.

Ever chimed in, looking at Kyleigh with keen interest. "Sadly, yours is closed off...which is what interests me. How did one of us end up out there?" They pointed behind her, past where the veil cloaked them from Celaria's view.

"Never mind," Ever said, waving a hand in the air before adjusting their coat, the sequin trousers rustling as they moved closer to her.

"Otherworlder? Very, very interesting," Rue said, eyes locked on me, a shiver creeping up my spine. I brushed back my silver strands to push the feeling away.

How long were we going to be in this fucking place?

Ever swayed over to a tree, leaning against its rich brown bark. "If you're wanting to speak with our leader, there isn't one."

"There's no leadership here?" asked Kyleigh.

"I didn't say that...just that there isn't one," Ever drawled, twirling a wrist before flicking it. "You'll need one of the Octux to call a meeting."

Octux?

Kyleigh crossed her arms, seemingly unimpressed by the weavers in front of us. "Where do we find this Octux?"

"No need to find them. They *all* already know you're here," Volett murmured. Her gaze stared dreamily above her, and I watched glimmers sparkling like tiny moving beads in her hair, rising up and pulling strands of her gossamer tresses with them.

Then I realized they weren't crystals at all.

They were spiders.

Dozens of tiny diamond-backed arachnids twirled up from Volett, hovering above us, climbing toward the purple sky. I blinked a few times, taking in the web nestled between the pillars denoting Alucinor's territory.

Just then, a larger spider plummeted down, landing on Ever's wrist. Scuttling up the black jacket, it scurried into the shell of their ear.

"Ah," Ever said, making no move to disinvite the creature from its new nesting place. "The Octux will receive you all tomorrow night for an exhibition."

"Exhibition?" Kyleigh questioned, eyes narrowing, the silver in them flaring a bit. "What is that?"

"An old tradition among weavers when we have guests," Ever said with a smile that didn't meet their eyes. "There'll be drinking, dancing, a feast—a fete to remember."

"Sounds festive." Kyleigh cut me a look before I could back out.

"Wonderful," the three weavers said in unison, clapping their hands together in eerie synchrony. "Let's get you situated with somewhere to settle in the meantime." Ever beckoned us to follow along the path, Volett and Rue trailing behind us until we came to a halt in front of a translucent dwelling, seemingly empty on the inside.

Ever's fingers ran along the crystal hanging against their chest, framed by the ruffles along the blouse's collar. Moments later, the nondescript cube in front of us warped into a cozy, familiar cabin, its door open, a beautiful fire crackling in its hearth. Luxurious fur rugs lined the floor, and hanging from the ceiling were icicle chandeliers like the ones I adored within Inverno's castle, the smell of fresh pine sifting through my nose.

My chest clenched at the sight.

It looked like the cabin my father used to take my mother and I to. An escape from Inverno's busy life and his responsibilities as commander. Living within the castle walls, he was always needed, always on demand. Those few days we could journey to the farthest reaches of our territory, staying in cabins nestled along our shared border with Cicatrix, were some of the best memories of my life. When my mother died, we'd stopped going.

And here it was, like decades hadn't passed.

Kyleigh shivered, wincing a bit, but shook it off almost immediately. Whatever was going on in her mind, it would be better to talk to her about it once we were alone. If that was even really possible here. I glanced up at the shimmering net above us, rain beginning to pelt down from the now-graying sky.

"Best if we all get some rest and shelter," Volett said, spinning away from us and linking hands with Ever and Rue. The trio glided swiftly away from our illusioned abode, and I moved inside, Mox trotting along behind me.

It wasn't until I'd had my hands held in front of the fire, savoring its warmth, that I realized I never heard the door shut behind Kyleigh. I turned to find her shivering, blouse drenched from the heavy rainfall.

"What's wrong with you?" I asked, trying to pull her inside with me. "You're going to freeze out there."

"Better than in there," she said, shuddering, the black lining her eyes beginning to run down her cheeks. Her face was two shades too pale.

"What are you talking about?" I said, scanning the room. Nothing seeming out of the ordinary. "I don't see anything."

"Be glad that you don't," she said, voice brittle, "because I don't see any of it."

"What do you mean?"

"The illusions. Their magic," she whispered. "They don't work on me."

I waved her inside, and she hopped over the threshold like it was a slithering snake between her boots. "So you don't see a cabin right now? No fireplace or a fur rug on the ground?"

"I most definitely do not," she said, huddling close to me, eyes darting frantically around the room. Mox moved to her side, and she gripped him possessively.

"What do you see?" I asked, patting her reassuringly on the back.

She stared off behind me, eyes shifting back and forth along the log walls. "You really don't want to know."

CHAPTER 28

Dru

I attached the strips of moonflower petals to the sturdy white stem I'd scrounged from the outskirts of Renegade Trench. There were many plants in the cave that I hadn't seen before, and according to Harkin, a few faeries with nurturing affinities spent their days tending to the wildlife, helping things grow despite the darkness and inhospitable climate of the cave.

I'd already tweaked the makeshift aqueduct the faeries had forged, veins from the walls now filling the pool to its brim. Faeries rounded up stone cups and bowls, collecting the water and carrying it to cleansers who'd purify it. They smiled in gratitude, and I swelled with pride at seeing my work in action. I always enjoyed making contraptions, engineering and fastening ideas together to create something better, but when those efforts were noticed—were appreciated and helped someone else—it meant all the more.

My father had instilled in me his love of knowledge, and I often wondered what he'd think of the work I was doing. Would he be proud of the ways I'd taken the research he'd spent his life protecting and used it to build and better things in Arafax? Deep inside, I knew he would be. Both of my parents would have

185

been. But I wished I could have shown him all that I'd innovated since his death.

"Wow." A gentle hand touched my shoulder, and I craned my neck, finding Wynnie peering over at the wing I was building. "And that will work? He'll be able to fly again?"

"Yep. We may have to do a few adjustments once he tries it on, but with some practice he should be able to. Your healers may need to work with him on getting used to balancing his body and restrengthening his other wing, depending on how long it's been since he's used it."

Travis sauntered over, all of a sudden interested in my work. "It's coming along great, Golden Boy."

Golden Boy? The taunt disguised as a nickname had me holding back the urge to smack the smugness right off his face. Considering he had ignored me and wandered off to check out his new home, I knew his curiosity had little to do with what I was working on and was all directed at the faerie next to me.

"Where is Harkin? I'd like to see if everything fits." I ran my palm over the wing, pulling on a few spots to make sure they would hold.

"We can go meet him back at home," Wynnie said cheerfully. I didn't miss the edges of Travis's lips crumple a bit at that.

Picking up the wing, I folded it into my arms and followed Wynnie toward an offset path heading up a steep slope. Perched atop a ledge was a set of four homes carved directly into the cave's wall. Unlike the other structures that had multicolor flower petals pressed into them, these were all decorated white, making them stand out among Renegade Trench's vibrant rainbow.

Travis and Wynnie flew ahead as I climbed slowly, my legs aching from the slope's impressive incline. The Trench was designed for flying, and I was glad that I'd offered to do this for Harkin. I couldn't imagine him doing this trek multiple times a day, though I doubted he ever complained. He didn't seem the type.

The valley below me snagged at the corner of my eye, and my boot slid against the dirt, throwing me off balance. I tried to hold tight to the crafted wing, clutching it in my grasp against my chest. My heart beat painfully, panic silencing my scream as I lost my footing, falling backward.

Hands gripped my shoulders, stopping me mid-fall. "Can't lose you, Golden Boy."

"I'm surprised you didn't try to push me over," I heaved out, shooting him a pointed look despite being grateful not to be a splatter on the cave's floor. "Already given up on being Kyleigh's champion?"

"Believe me, it's tempting to keep trying but we both know she'd singe off my balls," he replied smoothly, giving my shoulder a nudge with his own. "I'd prefer to keep them intact for when she changes her mind down the road and comes looking for some fun."

I groaned. "You're such an ass."

"You act like I'm not aware."

"Oh, I know you are. I just don't understand why."

He chuckled darkly to himself. "Be glad of that, Golden Boy."

I took a deep breath. "Well, thanks."

Wynnie held the door open for us. The white flower petals that glowed against the exterior walls had been rolled up, posted into various spots within the room to keep it illuminated. While this entire place was still very dark to my eyes, I assumed the glowing irises of the faeries who'd been born here and transplanted from the Pitch had an easier go of seeing things.

"Ah, you brought it," Harkin said, eyeing the bundle in my arms suspiciously. "Still convinced you can get it to work?"

"I may need to do some additional tinkering." I held the wing out to him while Wynnie smoothed out a few spots that had crumpled a bit when I'd stumbled. "But if you can slip it on, then I can do the rest once I know it fits properly."

Harkin held the prosthetic in his hand a few moments, inspecting it from every angle.

"May I?" Wynnie asked, arms outstretched.

He handed it to her and turned away as she looped his arm through the chest strap, bringing it across and tightening it at the buckle. Afterward, she stepped back, leaving Harkin peering over his shoulder at the wing sitting opposite his other. His body swayed toward it, and he took a moment to find his balance, adjusting his weight to make the wings sit even.

"That's incredible," Wynnie said, admiring him. "How do you feel?"

"A bit clumsy," he admitted, but he didn't move to take it off.

I ran the cord along his arm, attaching it around his thumb. "You can maneuver and adjust it when you fly by pulling on this."

He said nothing but gave it a few tugs, watching how the wing moved. Then he walked straight out the door, all of us following him.

HARKIN LED US TOWARD THE MOUTH OF THE CAVE, squinting from under his forearms.

"It's been awhile since we've come out this far," Wynnie explained, eyes darting toward the light. Her wings hummed next to me as she floated a few feet off the ground with Travis trailing quietly behind us.

He stopped at the ledge, climbing over the cave's lip that was littered with fluorescent wildlife. He pushed them aside the long, green-tipped stems leaning in various directions, weaving through their stalks to get outside the cave's walls. A bright fuchsia moonflower sprang into us, causing me to jump. Wynnie flew up to it, primping its petals. Then she held it in place while I passed, the petals blossoming further.

"So that's how affinities work?" Travis asked from behind us, his eyes pinned to Wynnie's affinity, looking a tad disappointed.

"Yes, outsiders won't notice it because it's so faint. Your affinity should come naturally, but you can push more forth at different times when you need to call on it."

"Oh."

"We will help you with it while you're here," she offered, giving him a small smile. Making our way through the maze of stems and grass lining the cave's edge, Travis seemed to brighten a bit, and I wondered if nurturing was her affinity, like Harkin had mentioned earlier. I didn't know if it was impolite to ask specifics, I was already asking so much of them to trust me by helping with the tome, so I stayed quiet.

"When was the last time he was outside?" I asked, sitting down next to Wynnie. Travis stood on the other side watching Harkin intently.

"The night he saved me. Saved many of us." She leaned back, drinking him in with the same adoration I felt watching Kyleigh. Wynnie sucked in a breath, eyes dropping to the ground. "It was the night Faerie Hollow fell."

The faerie leader extended his wings, playing with the cord to test it out. Practicing moving them together while still on the ground, he finally began to get them synched.

"What happened to him?"

"So many faeries died that night, but he tried to save as many as he could. He was the last one out, following behind those of us that survived."

He ran forward, bending his knees and springing off the ground, managing to beat his wings together a few times before tumbling across the grass. I stood up quickly, ready to have him yell at me or tell me what was wrong with the invention, but instead he brushed off his trousers, nodded to me, and went back to practicing.

"I was caught by Prince Ciaran, Deirdre's former lover—" Wynnie shot him a look I couldn't pinpoint. "Um, patron, I mean. His fingers were clamped around my wing, thinking he'd won. But I wouldn't let him capture me. I knew what they were going to do with the faeries that didn't make it that night."

"Drain them," Wynnie whispered between us.

Could Arafax really have done something so cruel? Had my father known about what had happened to the faeries? Did the Queen know?

"When was this Great Betrayal?"

"Over a few decades ago," Harkin huffed, rolling his shoulders and stretching his arms out before running and pushing off the ground again. This time he managed to stay airborne for about twenty seconds before dropping to the grass. "I escaped his hand and my wing ripped in the process. Wynnie and a few others saw me struggling to fly and helped me get back here. I haven't left since."

"We don't make it a habit of leaving The Trench unless we desperately need supplies or something," she added, waving him over to her.

"It's safer for our people that way." He bent down, pressing a kiss to her temple. Then he hooked his finger under her chin, pinning her gaze to his a moment. "You'd do well to remember that, Wynnie. The fact that a Revered one knew where we were could have been incredibly dangerous."

"Neve can be trusted," I said, gaze narrowing.

Wynnie gripped the collar of Harkin's jacket and snuck in a few kisses, making me miss Kyleigh more than I already did.

"And I suspect it's only because she knows we are desperate for answers," I added.

Harkin knelt in front of me, our faces level, his eyes dropping to the glove on my hand. "What will you do with this knowledge if I show you how to decipher the tome?"

"I only wish to find a way to remove the Enchan— Deirdre's threat." It was the truth. Most of it at least. But if I wanted to gain Harkin's trust, I needed to be as honest as possible, even with Travis here. "And to help some people who have been trapped by her...if possible."

Travis raised his brows at my admission.

"You've more than held up your end of the bargain," Harkin said, brushing some dirt splattered on his new wing and grinning. He extended his hand out to Wynnie, helping her stand before assisting me. "Time to hold up mine."

Leading us back inside the cave, he slid his hand around Wynnie's waist, kissing her a few more times. It took me a moment to notice Travis was standing still next to me, shaking his head.

"Well, isn't this an interesting turn of events," he said, looking at me with a newfound respect that had me loathing him more, if that were possible. "Looks like even Golden Boy has a personal agenda."

CHAPTER 29

Redmond

Bejeweled coral reefs flanked the winding path of pearlescent moonshells leading up to Equis castle. Jasper was at the head of our group, donning a sash of jade seaweed across his chest. Tiny conch shells were threaded through one of the strands, three of them, representing years of service in King Morrow's legion. Opal and Aurelia swam next to him, looking back every so often to make sure we were keeping up.

"You okay?" Sir Fergus asked, giving me a once-over.

"No," I muttered, low enough that our company wouldn't hear. "But that has little to do with providing mate bait for these mermaids tonight."

I glanced down at my shoulder, bandaged up with orange seaweed after one mermaid insisted on getting her lure directly from the source for luck. According to Sir Fergus, in their more primitive years, the mermaids would drag land dwellers near the edge of the Spuma and use their sharpened teeth to rip into their prey. Then they would cover themselves in its blood and present themselves to a prospective mate. They'd moved away from the barbaric practice once they realized it deterred land dwellers from nearing the sea, needing them to help produce the next generation.

I wondered if Sir Fergus had any teeth marks hiding away from the pair in front of us. Not that I'd ask, or want to know, considering I was still reeling with the news about him and Neve.

Unfortunately, I didn't have enough privacy to lick my wounds, my mind flitting back to the single bed awaiting us at Snatch of the Day.

As we neared the palace's entrance, a dozen guards lined the walkway on either side, each wearing matching seaweed sashes and a harpoon strapped to their back, showing them off as they bowed their heads in respect. Jasper returned the gesture to his fellow legionnaires.

"Greetings, Jasper. The Frenzy doesn't start for another hour," a tall guard with a long lilac mane and beard said, eyeing us suspiciously. "Not that you have much reason to be here for it. Shouldn't you be at home mating?"

"We did plenty of that earlier," Jasper bragged, giving a salacious grin to his buddy. "No, we are here to see King Morrow. This is King Redmond of Inverno, a rarity both in bloodline and magic. And this is his protection, Sir Fergus."

My protection. I wanted to roll my eyes.

"I'll let the King know you are here and see if he is willing to visit with you," the lavender-haired male said, pupils dilating as he scanned over Opal and Aurelia's friend who'd traced jagged lines along her arms and chest with the lure I'd provided.

I guess it worked.

"That would be much appreciated," Jasper said, bowing low and snagging back his colleague's wayward attention. He swam through the entrance to the Great Hall, turning off at a corridor near the end. Crushed aqua, peach, yellow, and sandstone shells cascaded up the columns and spires of the castle, making the walls glisten. Interspersed between them were pink and green gems that sparkled when the enchanted water rippled past.

Jasper shot back into the Great Hall, jetting toward us with his lips pressed in a thin line. "The King doesn't have much time, but he's willing to give you five minutes."

"That's all we need." I nodded, following him.

Oversized conch shells lined either side of the wavy carpet leading toward the throne room. Jasper had to stop every few tail swishes, realizing we couldn't walk as quickly in the water. Each step was becoming easier but my body still met resistance, pressure on my wings and chest constricting me as we continued forward.

When we arrived outside the throne room, Opal and Aurelia stayed back. We followed Jasper in, the doors groaning shut behind us.

The throne room was taller than any I'd ever seen, several stories high with little coves heading off in various directions, presumably to wings of the castle.

Carved into a jade coral reef was a wide-set throne with a matching one on its left. A beautiful mermaid sat with her tail tucked behind her, a set of small bedazzled starfish covering her chest. Her hair was done in a series of raven braids that floated around her shoulders, aqua gems embedded in their plaits. A large silver horseshoe clung to the base of her neck.

Queen Maren.

Her gaze flared when it snagged on my wings. Though I'd never seen her before, it was apparent she knew who I was—or more likely, who my father was.

"Welcome," she said, her eyes darting up a moment. "I'm Queen Maren."

"Thank you for seeing us, Your Majesty." I bowed to her, wondering if the King would be joining us or if this was some sort of tactic. A means of showing us we weren't worthy of his time.

A *neigh* rang through the Great Hall. Galloping toward us from above was a brilliant black stallion with a horseshoe seated between its ears, its hooves swimming through the water with ease. I looked to see the rider on its back, but instead found a long onyx tail swishing where its hind legs should be.

It wasn't a horse at all.

A kelpie.

I'd only ever heard of them in tales.

"I don't have much time, King Redmond of Inverno," the kelpie said midshift, leaving me stunned as I stared at the Mer King who now rested on his throne. I don't know why it surprised me, I was a fucking phoenix shifter. Suddenly the horseshoe emblem on the soldiers' arms made sense. They were a sigil in honor of their ruler. Were there even more shifters out there that I didn't know about? "What is this about?"

Sir Fergus's mouth was gaping. I shot him a glare, reminding him to bow, which he did hastily, lowering himself before the royal couple and snapping his jaw shut.

"The King has learned of your struggles with finding a mate for Princess Moray. He's offered to donate some lure for tonight's Frenzy." Jasper bowed his head to his king.

"How generous..." he replied, tone pompous, drenched in self-importance. He looked down at me from his throne, a slight peel at the corner of his lip telling me he was enjoying having the upper hand. "And what are you wanting in exchange?"

My father warned me that King Morrow thrived on his royal status. He was removed from the rest of Celaria and therefore easily overlooked despite having the largest territory. If I could win him over, almost three-quarters of the realm would be aligned against the Enchantress. Besides their size, the mermaids also dealt in trade, a useful resource for the future.

"May we speak privately?" I asked, still unsure of who I could trust. I was pretty certain the Enchantress didn't have any deals with the merpeople. There weren't any signs of them in her cabin collection and they wouldn't have any way to get near the Silent Woods, but that didn't mean I could speak freely.

"Everyone else, leave," King Morrow said with a flick of his tail. "Bring my daughter here."

Scurrying out of the room, Jasper left with Sir Fergus loping behind him.

"I won't waste time, Your Majesty." I strode up to the royal couple, placing myself between their thrones on the dais. "I am here because I believe soon there may be a time where Celaria's territories will need to unite to face a dangerous threat and I want to know whose side you'd be aligning yourself with if that were to happen."

His eyes narrowed, and he combed through his long black beard a few strokes before looking over at his queen. "Why would I concern myself with land dwellers when the only time you acknowledge us is when it suits you? Your father, King Reynard, was no different."

I bristled at the insult. Even though I knew my father was not beloved and could sometimes be more frigid than his kingdom, he was still the one who'd raised me.

Taking a deep breath, I continued on, wings tucked stiffly behind me. If I was going to secure this alliance, I would need to set aside my pride. "I admit I haven't taken the time as I should have when I became ruler to visit and build a relationship with your kingdom. For that, I am sorry. There is much to being a ruler that I've only begun to learn by no one else's fault but my own."

Queen Maren spoke, her tone delicate, like the chime of a silvery bell. "King Redmond, I don't know what you've heard about our people, but we do not concern ourselves with land-dweller politics. If there is a time when that changes, our people will float toward the side that will benefit our future most."

She twirled the braids of her hair between her fingers, giving her husband an uneasy glance, as if trying to diffuse something unspoken between them.

"The Enchantress, the one that you may have heard of through rumors over the years, is becoming stronger by the day since power was restored within the realm. She's amassed a collection of abilities from Celarians from most of the territories. If she's free, how many other powers will she steal? What will she do with boundless magic? She won't leave your territory, such a large portion of Celaria, untouched." Both rulers' lips dipped into frowns. "If you were to align yourself with me, with Inverno, you'd have our troops, our familiars, along with Arafax and their wielders. Their Revered."

"Ha! Arafax?" King Morrow sneered. "You want me to believe you are aligned?"

"It's true, though I understand why that would be hard to believe. Sir Fergus is here with me as part of our kingdoms' alliance." I nodded toward the door where the giant was no doubt waiting to reenter.

"Interesting..." the Mer King said, scrunching his nose.

The door peeled open, a flurry of bubbles bursting into the room. A mermaid with a long flowing mane of crimson and plum swam into the room. She wore a similar horseshoe necklace like Queen Maren's, only hers was more delicate.

Princess Moray.

"You wanted to see me, Father?" When she noticed me, her lips pursed and she crossed her arms. I was still getting used to the merfolks' white eyes and figuring out how to read their expressions, or where they were looking at exactly. My best guess was that she was glaring at me. Then her head turned back to her father, casting him the same look.

"Shit on a seaweed, this better not be another blind match you're trying to hook for me. I've already agreed to another stupid Frenzy—you're lucky I'm even showing up for it."

"You should be grateful I'm willing to throw one for you.

How many unmated mermaids would love for an opportunity like this to find a mate?" King Morrow threw his hands up before pointing at me. "Moray, this is King Redmond of Inverno. He has offered to donate lure for the Frenzy tonight. Unless that offer has been pulled since I haven't agreed to your terms?"

"No, I'm still happy to help," I said, noting that he didn't say he disagreed with my terms either.

"Who says I need lure?" Princess Moray asked, annoyance cresting her tone.

"This is the third event I've held to get you mated. I will not be hosting a fourth."

"Maybe that's what I want." Her razor teeth were clenched together, the words coming out in a hiss. "Maybe I have no interest in being mated or provided lure by some asshole king from another territory!"

"I beg your pardon," I chuckled, amused.

"Moray, that's quite enough." The Queen gave me an apologetic look, then bristled when her husband glared at her.

"I appreciate your willingness to assist, King Redmond, but my daughter has spoken her mind," King Morrow said, waving us away.

My not-so-subtle cue to leave.

I turned to leave, trudging toward the pair of guards holding the doorway open, Sir Fergus standing awkwardly between them.

"And as far as your request goes, the answer is also no," King Morrow called out from behind me. "I appreciate you taking the time to come down here, but Inverno would be the last kingdom I'd ever want to align myself with. Your father and I have never been on good terms."

"He never mentioned it." I glanced over my shoulder, the Queen's throat bobbing, eyes glued to me.

"I doubt he would," he said. "He brought our people safety

and the ability to help the next generation through Tesceillus's protective shell. For that, I will always be grateful. But that's as far as my kindness toward your father and Inverno goes."

"Well then, I apologize for taking up your time." I bowed my head, then continued walking. When I got to the door, I faced the King one final time. "You're sure there's nothing I can say or do to change your mind?"

"Unlike the tide, my position is unchanging."

His guards ushered me out, the door slamming with the force of the current, hundreds of bubbles spilling through the small gap right before it clasped shut.

"Thanks again for trying to help," I said to Opal, Aurelia, and Jasper. Then I continued striding forward, Sir Fergus catching up to me on the winding moonshell path.

"What's next, then?" he asked, placing a hand on my shoulder to stop me. "Will we stay and try again?"

"No." I brushed his hand away, ready to depart but knowing it was too late to head to the surface. "I refuse to waste more time here. First thing tomorrow, we're leaving."

"To Arafax to update the Queen?"

"Not yet," I replied. "There's somewhere else we need to go first."

CHAPTER 30
Kyleigh

The spiders were everywhere, frantically spinning threads up and down the clear cube encasing us. It was as if they'd created their own projector screen, casting whatever illusion Sloan was no doubt seeing now.

A log cabin. Fur rugs. A fire.

I fucking wish.

The way Sloan looked reverently on the scene when we arrived gave me the impression that this place was familiar. Someplace she knew and was comforted by.

Meanwhile, I felt anything but. Even though the spiders were outside—where they fucking belonged—the transparent walls made it feel like they were in here with us.

I wished for the sake of my eyes and sanity that I could be spelled into believing this place gave cozy cabin vibes instead of serving haunted house of horrors ones.

"What do you see?" Sloan repeated, looking at me with concern.

I gritted my teeth, still shivering. "You sure you want to know?"

The rain continued to pound against the glass, and the

spiders scurried up into the atmosphere, headed toward their suspended web. Thick droplets clung to their threads like crystal beads, creating a haunting prismatic necklace that spanned the width of Alucinor.

"Just tell me," she said, pulling the tiny packs from her satchel and setting them on the translucent floor. Worms punctured the ground beneath, wriggling out to enjoy the rain. I cringed, trying to focus on Sloan working the enchantment to enlarge our bags. I swallowed back the knot lumped in my throat, nausea surging into me in an acidic wave.

Sloan sighed. "The expression you're giving is unsettling, and I can't deal with much more of that today after seeing Aislin —faux Aislin."

Well, I'm an ass. Here I was thinking about slimy, creepy crawly creatures and the most frightening thing for Sloan must have been seeing Aislin only to have her taken away again. "I'm sorry. I'm sure it must have been hard. I can't even imagine."

"It was." She glared at me as I continued to squirm at things she was blessed to be blind to. "What do you see that I'm not seeing, Kyleigh?"

"Oh, just spiders floating up to their giant web. And worms crawling out from the ground. And a big glass house covered in spider silk."

She shuffled toward me, like something had nipped her in the ass, flicking her gaze to check over her shoulder.

"What is this place to you?" I asked. "The one *you* get to see."

"My family's cabin on the outskirts of Inverno."

"I'm jealous. I'm seeing a room as cozy as my cell in Inverno's dungeon and weavers in silken togas."

"Togas?" Sloan asked, bewildered.

I sighed, remembering that most people here had no clue what I was talking about. Just another frustrating aspect of being a visitor in the place I was apparently from. "It's like a bedsheet that's wrapped around you. I think theirs are made of the material the spiders are spinning."

"Well, I definitely didn't see people in *togas*, as you call them." Her eyes went to the doorway, where we'd last seen Ever, Rue, and Volett. "They were all stylishly put together. It made me want to get back to designing clothes again."

"I think the spiders would be happy to provide you with some thread," I tittered, trying to inject some humor into this awkward experience. "Maybe you can get one of them to illusion up something for the exhibition."

"Not funny." She took a deep breath, pinching the bridge of her nose.

We stood there silently a few moments, Sloan staring off at seemingly nothing. I was used to it now, though. When she was watching things through Mox's eyes, that's how she looked, but he was right here with us, so it wasn't that.

Her eyes softened, flitting to the ground a moment before their sharp gaze drew to mine. "How do you think they could see inside my head like that? To know our names. What Aislin looked like. What this looks like."

"According to Dru, to control their powers, usually they have some sort of talisman on the person whose mind they are looking into, but maybe that's not the case here?"

She began to pat around her body, feeling along her chest and in her pockets. I moved closer to her, scanning what I could see. Something glinted on the top of her boot, and I raised a hand to her. "Don't panic. Stay still."

She froze in place.

"You can breathe," I reminded her, and she released a sigh as I knelt down. A set of three charms hung around the lace of her boot: a prismatic rainbow, a rich ruby, and a gear. They each appeared to have been hacked away from something, the small tokens now attached to her lace with loops of iridescent string.

A spider had attached it.

I shivered, then reached out, thumbing the strand. It was slippery in some spots, sticky in others, but I undid the loop and held the set up to her in my palm.

"Fuck," she said, flicking each one with the tip of her finger. "How did that get on there?"

She picked up her boot, inspecting the bottom of it.

"I think their spiders are kind of like Mox."

She swung her arms around to cover his pricked-up ears with her hands, like I was somehow insulting him. "They most definitely are *not* like Mox."

"No, I just mean that it seems like they are connected to the spiders, almost like some sort of network. How else could the Octux know so quickly why we were here or see into your mind?"

"Yeah, *my* mind," she muttered, casting an icy glare that sent chills through me, heightened by my wet clothes. I needed to get changed out of them soon, but the fact that we were in a glass house wasn't the most reassuring thing.

"Believe me, there's enough fucked-up stuff going through my mind that I don't need their tampering." My mind would probably scare them if they could peek inside. "Guess that's one perk of having weaver blood. Though it sounds like it's much more enjoyable to be seeing what you are."

"True," she agreed, opening her pack and grabbing some clothes. "Well, if it's possible, let's get some rest."

"I'll try my best." My eyes flitted around the room, and I took a deep breath. "I can't guarantee I'll get any sleep on that cot."

"Cot?" she asked, slipping a fresh tank top over her head. "I see a sleigh bed with flannel evergreen sheets."

"Must be nice," I grumbled, pulling out a black shirt that I'd cut the neckline off of, swapping it with the wet blouse stuck against my chest.

"Yeah..." Sloan replied, continuing to change into her jammies, eyes cast to the ground. "Must be nice."

We finished getting ready for bed, and I grabbed out a blanket, laying it over the cot so I could pretend with Sloan that it was a sleigh bed. Closing my eyes, I imagined something out of the North Pole: snow flurrying against the glass instead of rain, maybe a cup of hot cocoa set on a table near the fireplace.

Sloan climbed in, and I opened my eyes, watching her lay a silver, delicately curved knife on the floor next to her. At least I was safer with her around. That thought lifted a weight off my chest, making me feel less like I was sinking into the silken cot made from something I didn't want to think about.

Despite the fear, I was handling this journey better than my previous one. We weren't locked away in a dungeon, after all, and I wasn't burning everything around me.

I wished Dru was here to witness this. He'd be proud of me.

It had me missing him even more, wishing we'd at least been able to bond so I could know how he was doing, yet partially glad we hadn't since he would have sensed my fear at just about everything I'd seen since we'd arrived here.

Shutting my eyes, I let my imagination carry me off to my own safe cabin, granting me the rest I'd need for whatever awaited us at tomorrow night's exhibition.

CHAPTER 31
Dru

Unbuckling the strap of his new wing, Harkin hung it from a branch-shaped hook in his office.

A long desk sat a few feet away from the wall, empty aside from a quill and a stack of papers set in the corner. Behind it, various maps were posted, lit by the petals that had been rolled up to line the perimeter of the ceiling. Some maps were so old that the browned edges were jagged with singed holes and missing pieces. A few were realms I'd never seen before. Where had he gotten them? The idea of other portals, other veiled worlds, wasn't far-fetched but it suddenly made me feel very small.

Off to the side was a circular map of Faerie Hollow that had various colored pins pushed into different areas around its outer rim, making my mind spiral at the thought of how much life happened within the Evergleam before the faeries had been driven out of its shelter.

"Was there ever an issue with the Evergleam when the faeries lived there?"

Harkin settled into his chair, draping his wing over its arm before pointing across from him for me to take a seat. "Hmm...

not that I'm aware of, but I can ask Wynnie if she's ever heard of anything. Is there something wrong with it?"

I took a seat, thinking back to the night Kyleigh and I tried bonding. "The bark is peeling off. In fact, the entire grove seems to be deteriorating."

"Interesting." He stroked along his jaw, his red wing furling and unfurling around the seat's cushioned arm. "The gem is there, right?"

"It is. And I know Celaria's magic is tied to it which has me concerned."

"The Evergleam and its roots spread magic through Celaria. All of the realm's inhabitants are connected to it. The crystals on its branches are powered by the Revered and their champions. The magic enchantments on the tree itself were put there by the faeries, carved into its design by our people's hands."

Could those billowing swirls and flames leading up the roots of the tree be conduits of magic?

"So, you know about the bonding ceremony?"

"Of course," he said, shaking his head. As if this fact that had been hidden away from the rest of Celaria was everyday knowledge. "The faeries used to preside over them. The Faerie King usually sanctioned any couplings that took place there."

I'd always believed the tree was a myth, not a real place that Arafax had taken by force. But it was easy enough to fix the maps, burn texts, and use weavers to erase its history. That was the scary side of magic. Unchecked, there really wasn't much you couldn't do—but it always came at a price. Having claim over the Evergleam would have given the Faerie King incredible political control over Arafax, especially if they could veto the pairs.

"Why does the pairing matter?" I asked.

"The crystals are powered by the bonds, even after death."

"Does that mean if a bond was severed by magic that it could be the cause of the Evergleam's issues?"

"I don't think so... Champion bonds can't be severed. It's impossible. Both people would be dead if that were the case. Their life essence is tethered to one another's when the bond is set."

Sloan was still very much alive, which meant that she and Aislin were still bonded. Somehow. She didn't believe they were, but maybe some part of them was still connected. That could be useful in going after the Enchantress. And if that were the case and Kyleigh and I hadn't done anything to the tree...that only left one other Revered who could have been responsible.

Neve.

Why would she hide something like that?

"Do you know anything else about the bonds? Our only text on it that survived The Blaze was taken and hasn't been located."

"Just that they have to be tended to, nurtured regularly."

That I already knew. There had to be something more to it, though. Something that would have caused the problem. "And if they aren't?"

He shrugged. "I suppose it could cause your problems."

Blazes. Heat prickled in my chest, but I brushed it away. That wasn't what I was here for, but I knew what I'd be talking to Neve about as soon as we returned to Arafax.

"So, you going to finally show me this tome?" Harkin asked, lifting a brow as if he could read my thoughts.

"Do you have a mind-reading affinity?" I half teased, still somewhat curious about what his was.

"No. But you're not far off." His wing curved over the desk, flitting to my chest. "Empathetic affinity. More of a heart reader, if you will. Helps me understand and know things about people not even they can see or sense."

"That is fascinating. The affinities are their own magic, but they don't seem to have to be conjured like with Arafax's wielders."

"Our magic is a part of us. Running through our veins at all times." His wing tapped at my wrist where my glove ended. "We are our own magic source. No fancy gadgets needed." His eyes drifted from my glove over to the wing hanging on the wall. "Not that your work isn't impressive in itself."

"Well, I'm a null, but I don't let it stop me." I pressed the third stud on my glove, feeling the weight of the text shove through its copper palm.

"You certainly don't." Harkin watched, transfixed with his eyes narrowed in a strange mix of shock and awe. I wasn't sure if it was from the sight of a massive leather-bound book erupting from my glove or the book itself, but his brows were pinned midway up his forehead. Once it fully manifested into my palm, I set the tome on the desk between us.

"It's true." He gasped, cursing at himself, body tensed. He shifted forward in curiosity before flinching back quickly. "You haven't used it yet, have you?"

"I don't even know how to read those symbols or speak in the ancient faerie tongue, so no. I try to make it a habit to learn as much as I can about doing something before just jumping in. Tends to be less perilous."

He sighed with relief. "Well, thank the stars for that."

"What is it?" His reaction had me curious.

"The *Validus Venenificium.*"

"Have you seen it before?"

"No." He shook his head, leaning forward again and reaching out a hand to touch it. "Never seen it myself. It was supposed to have been destroyed over two centuries ago. But here it is."

"Do you think the key to her power is in here?" I asked, pointing at the text.

"Oh, most definitely." His eyes met mine, any humor or light snatched away, the air hanging thick and murky between us. "And you'd do well not to tamper with it."

"What could she do with the power from this book?" I

needed to know everything he did about it. "She seems to be connected to it. From my source, she is showing the signs in the illustrations on this page." I thumbed through while Harkin held his breath, watching until I'd come to the image of a figure partially turned onyx. "Here."

"Those are the effects of a binding spell." He sat back, deep lines painting into his brows. "Stars, if she truly bound herself to this book, she could perform any dark spell from it without even thinking."

"That sounds dangerous."

"Oh yes. Once the binding takes effect, it needs a continuous stream of magic to give her power, though. Magic of that magnitude will pull from any source it can."

"So you're saying her need to consume power might not have to do with her own personal ambition? It could actually be feeding the magic to this tome?"

"I am."

If that were true, how much of the Enchantress's deeds were driven by her own decisions and how much was the tome steering? Depending on how long this binding had been in place, how much of the faerie remained? How much of Deirdre had been consumed by the Enchantress after she bound herself to this book? Her banishment had come after the forest around her had begun to die off... Could she have been taking from the magic running through the trees and their roots?

"You said it was supposed to be destroyed over two centuries ago. Why?"

"Emeric, the faerie who created that text, was one of the originals to inhabit these lands. He'd been cast out of his territory. There were many more of us back then and more faerie territories that were spread throughout Celaria.

"It is said he stole a piece of power itself and fled to Cicatrix where a demolier ground it to dust. Emeric took that dust and mixed it with his blood to use as ink. Then he hid away in exile, playing with magic until he'd created his masterpiece, the *Valídus Vénenifícium.*"

"What happened after that?"

"He bound himself to the *Valídus Vénenifícium,* and it continued to thieve from him as his power within Celaria grew. All the lands became barren around Cicatrix until the earth eventually cracked, swallowing him into its scarred valley. Power demands balance, and his life was the debt he eventually paid."

This definitely sounded like the same magic the Enchantress was harnessing.

"Many of Cicatrix's people referred to him as death himself, treating him as a god among their men. All of Celaria's fallen are believed to be swallowed by the Nefastus Valley, cycling through its cleaved core to continue powering the realm."

"You really believe that?" I asked, trying to think through everything he'd said. I'd heard so many rumors surrounding the Enchantress over the years. What made this story the truth? "That one person—or faerie, rather—could create that chasm?"

"Why not?" Harkin countered. "The trees you find your shade under back in Arafax, where do they come from? The faeries. Most of the world was created by our magic, our essence's power. That sap you harvest...it is ancient faerie magic, faerie blood, that runs through the bark."

So that confirmed my suspicions about the Silent Woods. Once Arafax stifled the Enchantress's abilities from reaching out farther...she would have needed another source. She had the wisps, but that wouldn't be enough all these years. "The faeries created Celaria?"

"Not just the faeries. All Celarians. Our magic, our energy, it doesn't disappear. It cycles back into the world, into magic's source itself, into our descendants. You cannot create something out of nothing. Someone cannot disappear without leaving traces of themselves behind in the world."

"I suppose that's true."

But if the book still existed, something had gone wrong. "Who was meant to destroy the book?"

"The leaders of the different territories came together to destroy it. Ultimately it was supposed to be done by the Revered. They were believed to have the power to." His eyes dropped down to the book sitting open between us. "Obviously that didn't happen."

"Any idea how they planned to do it?"

"Considering I wasn't alive and this is all just stories passed down from one faerie to another...no. We may have a longer life span, but not that long. I'm only eighty-nine."

"Eighty-nine?" I was shocked. He didn't look a day over forty. "I didn't realize faeries had long life spans."

"Have you spent a lot of time with faeries?"

"No," I admitted, my face heating a bit with embarrassment. "None, until Travis."

"Well then, you really know nothing of our people." He shook his head, disappointment filling his words. "Most can live up to two hundred years. Unfortunately, conditions for faeries in Celaria have historically been rough, so we are only starting to see the full capabilities of an uninterrupted life span now that we are hidden away."

"So, you're telling me that if I leave Travis here, he could live over a hundred more years?" I grimaced.

Harkin gave me a knowing smirk, reminding me that while he couldn't read my mind, he could sense my emotions about the new faerie I'd brought with me. "Yep."

"Do me a favor—don't tell him about that just yet."

"I wouldn't dare. There'll be no living with him once he knows that." He chuckled to himself. "Now, why don't we try and decipher these ancient faeries runes?"

Taking a key from his pocket, he stuck it into his desk and pulled out a drawer, withdrawing a large roll of parchment with symbols similar to the ones in the tome.

"You have a key?"

Harkin barked out a laugh. "You think just because I've learned an ancient language that I have every symbol memorized?"

"Fair point." I shrugged, trying to look over the sheet to see which symbols I recognized from my days of combing through the *Validus Venenificium.*

"Ready to learn its secrets?"

"Yes," I replied, flipping back to the front of the tome. "I'm ready to learn them all."

CHAPTER 32

Isla

Stars blinked back at me from a purple sky. Fluorescent lights illuminated the enclosed six-sided room that would gladly swallow me whole, surrounding me, engulfing me. Coves peeled off the main hub, each one representing the six territories claimed by Celaria: Arafax, Alucinor, Cicatrix, Spuma, Inverno, and wherever the faeries had hidden away to.

My head hung back, soaked hair stuck to the stone beneath me, dazed from the smoking sticks my father had secured for transport. *Might as well enjoy the goods my life paid for.* Shipments came each full and new moon as part of my dowry—pieces of home to be enjoyed by those who knew little to nothing about it.

But the Grymms would pay handsomely for them, along with the other founding families.

If they were bound by duty to stay here, *a few trinkets, delicacies, and a princess should suffice as payment.* That's what I'd heard my father tell Neve's when we'd snooped one night, leaning against a gilded column outside his study, the pair of us taking turns swigging from a bottle of faerie wine.

A week later, they'd announced my engagement to Seth Grymm, the son of Halston University's president.

Now I was here, helping them shape their bland world in Celaria's image.

A poor man's version of where I'd come from, now replicated beneath Halston's prestigious walls. Cooperating to hide myself. The truth of who I was, that was no secret. The truth of what I could do...that could never come to light.

Too much was at stake if it did.

I knew my purpose, my sworn duty as Arafax's Princess. It'd been ingrained into me since the announcement delivered on my seventeenth birthday.

Keep the Grymms happy by way of his son.

Sate the thirst for Celaria's knowledge among the unhappy outcasts.

Above all else, ensure they never come back.

Crystalline water rippled around the bodies drunkenly splashing through the cove-encased pool, a tray of vibrantly colored mushrooms perched on its ledge. They popped them in their mouths like bonbons, laughing all the while. I should've told them that having too many could kill them but, honestly, I was too numbed to care right now. And it's probably best that way. My vision shook, moving in time with his thrusts. *Christening the corium.*

Whatever that meant.

Pleased, he collapsed over me, sweaty and spent, shaggy wet hair tickling my neck.

Just lay there a few minutes.

Duty done.

"How incredible is this, Isla?"

My eyes darted up to his, finding genuine curiosity laced within them. *Insecurity.* He wanted the praise. Accolades for what he built. I paid him in smiles and a gentle hand across his cheek.

A cloth swiped between my thighs and hands helped me sit upright. Brushing my hair over my shoulder, I braided the sopped strands, tucking it back into the hood of my robe.

"Shall we?" Seth held out his hand, giving me a proud smirk. Taking it, I popped off the slab, watching Greyson and Kendrick round everyone up. Half muttering to themselves, the others stared expectantly, captivated by their leader.

"Brothers and sisters, our ancestors were given the sacred *duty*"—I scoffed to myself at the word—"to protect Celaria's people, our true people, but somewhere along the way that was lost. Our own world left us here to rot. They took the power for themselves, and we've spent years trying to take it back.

"But no longer will we be denied our birthright. Yes, some of our descendants tried. Tried and failed. There's never been a true collective presence of our people, and thanks to my extraordinary fiancée, I realize how fruitless our efforts have been because of that. Starting today—our founding day—we will become one. One purpose. One vision. To finally claim what is ours."

The group was nodding, staring at him reverently, and he ate up every morsel of their worship like the false god he believed himself to be. But egos were easy to manipulate. As long as I was smart, I could play this to my advantage—to my people's advantage.

The other founders joined us at the front, each from a prominent family representing part of Celaria. Only, when it came down to it, they were all ignorant of anything about the realm, another advantage I had.

Seth pulled me in for a deep kiss, earning whoops and cheers from his brethren. Hardening against me, he gave me a salacious grin that I returned through gritted teeth.

Keep the Grymms happy by way of his son.

Greyson came over with a box clutched in his hands. Seth

reached in, taking out a large wolf mask with gears pinned over the ear in a makeshift crown. "I had these custom designed."

He held out my mask, layers of scales circling the eyes, the onyx of it shimmering with coppery tips. "Come and stand at my side, where you belong."

Sate the thirst for Celaria's knowledge among the unhappy outcasts.

I did as I was told, and he stepped behind me, bringing the mask over my head. Tying the ribbon, he pressed a kiss to my shoulder before putting on his own.

Turning to face the crowd, he held my hand up into the air as Kendrick's voice boomed from behind us. "Bow to your President and *his* Queen."

Above all else, ensure they never come back.

A ripple of black, knelt before us, reaching within their robes. When they stood back up and applauded, all I could see was a sea of onyx animals staring greedily back at me.

A WAVE OF NAUSEA SURGED THROUGH ME. CLAMPED tightly by one of Craig's arms, his other held the bin under my face. Bile dribbled down my chin, splattering against the metal. Grabbing the bottom of my shirt, I used to wipe my mouth. "Sorry."

"Nothing to be sorry about." His voice was quiet.

"You don't just pull the memories. You see them too, don't you?"

He nodded, remaining silent but dragging me closer until my back was pressed to his chest.

There were few places I hated more than Vindicatio Vis's ceremonial chamber. Every time Craig brought me back there, weaving through the memories, it only reminded me how much I'd willingly sacrifice them if his magic malfunctioned.

Sometimes the memories that shaped us were best left in the recesses of our mind.

But I'd relive them. I'd take on their burden to help my husband so long as the memories after *him* remained. The rest were up for grabs, especially if they involved that chamber and all the sins that stained its corium.

"Well, I still remember, so you didn't accidentally remove anything. That's progress." I shrugged, not sure what else to say. Wishing I didn't remember it anymore. I knew not all my memories had survived, he'd told me as much, but I didn't feel like I was missing anything.

Tucking my knees into my chest, I stared down at the pristine laces of my red Chucks, feeling anything but. To be fair, I didn't know any other way to live back then...not until *him*.

"I remember that night myself, just very differently."

I rolled my eyes. "You were high on smoking stems, doing stars know what."

"This is true." He chuckled, pressing a kiss to my throbbing temple. Gentle fingers combed through my hair, and I leaned against his chest. "Just to be safe, though, you should probably sit over there."

My eyes went to the chair across the room, a whole world away from Craig's warmth. The first bit of warmth I'd had since...I couldn't remember when. "I need to get back to the fort. The Otherworlders that traveled with you still have to be trained, and I'm the only one left to handle it until Dru returns."

I stood up, striding toward the door.

"When will you be back?"

"I'll stop by tonight." I didn't even like waiting that long. Without knowing how often he needed to siphon his powers to preserve his own mind, I refused to chance too long between visits. As hard as they were for me, he'd been through enough. I'd go through it all again for him.

I owed him that and so much more.

Anger stung my eyes, tears filtering down my cheeks as I walked along the hallway, heading toward the fort. Having him here and unable to be with him without carving up old wounds... Having Kyleigh here but hating me...

It all felt like a punishment.

If there was one thing I'd learned, karma was real, and she was dishing me everything I was due.

CHAPTER 33

Travis

Buildings climbed up the darkness, like skyscrapers chipped from worn-down stone. Faeries whizzed past, going about their business, some heading into the various shops lining the lower levels, others soaring through the windows above, their outlines only visible from the neon petals pressed along their exteriors. "Was this place always so flourishing? You've built your own little cityscape here."

"It has always been bustling, but much quieter before The Great Betrayal, from what Harkin has told me. About a third of our population are transplants like me." Wynnie brushed her blonde hair behind her pointed ear. A row of tiny pink studs traced the line of its shell, connected to a larger pink gem in her lobe by a series of shimmering chains. A matching set hung around her neck at different lengths, some dipping into her cleavage.

My dick was going to land me in a lot of trouble if I didn't get it together. Wynnie was off limits. She was with the faeries' Overseer. I might have been cocky but I wasn't stupid.

Coughing, I turned my attention to the faeries huddled

around the large pool in the city center. All of their wings were bright, glowing in a neon rainbow of colors ranging from electric yellow to bubble gum pink. It was like someone had taken a pack of highlighters and painted their wings.

Meanwhile, Wynnie's were more like mine: muted gossamer with iridescent etchings. I searched for others with similar wings, only managing to spot a few. If there were many more, they were either hidden among their boldly colored brethren or tucked away somewhere.

"What is it?" Wynnie asked.

"Not many look like us." I lifted my wings, curling them forward for emphasis.

"Nope." She reached a hand, as if wanting to run it along the rim of my wings, before folding both her arms quickly into her. "Most of the faeries here are born with their fluorescence." Lowering her voice to a whisper, she discreetly nodded toward a group of faeries floating above us. "A few paint it on, but I'll never tell their secret," she said with a wink.

"But not you?" I guess wanting to fit in wasn't just an Otherworld concept. I'd quickly learned a sense of belonging wasn't possible for me. My father had made sure of it. Growing up in the shadows of a University President and elite society founder didn't grant you real friends. Followers, plenty. But not friends. I was fine with it, though. Once I realized I was never meant to fit in, it was freeing to just stand out.

"No." She shrugged, primping her wings a bit with a sigh. I had the urge to touch them, to trace along the etchings so similar to my own, but I remembered how quickly she'd retreated from mine. It probably wasn't appropriate. One of the many things I'd have to figure out during my time here. "I don't want to forget where I come from, if that makes sense."

"It makes perfect sense." I thought things would click into place when I finally got to Celaria. But everything was so different. Even my own body was foreign to me.

"What's your story?" Wynnie asked. We continued walking, her waving at many of the faeries as we passed. She didn't need glowing wings to stand out. Her presence alone demanded attention, and she'd obviously won over Harkin. "You're newly a faerie. I don't really understand how that's possible."

"The world I traveled from doesn't have magic."

Her brows lifted in surprise. "None?"

"None." I tucked some strands of hair behind my ear, flinching when I brushed against its sharpened tip. "I grew up in a crossroads area. Magic flits along the boundary, so there were a few things I could do, but not much. It was very limited."

"Did you know you were a faerie?"

"I had no fucking clue." I brought my hands to my pockets —before realizing they were still doll pants and didn't have actual pockets. Not trying to look like more of a fool in front of Wynnie, I tucked them into my waistband, pulling my elbows behind me.

"You seem disappointed."

"Would saying that I am get me killed?"

"No, though I wouldn't make it known publicly." She offered a comforting smile that sent a swell of warmth flooding through me. "Most faeries take their lineage very seriously."

Was she using her affinity on me right now?

"My father took our lineage very seriously too. Proud that we were descended from Richard Halston, the great founder of the school he was president of. The position I'm supposed to inherit."

"Do you know which of your parents is faerie?"

"I don't." A question that'd been gnawing at me since Odette had scooped me up in her palm and carted me toward Arafax's fort. Maybe it would have felt less shitty had I not been the only one. "And I'm curious to know if my father did. He always seemed like he knew everything."

"You could ask him?"

"Doubtful. At least I'm hoping so." The last thing I needed was him showing up and seeing me like *this*. Bet he would get a great laugh. He probably had some useful ability, like everyone else seemed to. Something better that I didn't inherit. *Fucker.* "He didn't come through with me. Still running the school and keeping up appearances over there."

"He must miss you."

"Nah." I shook my head. "We don't have that kind of relationship."

"I understand. I don't miss mine either." She placed her hand on my shoulder, then used it to redirect me down a narrow road. This area was more tucked away, dimmer with less petals lighting it.

"So, tell me more about Renegade Trench. How did you get all of this built in here?"

"Well, for one thing, we have our affinities, which helps. Lots of talented faeries." She pointed a finger at the windows of the shops along either side of us, faeries busy at work. Some were sewing clothes, pins pursed between their lips; others grinding herbs; and in the farthest window, I could see a faerie rolling up hair and pinning it into curls.

"We also, up until recently, had supplies left at the base of the mountain for us every so often," Wynnie added with a sigh.

"Up until recently?" *Odd.*

"Yeah. They stopped."

Improbable. But not impossible... "If you used the same transport for your goods that I had back in the Otherworld...it's closed for business. *Permanently,* if you catch my drift."

She halted, bringing a hand to my chest to stop me. "Permanently?"

"Yeah. Flynt and his whole network were killed," I shared, taking a step back and rolling my shoulders.

Her hand dropped. Her eyes dropped too. "Oh."

"Why?" My hand absentmindedly lifted her chin. I debated whether to let go once I'd done it, but she didn't startle—didn't flinch—so I left it. "You know him?"

"Yeah." She peered up at me from under her long silken lashes. "We went way back."

"I'm sorry." Bringing my hand up to her cheek, she cupped it at the wrist, holding it in place. "I didn't realize. He didn't strike me as someone who was close with many people."

"He was a very different man when we met." I pulled my hand down with hers but not releasing it, she continued to walk forward, swinging our clasped hands between us. "Time can corrode people if they let it."

A weight fell heavy in my chest, discomforting and comforting all at once. I'd never held someone's hand like this. Not even my parents' that I could recall, though they were usually too busy with parties and entertaining board members to care. I sure as fuck never held my father's hand. My mother's? Maybe a long time ago, before she'd decided drinking and fucking the gardener were better uses of her time than raising her son.

That's what nannies are for.

Not that I could blame her. She was married to *him*, after all.

"I was thinking..." Wynnie said, dragging me down another side street. "You should stay with us while you get settled."

"You sure Harkin would be okay with that?" Pretty sure if she kept looking at me like that I was going to be getting my ass kicked.

"Of course." She giggled, the sound vibrating through me like a delicate chime. "He always enjoys having company. Besides, you don't have any kin here that we know of. Where else would you stay?"

"I don't know."

I hadn't thought that far. Dru would be heading back to

Arafax, and I knew I didn't want to go back there until I could be useful somehow. I needed to figure out my affinity, then show how I could be a powerful ally like I'd promised. I probably wouldn't get to be her champion, but a friend like Kyleigh, Arafax's future Queen, would be valuable. If I could stay here until I found my faerie footing, it would also stop the pitying looks and near-death experiences I'd had at The Lavender.

Dropping my hand, Wynnie pointed to a small shop at the end of the road, eyes alit with eagerness. "Come on. How about we grab some food and bring it back to our place?"

"Sounds good," I replied, feeding off her pure excitement. "Thank you, Wynnie."

She gave a quick shrug, then pranced toward the sign boasting fresh bread and sugar buns. "Don't mention it."

AFTER WE'D TOLD DRU THAT I'D BE STAYING IN Renegade Trench for the foreseeable future, we headed to Wynnie and Harkin's place. She'd been kind enough to grab a few of Harkin's clothes so I could finally wear something other than fucking doll attire. After changing into a pair of black pants and a plain short-sleeved shirt with slits for my wings to slide through, I strode out to the living room.

We set the table, and I watched Wynnie flit from place to place excitedly. It was like everything lit up around her—even the plants seemed to lean in her direction when she was near them in the kitchen, building up a tower of sugar buns on a plate.

The door creaked open, and Harkin looked momentarily unsettled when he came in.

Fuck. Guess we'd see how this would go.

Wynnie jumped into his arms, kissing him boldly. He returned the kiss, arms looped under her ass, gripping it tightly. My dick perked up stupidly in my pants.

Down boy.

"Miss me?" Wynnie asked him, her lips slightly swollen, cheeks flushed as he set her down.

"Of course. I left Dru to keep working at the Council's headquarters. He'll be heading out shortly." Harkin strode confidently across the room, his red wings flaring a few times—even the shredded one—like he was shaking something off. His eyes roved over the food and then back over to me. My throat went dry. "And what do we have here?"

Before I could say anything, Wynnie chimed in, picking up a sugar bun and holding it up to his lips. "I figured since Travis doesn't have anyplace else to stay that he could be our guest until we sort out his affinity and he finds his place in The Trench."

Harkin's lips closed around the bun, filling dripping down his chin a bit. Wynnie caught it with her fingertip and went to lick it off, but before she could, he grabbed her wrist and brought it to his mouth.

When her finger popped back out, completely clean, I stifled a groan.

"I hope that's okay."

"The more the merrier," he said, eyes never leaving hers. She continued to feed him the sugar bun, somehow making it the most erotic display I'd ever seen.

"Of course you're welcome here. We have plenty of space," Harkin said, finally turning toward me. He wiped off the last bit of sticky residue from the corner of his mouth. He grabbed a bun from the stack and held it out to me. "Glad to share."

"Thank you." I nodded, grabbing the bun and taking a big bite.

Sweet sugary goodness burst across my tongue. Releasing my

previously stifled groan, I chewed the fresh-baked heaven, continuing to eat it in two more bites before licking up the left-over mess from my fingers. God, they were fucking heavenly. "I promise not to wear you out with my presence."

The corner of Harkin's lip curled up in a smirk. "Oh, I hope that you do."

CHAPTER 34
A Wisp

Clap, clap.

Twirling the vial in her claws, our Queen tapped her other hand on the table, deep in thought.

Jars were still amiss, the cabin emptier each time I saw it.

More of us disappeared from the cabin.

Not everyone returned.

Faceless visitors came, and our Queen stared at the window, focused on the husks.

They rose. A sea of gnashing, snarling ghosts.

Then, just as quickly, they crashed back into their heap.

The one who summons, he never spoke.

He tucked away with some of us when he visited.

I retracted into my coven.

Hidden.

A flurry of anxiety thrummed through us when he arrived today.

Unease struck me even before our Queen's hands met—

227

Clap, clap.

The white fox hasn't returned.

The one who erased them left some small pieces of bread on the sill, now all that remained were stale crumbs.

We should clean them up but we don't.

I remember him bolting away into the woods.

Silver strands whipped behind him, reaching toward me.

When was that?

Now all that rested outside the windowsill were shells.

Clap, clap.

As a coven, we've worked collectively to piece things together.

But some things feel imprinted, impossible to forget.

The white fox. The emerald scales.

The icy eyes that pierced like needles, stitching into my very being.

But I didn't dwell on the facets I held on to.

Because what if *she* noticed?

I was known as *the one that's struck many*.

They say I once touched the sky beyond.

I didn't know if I believed them.

But I'd hit the barrier, waiting for the pain.

Waiting to feel.

Anything.

Clap, clap.

Taking off her copper claw in the moonlight, our Queen's onyx finger dipped into the vial.

She knelt, blocking my view.

I flitted closer, wanting to see.

The coven watched, awaiting the signal to follow.

The next set of orders to obey.

They never came.

She wrapped her cloak around herself and stepped over the threshold.

CHAPTER 35

Enchantress

Our people are born in the shadows. Destined to die in their clutches.

I'd grown up hearing those words repeated, yet here I was, the iridescent swell of Celaria's moon beaming down on me, almost within reach.

Illuminating just how wrong they'd *all* been.

For years I'd longed for freedom, had begged for it, then realized how fruitless, how beneath me that was. I may have been born in the shadows, that I couldn't change, but I was destined for so much more than any of *them* could have expected.

They'd all underestimated me, but such was the story of men. Stroke their ego well enough and they didn't even notice their exposed jugular.

And I'd happily bleed them dry.

It was only fair—just—to leave them as hollow shells.

They'd been more than happy to trap me. Drain me. Use me. As long as it served their agendas.

Why not return the favor?

I clapped, summoning my wisps. Two began untying the laces of my boots while another set held me steady. I stepped out of them onto the thin layer of dust coating the porch, the few sets of boot- and footprints leading toward the door the only cleared spots. A flurry of more wisps filtered out to assist. All I needed was to call upon them.

They were beautifully obedient creatures.

And they were mine.

With another set of claps, I released my hold over them, a few returning to the cabin, others flitting into the woods. A small group of the coven stayed in place, watching me curiously, fearfully. I'd been through enough to know that curiosity would win out.

Lifting the skirts of my dress, I extended my foot into the trail of light, black glittering over the exposed skin. At first, I'd been shocked when it'd appeared, missing the previously milky pallor. It's softness. But this was more fitting. I'd shed that skin, that delicacy. Traded it in for obsidian armor.

And power.

The timing was perfect. The real battle was almost here. Every deal, every sacrifice along the way, leading me to this point.

Dead leaves ground into bits beneath my bare feet as I descended from the porch and into the forest. I twisted them into the dirt, enjoying the scrape against my skin, inhaling the rich earthy smell. I strode quickly to the nearest tree, palming the rough bark.

Continuing through the forest, I signaled the wisps to help clean up after themselves, brushing dirt back into the scattered holes. I didn't need any visitors seeing those, and Redmond would be returning soon, hopefully with my tome. Flynt betraying me after all these years wasn't a surprise, but I'd appreciated his ambition more when it was tied to serving me. At least the magic I carried hadn't been hindered, which meant the tome hadn't been used—at least not in any way that mattered.

Once Redmond retrieved it and I was free, I could end our farce of an engagement.

A king gave me fuck all when it came to power.

Not when I still had all my tome's magic seeping through my veins, indulging my desire for revenge.

It would have been more enjoyable collecting Reynard, the selfish ass who spent decades pining after his secret pearl. Not a secret to me, though. Love was a weakness, best ripped free and tucked away where no one could find it.

When he wished to garner enough land to rival the Mer King's territory, he all but begged me to help him.

So unimpressive.

Predictable.

He barely needed any persuasion to enter our deal.

Then he went and allowed his arrogance and greed get in the way of our bargain. Losing me the gem he'd promised, the blood that should have been mine to shed.

It took far too long for Redmond to finally answer my summons, stubborn to a fault. He may not have been able to keep hold of the gem for me, but he still had ample power to absorb. He'd make such a beautiful addition to my magic-filled menagerie.

And if everything went according to plan, the gem, along with the rest of the realm, would fall at my feet soon enough.

CHAPTER 36
Kyleigh

"Guess I should go ask for a spider-spun sack and a weaver-style makeover," I said to Sloan the next morning after getting about two hours of combined sleep through the night.

She yawned, turning to face me. "No need for that. I've got it covered."

I didn't know what that meant, but I'd trust her to handle our outfits.

She'd also been up through the night, every so often reaching for her knife, clutching her chest with the other hand. For the most part, we left each other in silence, not sure what to say about any of this. The rain had stopped in the early morning, making way for peeks of pale gray and lavender where the web wasn't obscuring my view overhead. The iridescent network above hung like an ominous veil, feeling heavy as the rain droplets clung to it, slowly dripping and splashing onto the glass ceiling.

I couldn't decide if this was all strangely beautiful or the precursor to a nightmare.

My stomach rumbled, starving, Sloan's joining in a moment later.

"Do weavers eat?"

"This one does," I said, peeling myself out of bed. "But maybe that's only because I'm only half weaver."

Tappity-tappity-tappity-tap-tap.

My gaze shot to the sky to see if the rain had begun pelting again. When it hadn't, I listened again for the sound.

"Ahem, figured you might be hungry," Volett's soft voice was muffled through the glass.

"Do you think they could sense our hunger?"

I shrugged. "Maybe their little eight-legged minions reported the growling?"

It was kind of creepy, but my stomach didn't care too much about that at the moment. I was starving. The last thing I'd eaten was some berry bake Leigh had given Sloan at the inn before we'd left.

Walking us toward a larger glass-encased building than the one we'd stayed in, I leaned over to Sloan. "What do you see?"

"A large mess hall. You?"

"Another glass building covered in webs with tables and chairs within," I whispered back.

About thirty weavers were inside what Sloan described as a *mess hall*, seated among the tables. Ever slid a plate onto the table, pulling out a chair for me.

"Thanks." I nodded to them, watching as they walked with Volett and Rue to get a few more full plates to bring over to the empty chairs with us.

"Bleh," Sloan said, throat bobbing as she stared at her plate.

"What?" My eyes dropped, nausea crawling through my gut, a small amount of acid rising in my throat that I managed to swallow back down. On the plate were a handful of colorful insects with a brown sauce pooled next to them. On the other side of the dish was a pile of leaves. Not leaves of romaine or spinach like I would occasionally force myself to choke down back home, but actual leaves. Crisp and brown, like they'd seen the end of autumn and then were collected to be served up as breakfast.

I shivered, staring at the plate. The screech of Rue pulling out the chair next to me interrupted my unpleasant thoughts.

"Evergrubs and pineweebles," he said, picking up one of the blueish bugs with beady silver eyes and dipping it into the brown sauce. Bringing it to his lips, he smiled as he crunched down, swallowing after a few bites. He licked his lips of the few leftover dribbles.

"Mmm. You're missing out." He looked over at Sloan who was shoveling the beige and brown leaves on her plate.

"Planteater," she said simply. "Never know when your next meal could be someone's familiar." She shrugged. "Made that mistake once when I was on an expedition. Never made it again."

Twirling a brown leaf between my fingers, my stomach garbled again, pissed at my hesitation to fill it up.

"You a planteater too?" Volett asked, popping a pair of bright pink—what I believed to be—evergrubs into her mouth and swallowing them down with a *slurp*.

"Um. Yes." I shoved the leaf in my mouth before grabbing a glass of water across from me and chugging its bland crunch down.

"You ready for the exhibition?" Ever asked, sandwiching some pineweebles between the leaves and dipping their makeshift sandwich into the brown sauce before taking a bite. That somehow seemed less gross to me—not that I had any intention of trying it myself.

"Have something splendid to wear?" Volett asked, braiding some strands of her white hair together, iridescent flecks glimmering from within. Once I remembered those were tiny spiderlings, a chill scurried straight up my spine, causing me to jolt in my seat.

Ever's gaze darted to me. "You okay?"

"Yep," I chirped, picking up another leaf and reaching for the water glass as I shoved it into my mouth.

"I have attire for both of us," Sloan said between chews.

"Wonderful," Volett exclaimed. "I can't wait to see what you come up with."

"I'm excited to see what you all come up with as well." Genuine kindness threaded her words. I knew she admired the fashions the weavers were donning, though all I could see were silken sacks and togas.

After we finished up our meal, which didn't take long, considering we could only pick from half the plate, we headed back to our quarters. Sloan went straight to our bags, moving things to the side and digging deep into the packs.

"Your excitement over this has me a bit nervous."

I couldn't complain, though. Sloan showing any sort of excitement had me grateful. If playing dress up for some strange banquet helped her morale, who was I to judge? Of course, I hadn't had the best track record with fancy dinners, but at least no phoenix king would be showing up with threats.

This was a step up already.

"Ah!" Sloan's lips peeled into a smile. She lifted out some white fabric with peach watercolor climbing along it. Rose gold was also mixed into the pile. "Here it is!"

"Is that for you or me?"

"You," she said, holding it out to me before pulling out some charcoal fabric and clutching it against herself. "This one's for me."

"At least one of us is excited about this exhibition."

"I'll admit, they are a bit odd, and I don't want to run into any more false Aislin's, but they are kind enough. And how many people in Celaria can say they've attended an event in Alucinor?"

"That's true."

While I admired Sloan's enthusiasm about tonight, some-

"ARE YOU SURE THIS ISN'T TOO MUCH?"

My eyes dropped to the plunging neckline that waved its way down the center of my chest, swirling strategically and stopping above my belly button.

"Never," Sloan said, surveying me. "Especially not for Arafax royalty."

"Well, they don't know that," I said, bringing my hands across my stomach, thumbing over the gauzy material. The dress was white for the most part, running into a short peach-and-red streaked train that pooled a few feet behind me.

I double checked to make sure my nipples weren't visible through the material.

"Don't worry, your tits are safe."

I coughed out a laugh. "Thank goodness for that! I was worried I'd be having a wardrobe malfunction in front of a bunch of strangers."

"Worst case, I'm sure they could illusion you something in a pinch, but you should trust my expert construction. They'll stay put."

"If you say so." I shifted my shoulders a bit to make sure it didn't mess with anything if they moved, feeling the weight of the rose-gold scaled armor capping my sleeves. Drawn across my collarbones were a series of thin chains that wove through each other, reminding me eerily of the web hovering overhead.

Sloan was in a plain fitted charcoal gown that was corseted at her chest. I remembered it was the color of mourning in Celaria. Had she chosen it intentionally? In fact, now that I thought about it, she'd been lacking color in her wardrobe lately. But I guess even if Aislin was still technically alive, Sloan had lost her. A different sort of grief, but grief, nonetheless.

A grief I understood all too well.

She snapped something around her neck, and I peered over her hands, trying to see what it was. Finally, when she'd situated the piece, my breath caught.

A silver dragon with scales tipped in purple curled around the base of her throat, leaving a small slice of skin uncovered.

"That's beautiful," I said, admiring it.

"Thank you." Pink stained her pale cheeks. "It was a gift."

The perfect gift for a champion.

"You ready?" I asked, nerves jolting through me in anticipation of whatever tonight would entail.

Moving the slit going up her leg to the side, she slipped her knife into her thigh holster and nodded up at me. "Always."

The trio of weavers were already awaiting us outside. Holding cobweb-wrapped lanterns in their hands, they led us toward the exhibition.

It was time to finally meet the Octux.

CHAPTER 37

Kyleigh

T he exhibition was to take place at The Cortex, nestled within Alucinor's nexus.

A shiny iridescent path led us into the belly of the building, the weavers' lanterns the only other source of light along the trek. Large satiny curtains hung from its ceiling at regular intervals, sashed in the middle so each one tapered in, revealing small coves with glass lounge chairs and cocktail tables.

Within each nook, situated against the wall, were shadow boxes with large spiders, their bulbous hind parts a crystalline prism of colors. The first one we came upon was spinning its own art, working quickly to create a thick opaque scene of snow-tipped mountains. It wove in layers, creating a three-dimensional masterpiece that left me stunned.

As we continued to wander with Rue, Ever, and Volett down the entryway, there were different similarly colored spiders, all looking like larger versions of the ones we'd seen throughout the territory. They each created their own iridescent renderings within their shadow boxes, rich imaginings from a coral reef-tipped underwater castle with bubbles peppering the background, to a forest spun with ghosts and a shrouded woman under the moon.

"These are beautiful," I said to Ever, getting an appreciative nod back.

"These are our *aranea*. The other spiders report to them, and they directly serve our Octux."

"Fascinating," I said, finding myself less repulsed by the unusualness of being surrounded by spiders. Like the people they served, they seemed to keep to themselves unless needing to connect with the weavers or each other. As we spoke, I noticed a few smaller spiders burrowing in the shadow boxes, nearing the aranea, before quickly leaving them to continue their work.

Overhead, a network of thick webbing cast its net across the ceiling, hanging lower in various spots. Spiders were gathered in their depths, touching it up.

"The trellis is spun anew for each exhibition," Volett chimed in, noticing my upturned gaze.

"It also allows our friends to attend without getting in the way," Rue added.

I wished I could know what he was donned in according to Sloan. The way she was gawking at everyone told me they all looked incredible. "How often do you have exhibitions?"

"They are rarely done at this magnitude. This is only because we have guests. But normally about every six weeks." He flashed a smile. "We've always kept to ourselves, so it gives our people something to look forward to."

"That's really nice."

Sloan placed her hand on my shoulder, leaning close. "What do you see?"

"Honestly, I'd rather stick with your version of things tonight."

She gave me a pointed look, pursing her lips.

"Come on, indulge me," I urged.

"Well, I do see all the spiders and their webs. Everything, I believe, is spun by them," she started, and I breathed a sigh of relief. At least some of what we were seeing matched up.

"What is everyone wearing?"

"Rue is in a tapered black suit, mesh peeking from under his jacket. Ever has a pair of charcoal trousers, a white button up, and sequined suspenders." Then she pointed over at Volett, who was mingling with a few other weavers, combing through the braids of her hair mindlessly with her fingers. "She's wearing a silver chiffon number that has beading and is hanging at all different lengths around the skirt."

"Sounds fabulous."

"Oh, it is," Sloan said, like a giddy schoolgirl. "I wish you could see it."

"So do I." All I could see was everyone in their sheeted garb—the only thing differentiating their looks really being how they wore them and the various talismans dangling around their necks, ranging from deep jewel-toned gems to gears and clocks to some with shards of rocks and sea glass. Each weavers' seemed unique to them and maybe their magic as well.

I walked over to Ever and Rue, who were chatting a few feet away from us, seeming to give us some privacy, though I'm sure the spiders hovering around us were reporting everything we said anyway. "Could I ask about your talismans?"

"What would you like to know?" asked Rue.

"When do you get them? How do they work exactly?"

Ever lifted a hand to Rue, giving me a curt smile. "When we come of magic age, we are gifted our talisman by the Octux who oversees our gift's branch."

"So the Octux who is a dream weaver would give a talisman meant for dream weaving to someone with that ability?"

"Yes." They nodded. "It's important we have them, especially before dealing with outsiders. They don't grow up with the intention we do, leaving their minds needlessly unguarded.

Until we have control of our powers, it can be especially dangerous to anyone we come in contact with."

Like what was happening with my dad.

"When we complete our training here with our Octux, we are sent out into Celaria to test our abilities and our control, usually with a mentor to oversee. We don't leave here otherwise. Haven't in centuries."

That answered my question about why I'd seen weavers at The Lavender. They must have been in town to complete their training.

A harp's chord rang out from one of the coves I couldn't see from my vantage point.

Ever held out an arm. "May I escort you in to join the clutter?"

"Of course," I said, smiling, craning my neck to spot Sloan on Rue's arm. Volett filed in behind them, twirling around as she did, arms held wide, six or so spiders flying into the trellis above. I still couldn't decide if the creatures' relationships with the weavers had me struck in awe or horror.

We moved farther into the Cortex, filtering into a circular room, the trellis overhead expanding out to span its diameter. Gathering around the large round table, I moved with Ever toward the front of the clutter of weavers, Rue, Volett, and Sloan catching up to us a moment later. Draped in hooded cloaks, the same silk material as their weaver brethren, the Octux took their place at the eight chairs surrounding the table.

The Octux in front of us removed their hood, exposing a shock of silver hair and an iridescent woven circlet. I couldn't see their face, but their voice carried a deep commanding tone that seemed to grab everyone's collective attention. "Please help us welcome our guests for tonight's exhibition."

The remaining seven Octux members removed their hoods in unison, all of them wearing matching circlets atop their heads. Placing their hands toward the center of the table, they remained still, and I rose up onto my toes to try to see what was happening. Dropping from the ceiling, each aranea landed centered on the circlets where they nestled into place, beady crystalline eyes looking out among the clutter surrounding them.

"Tonight, we've gathered to feast, drink, and dance together," an Octux with black braids cascading down her back said, her melodic voice trilling through the space.

"It is not often we are fortunate enough to have guests grace our hallowed grounds."

"And we are oh so honored you've come."

I wasn't quite sure who'd been the last few to speak because I couldn't see everyone around the table.

"Does that mean you have an answer, if you already know why we are here?" Sloan piped in over the crowd. The clutter of weavers around us began murmuring to themselves, and humming echoed from above, making me think even the spiders had decided to gossip at my companion's forthright question.

"We appreciate openness in Alucinor, so thank you for your candor, Commander Sloan," an Octux with thin ribbons of black tied into her silver strands said, holding her hands up to the room until the crowd hushed. "But such things cannot be decided until we've feasted."

The Octux who'd first spoken nodded in agreement. "Yes, we shall get our fill first, then discuss that which you seek."

The eight leaders sat down, turning their heads, looking at us expectantly.

"Where are the plates?" I whispered to Ever. "Bowls? Cutlery?"

I locked eyes with Sloan, who looked equally confused, hand poised near where her knife was hidden beneath the layers of her skirt.

"I see neither of you have learned of our ways," huffed a bald Octux, the only thing on his head the circlet and aranea glaring at me.

"Disappointing, especially for you, weavling." The black-ribboned Octux's lips pinched into a frown. She cocked her head to the side, inspecting me. "Tied to us by blood, yet you know so little of who you truly are."

"As if she's ashamed of her own lineage."

I had no clue who said it from the Octux, but the words pierced through me like lancing an already open wound. It wasn't my fault I didn't know about my lineage. That'd been withheld from me.

I was fucking trying, dammit.

My chest warmed, fingers igniting a moment before I could stop them, sending a collective gasp around the weavers. Even the aranea recoiled at the sight of my power.

Taking a deep breath, I extinguished the flares.

"I'm not ashamed. I was never taught," I said, scanning the room, sincerity laced through my words. "But I do wish to learn."

It was true. I needed to, not only for myself, but out of necessity for my dad.

"How can you learn when your people have only ever given us judgment? Fear. Disgust," she sneered.

"There are reasons why the Octux has forbidden our people from leaving without approval," Ever whispered in my ear. "Only to feast safely and when necessary."

The words didn't sound predatory, despite the meaning coming across.

"Feast?" My eyes went wide, trying to understand what was happening. "Like tonight's feast?"

What was I missing?

"Tonight, we will get our fill," said a lanky Octux with a crudely cut amethyst set into his talisman. He licked his lips in a way that intrigued and terrified me. What kind of mind magic did he wield?

"We will see if you are truly honorable," the angry Octux with black bows interjected, pulling my attention back to her.

"Truly worthy."

"Despite your inadequacies."

They were all talking too quickly, one after another, and I couldn't keep track of which one was speaking. It was almost like they were completing each other's thoughts, connected by something, possibly through the aranea perched atop their crowns.

"Our weavers have already sampled your friend. But we, the Octux, are more interested in you."

"In me?" I asked, taking a step back and bumping right into Rue, who was standing behind me. "Why's that?"

Ever crooked a finger, beckoning me forward. "Because, my dear weavling, we've never met one of us that's experienced a life outside Alucinor."

"But aren't your powers unable to work on me?" I asked, looking toward the Octux before returning my gaze to Ever and moving closer.

"Weavers cannot use their powers easily with each other," called out the lanky Octux. "It is a gift to be given among our people."

"They wish for you to gift us your mind to feast on willingly," Volett whispered from over Sloan's shoulder. The knight stiffened, and my eyes dropped to the knife poised in the palm of her hand.

"It is the only way they can see inside and fully understand your intentions," Rue added.

Ever slipped a fingertip under my chin, pulling my attention back to their lilac irises. "No harm will come to you. Weavers never spin lies."

It was as if they were reading my mind without being able to. As odd as the exchange was, as much as fear wanted to lay its claim, I was strangely calm.

I believed them.

And could I truly blame the weavers for wanting to understand? For wanting the truth? Hadn't that been what I'd sought since my mother had left a decade ago?

We wouldn't be able to get an alliance with Alucinor any other way, and an alliance forged in truths would always be stronger than one sealed in lies.

"Ah," the white-haired Octux said, grinning along with the rest of the leaders. "Your presence blesses us once again."

"What are you talking about?" Sloan asked from behind me, her blade-free hand clutching my wrist protectively.

Their eyes all went to me, speaking in unison. "They've come for you."

Who?

Sloan pulled me by the wrist to get behind her. No one moved. They simply stood there, eerily twisting their heads to stare at the room's entrance.

My eyes shifted to Rue in question.

"We shall wait for the rest of the guests to arrive," was all he said.

"Mmm, they are both quite a treat from what our aranea and their spiderlings have foretold." The Octux sighed, twirling a black ribbon between her fingers.

"You're not going to allow them to feast on your mind, right?" Sloan whispered, still shielding me with her body.

"It doesn't seem like we will get an alliance with them or help for my father otherwise." I patted her hand clasped around me. "They just want the truth."

I couldn't fault them for that.

What I wouldn't give to be able to do this to my mother. My dad. To know if there were any other deceptions hidden from me.

"Besides, you're forgetting that I can protect myself. And you." I stepped out from behind her, moving toward the front.

Sloan followed me until we were standing side by side, Rue, Ever, and Volett awaiting the visitors right behind us. "These people aren't a threat to us. And even if they were, I'm a greater one."

There would be no more cowering.

Anyone who came for me would regret being on the opposing end of my wrath.

As the weavers clustered near the room's entryway, a familiar face poked out from above the crowd.

"Ox," I said to Sloan, whose grip around the hilt of her dagger tightened. But before she could respond to me, a smoky timbre cleared the murmurs around us.

"We've come to join the exhibition," King Redmond said, stoic and full of his usual regal nonchalance. He stared at the Octux's members, wings splayed wide. "We've come to partake in the feast."

CHAPTER 38

Redmond

"I apologize that we are late, but we had business to attend to in Tesceillus." I walked straight into them, willing back any apprehension about the fact that I'd never been within Alucinor's territory before and had only a base-level understanding of their culture and its practices. We had already lost out on securing one alliance. I refused to stand by and have that happen again.

I peered up at the trellis full of shimmering spider silk, their creators bobbing along them as they continued to work and watch us all inquisitively. Everyone else in the room had two fingers pointed at their temple, a salute honoring their mind magic, but their eyes were wide in fear.

Not that I could blame them.

They'd seen Arafax after The Blaze. *My* blaze. But I wasn't there to harm them, so I bowed my head in submission, making sure to lower my wings. "I wanted to ensure we didn't miss the grand event after our associates arrived before us."

The crowd's communal gaze shifted, unease settling in at my words.

My eyes darted to the farthest wall, drawn to the coral-streaked strands that stood out among everyone else's black, white, gray, and silver. *Kyleigh.* Her head and chest were held high, outlined in gossamer white that slithered down past where I could see. The shoulder not blocked by the Octux standing in front of her was covered in rosy metallic scales. All she needed was a matching crown and she'd look the part of Arafax's Princess.

Blue flared behind my eyes, burning through them, my phoenix's magic clawing to the surface protectively. Her brows shot up quickly before she trained them back down.

An icy glare snared my attention, and Sloan stepped in front of her, looking pissed, though I wasn't sure if it was aimed at me or at the situation.

"Very well," the Octux said, eyes narrowing before they drew up to my traveling companion. "Welcome to you and Sir...Ox."

"We were just about to begin our feast, if you would like to join us," another Octux with long white braids crooned, tone dripping with honey.

"Of course we would." I smiled and took a few more steps toward the table, Sir Fergus following close behind me. I turned to look up at him with a shrug. "It would be rude not to."

The bald Octux catty-corner to us shook his head at the ceiling, the only thing on his scalp the circlet with a large spider poised atop it. "We appreciate you honoring our traditions, even if we do not appreciate your presence here."

I followed his focus, finding thousands of tiny spiders paused from their work, watching from the layered webs above. Their eyes glinted like diamonds in the light. Some seemed to be hissing at me. *Oh well.* I wouldn't appreciate me either—I could easily burn their beautiful handiwork to ash with just a flick of my palm.

Kyleigh could too, of course, but they didn't seem apprehensive or unappreciative about her *presence* at all. Granted, only one of us had actually done it to another territory, and that kind of thing didn't earn you much adoration.

Not that I gave a damn about having theirs.

"I understand. Forgive me for forgetting your people's aversion to fire," I said, lifting a hand. A few Octux recoiled, along with the weavers standing behind them.

"Yes. And a greater aversion to tyrants. Like you," he sneered, "and your father."

As much as I wanted to tell them how wrong they were, the reality was I'd allowed that perception to fester the last decade. None of my actions had been fair, just, or good. As far as the realm was concerned, I was their villain.

Maybe I always would be.

And I could live with that, if we were rid of the one who was much more formidable.

"Does it help if I promise not to ignite unless provoked?"

I tucked my wings tight behind my back, finally feeling dry after being dropped off at the ocean's edge by Opal and Aurelia. My temple throbbed from being prodded by the cluster of weavers around us, as if testing my mind, searching for something. A moment later the Octux in front of Sloan and Kyleigh nodded to his brethren, all of them seemingly taking a collective exhale.

"Bring the weavling to the center," he said, waving Kyleigh forward, pointing to the table in front of him. He, along with a raven-haired Octux next to him extended their hands and helped her to step onto the round glass table. "Do not be afraid, young one. Our aranea will prepare you."

The Octux all lifted their arms out to the side, then directed Kyleigh to do the same. The cluster of large crystalline spiders flurried onto the table, spinning in quick circles as they climbed over each other's bulbous backs. Then they were floating, building a helix around Kyleigh, reaching toward the trellis above.

The weavers around us clapped at the display.

Once the aranea neared the latticed stretch of ceiling, they split off into the depths of the patterns before spiraling down toward their respective Octux. All the while, Kyleigh stood preternaturally still, as if holding her breath.

Scalding pressure flooded my veins. I willed my phoenix away, its instincts becoming more pronounced, more demanding over the months since the gem's return.

The last thing I needed to do was accidentally decimate another population in Celaria.

"Do you serve your mind to us willingly, weavling?" they asked in unison.

An eerie chill spread through my wings. I glanced over, spotting a few iridescent spiders crawling between my feathers. I tried to ignore the sinking feeling in my gut as they crept along the structure of them, not wanting to offend these people and their beloved familiars of sorts.

They all stared up at Kyleigh, a hungering awe glinting in their violet eyes. "This is a reminder that we do not wish to harm you, only to feast with our collective power."

Diving from above, more spiders dropped down, climbing onto the clutter of weavers. Kyleigh's throat bobbed, and she held her silvery gaze above us, like she was drowning out the scene around her.

Sloan moved to step in, but I blocked her with a wing. "Can you explain what you will be doing to her?" I asked, feigning minimal interest despite the heat that rose in my chest watching the arachnids peppering my view. Some hung midair, others climbed into the hair of weavers or crept into their ears. "As an outsider, I would feel more comfortable understanding, as would my associates."

"We will all look into her mind, reaching into it with each of our gifts," the Octux members said in unison, their haunting harmony echoing against the walls of the Cortex.

"She is one of us. We cannot hurt one of our own, nor is that our intention."

A few twisted their heads toward me, violet gazes narrowing. "We never seek to harm the world around us."

"I see," I said, ignoring their pointed remark, ruffling my feathers a bit to get some of the spiders to escape their shelter. "And this feeds your power?"

"Like all magic, there is a give and take. We can more easily take from outsiders such as yourself, Sir Ox, and Commander Sloan. For the most part, your minds are open to us. While it is harder to breach the mind of a weaver, it is another way to exercise and siphon our gifts. The most powerful one."

"We still have more to replenish," the silver-haired Octux said, glaring. "For years we were unable to commune with our aranea and their spiderlings."

So, the missing gem had affected them as well.

"You're correct, King Redmond. Without the gem, we've had to take more from each other, leaving us weaker as a collective."

"I'm ready," Kyleigh cut in, but her voice wavered a pinch.

The rise and fall of her chest increased its pace, and my jaw screwed in place, watching her trying to suppress her anxiety. Despite their assurance that they didn't want to bring any harm, I didn't like this idea. I could feel my chest warm, my wings aching to splay wide and fling the spiders off them, disintegrating anything, *everything* that touched them as they ignited.

It would be that easy. My phoenix was on board, scraping at my insides with encouragement.

But just then, the crinkles around Kyleigh's eyes morphed from fear to determination. Her chest lifted along with her chin, facing the crowd.

If I did something with my phoenix fire right now, I'd only further perpetuate the hate I'd earned from The Blaze and put my allies in danger. Maybe there was another way, though.

Something I could offer them to give them this alliance without them having to take as much from her. I didn't know why I even cared. Maybe it was my own guilt over the things I'd done, for locking her away in my dungeon. But I felt like *I* should be the one put on display, fed from to increase their power.

Not her.

"That is admirable, King Redmond," the lanky Octux member said, adjusting his circlet, reminding me they were already listening to my thoughts without me saying anything. The aranea situated on top of his circlet adjusted to his movements before settling back in place. "We shall only need to feast from the weavling, though. As we have already feasted on the Commander and you all when you came into our territory. Don't take this the wrong way, but none of you—save perhaps Sir Ox's carnal escapades, which I may ask to be served later for... educational purposes—interests the Octux comparably."

Pink stained the warrior's cheeks before he broke into a grin, obviously pleased with himself.

"Only some offense taken," I conceded with a shrug. "If the princess has volunteered willingly, then we will, respectfully, stay close by for her safety and our own assurances."

Blue and white flames rippled along my wings before I smothered them out, and Ox and Sloan moved into a protective stance. The crowd parted from us, a few hissing while others' eyes went wide. "Anything untoward I will see as an affront to an aligned ruler and shall be met with my ire. Are we clear?"

Just because I didn't think they would do anything didn't mean I wouldn't remind them that I'd easily do something.

"Hmm... Yes, it's all very clear," said the Octux with a shock of white atop their head, the corner of their lip running upward before turning their attention along with the rest of the members to Kyleigh. "Very clear indeed."

The Octux next to them giggled, giving eyes to a few weavers standing around the table. Folks among the crowd tittered nervously.

"What's so funny?" I asked, pulling my wings taught behind me, fists clenched at my sides.

"Nothing you'd comprehend at this point, bluebird," she cooed, collecting herself.

"What do I need to do?" Kyleigh asked.

I took a few steps forward, Sloan and Sir Fergus coming around the edge of the table with me, standing between the Octux members.

"Are you sure about this?" I reached a hand out in case she wanted to make a run for it.

"Get your hand away from me before I burn it off," she gritted out in annoyance. Sloan shook her head and chuckled. Kyleigh's eyes softened a bit, her defensiveness in the moment waning. "Yes, I'm sure."

She waved us off with her hand, and we all took a collective step back.

"You come here of your own choosing, weavling," the Octux said in unison, attention pinned to their prey centered within the Cortex.

Kyleigh kept her focus forward, past the throngs of weavers around her. "I do."

The Octux then spoke, each member seemingly finishing the others' sentences.

"Then we will each reach inside."

"Feasting from your truths."

"Only taking a morsel of your energy to do so."

"To begin, take this potion."

"Free your mind to us."

CHAPTER 39

Redmond

"I can't believe you two are standing by while they do this," Sloan grumbled at Sir Fergus and I, knife still clutched in her palm.

"She's killed dozens of men before without any assistance. I have no doubt if she feels threatened she'd give them a worse fate than I would. Besides, she has the three of us here on her side, or have you forgotten the power you wield in your fist, Commander?"

"I haven't forgotten," she muttered, her grip tightening around the amethyst handle. "I can't watch her sacrifice herself like this and do fuck all about it. Not again."

"Look at me." It took her a moment, as if she was debating if she wanted to follow the request. When she finally did, I placed a hand on her shoulder. "They have given their word she is safe."

"Maybe physically safe but I've seen what they can do. I've *felt* it." Her eyes shimmered, and she blinked quickly before turning her head back toward Kyleigh. "Pain free doesn't equal harmless."

"You're right," I whispered. "And you don't have to like it, but you have to respect that this is what she's willing to do."

Sloan released a frustrated sigh.

"Just like you have to respect what Aislin was willing to do," I added, our gazes colliding for a moment before both going back to watch Kyleigh sip the potion they'd given her. She grimaced, smacking her lips together a few times then took another, this time pinching her nose. My shoulders pulled tight, and Sir Fergus leaned forward, as if he were ready to charge through the Octux at a moment's notice if things went south.

"Yeah, well, she was willing to do it to save *her*," Sloan said, nodding up at Kyleigh. "Now we're offering her up on a silver platter, excuse my pun."

"Shh!" Sir Fergus's attention shot to us with a glare. "You're missing it."

Kyleigh was still standing, the arachnids weaving around her to seemingly hold her in place. Her arms were posed a few inches away from her sides, palms up, the tiny creatures running along them. I knew she was already under the potion's enchantment because there was no way she wouldn't be reacting to this otherwise. Her eyes were mostly closed, only tiny crescents of silver glowing beneath her lids.

Sloan leaned in front of me, snapping at Sir Fergus. "She's your princess. And you're telling me you're okay with this?"

"I'm not. But while you two are arguing over there, I'm keeping track of what they are actually doing to our"—he gave me a dismissive glance—"friend."

"Fine," Sloan muttered, turning her attention back to Kyleigh.

One of the Octux leaders, along with about twenty weavers in the crowd, all clutched their onyx talismans, violet gazes glazing over. On the woven pale tapestry that spanned the wall, images began to spill, a series of repeating visions: flying above Alucinor, diving toward the Spuma, a boat in the curved shape of a yellow fruit I'd once seen flying over the southern islands floating along. A strange sight. Then a kind-looking man with black hair handed a plate down to her, piled up with flattened bread with rainbow specks and strips of meat.

In a swirl, black-hooded figures surrounded her, raising thin blades into the air before stabbing them into her flesh, the dream turning quickly into a nightmare. The figures scooped the blood from her skin, rubbing it onto themselves in smears.

A sinking feeling seeped into the pit of my stomach.

"She has some horrible dreams," I whispered to the two warriors. Sloan used her knife to point out a handful of weavers throughout the room, including one of the Octux members wearing a gear-shaped talisman.

My throat dried.

"That's not a nightmare, Red. It's a memory."

The memory weavers were smiling as the hooded figures drifted away. Other images came into view: my guards, a blue dragon crumpled on the ground, an icy wall.

We snapped views, staring down the staircase at a few of my men. Crude words left their lips before a fiery burst filled the vision. Then it was just crimson coating the floor and walls of my dungeon, sliding down the stone in stringy clumps.

Sloan's throat bobbed, witnessing her men die.

Knowing what happened was one thing. Seeing it was another.

"Damn," Sir Fergus said, eyes glued to the memories playing before us. It felt too private, too personal, watching these things without her knowing, so I dropped my gaze to my feet.

"Just tell me what's happening and if I need to set fire to anyone," I whispered to Sloan.

"There's nothing on the screen now," she whispered back, and I drew up my eyes to find Kyleigh's body moving while she was still under the weaver's thrall. Her nose scrunched up a moment before she shivered, then stuck out her tongue, as if catching something with it. About forty weavers seemed to be feeding from whatever she was doing.

I knew there were weavers that could impact dimensions, senses, balance, and other physicalities we experienced. It was strange to watch them puppeting Kyleigh, but nothing looked dangerous and it seemed less traumatizing than the images—memories—we'd seen prior.

"*Carath's lumen esi amharc tar soiléiratus.*"

"What is she saying?" Sir Fergus asked.

"I can't translate it all...something about *light through clarity*." I stared out among the clutter, noticing the weavers with talismans that boasted symbols on them seeming to be in a meditative state, eyes shut, *feasting*. "Those must be lingual weavers. They can manipulate sound and language."

"Which ones are left that haven't...feasted?" Sloan asked, not taking her attention away from Kyleigh.

"So far, we've seen dream, memory, sensory, dimensional, and lingual." I tried to tick the boxes off in my head, recalling what I'd read about the weavers and their mind magics. "That leaves illusion, euphoric, and..." I couldn't put my finger on the last one.

Kyleigh's eyes were still only slightly open, and I wondered how much she would remember of this. I waffled between wanting to make sure we were watching everything to keep her safe and feeling discomfort at her unwitting vulnerability.

Color washed across the screen again, a quaint home with blue shutters. Trees I'd never seen before framed it, gold- and red-pointed leaves decorating their branches. There was a porch that circled the bottom of the house, white columns connecting it to the roof, and a matching chair with navy cushions.

Movement snagged my vision away from the screen, finding Kyleigh, eyes open, walking toward something. Her legs lifted up one at a time, like the strands of the web supporting her were puppeting her. It was as if she were climbing something, and I watched the screen as she ascended a pale-wood staircase.

A picture hung on the wall, and I instantly recognized Isla

dressed in strange attire: a casual shirt, blue *jeans*—as Sloan had explained to me—and the same sneakers I'd seen Kyleigh wear, crimson with white laces. She was bent low next to a little girl with gray eyes and strawberry-blonde ringlets. *A young Kyleigh.* Behind them, a man stood with his arms wrapped around them both. He had black hair and blue eyes, and I remembered him from the earlier vision during the dream weaver's feast. This was her family. Her home. The one in the Otherworld.

Suddenly, Isla began to disappear from the image, fading away until only Kyleigh and her father remained.

"Your mother's gone, Ky," the man said with a frown.

"Where is she, Daddy?"

"I'm not sure, princess."

"When is she coming back?"

"I don't know."

The memory weavers were feasting again, obviously pulling from this memory that had been illusioned for Kyleigh. When I brought my attention back to her, she was standing in a puffy chiffon dress, layers of tulle flaring onto the table, white lace-up shoes covering her feet.

Her chest was heaving, glowing.

"It was all lies!" she seethed, clawing at the dress. "I'm not your princess."

Sparks began to rain from her hands, a few coral scales rising up over where her skin showed. The weavers began to murmur fearfully, aside from about six who were uncomfortably relaxed.

"I think that's plenty of feasting." Sir Fergus climbed onto the table, making it wobble under his weight. He pushed through the webs looping around her, swatting away the spiders, then gripped Kyleigh in his arms, trying to wake her. A few stray sparks pierced his skin, and he hissed, but refused to let go. The nearby spiders flinched away from the ignited rosy specks.

"Red," Sloan gritted out, knuckles white around the knife. "Do something or I'll send this dagger flying."

I lifted an arm for her to hold on to.

"Here," I heaved out a sigh, waving him over. "She can't burn me."

He hesitated a moment, then gently shifted her into my arms, cursing as a few more fiery flecks hit him. Her eyes were glazed, still under the effect of whatever they'd given her.

"Adrenal weavers, please reel in your work, for all our sakes," demanded the silver-haired Octux with black ribbons strewn through it.

Kyleigh shook, cradled in my arms, her dress returning to the one she'd been wearing earlier when I'd arrived. Sloan grabbed her shoulders, tapping at them to see if anything would wake her. She glared at the Octux leaders, jaw pulled taut. "How long will this last?"

"Not much longer. Once we finish feasting and our powers are restored, she should wake," they all replied, still as creepy as the first time they spoke in unison. Despite the sparks floating off her, they seemed calm.

The flecks prickled, a few holes burning into my shirt, their heat tingling on my skin.

"What's left to feast on? Haven't you had enough?" Sir Fergus asked, protective rage simmering in his tone. I understood his alarm, but she'd chosen to do this.

I reminded myself of that fact a few more times as she shivered against me.

"There's only one group of us still waiting our turn," said the Octux with amethyst set into his talisman.

"Just get it over with," Sloan snapped.

Grinning at us, a few dozen other weavers chanted together. "With pleasure."

At first, nothing happened.

Then Kyleigh began to squirm in my hold, twisting like she couldn't get comfortable. A languid sigh escaped her lips, freckled cheeks becoming flush.

My shoulders stiffened as I tried to adjust my positioning to accommodate her discomfort.

The corner of her mouth pulled up, a small smile shining through.

She was happy.

I sighed with relief. This was much better than the fear bursting from her mere minutes ago. Her fingers dug into my chest, and my body went still.

Then her legs began to twist, so I leaned back, trying to keep her in my grasp. She turned a knee in, gliding it against the other leg, rubbing them together, nails scraping my skin.

I hissed in a breath. Sloan quickly drew closer, feeling Kyleigh's forehead, which had begun to draw beads of sweat as her chest rose and fell with increased vigor. I couldn't seem to find a way to get her to relax. "Have the adrenal weavers stopped? She's feverish."

"She seems more than okay to me," Sloan murmured, her eyes shifted to the wall.

I traced her gaze.

"What—"

A head of dark-brown waves atop a bronzed forehead lifted up, revealing bright hazel eyes with golden flecks staring up at us from the silken screen. His tongue licked straight up—

Stars above.

Kyleigh continued to grip my chest, Dru's mirage eating her like it was the best meal he'd ever had.

I gulped audibly, moving quickly to politely lay her back on the table so she wasn't writhing against me. Her chest glowed, arching up from its surface, a few more sparks releasing from her fingertips. I grimaced, instinctively stepping closer so she didn't ignite the Cortex and destroy our chance at an alliance, despite not wanting to touch her in this state.

"Are you almost done?" I croaked out, unable to stop watching. Knowing it was wrong.

Kyleigh moaned, her hands grasping for purchase, legs tangling themselves up as the layers of her skirt lifted higher up her thighs. My eyes flared, heat surging through them a moment before clearing away.

A massive body moved in front of everyone, pushing me aside. Sir Fergus removed his jacket and laid it over her bared legs. His face was a deep shade of red. "I think you've all fed enough."

"Very well," said the Octux leader. The group of euphoric weavers opened their eyes, all glowing brighter than before. Those around the room were all lit as well, the aranea and their spiderlings filled to the brim with power, the trellis illuminated above. "We just didn't want to leave her wanting."

"That's very...considerate of you," I said, clearing my throat and stamping down my body's reflexes.

Kyleigh's eyes fluttered open, her chest and cheeks still pink. Pushing to sit up on the table, she crossed her legs, looking at the jacket thrown over her. Her face lost all its color, but before she could slither away mortified, which was the impression I got of what she wanted to do, the Octux spoke over the crowd.

"Thank you, weavling, for that delectable feast. Now, please enjoy the rest of your evening—food, drinks, and dancing—while we deliberate your request. The Octux must come to a unanimous decision."

Sir Fergus helped her slowly off the glass table. Kyleigh's eyes dropped to the ground. "What happened?"

We said nothing, the awkwardness of the weavers' feast settling thickly in the air.

"Do you remember anything that you saw?" Sloan asked, slicing through the silence.

Kyleigh gulped, eyes darting between us. "I don't."

"Nothing worth noting," I said, gesturing with my hand for all of us to leave and head out to the long entryway, giving the Octux privacy to deliberate.

Sloan and Sir Fergus's eyes bolted to me. The giant patted Kyleigh on the back before setting his jacket over her shoulders. It swallowed her up, hanging to below her knees.

A weaver wearing a prismatic talisman, a set of shimmering trousers, and matching suspenders with a mesh shirt beneath it, joined us. "The name's Ever, Your Majesty. Why don't we go enjoy the evening?"

"Sounds good. Lead the way." I stepped back for Sir Fergus to walk with Kyleigh, his arm around her as he rubbed her shoulder. She rested her head on his chest, looking sapped.

The feast had clearly taken a lot out of her.

As we walked into the festivities taking place in the Cortex's Great Hall, I silently vowed to never mention what I saw.

CHAPTER 40
Kyleigh

"I didn't do anything too embarrassing, did I?" I asked the others as we headed to a small cove off the main stretch of the Cortex. An aranea spun within its shadow box, a series of flame-like layers licking up the translucent enclosure.

"Not at all," King Redmond said, Sloan and Ox quickly nodding in agreement.

Too quickly.

I was pretty sure they were lying to me, but I didn't want to learn the details of what they had glimpsed. Some things were better left unknown.

My head pounded and my body ached like it had been hit by a truck. Everything was sore, an unfamiliar tingle paired with it.

"Are you okay?" Sloan asked, bracing me as I gripped the side of the lounge chair to sit down.

"Yeah. That just took a lot out of me." I inhaled deeply, leaning into the cushion.

Ox stood in front of us, brown eyes glinting with purpose. "Can I get you anything?"

"Here," Rue said, walking over with a small vial of lilac

liquid. "This should help. It's what we use when we feast on each other."

Ox sat back down, looking perplexed. "You feast on each other?"

"All the time," Ever drawled, sticking their hands into their white woven trousers that had apparently been illusioned to look like sequined ones with matching suspenders. They waved a hand over at Volett in the cove across from us. Her hand gripped the talisman of the weaver across from her, and he had a hand over her ruby one. The pairs' eyes were closed, as if no one else was around.

I popped off the cap to the vial, swirling the purple elixir a few times before drinking it down in one quick gulp. It was syrupy, coating the back of my throat. I swallowed a few extra times, trying to get it down. "What are they doing?"

"Continuing their feast, privately." Ever raised a brow suggestively.

A shiver ran through me, feeling like I was intruding on something too intimate to witness.

"Our people aren't as drawn to the physical carnalities like other Celarians." Their eyes ran over our group. "The mind is the epicenter of pleasure, after all."

Volett's chest rose and fell in quick succession, her body flushing with heat. Turning my attention away from the pair, I squirmed in my seat, trying to quell the desire that seemed to drift through me without a source.

King Redmond cleared his throat. "Well, that's certainly an enlightened perspective."

"Yep," Ox croaked out.

Sloan just stared off in the distance, distracted.

"You okay?" I asked. My energy slowly restoring, I noticed Mox at her feet, looking up at her with sad eyes, like a wayward golden retriever.

"No. I'm not." She leaned forward, stroking his fur a few times before nuzzling her cheek between his perked ears.

"I think I need some fresh air. Escort me?" Instead of responding, she simply stood, blinking away whatever thoughts swathed her mind. Ox moved to follow, but I held up a hand. "Can you stay here in case they come back with a verdict about the alliance?"

"Of course." He bowed his head, then sat at the opposite side of the cove, giving Inverno's King a wide berth.

"I wonder what's up with them?"

Sloan sighed, still petting Mox at her side. "Maybe their trip to see King Morrow didn't go as planned?"

"Oh shit." I hadn't even asked how it'd gone—not that we'd had time to talk since their arrival.

We passed along the stretch of coves, and I watched the various aranea weave their delicate artistry. One had spun a series of blooms, filling the expanse of its enclosure. On the opposite wall was an aranea building a gothic ivory tower, vines creeping along its perimeter. It reminded me of something I'd seen before, but I couldn't put my finger on where.

Finally, we passed the last nook, and my head snapped to the image woven into its display. A pair of breasts pointed to the sky, legs parted, the top of a wavy head of hair peeking between them. Heat swept through my cheeks, and Sloan looped her arm through mine, steering me toward the door. "Here, this is a great spot."

"But—" I said, eyes drifting back.

Sloan shook her head quickly, and my words died on my tongue.

"So, what had you wanting to get out of there so quickly?"

"You seemed distracted. Just figured maybe you needed to talk about it."

Mox came to my side, nuzzling into my palm.

Sloan stared up at the rich plum sky dotted with glittering stars that were partially obscured by the iridescent web above us. "I know I shouldn't be watching Aislin anymore. The things have been... hard to witness. But having Mox here, having my link to her cut... I'm suffocating. And I'm supposed to somehow just soldier on?"

"We're going to get her back, Sloan." I knelt next to Mox, looking up at her. He padded closer to his master, nudging her side. "Dru will find a way to save the wisps and take down the Enchantress. Have faith in him. In all of us."

"It's easy to tell someone to have faith when it's not yours being shaken."

"That's true," I agreed, knowing I would be a wreck if the situation were reversed—if Dru had been taken from me just as our story was beginning. "But *someone* once told me you can't fix what you refuse to face."

She shook her head. "Red can't take credit for that."

"Exactly. I'd never believe that moody asshole would think of it on his own," I replied with a smirk.

We both laughed, lifting the heaviness between us a bit. "We will figure this out, Sloan. No matter what happens with the other territories, when we get back to Arafax we will be going after the Enchantress."

A knock behind my head startled me. Rue poked his head out, Ever standing quietly behind him. "The Octux is almost done deliberating, but the dancing has started and you won't want to miss it."

I groaned.

"Come on." Sloan gripped my hand, giving it a squeeze. "You wouldn't leave me without a dance partner, would you?"

"You may regret this," I muttered.

"Probably, but if you're truly as terrible as you think you are, it'll at least give me a good laugh."

"Fine." I walked with her back into the Cortex, weavers cluttered within the main drag of the structure dancing in a variety of manners.

Some moved elegantly, waltzing along side to side or swaying in small groups around the room. Others were jumping around, knocking into each other. Then there were those swiveling their hips, dipping low suggestively.

I swept over the crowd, looking for Ox since he would be the easiest to find.

King Redmond's splayed onyx wings pulled my attention first. He was glued against the wall, arms crossed, seemingly glaring holes into the massive throng of weavers in the center.

The crowd continued to part as we moved forward, a cluster of weavers all dancing around one spot on the floor, the same spot the phoenix king had his eyes pinned.

Ox's head popped out among the throng, a smile spread wide across his bearded jaw, and he cheered loudly. I had no idea what he was dancing to, but as we got closer, we could see him grinding, breaking it down, then moving from above the crowd to dipping low to the ground, having the time of his life.

Not that I'd expect anything less from Ox.

"Do you hear any music?" I whispered to Sloan, still confused by the fact that everyone seemed to be moving at different speeds. Her head was gently bopping to a slower beat than whatever Ox was moving to.

"Yeah, one of my favorites," she said. "I'm sure you probably haven't heard much of our music since you've been in Celaria, but this is an old Invernish folk song."

"I don't hear anything," I said, observing everyone else enjoying themselves. "But I wish I did. I seem to be missing out."

"You're not," a rich voice drawled from behind me. I whipped around to find King Redmond looking bored as he stared out at the celebration.

"What do you hear?" Sloan asked the arrogant ruler she once served. Or currently served. The lines were all still a bit blurry.

"Doesn't matter," the King replied, running a hand through his hair, mussing it up with his brows knit. Pissed.

"I still don't hear anything," I said, looking back at Rue and Ever with a shrug.

"Our sensory weavers," Ever explained, pointing to the weavers who were wearing various yellow gems on the chains around their necks. "The music adapts to the listener. We've found this way helps keep everyone happy."

"Doesn't seem like everyone's happy," I replied, pointing at King Redmond who looked physically pained.

Meanwhile, Ox was on the dance floor, rolling his shoulders and hips with weavers crowded around him, feeding off his enthusiasm.

He was having a blast.

"I was promised a dance," Sloan said, extending her hand.

"Well, I hope you're not expecting any of that," I said, laughing at Ox, who was still grooving to his own beat. I wished I could hear it for myself. Other than what played within The Lavender, I didn't know much about Celarian music.

Ox looped his elbow with ours and began twirling us in a circle, threading between the weavers.

One moment Sloan was beaming, the next, she was leaving us behind, heading over to check on King Redmond. Every line in his angular face was pulled taut.

"What's got him in knots?" I asked Ox, pointing to the feathered wings peeking above the crowd.

"Well, we didn't get the alliance with the merpeople, for one thing."

Shit. Dru had mentioned how helpful that would have been, especially since they held such a large swell of territory. "Is there something else?"

He brought me toward him, humming, his feet moving some strange pattern that had me stumbling. Some sort of waltz, maybe? I stepped on his big boots a few times, but he didn't react.

"Well, yeah. There is actually something I need to talk to you about."

His words had me stunned at how serious he was, considering we'd just been galloping around the room. "Okay?"

"It's not all bad..." he began, the hand wrapped around my palm tensing as he spoke.

I halted in place, waiting.

"Okay. Here it goes," he said. I crossed my arms, my patience threshold for not overreacting wearing thin with each moment that passed. "Neve made me her champion."

"What?" My eyes grew wide, something clenching like a fist deep in my chest. I cleared my throat, attempting to blot away my confusion. "Congrats to you both!"

His lips peeled up into a huge smile, the cheeks of his ruddy complexion pulling in shades of pink.

I cocked my head at him. "How is that bad news? Other than King Redmond wanting to skin your balls."

"Yes. He didn't take the news...well, he didn't take the news as bad as he could have, to be fair."

"That's an understatement." Considering King Redmond had burned down most of Arafax over his believed loss of Neve, finding out she had moved on in such a bold way could have easily had him reacting terribly. But Ox was standing here in front of me in one piece. So it seemed like, aside from souring the King's mood, it wasn't that bad of a thing.

"Well, I'm thrilled for you. Both of you," I said, getting up on my tiptoes to give him a peck on his jaw because I couldn't reach his cheek.

"That's not all," he said sullenly, making me stumble a bit. He took a deep breath. "I'm pretty sure we broke the Evergleam."

"Pretty sure?" My face heated, mind wandering back to that

night with Dru when everything that should have gone so perfectly, so right...hadn't.

"How did you break it? Did you know when we brought it up at the meeting?"

"We didn't know when we bonded. Everything went...as it should. I still don't quite know how we broke it, exactly." He gave me a sheepish smile, one laced with apologies.

"Well, isn't that nice," I spat out before trying to swallow back my frustration. I took another step away from him before he could try to charm me. "Why didn't you say anything when we brought it up? Or even afterward if you didn't know what to say in the meeting with everyone there? I get not wanting to tell King Crankypants, but me? Dru? You didn't even give us a clue as to why the tree was broken. Sloan still thinks she and Aislin were the ones to mess it up. That's fucked up, Ox. I expected more from our friendship. From you."

He stood there, mouth half parted in stunned silence.

"I don't want to overreact." I kept my eyes on the skirt of my dress as I brushed it down. "So I'm just going to ask you to walk away now."

"Ky—"

"Go." Not waiting to see if he'd obeyed, I continued moving toward the central room of the Cortex. The Octux had plenty of time to deliberate, and the sooner I had an answer, the sooner I could get back to Dru and taking on the Enchantress.

The crowds of weavers scurried out of my way, and the spiders that hung from the trellis quickly ascended back up to their self-spun perch.

As soon as I stepped into the circular room, I expected to see looks of shock or anger that I'd barged in on their deliberations. Instead, I found them all turned to face me. Calm, like they knew I was coming.

"You can't read my mind," I stated, keeping my chin lifted.

"We didn't need to," the Octux replied in unison.

The member with long raven locks nodded behind me. "We could read theirs."

The walkway toward the circular room was cleared of all weavers and their spider friends, the only ones on the carpet Ox, Sloan, and King Redmond.

"Oh."

"Decided to get started without us?" the King asked, tone back to its annoyingly smooth drawl that made my skin crawl. Like I hadn't just watched him pout like a rejected teenager at a middle school formal while everyone else was dancing and enjoying themselves.

"Of course not," the Octux with silver scraggly hair intoned, surveying us all, eyes landing on Ox. "She was feeling...*motivated* to return to Arafax."

"Just in time, I might add," said the Octux with black ribbons through her silver strands.

"We've arrived at our answer."

"We will support your cause, if the time shall come, but we want something in return."

"Of course," said King Redmond. "What do you wish?"

Their necks all jerked to face me, speaking as one collective. "When the weavling takes the throne, she shall allow our people out among the rest of Celaria."

The bald Octux spoke next, the others nodding along with him. "We've been hidden away on this peninsula for centuries, people fearing us, filled with unnecessary hate. It has been harder and harder for our kind to survive without being able to safely feast, and it takes more from us to use our magics on each other, as you now know."

A shiver ran up my spine at the lost time when they'd feasted on my mind, still uncertain what they'd seen.

"I accept your terms," I said, giving a bow of my head, not even looking back at the others. "Now, if that is all, we will return to our guest quarters for the evening and be on our way at first light."

I didn't know if I would ever want to take the throne, but the weavers didn't need to know that. But they probably already did if they'd fished around as much as it seemed like they had during their feast.

"Of course, Your Highness," they replied.

And with that, I turned and walked down the carpet, taking Ever's arm as we led the others out of Alucinor's Cortex, another ally secured. They stopped abruptly, gripping my arm to halt me as well. A small spider hung low in front of us, blocking our exit. The weaver lifted their free hand to let the creature scurry up to their ear.

"I would be honored," was all I could hear them reply, then the spider retracted its thread and ascended to the trellis above.

Turning to face me, Ever swept a few strands of black hair behind their ear before speaking. "The Octux has requested I accompany you back to Arafax. I will be the one to train your weavers."

Hope bloomed in my belly. Not only had I secured us an alliance, I had managed to get help for my dad and Jet. Maybe we stood a chance against the Enchantress after all.

CHAPTER 41
Kyleigh

When Ever and Rue dropped us back at our guest quarters, we all sat there, silence gnawing between us.

Tiny spiders scurried along the outside of the space, an eerie moving backdrop. Swallowing down my unease, I took a few deep breaths, trying to get used to the creatures' presence. Once upon a time I would have simply said *burn it down* and run out of the place screaming.

King Redmond perched himself atop a glass stool in the corner, leaning back against the wall. His jaw clenched, one hand clasping the other in a white-knuckled grip.

Ox and Neve had merged their magics, their very beings together, and while I didn't get the sense the King expected to reconcile with Neve, they'd been in love. He'd set off The Blaze over the loss of her. Let Arafax burn.

Ox had taken up the couch, shifting on his heels, his hands clasped like the King sulking in the corner. Hunched over his knees, his eyes darted back and forth, face downcast, as if sifting through what to say next.

Meanwhile, Sloan had laid on the cot, not even bothering to take off her shoes. I sat at the edge of the paper-thin mattress, pulling off my heels and tossing them onto the floor. I grimaced, remembering it was glass. While the others couldn't see it, they still heard the abrasive sound of my thin stilettos *clinking* across the delicate ground.

King Redmond's eyes dashed to the spot where they'd hit, brows furrowed. "You don't see what we see, do you?"

"No. She doesn't," Sloan replied. I nodded in agreement. "Apparently being half weaver means their magic doesn't work on her like it does on us. She can see through all the illusions. But don't ask her what she sees—you don't want to know."

"You really don't." Luckily, since the rain had stopped, the worms had stopped wrestling in and out of the earth beneath us.

"I don't understand." Sloan's eyes shot across to Ox, her steely tone commanding everyone's attention when she spoke. "I didn't even know you two were together."

Apparently he or King Redmond must have spilled the beans to her on our walk back.

The giant merely shrugged. "Well, you've been a tad preoccupied. And we didn't want to make a big deal about it."

"Not a big deal?" My face and chest heated, the pale skin showing through the uncovered part between my breasts shifting into a deep crimson. I crossed my arms over myself, self-conscious now that the revelry of the night had subsided and things had become so sullen. I felt bared in more ways than one, still unsure what'd been disclosed during the weavers' feast.

The words were out of my mouth before my head could catch up. "You've been sleeping together."

Oops.

"You're tied to each other for eternity," Sloan added in a hushed gravelly tone, conveying nothing but her devotion toward being championed to one of Arafax's Revered.

My heart ached for her.

For them both.

Didn't Ox understand how sacred a bond like that was?

"Were you *together* just the once?" Sloan asked him, her head cocked.

Ox lifted a giant palm to his chest as he sat up. "Now that's insulting." He cleared his throat, arching a brow at me. "There's no such thing as *just the once* when it comes to my lovemaking, thank you very much."

"Thank *you* for the clarification we didn't need." King Redmond's wings flared, making my eyes go wide. He took a deep breath, the muscles along his chest tightening as he pinched the bridge of his nose.

Shaking his feathers out, they returned to their usual onyx. My eyes stung from the heat, and there were a few brown streaks where the feathers had touched the glass. Rubbing my dragon orbs of their momentary shift, I blinked a few times, turning my attention back to Ox.

"I have heard many of the tales of Ox's midnight snacks," I agreed. A deep and annoyed groan came from the corner. Ignoring its originator, I smirked.

Sloan released a sigh before standing and making her way over to our packs, rifling through them. She pulled out a pair of maroon sleep shorts and a matching long-sleeved shirt before throwing them to me. Turning to Ox and King Redmond, she waved her hand for them to look away. "When did this start up, Ox?"

Keeping his face trained to the floor while we changed into our pajamas, his fingers fumbled over each other. "Erm...we started spending time together when we were both going to the healers."

I nearly fell over trying to shimmy out of my dress after Sloan had unzipped it. When the men in the room flinched, I brought my hands across my body quickly, taking a few moments before I continued to change my clothes.

"Are you in love?" Sloan asked, now changed into her gray

pajamas. She plopped back onto the cot, rolling onto her side and propping herself up on her pillow.

"Maybe he'll actually give an answer this time," King Redmond grumbled, as if to himself.

I finished pulling my sleep shirt over my head and climbed onto the cot, sitting upright with my back resting on the glass. A few spiders crept along the edge behind my head, and I shivered, startling the rest of the group. Their eyes snapped to mine, but I just shrugged, not wanting to share my burden of true sight with them.

"Well, are you?" I asked, curious of the answer myself. I still couldn't believe they'd done this all behind our backs.

Ox looked like the air had been sucked from his lungs. His gaze shifted around to each of us. "That's personal."

"Seriously? You made it personal when you lied to our faces."

My face heated and my palms became clammy, so I clenched them tight, ignoring the sting of my nails digging into skin.

"I never lied. I wanted to tell you all, but Neve..." Ox scraped his hand across his cheek. When he moved it out of the way, the skin was raw beneath his auburn stubble, like he'd been rubbing it to the point of irritation. "She asked that we not."

"Why?" Sloan rolled to face the ceiling, brows scrunched together. "I don't understand. You let me think that Aislin and I broke the Evergleam. That it was from when our bond was severed." Her face pivoted back to him. "How could you?"

Ox paled, his gaze dropping between his boots. "I'm sorry."

Combing my fingers through my coral hair, I untangled the braids that Sloan had plaited earlier. "I'm not surprised Neve kept a secret like this to herself. She's been through a lot." Tears threatened the backs of my eyes, and I blinked rapidly, willing the pressure away. "But you? You've never been dishonest with me."

I wouldn't cry. I refused. It wasn't Ox's fault that everyone had lied to me—or at least what felt like everyone. The list of people who'd been honest since I'd known them was quickly dwindling. Hell, even Dru had secrets when we first met. Luckily, since we'd come through the portal, everything with him had been the truth.

Sloan craned her neck toward me. "Well, Ox here was planning to kill Aislin on orders from the Queen. Pretty sure he's kept secrets."

"What?" Taking a deep breath, I tried to not allow my shock to overtake me. "Tell me that's not true, Ox."

"I—er—yes, it's true, but I obviously didn't follow through."

More than ever, I *hated* secrets. They had no place in my life, from him or anyone else, and I was quickly realizing that I was tired of making space for people who hid things from me.

I wiggled my fingers, willing down my power's desire to flare into existence. "Will you tell us how this all came about, now that we all know?" I wasn't mad they'd gotten together, I was surprised.

"Fine." He sighed. "When we were both spending our days with the healers, we started getting to know each other—as friends," he clarified with a cough. "After Kyleigh and I returned from the Otherworld and we found out what happened to Aislin, Neve and I moved to The Lavender to keep an eye on Sloan—"

"You make it sound like I'm a child," she glowered.

"You're not. But you needed us." He stood and walked over to our cot, kneeling in front of Sloan. "You may be mad at me right now, but don't pretend you didn't."

He held his hands out in offering. The gesture was one of the things I loved most about Ox. Those giant hands could tear an enemy in half, but for his friends they offered gentle protectiveness. His formidable strength was deep, brutal and equally as loving as it was fierce. Sometimes I wondered if he'd been born large so that his body could house such a massive heart. "One night, with a little liquid mettle, we ended up—you know. After that, we kept on."

"How often?" Sloan asked him, hands clasped around his.

"Just about every night."

"Damn," she said, sitting back up next to me, looking stunned. "How did I never catch you two?"

He shrugged then cleared his throat. King Redmond remained silent, but I could have sworn there was a flare of heat coming from his corner of the room. "We always made sure to be in our respective rooms before day's light."

"But how did you go from that to being her champion? Was it her idea or yours?"

"Hers."

"But when I asked her about champions—if she'd ever have one—she didn't sound like she ever would." I couldn't tell if the statement came from my own jealousy over their bond or genuine curiosity. She'd said she didn't think she wanted to tie herself to someone in that way. Meanwhile, I wanted that with Dru more than anything. Now we couldn't have it until whatever had broken the Evergleam was rectified. And I didn't see that happening before we needed to take on the Enchantress.

"I think her mind changed when she realized we were down a champion set with how powerful the Enchantress was getting."

"So she asked you to be her champion? Tied to her for the rest of your lives? And you just said *sure*?"

"Well...yes." Ox shrugged, still planted on the floor in front of us. "She had a lot of strong arguments why it made sense."

"Bullshit," King Redmond's deep voice soared over the giant's shoulders. "It's obvious you're in love with her."

"I—"

"You are," the King continued, clear he would ignore any word otherwise from Ox. "Just admit it."

"I really don't feel comfortable having this conversation right now. Especially with you," Ox replied over his shoulder. He slunk back to the make-believe couch, taking up most of its width.

"Fair." King Redmond puffed out his wings a bit, tone boastful despite how sour I'm sure he was within. "I was in love with her first."

Sloan's head tilted at Inverno's ruler. "Was?"

"Maybe still am. I don't know. Not that it matters. She chose her champion." He released a long sigh, keeping his eyes averted from all of us. "I don't have to love the concept to accept it."

Ox glared. "That's rich coming from you." Turning back to us as if Neve's former fiancé wasn't in the room, he continued, "She's been very clear that she's not in love with me."

"She sure as shit isn't in love with me," King Redmond muttered.

"Maybe she's not in love with either of you." Their eyes shot to me. "Maybe she is," I said, looking between the two of them. "But maybe it's more than that. Maybe she's just trying to love herself."

I lay back and pulled the thin sheet over me, pretending I could see it was a quilt or whatever the fuck Sloan thought it was. I watched the spiders creep overhead, the stars peeking between their strands of iridescent webbing. "Maybe that's what matters when it comes to her right now. Because I can tell you what doesn't matter...you two idiots bickering over this."

"There's nothing to bicker over."

I turned my gaze to Ox. "You need to fix the Evergleam. Whatever is messing with it is *both* your faults. So help me, if I fuck Dru against that tree again to no avail, I will ensure you'll never be able to enjoy a midnight snack again." Ox's throat bobbed. "We clear?"

King Redmond's eyes jolted a moment at my words. Then he dropped his gaze to the floor, blinking rapidly.

"Crystal," was all Ox managed to croak out.

Sloan took a deep breath. "Why don't we try to get some rest before we get moving tomorrow? Kyleigh, are you up for flying Ox and me?"

"Yep. We'll have Ever as well, since the Octux is sending them to help our weavers. Just make sure we pack an extra sack for Ox in case he gets sick like usual.."

The King chuckled from the corner, fluffing his feathers a few more times before wrapping them around himself. "Some champion."

Ox lay back on the sofa, disappearing from view, but I didn't miss his retort in the darkness.

"Some king."

CHAPTER 42

Redmond

Kyleigh had been the first to drift off, most likely exhausted from a combination of the weavers' feasting, the celebration, and the revelations. Sloan slept next to her, over the evergreen quilt with her amethyst dagger within reach, probably to protect the Princess. Not that she ever seemed to need protecting.

Meanwhile, Sir Fergus's snoring made sleep impossible, yet again. The sound reverberated through the small cabin, making it shake every few breaths he took. I guess the others were used to it. Between sharing a room with the oaf during our travels and my own agitation, it'd been days since I'd had good rest.

I glared at him, watching how peacefully he slept. How unburdened.

Lucky bastard.

After spending this time with Sir Fergus—Ox, I had to concede, he was the better man between us.

A good man.

He could give Neve things I never would be able to. Things she deserved, but not from me. I'd witnessed firsthand how protectively he watched over and cared for Kyleigh. The kindness he exuded. The bravery that came with years of fighting for his kingdom despite its shortcomings after The Blaze and its destruction.

Destruction by my fucking hand.

Being with her wasn't something I mourned, though. I never expected us to be together after I'd learned the truth about what I'd done and what she'd done to my father.

I still loved Neve. Maybe part of me always would, in a way. But I loved her enough to see the life she could have with Ox. The ways he would complement her. Devote himself to her.

He loved her too, even if he couldn't admit it yet.

I didn't deserve her love—or anyone's for that matter. That was something a much younger Redmond craved. Now I just craved repentance. Justice and safety for my own people that I'd betrayed, even if unintentionally.

I stood from my chair and opened the door to the cabin. Walking outside, I stared at the crisscrossed strands, dipping and hovering and glinting above me. The moon shone between the slats, illuminating the path out of Alucinor's territory.

I headed toward the edge of the village, ready to shift and fly back to Inverno, when a crunch on the ground behind had me halting in place.

"Leaving already?"

"Couldn't sleep." I glanced over my shoulder to find Sloan standing there, fully dressed in dark trousers and a pale tunic, dagger tucked into her waistband. Giving a shrug, I continued my trek, keeping my pace slow enough for her to catch up. "Figured I'd get a head start. Kyleigh is taking you all and the weaver back tomorrow anyway. It's better if we aren't seen together."

"Fair point," she replied, eyes darting skyward to the glowing web above us. Then she stopped in her tracks, pivoting to face me. "Can I ask you something?"

I met her stare, taking in the furrow of her brow. "Of course, Sloan."

"Why are you doing this?" she whispered. "What's changed?"

Her eyes shifted around us, taking in the tiny spiders dropping from above to listen in. It was pointless to think there were any secrets in a place like Alucinor, not with the way the weavers had access to our minds, or the way their companions were everywhere, spinning a network for them to communicate with one another. "A year ago you wouldn't have even entertained bending over backward like this for another territory. Even for Inverno, to be honest."

"*Everything* has changed."

And it had. The day I'd found Neve curled up in my dungeon, it was as if a rage-filled blindfold had been ripped away.

"It won't change her mind, Red."

"I'm not doing this for *her*."

She huffed out a laugh.

"I mean, I'm sure part of this is for her, but not because I think it will win her. We both know that isn't possible anymore, but even before then, I didn't expect anything to change with where I stood with Neve. That doesn't mean I can't do whatever is in my power to fix things. To stop the wound I created from bleeding into something worse—something fatal to the realm."

I was beyond repair, but this world wasn't. Its people would thrive, grow, and create a realm far better than the one I'd ruined.

"How are you going to keep up this charade?" Her voice lowered further, not that it mattered. The weavers had seen everything from us the moment we walked through their illusioned walls. "The Enchantress isn't a fool. She has spies everywhere. How do you know she hasn't already realized that you're working against her?"

"I don't." I placed a hand on her shoulder, giving it a small squeeze. "But I still have to try."

Wrapping her palm around my wrist, she squeezed back, icy-blue eyes glittering in the moonlight above. "You're going to get yourself killed, Red."

My free hand clasped over hers. "Better me than those undeserving of such a fate."

"I'm so tired of everyone playing the martyr," she said, stepping back out of my reach.

I knew she wasn't talking about me anymore. "Sloan, she did what she had to do."

"What was the point? She protected Kyleigh, but Kyleigh doesn't seem to get that." She cursed at the stars above us, pacing. "Putting herself in harm's way coming to Alucinor. Offering herself up to the weavers to prod. That's not her job. She's a princess, not a warrior."

"Why is it one or the other?" I asked her. "Can't someone stand for something and fight for it as well?"

"Yes. Just not her. Not after everything Aislin sacrificed." She groaned, stomping toward one of the totems edging the weavers' territory and sliding down it. "I hate that she did that without telling me. We could have figured it out."

"Well, you can kick her ass when she's back." I sat down next to her, patting the knee she'd propped up. "But don't judge how others fight their battles. Whatever happened, she had her reasons for her actions, and she knew the alternative was a worse fate."

"Oh, I will be kicking her ass." Sloan laughed, a sound I'd missed hearing. "Assuming we figure out how to get her back safely."

"I promise you, Sloan, we will find a way."

"I'd love to believe that, Red," she said, finally making eye contact, the rims of her eyes glistening with budding tears. "But she promised to weather these storms together. Promises don't mean much to me now."

"Did she really break her promise?" I asked her, thumbing away a tear as it tracked her cheek. "She's no less yours than she was then, even if she isn't *here*. Your bond may have been tampered with, but it's still there. *She's* still there."

"How do you know?" Her brows knit in frustration.

"Because I do, Sloan." I gave her shoulder a gentle punch, then leaned back, looking up at the stars and thinking about the last time I'd been at the cabin. When I'd learned what had happened to the assassin that'd somehow chosen to spare my life despite my faults. Despite my part in her family's demise. "Because I've seen her."

"You have?"

"I have. And part of Aislin, she's still in there."

"Maybe you're right."

"It happens." I shrugged, giving her a thin smirk. "Not frequently as of late, but it still happens."

"I want to believe she's still in there somewhere. That we'll be able to bring her back."

"We will." We had to. I wouldn't fail Sloan again. Not after how much she'd stuck by me over the years.

"But the part of me that doesn't know if we can be success-ful, *that* part begs the stars that she isn't there anymore. That she can't feel. Understand. Because if she does...I don't want to imagine the horror she's facing trapped by the Enchantress."

I prayed to the stars on behalf of my friend and her Revered, despite the fact that those glimmers would probably never listen to my pleas.

"Are you sure you don't want to wait until morning to leave?" Sloan asked, tilting her head. "You could easily get a few more hours of sleep."

"Not with Sir Fergus's snoring."

We laughed, and I stood back up, brushing off my trousers. "Too much for me to do before the Enchantress summons me back."

There was too much at stake.

And too many people to keep safe.

CHAPTER 43

Neve

Dru had been silent the entire ride back. I normally didn't mind, but there was something different about this quiet. It was uncomfortable. Intentional.

Concerning.

I landed in the arena, and he slid off me, eyes pinned to the dirt. He pressed a stud along his glove's edge, and my slip pooled in his palm. He held it out to me, keeping his gaze averted. But it wasn't just some polite gesture, a way to grant my privacy.

He *wouldn't* look at me.

"You going to tell me what's got you giving me the cold shoulder?" I asked once I'd dressed, shooting a few flecks of snow in his direction. He lifted his hand up, sucking them up into the coppery center of his palm.

"It was you." His eyes flicked to mine, the gold in them more vibrant than usual, as if ignited.

Tension gripped the fragile thread of my bond. It was a sensation that had been coming in and out over the last day, but not enough to have me alarmed. Just uneasy. I wondered if my own emotions had slipped through to Ox despite my attempts to freeze them within the icy confines of my chest. Tugging that knot tighter, I choked out the steady flow of the bond's magic.

"I'm sorry, you're going to have to be a bit clearer because I feel like I entered into the middle of a conversation I wasn't included in."

"You're the reason the Evergleam is broken." My throat dried at his accusation, the disappointment pricking through his tone. "Not Sloan and Aislin. Not Kyleigh or me. That leaves you. You and whoever you managed to bond or not bond with."

"Dru, I—"

"Did it at least work? Do you have a champion?"

"I do," I said, lowering my voice. "But I don't know what's wrong with the Evergleam. It worked during our ceremony."

I'd thought everything would be easy making Ox my champion. Being with him was invigorating, and I felt lighter than I had in ages...maybe ever. But I was still rebuilding myself, one shattered piece at a time.

Anything *more* than that was too much.

"Well, according to Harkin, who explained to me how the Evergleam's magic works, it means one of you is interfering with the bond."

Just then, a flash of blue dove from above, landing in a large puff of dirt. Luckily, Redmond had at least covered himself with his blue fire. I was grateful for his new parlor trick.

Dru groaned, looking between us. "Neve, please don't tell me—"

"Not me," Redmond cut in, lifting a hand. "But thanks for the vote of confidence."

He nodded back toward the labyrinth leading to the fort's entrance. "Why don't you head inside, Dru? Kyleigh should be back later, and I'm sure you have catching up to do."

"Dru, wait—"

He turned, speeding off like he couldn't get away from this conversation fast enough.

My chest clenched, the knot there pulling taut as I stared at my former fiancé.

He cocked his head, arching a brow. "We need to talk."

"Sounds like someone already talked," I seethed, forcing some assurance down the bond that everything was fine. Bubbles fizzed along its wiry strand, light and happy. The feeling instantly set me more at ease, and I looked around, wondering if he'd arrived to save me from this exchange.

"He's not back yet, if that's what you're wondering." Disappointment flooded the bond before I could dam it from bursting through. "He will be getting back with everyone else later."

"So you just left them behind?"

"They weren't in danger." The black feathers along his wings shook a few times, bristling at my words before he puffed out his chest, always the kingly presence. "And I still have a kingdom to run. People to protect."

"Then what are you doing here? Shouldn't you be off running? Protecting?"

He pinched the bridge of his nose, then released a sigh. "Why did you do it?"

Why did you pick him was what he meant to say.

"A champion and their Revered are much stronger together," I defended. Not that I needed to. "We need all the strength we can get."

"Is that how you feel?" His tone was smooth, relaxed, which only irritated me further. "Stronger?"

His brows lifted. "Because I've been with your champion, and he seems far from *strong* right now. And based on the Evergleam's damage, I'd say something isn't right." His eyes darted in the direction of the hidden grove. "From what I just overheard... if one of you is interfering with—"

"Our bond is none of your concern." Ice shot through my veins, glowing under my skin.

Redmond tilted his head, eyeing me curiously. He chuckled darkly, taking a few steps closer and lowering his voice. "Oh see, that's where you're wrong. Because your hasty little stunt and the fallout does concern me."

This man's ego knew no bounds. How dare he think this had anything to do with him. I had chosen Ox for myself, and if Redmond was deluded enough to think he had somehow stood a chance, I had to rip away the blindfold. "It was *never* going to be you."

He staggered back a step, like I'd shot him with a dozen icy arrows. "Are you saying that to hurt me? Is this all to hurt me?"

"If I wanted to hurt you, why would I have kept it a secret?"

"I don't know. And I guess I never will." His eyes dropped to his feet, hands clasping together a moment before he released them with a resigned shrug. "I'll add it to the list of mysteries when it comes to you."

I didn't owe him an explanation.

I didn't owe him anything.

But I'd decided back at that ledge that I'd been ready to forgive, and the best way I could do that was give him the truth.

"The night before The Blaze, I was ordered to kill you. After our wedding."

Blue flared from his fingertips, and he clenched his fists at his sides, smothering it out. "I don't understand."

I took a deep breath, softening my voice. A tug came from the bond, but I relaxed the grip on the knot in my chest, unfurling reassurance. I didn't need Ox to worry on his way back here.

"Our families weren't supportive of the marriage, Red. Arafax wanted to use it as a way to claim Inverno's throne instead of sharing power. Who would oppose Arafax taking the reins? They had three dragons. And who would question the grieving queen consort of the crowned prince ruling over their people? Your father was the only one strong enough to oppose King Laisren."

"My father—"

"Had his own agenda. He told me he had learned of Arafax's plan to remove the phoenix line from the equation—opening up the throne to whoever would claim it for their own."

"*You?*"

"I tried to tell him I wouldn't do it. Couldn't do it. That I truly was in love with you. The marriage to me was real. It always was." I could feel the stinging pressure of tears forming behind my eyes, but I froze them in place, refusing to blink. To cry. To shed another tear over what had happened. I wasn't that naïve woman anymore, and I refused to continue mourning what she'd lost. "He didn't believe me. He had his men attack me, and I shifted, trying to get away."

"And that's why you killed him," Redmond offered, filling in the gaps I didn't want to speak aloud. Admit. "Why didn't you just say that before? Why didn't you tell me?"

"It doesn't change the fact that I killed your father, Redmond. It doesn't change the fact that I spent the last decade locked away at your hand. It doesn't change the fact that I'm bonded to someone else now. Ox is—"

"The champion you deserve."

My tears disobeyed me, a few tracking down my cheeks. Redmond stepped closer, the tip of his wing brushing them away. "Neve, I know things are over for us. There have never been any illusions for me otherwise. I just wish I would have found out differently—about everything."

"I wish that too."

"I'm glad you found someone. And whether you want to admit it to yourselves or not, there's more going on than merely bonding for the sake of some power boost."

"I don't want to talk about this with you," I said, wiping a few extra rebellious tears from the corners of my eyes.

He chuckled with a sigh. "I know you don't. But you need to at least listen to what I have to say because it has nothing to do with our past and everything to do with Celaria's future." He waited a moment until I'd met his gaze. "You need to fix the bond. You may be our only champion-bonded pair going up against the Enchantress."

"If I knew how to fix it, don't you think I would?"

"I think you know how to fix it. But you're stubborn enough where you won't." He shook his head. "Whether or not you believe it yet, you deserve a happy ending... I think you could have it with him."

The admission stunned me.

I'd thought he'd be mad. But he'd said it all along: *I hope one day to earn more than your hate.* He'd never believed we'd be together, he just didn't want things left so broken.

Didn't want *me* left so broken.

Maybe forgiveness wasn't as simple as accepting I'm sorry. Maybe it was accepting another person's broken bits and still wanting to see them whole.

"I still think you deserve one too, Redmond."

"I'm not meant to find happiness, Neve," he said, giving me a pleasant smile that reminded me of the Redmond I'd met when he was a teenager. A second later it pressed back into a firm line, that carefree prince gone just as quickly. "But hopefully, one day, I'll find peace."

CHAPTER 44

Flipping another page of the *Valídus Vénenifícium*, I held out my notes next to it, working through the translation.

Unlike our written language, ancient faeries wrote theirs to be read from bottom to top and then top to bottom, starting in the lower left corner. I supposed it would be easier to flit over the words as they read. It also explained a huge part of why no one had been able to decipher the tome's meaning all these years. Even if you knew the runes and the translations, you'd end up with a muddle of words and sounds that didn't equate to anything usable to the caster. A few of the incantations, once I'd learned them, were more familiar to me than I'd realized.

I murmured some of the words, rolling them off my tongue. "*Neth anéiavan só—*"

The door to the study creaked open, and my chest tightened a moment, worried it was the Queen. I needed to find a way to transform the wisps before we discussed a final plan to go against the Enchantress. The key was in here. I could feel it. I just needed to decipher it all first.

Kyleigh's head peeked through the slat, a smile brimming on her pink lips. "I figured I'd find you here."

I was out of my chair in an instant, dragging her into me, kissing her deeply. It had only been days but I'd hated the separation.

"I missed you terribly," I whispered against the shell of her ear, brushing back some strands of her coral-dipped waves. Sliding my other hand along the door to find the knob, I listened for the faint *click* to signify I'd locked it. "How are you? How'd it go?"

"I'm good," she said, giving me a quick kiss. "I won't say it was easy, but the weavers will join our cause. And better yet, one of their own has come back with us to help my father and Jet with their powers until they can safely go train more extensively in Alucinor."

"That's incredible, Ky. I'm so thrilled to hear it. Have you told your mo—"

"No. I figure I can deal with my parents and all of that *mess* tomorrow. How did it go with the faeries?" Her eyes trailed over the open tome and sheets of notes on the desk.

"They helped me translate some and I memorized the key for the rest. Which is a huge win, considering Neve wasn't lying about their distrust of outsiders. They wouldn't even let her come with Travis and I."

"Then it is lucky they were feeling kind enough to allow you in."

"Definitely. Speaking of Neve," I said, wanting to give Kyleigh the truth about the Evergleam. "She and—"

"I know." She took a deep breath, shaking her head. "When Ox told me, I couldn't believe it myself."

"Ox?" *What?*

"You didn't know?" She rested her palms on the straps of my chest harness. "I'm sorry. I just assumed when you brought it up."

"I found out she had completed the ceremony. She didn't say it herself. One of the faeries told me more about how the Evergleam's magic worked and I narrowed it down from there. I was about to talk to her about it, but Redmond interrupted and said you'd be back soon."

"*Oof.* I'm sure that was a fun conversation after you left."

"I'm glad I got out of there when I did. Besides, I was too excited about getting to see you."

"Same. Would have been nice to have had that champion bond so I could at least sense if you were okay."

She tugged at the hem of her plain white shift. Color bled through from whatever she wore underneath, pulling my curiosity.

"Agreed. Hopefully Neve and Ox"—it felt weird to say aloud—"can get it together and then we can complete the bond. In the meantime..." Caressing along her silky thigh, I started to lift the hem of her shift.

She swatted my hand away, then strode over to the desk, scooting next to the tome and papers spread across it. She crossed her ankles, swinging her legs back and forth, having way too much fun toying with me. With a coy smile, she pointed to the chair. "I know you have work to do, and I don't want to distract you."

"Being inside of you isn't a distraction." I guided her legs apart, pressing myself against her so she could feel just how serious I was. "It's a necessity."

Her breath caught at my words, hands warming as they paused at the waistband of my trousers. She wanted this, too, but instead of undoing the buttons, she pushed me back forcefully, playfully, my ass landing in the chair.

She lifted the shift above her head, revealing deep-coral flowers scattered along the nude mesh covering her bra and thong, strategically placed over her nipples and core. I gripped the sides of my trousers, unsure how to respond. It was clear she had something planned, and I was beyond eager to participate. "Are you here to torment me?"

She widened her legs, and I traced up her thigh to the damp spot budding on a pair of overlapping coral tulips. Biting her lip at my response, she lowered her voice to an octave that had my dick jolting against the zipper restraining it. "Are you feeling tormented?"

I groaned and shifted in the seat to alleviate the growing ache for her touch. Not taking my gaze off her smirk, I rested my palm over my heart. "Tortured."

I leaned forward, but she stopped me, the ball of her foot digging into my chest. Catching it between my hands, I gripped her ankle, stroking up along her calf, her eyelids fluttering a moment. Her lips curled mischievously. "I don't want to stifle your productivity."

"I can think of a lot of very productive things I'd like to do to you right now," I said, matching her expression.

She cocked her head, eyes shooting up to the ceiling, enjoying this game. Not that I minded. Things had been so heavy since our failed ceremony and visiting with the faeries. While I should have petitioned Harkin for support against the Enchantress, it seemed wrong after everything was stolen from them by Arafax's hand. Giving me the key to unlock the *Validus Venenificium* was a big enough ask.

Kyleigh's gaze narrowed, caught on to the fact that my mind had done its usual spiral. She was never frustrated by it, though. One of the many reasons I loved her. She saw me. Knew how much my work, deciphering this tome, all of it meant to me. She also knew I'd allow myself to burnout in search of answers.

"How about a compromise?" A smile kicked up the edge of her lips, and she lowered the leg that'd been holding me hostage.

"If the compromise gives me access to that damp spot between your thighs, then I'm all ears."

I scooted the chair closer between her legs, looking up at her. My lips only mere inches from her breasts. I brought my hands to her waist. The scales climbing up her sides were slightly distorted now, scarred from Flynt's crossbow. The other scars were only visible in her dragon form, breaking up the red veins of her wings.

She scanned the open tome on the table, lifting up a few of the pages and letting them fall back down. "You still have a lot of pages to translate."

"I do." I sighed. *Seventeen.*

"How about we pull an all-nighter to get them done?" Stroking my cheek with her hand, she captured my face with her palms.

"You want to pull an all-nighter studying the tome?"

"Hey, I never got to pull one at Halston." She shrugged, the flowers on her bra snagging my attention as she leaned back on the desk.

And just when I thought I couldn't possibly get any harder.

I willed my hands at my side, desperate to rub over the coral fabric until she was begging for me to rip it off.

"Besides, I figured we could make it more fun."

"What did you have in mind?"

"Show me how to interpret the runes. For every page I translate first, I will choose a reward. For every page you do, you'll choose."

I ran my palm up the inside of her thigh, tracing the stitching along her thong. "And what kind of rewards are we talking about?"

She slid off the desk, landing in my lap and wrapping her arms around my neck. "Anything your heart desires."

"I must say, I like the way your mind works."

"The feeling is more than mutual."

I kissed up her neck, my hand stroking the strap of her bra. "Well, let's get to translating."

"Someone's eager."

"That's an understatement. Have you looked at yourself?" She'd have this effect on me whether she was in this delectable lingerie or a pair of jeans and her faded Halston hoodie.

"I have. But I much prefer the way you look at me."

She kissed me a few more times, sinking against me and unbuckling my chest strap. Taking a vial of contraceptive tonic, she popped the lid, swigging it down before letting the harness fall to the floor. Then she moved along the buttons on my shirt.

"Here is the key," I breathed, already ready for my reward and to skip the game if we didn't start translating soon. Sliding my hand across the desk, I grasped for the sheet, peeking out of the corner of my eye. She licked up the column of my throat, the heat at her center an inferno against me, making me groan. "I'll give you a head start on the first one..."

She nipped my bottom lip, then pulled back, taking the paper from me. "Aren't you generous."

"Translate the page and I'll show you just how generous I can be."

"So, this is a spell for creating a protective barrier?" Kyleigh asked about fifteen minutes later, once she'd finished the translation.

The longest fifteen minutes of my life.

"It would seem so." I'd kept quiet, not wanting to let on that I'd figured it out about eight minutes prior.

Undoing the buttons of my trousers, she stood from my lap, wiggling them off until they were heaped around my feet.

"Now for my reward." She sank down to her knees before kissing up my thigh, peppering bites along the way. Then she continued, tracing up my shaft with her tongue.

My eyes rolled into my head as I leaned against the back of

the chair, gripping its arms. When I felt enough control, I watched her suck me into her mouth, her tongue lapping at the sensitive ridge around my tip. *"Blazes."*

She released me from her mouth, precum leaking down my tip until she licked it up. I groaned. "I want to be inside you."

"Then you better get translating."

I dragged the tome over to me, gritting my teeth against the urge to give in to the pleasure and come right then and there. Kyleigh sucked me in deeper, angling herself so I was hitting the back of her throat.

My hands shook as I reached for the key.

She paused, giving me a moment to catch my breath.

"Stars above," I prayed, trying to find the strength to keep translating, needing her body against mine like I needed air.

Scanning the key, I gripped the pen tightly in my clenched fist, knuckles white as I jotted down the translation, one messy letter after another... "Done," I rasped.

Her eyes popped up a moment to meet mine, and I stroked her cheek, waiting for her to release me from between her lips, even though it felt beyond incredible. Helping her up to stand, I lifted her and set her back on the desk, kneeling before her and licking up her center, tasting her through the damp coral tulips. Then I pulled her thong to the side, swiping the pad of my finger through her glistening release, bringing it to my lips. Wanting to savor every drop as her hips squirmed above me. I picked up the intensity, pumping my fingers slowly in and out of her.

"Not fair," she panted, clenched around my fingers. "How —am I—supposed to—translate—like this?"

I chuckled against her, making her shoot a few sparks from her fingers that I quickly caught in my glove. "Sounds like I'm going to get to choose another reward after this one."

"The fuck you are." She twisted, trying to turn toward the tome and its key.

"We'll see about that." Gripping her thighs to steer her body back to me, I switched hands, curling my fingers into her. Placing the center of my palm over her clit, I played with different pressures, using her sparks as they fed back out from the leather.

Her body convulsed, and she screamed a slew of Otherworld curses.

As she caught her breath, I began translating the next one...

"Ready for my next reward," I said a minute later, tapping the written translation with my finger. "Do you need some rest?"

"I was promised an all-nighter." She sighed, head resting on the table, coral waves framing her face. "Giving up already?"

"Never." I stood up from the ground, leaving her legs resting against my chest and I shucked away my shirt. Running my tip through her folds, I lined up with her center and pushed in just a few inches before moving slowly in and out.

She wriggled in protest. "*More.*"

I brought my fingers to her clit, silencing her as she sucked in a breath. She fumbled for my gloved hand, feeding some power into it so she didn't burn me or the desk beneath us. I pushed deep inside her, the warmth of her body enveloping me.

Whispering into her ear, I continued to thrust. "An all-nighter means I'll take my time with you."

CHAPTER 45
Isla

Lacing up the low-top sneakers, I stared at the mirror, finding myself unrecognizable.

I'd avoided my reflection for so long, afraid of what it'd show me. My silver eyes glowed in the dim light, I looked nothing like the woman I'd allowed myself to become over the last decade.

Once upon a time, I traded my Chucks for stilettos, my denim and cotton for velvet and chiffon.

I thought I could trade it all without changing who I was. But standing here in my old garb, the reflection of a life I'd sacrificed, reality punched into me with bloodied fists.

I'd left that woman and her life behind.

Kyleigh had every right to hate me.

I'd witnessed my family parade their royal status and power over Arafax, over Celaria, for almost two decades, vowing I'd never become one of them. As much as I hated being discarded to the Otherworld, I was grateful I'd never have to take the throne. To never have to follow in my family's royal footsteps.

Yet here I was.

It didn't happen overnight. I'd arrived back here with plans to get rid of the Enchantress. To resuscitate Arafax to its former glory, then bring my family here and prepare Kyleigh to one day rule.

How quickly time passed. How little progress I seemed to make. Before I knew it, she'd been preparing for college, and I had to ensure the society I'd founded still remained in the dark of what she could do.

What our bloodline could do.

Dru had been sent to help ensure this, without fully knowing his purpose. Yes, the technology he could implement here was useful, but protecting my daughter, the last Arafax royal—that was his real assignment. Even if he didn't know it.

I couldn't be angry that he'd brought her here. Getting to see her, the woman she'd become, it was something I began to think would never happen.

Of course she couldn't stand the woman *I'd* become.

I didn't know if I could stand her either, but it's who I needed to be to survive this realm and everything that came with it.

Maybe I was always this person. Maybe my title made me this way. Under the layers, it was hard to know who ruled my identity: the woman who'd protected Celaria from afar, forging herself a family without magic, or the queen that sacrificed a life with them to rid the realm of the Enchantress and rebuild.

Two impossibly different facets warred within me, and it was hard to pinpoint the scarred ledge where one began and the other ended.

I poked my nail back into the fresh puncture I'd made earlier, using it to close the room back up before heading toward room VI. I halted when I spotted two figures standing in the hallway, coming from Jet's room.

Kyleigh and Dru stopped short, their eyes scanning me. Dru's ignited with surprise. But not Kyleigh's. She was eerily calm, considering our last interaction.

"Your Majesty," Dru said, bowing his head. Kyleigh didn't follow suit. "May I ask why you're dressed like that?"

"It's for Kyleigh's father," I replied, eyes dropping to the Halston tee and jeans.

Kyleigh's eyes narrowed on the insignia before she cleared her throat. "Nice shirt."

"It's been helpful to pinpoint which memories for your father to pull from. To keep him safe," I added, feeling a bit defensive. "I realized his ability, like ours, requires steady usage. Better to pull from my memories, ones that are a bit more...expendable."

Kyleigh's lips parted, as if she were about to speak, but before she could become brave enough, I continued, trying to shift the conversation back to them. "I didn't expect to see you here so early."

"We waited for Ever to get up so they could meet Dad and Jet this morning," Kyleigh said, looping her hand through Dru's, clutching it tightly. "Figured it was better they begin working together and get help on their skills as weavers."

"Good thinking." The weavers were such a mystery to me, other than very few encounters with Reve. Kyleigh now had much more insight, something maybe she'd impart on me if she were to allow me any closer.

Someday.

For now, I wouldn't push anything—not unless it was necessary for dealing with the Enchantress. "Has Ever met with your father already?"

"Yes. They've had their first session of training. Ever brought him a talisman that should help control the memory weaving until Dad becomes more practiced with it." The tension strung through her face softened a bit. "As long as he wears it, it should keep his powers at a safer level. Controllable."

"Is Ever a memory weaver?"

"No, Ever is an illusion weaver. I'll introduce you after Jet's done with his lesson."

Having never met an illusion weaver, I was very curious about how their powers worked.

Kyleigh began walking toward her father's room. "The weavers were willing to let Ever come back with us and agreed to an alliance. They'll be our point of contact with Alucinor for our upcoming plans."

"What were the conditions?"

"Nothing unreasonable." She held out a finger to Dru, who gave it a gentle caress before quickly pricking it and pushing the pad so red bloomed from the tip. "They want to have a place within Celaria without prejudice."

"That won't be an easy undertaking." People feared the weavers for centuries, not wanting their minds tampered with. But if anyone understood that fear sometimes provided the best mask, it was me. "It's a fair request, though."

"That's what I thought."

"What did you have to do to get them to agree?"

"That's a story for another time." Kyleigh turned away from me, placing her pad on the doorway. It dissolved away, and my eyes met Craig's. "In fact, I wanted to see if we could maybe have dinner together tonight...in the main dining room, since Dad should be safe to come out. I can tell you more about my visit to Alucinor."

"Really?" I was pretty sure my brows had reached my hairline. "You want to have dinner with us?"

Craig gave a smile from behind Kyleigh, obviously thrilled at the idea. Warmth flooded my chest, but I tamped it down.

"I think it's important we talk. Now that we are all here and it's safe to."

"Of course." *It's important we talk* had a terrifying appeal to it, but at least we were finally going to be talking. I'd take what I could get. Aislin's words before she'd been taken had kept playing on a loop in my head: *When will you realize that all your sacrifice did was lose you the very thing you sacrificed for?*

Maybe all wasn't lost.

"I'll have the cook prepare something special. Any particular requests?"

"Breakfast for dinner," Kyleigh said with a smile. "Unicorn pancakes and dragon-fire sticks."

My heart lurched at the memory of our Sunday morning tradition back in Dorset. Did they still keep it going after I'd left? Or had that disappeared too?

I finally had my family back together and tonight would be an opportunity to salvage things, even if I didn't have a clue as to how to even begin.

But stars above, I would try.

CHAPTER 46
Kyleigh

"Thank you so much, Sloan," I said, looking at the crimson outfit set out on the bed. While it wasn't my usual t-shirt and jeans, it was more *me* than most things my mother had selected for my secretly royal wardrobe. Since Sloan had arrived, she'd been a lifesaver helping me feel comfortable—and designing a few pieces that would be easy to remove if I needed to shift quickly.

I guess creating outfits over the years for King Redmond helped.

"No problem." Sloan looped an arm around my shoulders before leaning in to whisper, "Thank you for doing this."

"Just get everyone back here safely or there'll be hell to pay."

"Hell?"

"Never mind."

I hated that they were doing this without me, but I also knew my mother would get in the way if she wasn't occupied. Tonight, I'd play the part of diversion while the people I cared about were out risking their lives.

It sucked.

Dru had been right, though, if it came down to it, we all

knew what my mother would prioritize for the good of the realm. And maybe she was in the right, in her way, but it didn't mean that was an outcome I agreed with.

"You Otherworlders and your strange expressions." Sloan chuckled to herself, walking with me toward the door to Dru's room. "Just yesterday during training, Athena was talking about The Lavender being *lit*. I was highly concerned until she explained. I'm constantly needing translations."

"Believe me...the learning curve is mutual," I replied with a small smile. It quickly dissolved as anxiety bubbled through me, acrid and sharp. If something happened tonight—

No. I refused to even think about any outcome other than a positive one. "Anyway, you better get going. Dru already headed out to meet with the others, and I need to finish getting ready."

Giving me one final squeeze, she released me, taking a few steps out the door before turning around to grip its frame. "I'll see you later."

"You better." A prickle of sparks edged along my fingertips, but I clenched my fists tight, unwilling to let her see my nerves. She didn't need that. Even if Sloan presented as calm and collected most of the time, I'd seen her at rock bottom after Aislin had been taken. The last thing she needed was my nerves compounded with her own, no matter how cleverly hidden.

"Sloan?"

Her head peeked back in the doorway. "Yes?"

"Good luck."

"I'm not sure who'll need more luck tonight, us or you." She gave me a roguish grin—one I'd associated all too many times with Ox. Maybe it was a warrior-confidence thing.

"Truer words have never been spoken." I took a deep breath to steady myself.

Then she was gone, and it was just me, left with her carefully curated outfit to prepare for dinner tonight. A dinner that included a discussion I desperately wanted to have and avoid all the same.

My heels clacked against the marble floor leading off the main hall and into the dining room. I tucked my hands into the pocket of my crimson waistcoat that flared at the hips, accentuating my curves. It was paired with matching fitted trousers and corset. It was a good compromise—not as uncomfortable as a gown for dinner in the Banquet Hall, but still much fancier than my usual attire.

I smiled to myself, thinking about the maroon leather jacket I'd found concealed beneath my clothes. Another Sloan masterpiece I couldn't wait to wear. As soon as I finished dinner tonight, I'd have to try it on and thank her in person once she was back.

She would be back.

They all would.

A flare singed the inside of my pocket, making me flinch before recovering. My parents were already sitting at the long table, my mother situated at the head, her hand atop my dad's, who was seated next to her. They were talking and laughing. A memory flashed through my mind of them looking just the same, albeit a bit younger, eating at the circular table in our breakfast nook.

The smell of unicorn pancakes and dragon-fire sticks wafting from the kitchen didn't help matters much. My throat dried at the momentary déjà vu.

"I'm so glad you suggested this, Ky," my mother said, taking her gentle gaze off my dad. A gentleness that hadn't existed since

I'd found her. She stood up, my dad joining her, and a servant went to the seat opposite his, pulling it out for me.

"It's been too long since the three of us spent time together." My dad gave me a big smile. Warmth flooded my chest having him back, and I couldn't help but return it. While I was so angry about the lies, it was comforting not worrying about him in Dorset anymore.

"This looks great," I said, scanning the spread as servers placed dishes on the table. Pancakes with multicolored specks were heaped high, and enough bacon to feed this whole fort mounded a tray next to it. A small carafe full of syrup sat in the center of the table, along with butter molded into the shape of Arafax's billowing flame.

The servants walked around dishing out food until my mother lifted a hand, flicking it toward the door to have them leave. Our golden goblets were full, and I peeked over mine to see what was inside. The drink fizzed, pale yellow with a tinge of lilac in it. "What is this?"

"It's sparkling faerie wine, a squeeze of lemon juice, and some muddled lavender," my mother replied, lifting the chalice. "A toast?"

"Sure." I held up my own, my hand shaking a bit. My mother's eyes snapped to the movement, but I steadied it quickly.

Stupid nerves.

This was going to be a long night if I didn't get it together.

"May I?" my dad asked, picking up his drink.

My mother bowed her head to him. "Of course."

"To being together again. Finally."

We clinked our goblets and brought them to our lips. My parents were both smiling at each other like suddenly everything was okay.

Acid rose from my gut, and I washed it away with faerie wine. Anger fizzed along with the drink down my throat, its heat pumping into my chest, my heart beating wildly.

"Where is Dru tonight?" my dad asked innocently, though there was another emotion threaded in there that I couldn't quite place. "Figured you'd bring him along since he's almost family and all."

"Hanging out at The Lavender with everyone tonight. He'll be back later."

He better be.

"Craig, you're going to love him. He's taken so many things from the Otherworld and implemented them here. A truly resourceful young man," my mother said, and I almost laughed at her, considering how little she'd seemed to value his return when he'd been taken to the Otherworld a few months back. "And most importantly, he loves Kyleigh dearly."

The urge to gag at her false sincerity nearly won out, but I swallowed it back. "Dru's amazing."

"I'm sure he is." My dad began cutting into his pancakes. "Don't get me wrong, he seems wonderful, but way to give your dad a heart attack between being worried sick over if you were okay and then coming here and finding out you're a Revered *and* you've already found your champion."

It was so weird hearing those words from him.

Avoiding thinking much more about it, I picked up a piece of bacon and took my time chewing the smoky deliciousness. Dragon-fire sticks definitely had a whole new meaning for me, but bacon was no less delicious.

"Discussing my love life is not why I asked to have dinner together." As much as I looked forward to my dad getting to know Dru, there were more pressing things on my mind when it came to my parents.

"Okay..." My mother put her utensils on the table.

"I want to know the truth," I stated. Dad immediately stopped chewing. "I spent years wishing our family could be together again."

"We all wished for that, Ky." He put his fork down and swallowed the rest of his pancakes. "Your mother and I—"

"Lied. You both lied to me. For years." I chugged the rest of my lavender drink, wishing the staff was in here with a refill. "I can't just forgive that. Expecting that I should be able to is asking too much."

"You're right," my mother agreed, taking me by surprise. "You deserved the truth. From both of us."

"That's all I'm asking for now. Please."

She clasped her hands together, eyes darting quickly to Dad before coming back to me. "As you know, I was meant to marry Seth Grymm and live the rest of my days in the Otherworld. My father had made a deal with his, provided a dowry, and I was sent to keep the peace between the worlds." She swallowed hard. "But beyond that, I had to ensure they never figured out how to get to Celaria."

Figured out that our bloodline was the key. And I guessed it had worked, considering they'd never come here until recently— thanks to me. They seemed harmless enough, though, minus their ringleader, Travis. Luckily his tiny-winged ass was far away now, hopefully gone from my life forever.

"Long story short...I met your father and we fell in love." He gripped her hand, eyeing her with the same devotion he had all those years ago when I was a kid...maybe even more. I wanted him to be happy but I didn't get it. How could he still be so in love with her after everything her disappearance had put us through? "This was all much to the Grymms' displeasure."

"It was one of the reasons I suspect you didn't get in to Halston the first few years you applied," my dad added. "Though I'm not sure what changed."

He might not know, but I was pretty sure I did.

"Travis." *The frat-boy-turned-faerie.* "He figured out my blood would open the portal." I swallowed thickly. "How could you have kept this from me all these years? You let me think she could be dead."

"To be fair, I didn't know if she was alive or not." He shrugged. "I prayed every day that she'd come back to us or send word it was safe." Grabbing his goblet, he took a sip, then went back to cutting up his pancakes. "But we both agreed we wouldn't do that until we knew the Enchantress couldn't collect on her bargain."

"Why not free her?" I asked, looking at my mother. "If you had that as another option, you could have removed her banishment and brought me back."

She shook her head. "You have no idea what she is capable of."

"Neither do you." Unless there was more she wasn't telling me, she really didn't know much about the Enchantress. How could you decide how bad someone was without truly understanding them? "Have you ever thought to find out what she wants?"

"She wants power. She wants Celaria."

"And how are you any better? Do you not want power? Did you not take part in a war against King Redmond and Inverno?" My heart ramped its pace, so I took a few deep breaths. I brought my hands beneath the table, sparks twisting along my wrists, the need to expend some magic growing increasingly harder to ignore.

"What are you trying to say?"

"Everyone can be the villain in someone else's story." How many people out there now cast me as the villain in theirs? I'm sure there were families, ones here and in Inverno, that would be happy to see me killed for the loss theirs endured, no matter if it was warranted or not.

One woman's evil was another's beloved.

"Is that what you see me as?" my mother asked, arching a brow. "The villain?"

"No," I said, probably too hastily, but my nerves, my thoughts, were compiling into a jumble that was too hefty to wade through at the moment. "I just think I'm starting to see that not everything is so black and white." The sparks dancing along my fingers vanished, absorbing back into their tips. "If we understood what she wanted, maybe we wouldn't need to rally allies and ready ourselves for a potential war."

"By all means, why don't you take a stroll through the woods and ask her yourself?" *If only she knew...* "The Enchantress does love her deals."

"Like you'd ever let that happen," I spat back at her, picking up the goblet on instinct and sipping from it, only to be reminded of its emptiness.

Her eyes turned icy. "I won't always be able to protect you."

"I'm not sure if you've realized this or not, Mother," I shoved another slice of bacon in my mouth, chewing over my words before I said them, "but I don't need your protection. In fact, I survived many years without it in the Otherworld. Not to mention that I now have magic in me meant to protect you and everyone else in Arafax."

She released an exasperated sigh, then took a sip from her chalice. "What do you want from me, Kyleigh?"

"Something that isn't possible."

"Say it anyway."

"I want my mother back. The one that loved us. Not whatever version of her sits across from me, barely a shell of the person she was."

"That's where you're wrong." She gritted her teeth. "I loved you more than anything. I still do. None of that has changed."

"Everything has changed," I sneered. "You are nothing like her. Maybe right now in front of Dad you can play pretend that we are all some happy fucking family, but we aren't. What about all the years you were gone? What about the months I've been back and you've pretended I'm not your daughter?"

"To keep you safe!" She stood up, and my dad's brows shot up in alarm, but he remained silent. Probably too afraid to get in the middle of this, but he clutched the talisman tightly between his fingers. "I loved you enough to want to build a life for us here."

"What life?" My fists clenched as I stood from the table. "I'm grown now." Waving my hand over myself, I tried to emphasize that I was no longer the eleven-year-old girl she'd left. "We've *lived* over a decade without you. Dad took the pieces you left behind and *he* built us a life in Vermont."

"Kyleigh..." he started, voice soft.

"No," I said, putting my hand up to him, a few sparks dancing along their fingertips. His eyes widened. I didn't want him defending her. Not now. Not after everything we'd been through. "You could have come back at any time. Even just to tell us you were safe. You had the ability to—"

"You're right." She lifted her hands by her shoulders, stopping me before I could continue spewing truths at her. "I could have sent for you. I could have visited. I chose not to."

"Do you not see how fucked up that is?" I was stunned she'd admitted what I knew deep down was the truth. She could have come back to us. She'd chosen to leave. To stay away.

"Every time the portal was opened, it came with risks. I loved you too much to risk you. If I had gone back, the Enchantress could have learned of your existence." She sighed. "Beyond that, I had a duty to my people to keep them safe, especially after everything they'd been through with The Blaze."

Pressure stung at the backs of my eyes like a thousand tiny darts pelting toward a water balloon. Just one prick and the tears would burst from them. I didn't want to give her my tears but they came anyway, streaking down my cheeks. I was tired of hiding the tears, though—of brushing them aside and pretending they didn't exist.

My mother was beside me in an instant, taking a napkin to wipe them away.

"She learned about me anyway. And guess who paid for it?" I pushed her hand away. "Aislin. The one person who had no reason to protect me."

My mother had trained her whole life to wear a mask. I'd grown up seeing her without one, but somehow she'd managed to place it right back on when she'd returned to Celaria. That was one of the many stark differences between us. I could never hide behind a mask. I didn't want to.

"I'm sorry." She placed a hand at the base of my neck, brushing at my hair, voice low. "You'll never know how sorry I am for all of it. It killed me to be away from you and your father. I know you'll never forgive me for leaving. For not returning. I don't expect you to."

It was the voice that lulled me to sleep all those years ago. The voice that reassured me when I'd fallen off my bike. And as tired as I was of her lies, I was also tired of ignoring the traces of my mom in the woman that stood next to me. "But I'm begging you, please give me a chance to get to know you. The you now."

She swept back a few strands of my hair and I took a small step closer to her. As she continued stroking my waves, I dropped my head to her shoulder. "Does that mean you aren't going to keep trying to parent me after taking a decade off?"

"I promise...to do my best not to," she offered with a small shrug.

"I'm still laying claim to parenting," my dad said, coming around to kiss the tops of our heads. "Speaking of...we wanted to talk to you about something and now's as good a time as ever."

I looked up at them. "What is it?"

My mother brushed away the tears clinging to my cheek. "After we've taken care of the Enchantress's threat, I would like to make a formal decree, introducing you as Arafax's Princess. Its future queen. My daughter."

I didn't know what to say.

"No more secrets. No more hiding. All of us in one world." She cocked her head to the side, waiting for my response. "Isn't that what you want?"

My dad's brows furrowed, lips pursing as he looked over at my mother. "We thought you would be happy about this."

"Of course," I said slowly, not wanting to admit I hadn't thought much about anything past dealing with the Enchantress. I was still scared to think past tonight. Not until everyone was back safe and Dru was in my arms. "I just...hadn't fully decided on staying here."

"What decision is there to make?" she asked. "Your father is here now. We all are. Dru wouldn't have to leave his home and you could keep your magic. Help rebuild Arafax as its Princess. Its Revered. We could do it together."

"Can I think about it?" That wasn't a decision I'd make without talking to Dru, and there was too much at stake for us in the next twenty-four hours.

"Of course."

Sitting back down at the table, we continued to eat, filling my dad in on everything that'd happened since I'd arrived, mixing in some nostalgia of our favorite family memories past.

The future?

It remained a subject we avoided. And I couldn't have been more grateful for that.

We needed to get through tonight first.

CHAPTER 47

Sloan

My body was a live wire, adrenaline coursing through me since I'd begun plotting tonight's mission. When was the last time I'd faced a worthy opponent? My body itched for the fight. To swing my blade.

To cut down an enemy.

Sure, I'd been training the Otherworlders and sparring with Ox prior to visiting Alucinor, but it wasn't the same as training an army. Training *my* army. I missed it fiercely, and while I knew Red would have me posted back as his commander and military advisor if I asked, I wasn't ready. My allegiances were now split even with Arafax and Inverno currently on the same side. What happened if they went back to being rivals?

I'd promised Aislin we were in this together. Until the end. Our lives were tethered when I'd become her champion, and when one champion fell...the other soon followed.

But I was here. Alive.

Meaning, so was she, even if it looked different for her right now.

As long as we drew breath, there was hope of getting her back.

Dru heaved a deep sigh, looking skyward. I bristled, watching Neve's sapphire form glide across the fading moon with Ox knelt between her wings, imposing and strong. She landed smoothly next to us, waiting as Ox hopped off her back.

"Surprised you're not hurling over a log right now," I snickered at the giant. A full foot and a half taller than me, the fact that I could put him on his ass was something I took pride in.

"Same." He curled up the bottom of his sleeve to show a small square bandage and nodded to Dru. "This one. Working his magic, as usual."

"You're welcome," Dru replied before quickly dropping his gaze, as if he'd just remembered he was decidedly pissed about Ox and Neve's secret bonding.

I cleared my throat, and their attention snapped to me. "Thank you all for putting aside your personal shit so we can do this."

"Of course," Dru said, scanning over the studs of his glove then pressing one. A small vial fed through the center of his palm, marked with a handwritten *K*. He slipped it into one of the slots on his chest strap, swallowing so hard I could see the bulb in his throat bob.

It was the one part of the plan for tonight that had us the most nervous. If things went accordingly, we'd never talk again about the risk we'd taken, but it was the only way.

"The most important thing tonight is we aren't detected." *Go in. Find what we need. Get out.* "Everything hinges on that."

"Everyone know what they're doing?" Dru asked, a slight quiver in his usually confident tone. The planning, the plotting, it all came naturally to him. Being on the other side of it, though —the execution—he'd only dealt with a few times. Luckily, Ox and I would be right by his side, both experienced warriors. Probably the best in the realm.

Mox gave an anticipatory growl. Always ready for the fight, like his master. Ox's gaze darted to his Revered. The sapphire dragon merely huffed in response. Neve had been pissed about her role in this, but unfortunately, a dragon hindered the stealth needed to be successful tonight, and she was integral to our escape.

"You'll have your turn later," I said to her with a smirk.

Ox took a few moments while he ensured the connection to Neve's magic was strong, frost coating his fingertips. Behind him, Maeve and Maisie peeked above his shoulders, making me wonder how much practice he'd had between his former weapons and his new ones. "Ox, remember, as soon as it's done, you need to get to Neve and head back to the fort. I will make sure Dru and I get out safely."

Dru scoffed, sending some sparks out from his glove for practice. "What makes you so certain I won't be the one saving your ass?"

"Keep that confidence up and we may have a warrior of you yet." I chuckled, making him frown. Putting my arm around his shoulder, I lowered my voice. "Let's do this."

AFTER TREKKING FARTHER INTO THE SILENT WOODS, marking the trees with my blade as we went, I brought a fist up by my ear, halting the others behind me. Bending, I tucked the knife back with the other two, their silver glinting briefly in the dull moonlight. Turning to face my partners, I pulled my sword out of my scabbard, gripping it with both hands. Mox bent low next to me, eyes darting around the darkened forest.

Ox opened his palms, ice shooting in rivulets, creating the base of an oversized cube. The top he constructed was closed for the most part, minus an opened circle in the center.

Our trap.

He placed it down at his feet, then waved his hands from side to side, coating the dead branches surrounding us with frost.

Dru's knees were bent, gloved hand extended out in front of him. Sparks floated slowly up, hovering around him in a circle. While we wanted to attract the wisps to us, we didn't want to set fire to the trees. Drawing attention to ourselves more than necessary would be detrimental, especially since we needed to save the element of surprise for tomorrow.

This was risky, but we had to. I fucking had to. The Queen had been clear what her priority was, and there wasn't much time to take action. While I'd given my life to protecting my kingdom, doing my duty, I also had a duty to my Revered.

And duty could fuck off if it meant giving up on her.

So here we were, attempting to salvage the wisps. I knew Dru would be on my side. He had his own personal investment in figuring out a way to change them back before we were rid of the Enchantress—his sisters, who'd been taken by her the night of The Blaze.

"See anything?" I asked, squinting in the darkness at Dru. His eyes were covered, a set of night vision goggles attached to his temples.

He didn't move his gaze away, continuing to twist his neck and slowly turn to look around. "Not yet."

Ox curled his fingers in, an icy spear expanding out from his grip. "How come nothing's happening?"

I lifted a hand. Patience was key in ensuring you didn't get yourself killed. As much as I wanted to get this over with and get the fuck back to the fort, stealth meant biding our time. Waiting for the perfect opportunity to strike. "They just need to catch on to the magic being here."

Digging the base of his handmade spear into the ground, Ox shifted his weight. "Should we stop?"

"No," Dru raised his hand, the sparks curving around his

knuckles. He whispered just loud enough for the rest of us to understand him. "Hear that?"

I didn't hear anything at first, but my mind was full of rampant thoughts.

Thoughts of the fight ahead.

Thoughts of the Enchantress.

Thoughts of *her*.

Those thoughts were the things that would get me killed, and if I died...I sure as fuck wouldn't allow her to come with me. Clamping my eyes shut, I inhaled deeply. Those thoughts were my greatest enemy right now, so I hacked them away, silencing them, my instincts surging up. The ones I'd refined over two decades of training.

A faint hum slithered through the tree line, coiling around me like a snake ready to cut off my air supply.

She's coming.

I knew tonight wasn't about finding Aislin. But was it possible? Would she recognize me? Reveal herself?

We quickly stuck the plugs into our ears that Dru had supplied, ensuring the wisps wouldn't be able to entrance us with their glamour. The last thing we needed was someone wandering right into the Enchantress's clutches.

A solitary wisp fluttered toward us, wings beating excitedly, detouring every so often to rub along the frosted trees. Ox painted a floating river of snowflakes, drawing the wisp closer, its dusky body rolling through the path he'd created, coming closer.

It was merely curious. Ashen locks floated from its form, and while I couldn't clearly make out what the wisp was looking at, it felt as if its gaze was pinned to me.

"Aislin?" I whispered into the darkness. Mox moved protectively in front of me, teeth bared, bowing back on his hind legs. "Is that you?"

"Sloan," Ox warned, lifting his spear up defensively. "Be careful."

"Remember, it could be a trap," Dru added, shuffling closer, like he'd protect me.

Adorable.

He'd said our bond was still intact, no matter how shredded it might be from the Enchantress's magic. Could Aislin still sense it too? Sense us in the depths of whatever was left of her?

I had to see.

Reaching deep within myself, I searched for the threads of our bond, rifling around for whatever I could salvage. But there was nothing to hold, to grasp, to pull her to me.

Fuck.

The wisp floated to Mox, extending out a dusky hand. He growled, inching back a few paces and bumping into me. Attention moving to me, she floated closer and swept back the strands of my hair hanging limp in my face. Her faded body was a gentle caress against my skin, one that I missed so fucking much. I sketched her path into memory, just in case this was the last time, the closest I'd get to having her again. "Ais?"

It was her. I just knew it. Deep in my bones, in the empty hollow of my chest, a thin thread glinted in the darkness. I leaned toward the wisp, toward *her.* My chest spooled tight, grasping for that faded strand, watching the wisp as she flitted along the blade of my sword, wrapping herself around the hilt and my hands. Pouring every ounce of love, of energy, of whatever I could fucking find into that cavity, I drenched that gaunt tether.

Clap, clap.

"Blazes!" Ox shouted, and my eyes snapped over to him just as dozens of wisps shot toward us. "There's so many of them."

The longsword was knocked out of my hands, and the wisp jolted forward, surging into my chest like a blade. I screamed out, clutching where it'd pierced my flesh. Falling back onto the underbrush, I twisted my head, scrambling on my back, using whatever force I could leverage from my feet to get me to my longsword.

Finally, I found the comforting steel, swinging it up in time to slice through two wisps diving for me.

Teeth clenched around the back of my collar, and I was dragged back.

Blood oozed down my chest plate, the wound just above its protection. I tried to grip the sword in my hands, but it was too heavy.

Pain sliced through my torso, and a desperate yelp snapped my panicked gaze to Mox. Two wisps encircled him. He staggered, then reared up on his hind legs, swiping at them. His white fur was stained crimson, a large gash carved across his ribs.

Duck.

Mox obeyed, whimpering as he knelt low.

Dragging my heel into me, I grabbed a knife from my ankle holster, sending it flying at the wisps. It cleaved right through them and sank into the bark of a dead tree stump. Orange flecks ignited across my vision, colliding into wisps and disintegrating them a moment before they reappeared.

My chest heaved, gasping for air, eyes blurring. Then darkness drowned out the sea of shadow, sparks, and frost surrounding me.

CHAPTER 48

Dru

"Where did she go?" Ox asked, frantically looking around as he swung his spear into a group of wisps. They collided into the trees, disappearing a moment, then peeling out of the blackened bark to return and fight.

"Now isn't the time to be picky." Sparks flew from my hands, the ashen figures flinching away. I knew it wouldn't destroy them, and I was grateful for that. I needed to buy us time. Gritting my teeth, I cast out another quick wave of sparks, not wanting to run out of Kyleigh's borrowed power before we were out of the Silent Woods. "Get one and go."

Mox yelped, then leapt into the air, claws slashing at the shadow wisps. He wrapped his teeth around one and dragged it by its translucent wing to Ox. Coming back beside me, he drew up on his hind legs, his midsection covered in red.

Fear grabbed me by the throat, but I swallowed it down, his persistence to keep fighting driving my focus. We needed to get the wisp and get out of here.

Becoming as large as the giant, Mox blocked the others while Ox finished wrestling the wisp into the ice box. "Got it!"

"Leave!" I commanded. Ox bent down, grabbing the box

around its edges. Out of the corner of my eye, Sloan used the tree to push herself to stand. Crimson oozed from under her hand, just above her breastplate. She held Aislin's amethyst dagger in the other.

Blazes.

Scuttling backward, I nudged her hand away and gripped over the seeping wound with my glove. "This is going to hurt."

"Do it," she spat out, blue eyes striking me with determination. When the sparks began feeding through the glove, cauterizing the wound, she gritted her teeth, grunting through the pain. "*Fuck.*"

The angles of her jaw pulled taut, spit flying through the cracks between her teeth.

I lifted my hand off her, ensuring that the bleeding had stopped, and she heaved a deep breath before holding up the dagger.

I shot out more sparks, weaving them tightly so that the wisps couldn't pass through its mesh wall without needing time to reform. It had to be enough to hold them off.

"Let's go," I said, dragging Sloan backward with me as we sprinted through the tree line. Mox followed, crunching along the underbrush, growling every so often. Blue scales glinted in the pale moonlight, along with a looming giant figure, box clutched in his palms. My lungs filled with air. Relieved. We were almost there. Just one last step and we'd be gone.

Sloan halted at the edge of the woods, where the decay stopped, the only indication of where the Enchantress's barrier lay. Kneeling low, my eyes darted up to her. No blood spilled from the angry red flesh near her shoulder. Mox keened, the red splotches marring his white, fluffy coat capturing my attention again as he limped on his hind leg.

"Head to the fort. To the infirmary," I instructed. She nodded back at me before guiding Mox out of the forest.

I pulled the partially empty vial from my chest strap, and Ox shifted like an impatient shadow over me. "They can't be far," he whispered, panic threading his voice.

I hurried through the incantation, watching the grass turn bright emerald, a vibrant-purple mushroom springing out of the ground where I'd smeared Kyleigh's blood, opening a space wide enough to slide the box over the threshold. It was the only way to take the wisp, to take part of the Enchantress's magic beyond the boundary that'd been created when she was banished.

Ox shoved it another step, then picked it up, hoisting it over his shoulder, his massive weapons shifting to make room for the icy box.

"I'll meet you there."

Ox gripped Neve's scales, fumbling up her back with one arm, using his feet to propel him. I scanned my memory for the other incantation, the one meant to reverse what I'd done.

While the mushroom didn't disappear once I'd finished, the green grass stopped winding further into the dead, root-covered ground of the Silent Woods.

The magic wasn't spreading.

It had worked.

We'd smuggled a wisp out.

There was still so much to be done tonight, but first—

"Well, well, well. Who do we have here?"

The lilt was unfamiliar, yet terrifying.

I stilled, hunched over the path of bright grass spilling into the Silent Woods.

Her domain.

"Don't believe I've met you before, have I?"

I turned slowly, standing as I did to face the Enchantress.

Sweat beaded at my brow, a few drops streaking down my cheek.

She shouldn't be here. How was this even—

"Wondering how I escaped my cabin?" As if in one step, she gripped my throat, pinning me against the ragged bark of a nearby tree. Her head cocked sharply to the side, then she eyed the emptied vial nestled beside the newly grown grass. "I, too, wondered how it was possible."

Her eyes snapped back to mine, completely onyx, making her expression hard to discern. I rasped into her palm, struggling to draw breath. The sharpened metallic tips of her clawed fingers pressed into my throat. I couldn't form words, my breath stuttering.

"Shh..." she cooed, tilting her head in the opposite direction and stepping closer to me. Squinting in the darkness, she took her other clawed hand, feeling around the edge of my night vision goggles and ripping them away, leaving a few scratches that seared along my temple. She inhaled sharply, her palm twitching against my pulse ever so slightly, pricking into my flesh. Her gaze followed the movement, the reflection of the crimson blood dribbling down my throat.

Frozen in fear, I watched as she swiped the bead and smeared it between the pads of her glinting metallic fingertips.

"I don't fear you," I lied. I knew without a doubt she could kill me if she decided. Probably make me a husk since I had no powers to offer. My body shook in place. I needed to do something to set her off her axis, even for just a moment. "Deirdre."

The edges of her sable eyes crinkled, then disappeared just as quickly.

"Don't fear me? Is that so?" Her mouth flipped into a smirk, and she continued, ignoring my use of her name. "Isn't that why I was trapped here in the first place? Fear?"

She arched an eyebrow but didn't release her grip.

Quivering in her grasp, I raised my glove, blasting as much power through it as I could muster. She hissed, and I dropped, crumpling to the ground, gasping for air.

"Interesting parlor trick you've got there with your little gadget."

I scurried backward toward the boundary, watching her

bring a hand across her stomach and the singed dress there, the fabric stitching itself back together, much like the wisps did when Sloan split them in half earlier. "You know, you're bold, considering—"

"I'm a null?" I spat the term at her that I'd heard a million times since I'd come of magic age. It didn't bother me like it once did.

"Oh, you're much more than that," she said, watching me cross the threshold separating Arafax from her domain. "But do you even realize?"

Confusion threatened to spill over my features, but from everything Aislin and Sloan had told me about the Enchantress, I couldn't let that show. She was a master of deception. Manipulation.

I continued taking steady steps backward, holding up a glove that I knew had nothing left to save me if I'd fucked up the enchantment.

She walked until the barrier stopped her, making me jolt back on the off chance I'd been mistaken. Her hand pushed against the invisible boundary, recoiling off its edge. She pursed her lips in frustration but stayed silent.

Finally able to catch my breath, knowing the incantation had done its job, I darted away from the twisted faerie, refusing to look back.

CHAPTER 49
Sloan

I rooted my knees to the infirmary floor, hunched over Mox who lay still, aside from the slow rise and fall of his abdomen. Its rhythm was the only thing keeping me sane and my hand steadied as I sutured the gaping slices exposing his ribs.

Just keep breathing, boy.

I'm nearly done.

There was no emotion returning from the other side of our connection. It merely existed, its rope-like structure saturated and heavy. So fucking heavy. Even if he couldn't hear me, I continued to coax him through my mind.

Open your eyes, Moxy.

"You sure you don't need me to do that?" Brighid's gentle voice filtered into the room, making me want to swat it away. Ignoring her train of thought, I narrowed my gaze and went back to my work, pulling the strand of white through Mox's taut flesh. I didn't need her interruptions.

I need you.

"I doubt you'll find someone who can stitch better than me in all of the six territories." Other than maybe the araneas, but I preferred not to think back on my time in Alucinor. "Just keep working on his leg. Once he wakes up, he won't be easy to keep down."

Not my fighter.

Mox's body stuttered against my palm holding him in place.

"Please," Brighid urged. "You still need to be tended to."

"I'll be tended to when he's done. I'm fine," I gritted out, willing away the lash of pain I'd been ignoring while I took care of Mox.

Dru had stopped the bleeding. That was enough for now.

Tomorrow we moved forward with our plans. There was no delaying them, and I needed Mox. Aislin needed Mox.

Looping the thin strand through itself and knotting it securely, I cut off the excess, then set the spool on the ground. Melting onto the floor so I was flush with his back, I wrapped my arms around him, savoring the comfort of his fur against my palm. Normally he'd hum getting scratches in his favorite spot, but now?

Nothing.

Just the frail reassurance of his ribs lifting toward the ceiling before contracting in.

Nuzzling my face into the crook of his neck, I tasted salt water on my tongue, not even realizing until that moment that I'd begun to cry.

I couldn't lose him.

I'd lost enough.

And I refused—I fucking *refused*—to give up on them.

Either of them.

Come the fuck on, Mox.

Another stuttered beat had me stilling in place. My breath suspended somewhere outside my lungs.

Waiting.

Wishing.

Begging.

"Commander..." Brighid whispered, using a title I no longer claimed, "look."

Lifting my head, I watched the slow flutter of white lids peel open. I pushed up to sit, too quickly, the sting of my injury surging through my arm.

"Hey, Moxy," I managed through a wince.

His onyx nose scrunched up, probably because we both smelled like dirt and the metallic stench of blood. Then it wriggled, his eye darting up to me, he gave me a lick on the cheek.

Brighid slid over some crackers, holding them cupped in her palms as Mox ate greedily. Messily. Savoring every morsel until he released a *harrumph,* signaling the healer to grab more.

When he was done, she stood and went to the sink, washing her hands. She glanced over her shoulder at me, eyes darting to the angry mess of blood and tissue near my clavicle. "*Now* will you allow me to tend to you?"

I quickly scanned over Mox, making sure she'd finished stitching up his leg, then I nodded to her.

Gripping my familiar around the neck, I pressed a kiss on his snout. The constricting weight on my chest, the pause in my lungs, retreated, filling them with ignited air. With hope.

I love you.

The twines encircled. Our connective rope strengthening with each breath we took.

I refused to leave him, twisting only slightly to allow the healer access to my wound. Pressed into Mox, he nudged me with his nose, taking some of my weight as I gritted against the pain of Brighid's work.

We're gonna be okay, I sent through our connection.

He nipped at my hair, curling toward me, his eyes meeting mine as if to say, *We're all gonna be okay.*

CHAPTER 50

I crept across the red carpet, up the stairs, and tiptoed as quickly as I could toward the study. The sounds of talking filtered from the Banquet Hall. Not shouting, so I took it as a good sign, still not wanting to attract any attention to myself.

Back pressed against the wall, I reached over and twisted the knob until the door swung open. Slipping into the room, I turned to find Ox's massive form stuck in the windowpane. I struggled to contain my laughter as I locked the door behind me, then crossed the room, assisting him. He fell into the study with a *thud*.

Neve hovered outside the window, her sapphire wings beating gently. Once Ox had grabbed the box off of her, she descended out of view.

"She's just going to go check on Sloan and Mox."

"Good." A shiver trilled through me—from the cold or the close encounter with the Enchantress, I wasn't sure I still couldn't get our exchange out of my head or understand how I'd survived it. We had our wisp, but I'd also come face-to-face with the very person we weren't supposed to engage. How was she able to roam the Silent Woods now?

"You okay?" Ox asked, concern drawing his bushy brows together.

Should I tell him?

Had I just put us all in even more danger?

Did she know that we'd taken one of her wisps?

I shoved a cork into the barrel of questions threatening my confidence to its core. That was the last thing I needed right now. Not when we were so close to figuring out more about saving the wisps.

Saving Aislin. My Sisters.

"I'm fine. Just glad we got what we needed."

Ox set the cube down, the wisp jolting erratically in a blur beneath the walls of ice.

"You don't have to stay," I said to him, knowing he probably wanted to check on Sloan and Mox as well. I did too, but my role was too critical, too time sensitive right now to stop.

"Neve will get us an update." He crouched next to the cube. "Besides, I'll need to make sure this doesn't melt until you have things figured out."

I'd forgotten he could manipulate her element even when she wasn't in dragon form. That would at least make things easier than trying to grab Neve later or figure out how to keep from having a puddle form in the middle of the study.

"Then I better get started." I brushed my hands on the sides of my trousers, then walked over to where I'd translated the *Valídus Vénenifícium*. Right now, us having the book gave us an advantage. If the Revered were supposed to destroy it all those years ago, then we potentially had a way of stopping her.

Or at least weaken her.

"I'll just keep quiet so you can do all your tinkering." Ox brought his thumb and pointer finger together, zipping up his lips with a determined nod. Our final meeting with King Redmond was first thing tomorrow and going into it with all the information I could uncover was paramount. Any discoveries from tonight would be crucial in formulating a plan.

The Queen would prioritize eliminating the Enchantress and the threat she posed above all else—including saving Aislin, not to mention the other numerous wisps in her blackened clutches. If it came down to it...I didn't know if I could deliver on that expectation, even if it was what my Queen demanded of me.

If the Enchantress's magic was tied to her wisps and we found a way to kill her, there was a good chance those she'd taken from would disappear as well. She'd pulled from their very essence somehow, transforming them into shades to do her bidding.

If that wisp we'd seen earlier was really Aislin...then she really had no idea who she was. That much of her had been ripped away. There was no other explanation to defend her attacking her own champion. If she'd killed Sloan, any trace of Aislin would quickly die with her...at least from what I understood when Harkin explained it.

Unless she could remember and she was just overly willing to die alongside her champion.

No. I flicked the thought away like a nasty pebble stuck in my boot. Aislin wouldn't have done that willingly. It was after the claps. After *she'd* taken control.

The wisps didn't seem to have any autonomy when she called upon them. My mind flitted back to the golden scale hovering over the map that now hung on my wall. The spot where I'd marked. Where I'd located my sisters.

How many horrible deeds had they committed on behalf of the Enchantress? They'd been in her clutches for over a decade now, just teenagers, barely knowing their magics. Fiona had only discovered her affinity for wind a month prior.

The deadened stares of Imogen and Enid as they trailed

behind her, walking as if in a daydream toward the Enchantress's cabin.

The others, including one bedecked in a crimson cape shuffled through the blackened trees.

I'd lost so much with my family's absence. But them? How much of their life had been stolen away at the hands of the Enchantress?

It wasn't fair.

My fists clenched, recalling how I just watched them go, calling out to them in frightened whispers, pinned in place. A coward.

Never again.

This was my chance. Starting in this room tonight. There was no alternative. I had to figure out how to override the Enchantress's spell over them.

I sorted through the papers Kyleigh and I had transcribed onto. Some were almost illegible, probably due to our all-nighter.

I smirked at the memory.

"Find something?" Ox asked, voice perking up in hope.

"Not yet." I cleared my throat, eyes narrowing on the page denoting an incantation for transformation. If I set the intention to transform the wisp back into its original form, maybe it would work. Bringing my thumb to my cheek I scraped over the stubble building there.

Unlatching the portable cooling box I'd hidden away earlier, I tapped the head of a vial, tipping it a bit to see the label. The most potent blood that I'd collected belonged to Kyleigh. She'd even helped me stock up more when we'd hatched tonight's plan.

Taking the vial in my hand, I carried it over toward the box, kneeling down and waving Ox to assist. He snapped out of whatever daydream had him occupied, the deviant grin stripped off his face in an instant. "What do you need me to do?"

"Give me a way to slide some of this in there. I'll say the incantation a few times and then you open the box enough so the wisp has to touch the blood on my hands before it can move out of reach."

"Hold on," Ox said, jumping to his feet and shuffling to go lock the window. "Just in case."

"Good thinking." I must have been feeling off after tonight's mission—tonight's encounter—to make a rookie mistake like that.

"*Neth anéiavan só iánu ríth.*"

I nodded to Ox and circled with my hands around where he was touching the box, melting away part of its lid. Slipping through the opening, the wisp flitted out quickly, rubbing against my hand, smearing crimson along its side and the rim of its wing. I continued, keeping my hands outstretched, slowly following the wisp as it frantically moved about the room. "*Neth anéiavan só iánu ríth.*"

I heaved out a frustrated sigh. "Well, now we have a wisp trapped in this room and we can't leave."

Ox grabbed a large satchel of supplies sitting in the corner and emptied it, holding it between his hands to ensnare the wisp. After a few clumsy attempts he was able to grab it again, the satchel punching out in different angles as the wisp tried to escape.

"What now?" Ox asked, giving a small shrug while he clamped the moving satchel in his hand.

"Just tie it up and go check on the others for me. Make sure no one comes in here until I'm finished."

"Not even Kyleigh?"

"Not even her." If I couldn't figure this out, then I'd have to concede.

And that was the last thing I wanted.

"You sure?"

"Yes," I replied, already combing through the other translations to see if I was missing something. "Just tell Kyleigh to go ahead to bed without me. She needs her rest for tomorrow. I'll meet her."

"Oh, I bet you will," he said with a wink, making me groan.

"Speaking of—tomorrow is a big day for all of us."

"I'm ready."

"Are you?" I asked. "Because you are our only champion-bonded pair that's currently intact. You should know the significance of that."

I hadn't forgotten how pissed I was at him and Neve but there were more important things to worry about.

"I do know. And I've always sworn to do everything to protect Arafax. Tomorrow is no different." He gave a heavy sigh. "We may not have our bond...figured out, but we are on the same page when it comes to our duty."

"Well, that's something," I said, trying not to get annoyed that he made something sacred seem so *sterile*.

Without another word, he left the room. As soon as the door shut and I'd clicked the lock in place, I slid down it, only the sound of the wisp fumbling around in the satchel filling the space.

Kyleigh's blood should have been enough, she was from one of the most powerful families in Celaria, a Revered, the strongest wielder we had. Crawling over, I clutched the contained wisp, then continued on my knees until I'd grabbed the cooling box, dragging it toward me.

I wondered what the wisp could understand if it wasn't under the thrall of the Enchantress. The wisp earlier had seemed to understand Sloan. "I'm here to help you. If you understand what I'm saying, stop moving."

The bag stopped shifting immediately.

"If I let you out, will you stay still so I can help? Beat your wings once for yes."

A slow clap of the satchel told me the wisp was in agreement. Now I just had to pray it didn't make me a fool.

Untying the knot, I opened the top, releasing the wisp. It quickly zipped out of the bag, floating midair until it twisted and saw me. I held up my hands defensively, but it merely flitted closer, as if curious.

"Stay still, please."

A nod. The wisp hovered in front of me, only slowly beating its wings to stay in place. Repeating the same incantation, I thumbed through the other vials, taking them out one by one to test them.

First, I tried it with the small amount of Aislin's blood I had collected prior to her being taken. Then, I tried with Neve's and even stooped to using King Redmond's that he'd had sent here with his healers as a show of faith that he was willing to concede some of his power to work together. Finally, I tried with faerie blood, even though the sight of it had me cringing after learning more about them from Harkin.

None of them worked.

None.

And none of the other incantations seemed to make sense for fixing this problem.

My chest tightened, the threat of failure a noose wrapped around my still-tender throat. My hand fumbled to the cut there.

I had no clue how to rectify this.

For the first time in as long as I could remember, my mind might not win this battle. I'd always believed everything was fixable. *Everything*. But I didn't know where to go from here. How to undo her handiwork.

Her words pricked at me like the tips of her sharpened claws, scratching at something in corners of my mind.

Oh, you're much more than that... Do you even realize?

A crazy idea formed, and I was just desperate enough to try anything.

Scooting the vials around, I found the one I was looking for. Uncapping it, I poured it onto my bare palm, running it over the wisp's wings. *"Neth anéiavan só iánu ríth."*

The wisp's wings curled in, its limbs began extending out. My heart pounded as I scooted into the corner of the room. Like a piece of clay molding itself, the wisp began to solidify, shifting color until a naked woman stood in front of me. She crumpled to the floor and clutched around her knees, looking up at me through faded-lilac eyes. She opened her mouth as if to speak, but then clamped her lips shut.

I unbuttoned my shirt, handing it to her to cover up with.

"Can you tell me your name?" I asked, feeling a strange sense of déjà vu, though I wasn't sure why.

I clutched the vial in my hand, staring at her. A dark realization was curling around me, pulling me under, saturating my lungs, stifling my ability to breathe.

She moved her mouth, as if tasting the word on her tongue, unsure of how to get it out. "Z-Zara."

Her eyes darted around the room frantically.

My mind swirled, nausea taking hold. But I didn't want to scare her. Who knew what she'd been through? How long she'd been like this?

"I assure you, you're safe. You're at Arafax's fort." She didn't seem to be comforted by that. "Stay here," I insisted. "I'd like to get a healer to help you and get you a fresh set of clothes."

She shook her head violently from side to side, scooting over to me and gripping my hand, pleading. "N-n-no."

White and glowing, the moon hung above. Warmth flooded my chest. It beamed its brilliance like a beacon I yearned to reach for. To cradle. A voice pulled my gaze, something gentle and bright sweeping my cheek. A pair of fluorescent eyes—rich magenta—

stared down at me, soft and comforting. "My sapling," she cooed, voice threaded with awe.

The weaver's lilac eyes widened.

The vial was still in my shaking hand, and I dropped it to the floor. It rolled a few inches away, landing with the *D* staring back at me, bleeding me of my sanity.

Of everything I'd ever known.

I whipped my head away, scooped under Zara's shoulder and carted her toward the infirmary. Every step in that direction automatic, my mind somewhere else completely, trying to understand what this meant.

Knowing what it meant.

For the first time, I wished for ignorance. Begged for it.

Oh, you're much more than that... Do you even realize?

I wished I didn't.

Harkin's words filtered in as well, spearing me with understanding.

Well then, you really know nothing of our people.

Our people are wary of outsiders.

Our people.

Not an outsider. Not lumping me in with them. He meant *our.*

We crashed into the infirmary. Ox and Neve were talking with Brighid, all of their eyes snapping to me. The healer hurried over to take Zara out of my clutches. As soon as she did, I fumbled for the wastebasket, throwing my head in it, bile surging up in waves until I had no more to purge.

Ox and Neve were next to me when I finally wiped the putrid remnants on my sleeve. A big hand spanned between my shoulder blades, giving me a few soft pats. "You okay?"

The rims of Neve's caramel irises were ignited, her voice firm with concern. "You look like you've seen a ghost."

I had. The ghost of a truth I wanted to deny.

"Incantation took a lot out of me, I guess." The half lie slipped eagerly off my tongue.

The incantation had undone the Enchantress's work. Using *my* blood. *My* fucking blood.

The blood of a null. Lacking power, strength. The least potent—at least it *should* have been. But it had worked. I was *just* a null. But I also wasn't.

All Celarian blood enchantments could be altered or undone by their kin.

My sapling.

The evil that haunted the Silent Woods, the wicked faerie that'd betrayed her kind, the one who had ripped away my sisters, Aislin, and countless others...the Enchantress...

Was my *mother*.

CHAPTER 51
A Wisp

Clap, clap.

Muttering filtered from the bedroom, the floorboards askew once again.

"It's him. It's him. It's him."

Was it a chant? A curse? A prayer?

She'd shut herself away.

Alone.

Holding the copper vial, her eyes were distant. Glazed.

Only a drop remained.

The moon winked light into the room, a tiny dragon dangling from her claws.

Clap, clap.

We flitted about the forest, brushing against the trees, playing with their peeling bark.

Others glided around the edge.

A sliver of green unfurled where it didn't belong. Where it'd never been before.

We'd remember that. Wouldn't we?

Moving closer, I brushed the ground while the one that moved mountains dug at it.

They noticed it too, the glint catching our attention.

Hers too.

"Aren't you good little pets," she cooed before taking it and heading toward the cabin.

Clap, clap.

She held the empty vial in her hands, sticking her pinky in, scraping.

Looking at her finger, she frowned. "Not enough."

Throwing it against the wall, it shattered across the floorboards.

The one that blew tempests scooped them up, tossing them out the window into the heap.

I avoided that window now. No one sniffed there anymore.

And the gnarled shapes stared at me even when they lay. Unmoving. Still.

For now.

Clap, clap.

Something's under the surface, drilling at me.

But I returned here, soiled once again. Dank.

Clap, clap.

There's a gentle tug from the inside.
I didn't know where it led.
Every time I tried to follow, it snapped quickly out of reach.
Maybe one day I'd grip so tight I wouldn't ever let go.

Clap, clap.

CHAPTER 52
Neve

I t was the middle of the night by the time we left the infirmary. My bare feet dragged along the fresh grass springing from the thorny, root-covered ground. Bluebell and moonflower buds peeked from emerald stems lining the path leading toward The Lavender. Every day, Arafax was returning to the way I'd remembered it before The Blaze. Winter's clutch releasing its grasp to spring's claim of the realm.

The dark border to our territory pulled my attention. The Silent Woods, its dead trees stabbing up into the belly of the deepening purple sky. Once the Enchantress was gone, would the Serene Woods return to the splendor it'd boasted from my childhood? Would copper-encrusted bark coat their trunks? Sweet sap run through their veins?

Ox was silent as we walked, our bond prickling with heat in my chest.

A few of the lights were still on in The Lavender, shining against the darkness when the comforting crunch of boots next to me hushed.

I turned to find Ox planted in place, a statue of brawn, face contorted into a serious expression that didn't suit his demeanor. "What's going on with you?"

"What's going on with *me*?" His voice was a deep rumble, rich warmth crackling against my frigid walls. "I can't believe you're asking me that after everything."

He scooped me up, throwing me over his shoulder. "What are you doing?"

I didn't even try to resist...partially because I knew I wouldn't win and partially because, in some strange way, it thrilled me. Desire pooled between my thighs, anticipation at what he had in store for tonight. He was angry, but he would never hurt me. It was part of the reason I'd chosen to be tethered to him.

Besides, an angry Ox could be coaxed into a wanton one.

I loosened the knot in my chest, thinking back to the night before when he'd driven into me from behind, toying with the sensitive ring, heightening the sensations.

"Blazes, mó venéro," he growled, earning my prideful smirk. He heaved a sigh, finally putting me down on the ground, adjusting himself as he glared at me. "I know what you're doing."

We stood on the circular patch of stones at the edge of Arafax's main village. He took a dagger from his holster, grabbed my hand, and pricked my finger before saying the incantation he'd surprisingly memorized. A moment later, the entrance into Everwood Grove appeared, and we stepped through, closing Arafax behind us. "I know the Evergleam isn't working right now. We don't have time to worry about this."

"When is the right time to worry about this?" he asked, taking my hand and walking along the grove, its trees flickering an unsteady beat as we passed. "When Arafax goes back to being unable to have bonded champions protecting their people? When Ais is back and her bond is fucked up with Sloan? When the decay on these branches starts rotting Celaria's magic after we just got it back? WHEN?"

The Evergleam was still glimmering, but its illumination had dimmed, the crystalline leaves hanging from its branches like sullen teardrops. When we were close enough, I scanned the branches for ours, finding it a cloudy-rust shade. "You're right."

He pulled back, dropping my hand with his eyes wide. "I am?"

"Yes." I looped my arms around his neck, chin lifted almost uncomfortably so I could meet his gaze. "We should strengthen it. Fix it."

His head dipped low, thumb cupping my cheek, lips hovering over mine.

Waiting.

My heart pounded a rhythmic plea in my chest.

"Then let me in."

"Okay," I said, not even thinking. My pupils split down the middle of my golden orbs, reflected back to me in his chocolaty pools. My hand clasped around the collar of his shirt, moving me closer, lips drifting toward his as I undid the top button of his shirt.

"No." His voice was a harsh whisper, a massive hand wrapping around my wrist, holding me in place. "That's not what I meant and you know it."

I lifted my lips away from him, my body begging me not to. The bond swirled in anticipation, wanting to close the distance. Tears pricked at the backs of my eyes, and I went to freeze them too late, frosted streaks lining my cheeks. "What do you want from me?"

He continued to hold my face in his hand, thumb brushing over the frozen tracks, melting them away. "I want to make this work."

"This is working," I said, lip trembling with traitorous intention. I wanted to kiss him so badly. To not feel weak if I let my icy wall down. To find strength in being unguarded. Truly exposed. Our bond begged for it, parched for the nourishment that connection would provide.

But I needed to deny it. Deny this. To give in would be to break and I promised myself I'd be unbreakable. "Everything was fine between us until they brought up the Evergleam."

"Was it?" He raised a brow, cracking into my resolve.

My gaze narrowed. "What are you saying?"

"Maybe things weren't fine between us." My lips pressed together, and his eyes zeroed in on them before darting back up. "And I don't want just *fine*." His forehead pressed into mine, as if to stop himself. "I fucking want it *all*. All of it. All of *you,* mó venéro. Not some clipped connection that stops here." He placed his hand on my chest, his fingers spanning between my breasts. "This bond, it runs two ways. You wanted me as your champion because you trusted me. But you're not being honest. Not with me. Not with yourself."

"How dare—"

"I know you are tampering with it."

"You don't know that," I defended, stepping out of his reach and crossing my arms. Wanting to physically block the connection between us, though I knew it was impossible.

He shook his head, looking defeated as he threw up his hands. "I know you have a one-way connection to everything I feel. *That* isn't reciprocated. But whether you stop choking that cord or not, I know you. Better than you want to admit I do."

As if pulled by an invisible string, I pinned Ox to the wilting bark of the Evergleam. More accurately, he let me pin him. "What do you want from me, Ox?"

He slid his hands up my waist, making my breath hitch. Coasting along the sides of my body, the curves of my breasts, his fingertips traced the rise and fall of my chest until they stopped over my heart.

Ox's voice was firm, a possessive plea. "I want in here."

I stood there, unmoving. "I don't know if that's something I can give you."

"Well, I'll be here when you figure it out." He knelt, unthreading himself from between me and the Evergleam and giving a shrug before starting down the path of the grove. "Assuming we make it through tomorrow."

"Ox—"

He lifted a hand to silence me, unwilling to hear anymore.

It was probably for the best. It would have all been lies.

The bond. My body. My heart. It all wanted so much from him.

And the truth that threatened to shatter me: deep down, I knew he could give it all to me...and more.

CHAPTER 53

Redmond

I scanned over the tactical map, memorizing my bird's-eye flight for tomorrow.

Making sure I had each route navigated from best- to worst-case scenario. If everything went well, the Enchantress would be gone from our lives, Sloan would have Aislin back, and maybe she'd return here as Inverno's commander.

If it didn't, my fail-safe was ready to go.

A faint blue light shone through the veins of my chest. My phoenix certainly had its own feelings about my intentions.

While the gem hadn't hindered me in the same way as my people, since Inverno's Kings didn't bond familiars, I now realized how misaligned I'd been with my phoenix and its magic. Looking back at when I thought I'd lost both my father and Neve in one vicious swoop, that was the most out of control my power had ever been. I'd assumed it was because of my grief, my rage unleashing itself in one horrific blow.

But now I knew the truth...

The gem had destabilized my magic, the land's magic, in a multitude of ways that I'd probably never understand. My pain and selfishness had cost Celaria. Bleeding myself these weeks, laying the foundation to keep my people safe and protected, it was a small price in comparison to the wreckage I'd left in the wake of The Blaze.

The strange bursts of vision since the gem had been taken by Aislin were becoming more frequent, not just when my phoenix was trying to protect me. Entries I'd scoured for in the royal archives were starting to make more sense now that my phoenix had claimed more of its power. It'd been subtle at first, becoming increasingly apparent with each passing day as the power slowly spread from the Evergleam's hidden grove.

Knotting the parcel, I tucked it under my arm and headed out into the hallway, blue-flame sconces guiding my walk. Two rooms away, I rested my hand on the door's latch, disappointment sweeping through me.

I knew the room would be vacant. It had been for months. And I felt like an idiot doing this... It would probably remain empty.

Twisting the knob, I opened the door and turned on the light. Everything was still in its place. This room used to be my favorite spot to go to laugh, to escape within the walls of my own castle... To just be *me*.

A half-finished pair of navy trousers hung over the table next to a blue cushion stuffed with a hundred glinting pins. The perfectly made bed was silver with embellished quilted swirls floating along the comforter. So many questions ran through me, but I brushed them aside, placing the parcel at the foot of her bed. It would be here if she ever needed—wanted—to come back.

My hip seared in pain. *Another summons*. After inserting herself in my nightmares last night, I knew this was coming. She was not happy that I hadn't delivered on her suspected thieving by the mermaids. She'd want to regroup. To find someone new to blame.

A new focus for her infinite wrath.

I needed to distract her enough for our plans—ones we'd be confirming shortly.

Leaving Sloan's room, I halted when I found Cormac waiting for me. "Anything else before you head out, Your Majesty?"

"The plans have been set," I told him. I'd done everything I could to prepare Inverno for any outcome from my actions. "Now is the time to execute them."

He nodded quickly, scurrying out of the way.

The phoenix within rose to the surface, igniting my veins as I shifted. Careening through an open window lining the castle's wall, I followed the waking lavender sky, soaring toward my final stop before visiting the Enchantress.

I SOARED TO THE FORT AFTER FINDING NO SIGN OF Sloan at The Lavender. Poking my beak into a handful of windows, I finally spotted her in the infirmary. It was Mox's white fur that'd initially pulled me in, noticing her arm wrapped along his midsection, otherwise hidden from view.

They seemed peaceful like this, sating me with the confirmation that they were together and safe—until I spotted the bandages at her collarbone and around his hind leg, tucked beneath her palm.

"What happened?" I asked, louder than I intended, fury kindling in my chest as I shifted and moved closer. Sloan's eyes popped open, and I flew back when she drew her blade to my throat. When she realized it was me, she took a deep breath, sheathing the knife with a groan.

"You're wounded."

"No shit." She yawned. "Your observational skills aren't too impressive, Red." Sliding back down behind Mox, she waved me away. "Fuck off so we can get some more rest before our meeting later."

"I can't do that." Placing a hand on her injured shoulder, I leaned over and whispered, "Tell me what happened?"

"Fine," she grumbled, then began to walk through the encounter in the Silent Woods, pointing at the sleeping woman tucked under a blanket in the darkened corner of the room, her raven tresses covering her face.

"So, she was a wisp and Dru was able to change her? How'd he do it?"

"Using Kyleigh's blood and one of the translated incantations from that tome you snagged him."

"Well, that's something." Hope lit my chest. If he could fix the wisps, maybe there was a way to get rid of the bond marks.

"Why are you here, Red?" Sloan asked, voice less groggy than it had been minutes ago. She peered over at the clock. "The meeting's not for another three hours."

"I finished getting things ready with Cormac. And I needed you to know that I left something for you. In your room."

Her eyes shot to mine, glinting against the sliver of morning's light pouring into the room. "What is it?"

"A contingency."

"Contingency for what?" She pushed up to her elbows, wincing as she did. "I don't like when you talk in code, Red."

I nudged her to lay back down, not wanting her to stifle any healing. Healers were amazing but fighting against their magic too early could hinder its progress. "Just promise me, even if you don't return to Inverno for good, you'll retrieve the parcel if necessary."

She yawned again, rubbing her eye with her fist. "If I say yes, will you let me go back to bed?"

"Of course." I smiled, my arrogance smoldering out any other emotions flaring within me.

She tucked herself further into Mox. "Then fine."

"Thank you, Sloan," I said, brushing aside a few clumps of silver hair from her cheek before pressing a kiss to it. "For everything."

CHAPTER 54

Kyleigh

The bed dipped with a groan, Dru curling around me, draping his arm over my waist. My eyes squinted in the near-complete darkness, adjusting after a few moments. The sky was still inky purple, the faint glint of the day's moon beginning to wake across its illuminated surface.

"Hey," I keened, burrowing into his shelter.

Dru's warmth enveloped me like a comforting blanket, and his lips brushed against the crest of my ear. "How'd it go?"

I twisted around, needing to see his face and know he was okay. "Shouldn't I be asking *you* that?"

It had taken me a few hours to fall asleep after dinner. I was pleasantly surprised at how well it had gone, despite feeling like I would throw up. Anxiety punched through me as I waited for everyone to get back from the Silent Woods, until I'd become so beat down by exhaustion I'd fallen asleep.

"Well, I'm here, aren't I?" he chuckled, the sound feeling oddly forced.

"Yes, you are." I gave him a brief kiss before pulling away, catching the time on the clock. "And I'm so glad. But you better get some sleep before our meeting in the morning. Tomorrow is—"

"Technically today," he said, brushing his nose against mine, shushing me. "But right now, I just want to be here with you. Last night was successful enough. The wisp we rescued is in the infirmary now, a wisp no longer."

"Dru! That's amazing!"

My heart lightened at the news. If he'd been able to do that for one, that meant he could hopefully do it for Aislin and his sisters. "I knew you would figure it out. Is that why it took you so long to come to bed?"

He ran a hand through my hair, the golden flecks of his eyes dancing in the darkness. "I would have been here sooner, but I needed to get some plans in place so I'm ready for the meeting later. It will at least be easier to get the Queen on board now that I have proof the wisps can be returned to their former selves."

"Did you tell Sloan?" She would no doubt be over the moon to know there was a way to get back Aislin.

"I did. I was able to visit with her for a bit in the infirmary when I got there with Zara—the former wisp."

"Sloan's in the infirmary?" I asked, pressing up on my elbows. "Is she okay?"

"Yes. She and Mox sustained some injuries, but they are all stitched up. The healing balms should quicken things so they are ready for our plans." He gave a small smile, not as genuine as I would have liked but still breathtaking. "Now tell me, how did it go with your parents?"

"Better than I expected, actually." I sighed, grateful everyone was at least under one roof and as safe as I probably could have hoped for. "We all made it through dinner unscathed."

"That's a step in the right direction," he said with a laugh, this one slightly lighter than before.

I didn't want any secrets between us, so I decided to dive right in, bracing myself. "My mother...wants to formally

357

announce me as Arafax's Princess." I paused a moment. "As next in line to the throne. Once we've killed the Enchantress, that is."

Dru's expression never faltered, shocking me more than my mother had when she'd originally stated her intention. He cradled my jaw with his palm. "What do *you* want?"

"I don't know. I was kind of hoping you'd help me with that." I gave him a quick smirk, hoping to offset how torn I was over the idea. "Vermont has been the plan. It's where I grew up —what I've always known up until a few months ago. But now my dad is here. And we could really make a difference."

Dru had spent years plotting ways to rebuild Arafax, to see it have a bright and vibrant future. What would happen if we left? The fact that he'd been willing to give that all up for me meant everything. But the idea of Dru without *that* purpose, without the fire to innovate... That was unfair to him. "And obviously you must have feelings about it. Your life has been here, other than those few years at Halston. This is your home."

His palm slid where the marred scale markings etched my side, rising until it rested atop my chest, my pulse quickening beneath his featherlight touch. "Home is where my heart is with yours."

He smiled, kissing me slowly a few times before nuzzling my nose with his own, his golden eyes drinking in the silvery light of mine. "The location's just the backdrop."

My fingers crept down his spine, stopping at his waistband. I skimmed its edge, listening to Dru's breath hitch as the length of him pressed against my stomach, straining through the fabric. Just as I went to wriggle it down around his hips, he dragged his fingers along my body to gently clasp my wrist. "Before I forget, I wanted to give you this."

He twisted behind himself, grabbing something off the nightstand. Holding it in front of me, I studied the intricate detailing of a filigree heart dangling from a delicate golden chain. It was the most beautiful piece of jewelry I'd ever seen. It stood out but wasn't gaudy and looked like a treasure you'd find in an antique shop back in the Otherworld.

Undoing the clasp, I dipped my chin forward so he could bring it over my head, fumbling a bit as he moved my hair out of the way to secure it. The charm rested between the swell of my breasts, and I brought my hand up, rubbing the metal between my fingers.

"What's this for?"

His eyes lingered over me wearing his gift, voice catching on something unseen as he spoke. "I had planned to give it to you the night of our ceremony, but with everything that happened, I got distracted."

That night seemed so long ago, time blurred by with everything going on during our time away from each other. While Dru wasn't my champion forged in blood, the connection I had with him felt no less strong. He'd saved my life, taught me how to exist in this new world, loved me in spite of my mess.

His finger traced the edge of the pendant. "It's an enchanted heirloom, similar to King Redmond's, so it will stay with you, even when you're shifted."

"It's beautiful."

He smiled, the full beam of it filling me with warmth. "It pales in comparison to you."

"I love it, and I love you." Pulling him close, I ran my fingers along his waistband again.

"I love you too, Kyleigh."

As I hovered over his lips, a pool of want threatened to drown me if I didn't have him right now. "I know we should both probably go to sleep…"

"Sleep can wait." His hand drifted to my shoulder, pulling the lacy strap of my nightdress down. "This can't."

I tugged at his pants, and he wriggled himself free before I took him in my palm, stroking him slowly. He sat up, then lifted me over him, setting me onto his lap. He kissed and sucked along the column of my throat, working his way down my breasts, cupping and massaging one while he laved the other with his tongue.

I lowered myself, inch-by-inch, taking him deep, savoring his groan.

It was the strangest blend of urgent need and languid want. Like I had to have him but never wanted this to end.

He took his time exploring my body, kissing and caressing every inch he had access to while I rode him like we had all the time in the world.

Knowing tomorrow would come regardless.

CHAPTER 55
Redmond

Descending into the Silent Woods, the glowhoppers scattered in all directions, their bodies frantically jumping out of my vicinity. I knelt against the deadened ground, taking a final deep breath, head downcast, knowing when I looked up the cabin would be in front of me. I never had a problem finding it... not when *she* summoned. In here, the Enchantress ruled, and I was merely her subject.

Her devoted fiancé.

My phoenix's hackles were raised, heat radiating through my ribcage, threatening to spill out and ignite my wings. He'd become such a tricky bastard over the last few months. I hated these moments of pretending with her, but my phoenix fucking loathed it. Now I was fighting not only my own feelings but his instincts.

Had our connection always been like this? I couldn't remember... It had been over a decade, after all. Maybe I'd just been more willing to cooperate with his magic? Not rallying against my *nature* like I was about to right now.

Humming enveloped the empty woods, vibrating off the trees, an ominous battle hymn guiding each forced step.

One last time.

A final distraction. After this, she'd know I betrayed her. Would she change me into a wisp, or drain me into one of her horrific husks in the pile behind her cabin?

Best-case scenario, she'd be dead by the end of the day. Worst case, I'd keep my people safe. I'd resolved to be the ruler Inverno deserved all these years, and I knew where I'd be heading as soon as I assisted Sloan in getting what she needed.

The spectral beings pushed open the door, letting it shut behind us before they twisted the lock.

The living room was empty. Even the shelves that once were full of jars had only a thin layer of dust covering them.

"Hello?" I called out, finding the robe she usually left me draped over the chaise.

She knew I was coming.

Of course she did.

There was no response, just the incessant buzzing around me. The wisps grabbed the black satin and brought it over, but I waved them away. My phoenix pricked at me, a hundred flaming needles sending a warning.

Something's wrong.

A flash of white caught my attention, Mox's lithe body in the distance. He and Sloan were nearing. They'd come for their part of the plan.

I needed to find the jar with Aislin's lightning.

"Hello, darling," the Enchantress said, hastily slipping out of her bedroom, shutting the door behind her, twisting the knob a few times to ensure she'd locked it.

Interesting.

I sent a flare of my power in that direction, the blue smoke quietly drifting out the window.

"I know you said your visit with King Morrow was unsuccessful—"

"Yes, I'm sorry, my dark queen." I gave a quick bow in

supplication, then stepped toward her, willing away the kindling in my gut telling me to run; to get far away from this fucking cabin. "He said they never moved it for Flynt, and I'm inclined to believe him. The man's dead now, along with his network. There was really no reason for King Morrow to lie."

"There isn't," she agreed, bringing a clawed fingertip to her chin, scraping against the hardened coating there. The sound grated at my skull, acid igniting up my throat before I swallowed down some bile. "Though, I was thinking about it, and it is possible that Flynt wasn't the one to steal the tome."

I willed my phoenix to back down as he threatened to punch his fire out from my insides. "What do you mean?"

"Flynt wasn't the only one here that night."

Fuck. "Well, yes, the assassin was here—"

"We both know she doesn't pose a threat to me. Not any longer." She waved her arm to indicate the wisps flitting about the room. "You, however—"

"Have aligned myself with you. Am betrothed to you," I said, striding forward until I was pressed against her. Gripping her neck with my palm, I ignored the abrasive glittering onyx covering it, kissing her with as much false passion as I could muster while keeping my phoenix contained. "Why would I threaten that when we are so close to ruling Celaria?"

She deepened the kiss, nipping at my lip and lapping up the blood. Then she wiped away some, wandering into her room before coming back out with an ornate purple box. "What are you doing?"

She reached into it, smearing her finger across what I knew were the gears inside. When she dangled the clockwork talisman in front of me, I swallowed hard.

"Prove it," she taunted, walking it toward me, holding the chain out in front of her. The gears were still, their copper and silver grooves nestled into each other, the rhythm of their turning engrained into my chest.

"Prove what?" I asked, dipping my chin.

She threaded the talisman over my head, letting it hit against the empty cage settled below the column of my throat. Her hands lingered over the chain, strumming it between her fingers. "That your loyalties belong to me."

"Satisfied?" I focused my mind on the memory she'd seen, the one from the worst night of my life. She could have that one, torture me with it, but I couldn't let her see anything recent... anything that would give away my work with Arafax.

She waved the box around in the air, looking at me quizzically. "Would it work?"

"I don't know."

I really didn't. Now that Dru had saved Zara, the memory weaver, would the Enchantress have access to her magic? Did she have others?

Instead of bringing the box over, she threw it against the wall, letting it splinter into bits of gears and painted-wood chips. Before I could react, she wrapped the chain around her fist, dragging me toward her. She lifted me off the ground, as if I wasn't larger than her. "Bring me the boy."

"You'll have to be a bit more specific."

"The one *you* gave the tome to," she sneered, pulling the chain tighter around my neck. I gasped for air, the metal stamping divots into my throat. "He used it. And since he's never been here, he'd have to have gotten it from someone. I think that *someone* was you."

"I don't—know—what—you're talking—about," I rasped, my phoenix begging to obliterate this entire fucking cabin and its inhabitants.

But I couldn't allow that to happen.

Struggling against the binding, I reached up and gripped the metal chain with my own hands, pushing her away. I staggered to the floor and ripped it off my neck, breaking it and sending the talisman skipping across the wood.

I stumbled out of the cabin, out of her reach, hoping Sloan had followed the thin blue trail of smoke I'd marked the outside of the Enchantress's bedroom with. Aislin's magic had to be in there, somewhere.

"Don't play the idiot, Redmond. It doesn't suit you," the Enchantress taunted, shaking her head at me from the doorway. Her hands shot forward and black vines twisted around my body. "While I'm sad we won't get one last sensual round, I'm afraid this is where I dispose of you."

Silver and white flashed from the corner of my eye as I slowly loosened my hold on my magic, letting it unleash. "I'd like to see you try."

In a blink of blue, I'd shifted.

Heat radiated from my body, and I shot into the sky, sending cobalt flares in all directions. The hum of the wisps clamored after me, spurring me to move faster.

This hadn't been the plan.

Not exactly.

But I could still work with it.

My heart pounded, its pulse so erratic it worked against the beat of my wings. In a rush of adrenaline, my body broke through the barrier, a wave of relief surging when a set of water-color wings rose into the sky.

She'd seen the signal.

Whether or not we were ready, it was time.

CHAPTER 56
Kyleigh

King Redmond's phoenix hovered above the blackened canopy of the Silent Woods.

My dragon rose to the surface, and for the first time, I didn't fight it.

When my bones cracked, I didn't feel broken. When the scales burst from the scar-covered markings on my sides, they rippled seamlessly, like a flame in the breeze. When my eyes shifted into their silver-slitted orbs, they didn't sting. They burned with anticipation.

This may not be the form I was accustomed to.

The body I was born to.

But this magic, my dragon magic, was forged for moments like this. I could feel it in my very soul—the *rightness* of it.

We were ready for battle.

Destined for victory.

I huffed, taking to the sky with Dru on my back, a few fiery specks of orange and pink twirling with the smoke that billowed from my snout. Feeling a shift along my spine, I craned my neck to find Dru crouching, his bare hand gripping one of my coral scales, his gloved one held out, releasing a crimson spray from the copper-painted circle on his palm.

Blood.

My blood.

It'd been spread over the center of his palm after Dru's glove had been fed power from Sweeney and one of the water wielders from the outskirts of Arafax Village. He nodded toward me, his Adam's apple bobbing as he swallowed. "I'm ready."

It was moments like these that I truly hated he wasn't my champion. That I couldn't respond other than with a nod or huff.

The incantation he cast flitted along the wind. "*Ceáltair dhraíochta iálu ach ríu in ráth.*"

A handful of wisps beat against the border, giving us the perfect visual of where the Enchantress's territory stopped. We were pretty certain she couldn't fly, which meant opening the boundary here would be an easy way to get the wisps out in a contained manner while still keeping her trapped inside.

"*Ceáltair dhraíochta iálu ach ríu in ráth.*"

I leaned slightly, the wing Dru was closest to lifting a bit. He gripped it as he hung over the barrier, spraying crimson in a wisp-sized circle. Then he pulled out another vial and broke it against his palm, the glove absorbing it.

As the wisps began shooting out of their invisible prison, the phoenix screeched, his blue and white flames radiating out, herding the shadowy beings toward Sweeney. A few collided into my wings, piercing them in quick, sharp movements, searing pain puncturing the veins mapped across them.

I gritted my maw, refusing to move while Dru finished the veiling incantation to close up the temporary hole we'd created in the barrier protecting Celaria from the Enchantress.

"*Nes in ceáltair dhraíochta.*"

We followed the trail of ashen wings flitting away from us, guiding them with our combined pink-and-blue flames toward the tornado spiraling ahead. Streams of violent charcoal wind released from Sweeney's outstretched hands, expanding up into the purple, star-blotted sky. It was our best bet at keeping the wisps contained while Dru worked.

Sloan was beneath us, jar clutched tightly. She lifted the lid, reaching inside tentatively before scooping out a handful of bolts. Her eyes squinting, they shifted into long strands with jagged loops at the end. Swinging her arm around, she threw one into the sky, catching a wisp and dragging them into the cyclone.

Pride swelled in my chest, and I flew closer, herding in a few more wisps as peeks of violet lightning wrangled more beneath me.

Crimson released into the air, crashing into the confused spectral forms, Dru's voice shouting the incantation above the rough winds. *"Neth anéiavan só iánu ríth."*

CHAPTER 57
A Wisp

Clap, clap.

Heat spurred me forward, my coven tightly nestled around me.

But would it hurt to stop? To let it burn?

Or would it sear me into ash before this hold on me reignited?

The urge to stop, to find out, beckoned me—tired of the numb.

Clap, clap.

Bright-violet streaks coiled around me.

Prickling.

Vibrating warmth as I squirmed against them.

A familiar tug, then dragged into harsh, unforgiving wind.

The others spun next to me.

Above.

Below.

There's no end to this violent spiral.

The ancient words wrapped around me like sacred vines.

Clap, clap.

I heard the sound again, but there's no blank space.

No emptied pause.

Red blurred around me, smearing over my wings, my arms, the shadowy strands of my hair.

It pelted me, stinging like poison-tipped arrows.

Hitting my *skin*.

Making me *chill*.

I fell, slowly, as if held up by some other force.

Colliding into the ground with a steady *thump*. Never more grateful for the pain.

Tears stained my cheeks as I was dragged naked across the grass.

In one movement, I was spun around, pulled and cradled into strong, familiar arms that I refused to let go of.

Sloan.

CHAPTER 58

Sloan

I t was really *her.*
   Aislin.

I clutched her tighter to remind myself that we'd done it. We'd brought her back.

"You came."

"With backup," I replied, nodding at Sweeney who grinned at us both, hands still outstretched, "as promised."

I was tempted to tell her this wasn't the first time. That *of course* I'd come for her—not that she would recall. Who knew what she would remember from her time trapped in that translucent hollow shell. For me, there was no other option but to try until I persevered.

There was no future I'd design without her.

A streak of electricity bolted me to her, the comforting reconnection of our bond.

I'd never fucking let it go again.

Its braid wove back together, my body exhaling in relief, like I'd been holding so much tension it'd zapped my ability to breathe since she'd been taken.

Men and women were slowly guided down to the ground

with a wave of the breezetender's hand, the other held in place as Red herded the last few wisps into the spiraling wind that reached up into the sky. A loud screech from above told me he and Kyleigh had finished guiding them all where they needed to be.

His blue phoenix flew off toward Inverno's boundary. He needed to ensure the wielders there were ready, along with the troops lining the territory's perimeter.

It was time for the next part of his plan—one he still hadn't fully included me in.

It left me uneasy, but right now I needed to focus on my Revered.

Aislin's electricity crackled along my fingers, and I pulled back the strands I'd wrangled the wisps with, never more grateful the Enchantress had hoarded some of her power away. It surrounded us while I kissed every inch of skin I could get to with her in my arms. She shivered against me. From the cold, from shock, I didn't know. I shrugged off her leather jacket, the one I'd worn just in case, tucking it around her shoulders.

As much as I wanted to hold her here, to savor this moment, we still had an Enchantress to defeat.

Keep her safe.

"No," Aislin pleaded. Hope fluttered in my chest when I realized she'd heard me call to Mox. Our plaited bond resurfacing. "I don't want to leave you right now. I need to stay. This is my fight."

She moved to stand, legs wobbling and sending her back into me. She was covered in dirt, in her bloody antidote, and those were the things I *could* see. What marks had been left behind that I couldn't? That she *wouldn't* show me.

"You've fought enough."

She growled in frustration, clenching and unclenching her fists, brows stitched together, concentrating. A few tiny streaks of indigo flared from her fingertips before fizzling out.

She was weak. Too weak.

"I will be right behind you," I promised. "After."

Mox nudged her with his snout, laying on the ground so she could lean against him as I helped her onto his back.

"I'll be brave for the both of us. Remember?"

Aislin nodded but didn't speak, emerald eyes dimmed. She allowed Mox to take her without resistance. That was probably the best answer I could have hoped for.

Kyleigh lowered to the ground with a wild roar, her battered wings stretched wide.

"You okay to take everyone?"

Her opalescent snout bobbed up and down. Sweeney and I helped load the other former wisps onto her back. They were all struggling, needing to be carried or held in place. It would take a few trips to get them safely to Arafax's fort. Neve and Ox would be here shortly to transport more after they'd finished moving civilians to the bunkers. Then we'd go take care of the Enchantress.

Destroy the tome. Weaken her enough to vanquish.

As we lifted off into the air, my eyes darted to each person who'd been transformed back to their former selves. They could have been wisps for a decade or two. Some of them cried, others were dazed, eyes glazed over, silent. One man with brown hair was tucked into Sweeney as the breezetender sobbed over him.

Who was he?

I'd have to find out later, but it was a beautiful reminder amid the solemnness. Many had been lost, but today, some had been *found*.

Looking down as the world became smaller, my attention snagged on someone streaking across the emerald terrain.

It was as if a boot had stamped the air straight from my chest.

I whipped my head around, taking another inventory of our

passengers, then frantically scampered by Kyleigh's wing, hanging off of it to look closer.

To confirm what I didn't want to believe.

His white shirt blurred into the blackened canopy of the Silent Woods.

Dru.

CHAPTER 59
Dru

"*Neth anéiavan só iánu ríth.*"

My body quivered, and I stared at the crimson dripping down my palm. I'd run through the last of the vials I'd scrounged from the cooling box, along with a few fresh ones I'd taken this morning—marked *K* to not arouse suspicion.

When the last drop had seeped through and all that sprayed out was a clear mist, I had to take matters into my own hands. There'd been more wisps than I'd anticipated.

More people to save.

More I needed to *give*.

Pressing the silver stud, I fed out the small dagger, clutching it tightly. My hand shook, weakness threatening my task, but there was no time for hesitation. Kyleigh, King Redmond, and Sloan had herded them all into position. Now I just needed to continue to deliver the antidote.

Slicing bare palm, I clenched my trembling fist, opening when I could see the crimson seeping through my fingers. Smearing it onto my glove's coppery circle, I aimed it at the swirling shadows above, continuing the incantation.

"*Neth anéiavan só iánu ríth.*"

I watched in awe as the translucent forms shifted from ashen-gray phantoms to flesh, pride swelling in my chest. Slipping the blade into the back of my trousers, I drank in the beauty of seeing these people freed after much too long, excitement trilling through me.

Relief washed through me watching Sloan and Aislin embrace, reunited. I'd saved her. She was finally back after sacrificing herself to protect Kyleigh. To protect us all.

I wanted to hug her. To thank her. But my work wasn't done.

After the last person had descended from Sweeney's cyclone, landing in the grass, I hunted among the faces, searching for three familiar ones. *My sisters.*

Only they were nowhere to be found.

A decade without them and I wouldn't give up. Not now. We were too close.

I counted off the returned, interrupted by dark shapes floating through the trees.

They were still in there.

I had to go back.

Pulled by purpose, I trudged across the grass, my boots squishing the fresh greenery until their crunch told me I'd passed into *her* territory.

Keeping what I'd learned from Kyleigh felt like the worst thing I'd ever done. The guilt gnawed at me, like a beast foaming at the mouth, reminding me how fucked up it was to lie to the woman I loved. The one who had chosen me time and time again.

I turned briefly, watching her ascend into the lilac-kissed clouds, taking the rescued back to safety, hopefully returning them to their loved ones. She was so brave, so beautiful, spread across the sky like a coral-washed beacon of hope, doing what she was born to do—protect the people of Arafax. The people of Celaria.

Her love was my greatest gift. And the lie dividing us—my greatest curse.

But I couldn't go back.

Wouldn't.

Not when there was still a chance.

I released some crimson spray, not wanting to waste too much, hoping to draw them toward me. When nothing happened, I tried to send out more, the spray coming out in pallid-pink droplets.

Not enough.

"I know who you are," I shouted into the silent tree-filled forest.

What was I doing?

If anyone knew where I was right now, they'd drag me away fighting. Or if they viewed the Enchantress as a bigger threat, which she most definitely was, they'd likely use me as a pawn to kill her. They couldn't know the truth—why my blood was the only one that could shift those trapped wisps and undo what the Enchantress had done.

A few dusky shadows flitted along the path, ignoring me as nothing more than a null.

The irony wasn't lost on me.

"I'd created them to sense magic," the Enchantress said, stepping out from behind a tree. Her neck was covered in what looked like a coating of shimmering jet-black sand that traveled up to her chin, streaking up the hollows of her sharpened cheekbones. She gave me a smile, canines glistening against the scarlet of her lips.

It was unsettling.

"If I'd only known, maybe I would have found you sooner."

My instincts told me she wouldn't hurt me. She easily could have before, when she'd gripped me by the throat. But she'd let me leave. Let me go.

Even black widows were protective of their young.

Her wisps twirled in the darkness, moving so swiftly it was hard to make out their shapes. I stayed still, willing my body in place. Fists clenched at my sides. Resolve tightening in my chest.

Every last one needed to be returned.

"What name did they give you?" Her eyes searched for something before pinning to the moon hanging above and shifting back to me.

"Dru," I answered reluctantly. "Druce."

"Druce," she said, as if testing the sound on her tongue. "I never got to choose one."

"Why?"

"He took you before I could," she seethed, not at me but at the name as it escaped her crimson lips. "Prince Ciaran."

My own curiosity had me in a chokehold. "Why would he do that?"

"Why do leaders do anything?" She let out an aggravated sigh. "To secure more power."

"I don't understand. What does that have to do with me?"

"You're half faerie. That blood in your veins was very valuable. Still is."

The Enchantress arched a blackened brow. "Do your friends know you're here? Who you are?"

I only had a short amount of time until Kyleigh and the others would realize I hadn't ridden back with them. I needed to do something soon to help the wisps here. I couldn't put everyone else in danger or risk them joining the Enchantress's mindless coven.

"No. They don't know I'm here," I said smoothly, bringing my hands behind my back and fumbling for the blade tucked into my waistband. "And I don't know much more than them, other than the fact that you're the one who gave birth to me."

"I'm your mother." Her onyx eyes glinted, but the words were impassive. Distant.

"I had a mother. And a father, for that matter." Venom

seeped into my tone, a poison that'd been eating at me, every question that stood unanswered flooding my mind all at once. "*Sisters.*"

"And you were happy?"

"Yes. I had a great childhood...until The Blaze." My hand shook against the hilt before I wrapped my fingers around it. "Until *you* took them from me."

"I see," she replied, the syrupy tone of her voice hardening like the onyx shimmering over her skin. She brought an arm across her abdomen, tapping her clawed fingers against the lace of her dress. "Are you here to kill me?"

I had the power to eliminate her threat in the palm of my hand, running through my veins. But first, there was the matter of rescuing my sisters and the others.

"I'm here to free *them*," I said, shaking as I watched the shadowy figures flitting around us. "What I have to do to make that happen is entirely up to you."

"Unfortunately, I really need to hang on to the few you left me. There are things to rectify. A better world to remake." She clapped twice, making the wisps jerk at her summons. She sighed.

Pivoting away from me, she began moving toward the edge of the woods, her unwitting minions trailing behind her.

Where was she going?

"There's a better world to make, but not by your hand."

I was rooted in place, my mind sifting through the pages of translations we'd done. The wisps were flitting away quickly. *Too quickly.*

"Join me. Or, if they've sunk their claws too deep, just stay out of my way," she called back to me over her shoulder. "Last chance, Druce."

And she wasn't wrong. It was my last chance to do something. But I wouldn't join her, and I refused to stand idly by.

I flipped through the tome's pages in my mind, glad to have

memorized so much last night...even the things I'd been warned not to. But if I could shift the wisps into my control, I could help them. I needed to draw some of the book's magic away from her.

For once in my life, *I* had the fucking power.

Dread gnawed at my chest. My body, depleted. Weak. But the Enchantress had a weakness too, something no one else knew about.

A hidden vulnerability.

I finally understood what it took to be one of Arafax's champions. I may not have claimed the title in any official capacity, but I'd give my blood to the cause regardless. Only mine would do.

A silver glint.

A searing slice of crimson.

A final wish before I unleashed the lethal words.

"*Thoir suas mó dunas gwer a in nithem de Validus Venenificium.*"

CHAPTER 60

Neve

My back ached, the weight of my passengers a new sensation, considering I hadn't carried more than two or three people at a time before. Beating my wings against the sky, I neared the fort, lowering myself to the ground in the arena.

Ox slid down my tail, not making eye contact with me as he unloaded villagers, escorting them toward the bunkers well hidden by Ever's illusion magic. This would be the safest spot for everyone until the fight was over.

Guards lined the fort's walls, spread along its maze to help civilians and fight any external threat that might arise. A few of them watched me in awe, giving a grateful nod of their heads.

My chest swelled with pride.

They each wore a talisman, and next to them stood their twin, a double created by the weavers. Standing on the other side of Arafax's stream, they held hands, magic thrumming through the air in our direction.

Frosty specks released within my pallid breaths.

We're here. Kyleigh's coral dragon came into view, flying in from the other side of the stony structure and landing with a thud next to me. Sloan sprung from her back, then reached a

381

hand up to help the men and women off her. There were a few dozen people crammed together, and I knew the trip had to have been tough for her, especially seeing her wings pocked with tears and bleeding thick drops of red.

You okay?

She released a long sigh, a few fiery specks peppering the air. *Exhausted. Just finished my second trip.*

I looked over at Sloan, then back to my dragon sister. *Aislin?*

She's herself. Safe with Mox.

A giant tear splashed the people below me, making them shriek as they shook off its chill. I gave them an apologetic nod. *Sorry.*

Not that they could hear me.

Sloan stood on her tiptoes, whispering to Kyleigh, whose damaged wings were pulled taut behind her, tensed. Crimson dribbled from their thick veins, seeping into the ground.

What's going on?

Dru isn't here. Sloan saw him heading toward the Silent Woods.

My head whipped around, making sure he wasn't hidden among the crowd. There's no way he would do that—he was smarter than that. *Why would he—*

"Maybe his sisters? I think if they were here, then he would have come with them," Sloan offered both of us.

That was true. Dru always followed orders, obeying the Queen he served on behalf of Arafax. But this was personal for him. And while he'd nodded along at the meeting this morning, that the priority was getting the Enchantress and saving our third Revered if possible, who knew what cogs were turning within his mind. *I'm sure he has a pla—*

A loud *boom* shook the ground, dirt exploding in all directions, sending people stumbling and falling as they continued to scurry toward the bunker.

The illusioned guards disappeared in an instant, our imposing army cut visibly in half.

Craig and the new Celarians Kyleigh had brought over were protecting a small group of children huddled in a circle. They moved them quickly toward the bunkers, ushering them to safety.

"Shit! I'll help get the rest there," Sloan called out, running to pull a few people up to stand before moving them toward the maze beyond the arena's walls.

Ox was gripping my side a moment later, taking a few tries to climb onto my back. "Blazes! What is going on?" he asked, frost coating his hands as he prepared for any attack. The sky filled with darkness, ashen shapes shooting into the air like contorted humanoid arrows raining down on us in a wave of gnarled teeth, claws, and horns.

I sprinted to the side, avoiding a few before lifting off the ground.

The husks, Ox said through our bond, rage prickling heat along its delicate tether. *Time to fight, mó venéro.*

Let's go, champion.

It was the most we'd talked since Everwood Grove, but when it came down to it, in moments of peril we would fight for our kingdom, for each other, to the death.

Now was the time to set down our vicious words aimed at each other and pick up our spears. There was no greater sacrifice than duty. No greater force than love.

Arafax didn't worship the Revered without reason.

We'd fight.

We'd slay.

We'd *conquer.*

CHAPTER 61

Kyleigh

Descending, I tore into some husks, shredding them, licking my razor-sharp teeth. They tasted foul, like rot drenched in sour milk and cheap beer. I spat them out, sending the first back into one of the deep black holes that now pocked the landscape of Arafax. The second hit the ground with a loud *smack*, body scattered in pieces. I watched for a moment, curious what would happen next. When the bits didn't merge back together, I let out a relieved huff.

They didn't reanimate it seemed.

Small blessings, Neve growled, shaking her massive blue maw. A handful of husks dangled between her teeth, their bodies fraying before she swallowed them.

Gross.

A moment later, she snapped open her mouth, releasing ashen-colored snowflakes that twirled within her smog, drifting toward the ground.

Well, that's one way to get rid of them.

Ox stood tall between her wings, Maeve and Maisie slicing through any husks that made it too close. Then he tucked the weapons behind his back, forming icy spears in his fists and throwing them at the husks hurtling toward Neve and I.

I clamped my teeth around another husk, crunching through its horns. Tearing up its mangled body, my claw wrapped around another and squeezed until I felt a deadly *snap*.

My shredded wings were barely cooperating, the attacks leaving open gashes across their span. They pumped furiously against the wind, frantically trying to get out of the husks' line of vision. This army of hers wasn't as finessed as the wisps had been, simply ripping through blood and flesh in a blind rage.

Despite how much my chest ached, exhausted from fighting my body's need to heal, I blew a wave of fiery coral sparks, searing holes into the husks that continued to surge like a persistent flood. I needed to shift back but with the constant swarm, it was too hard to pinpoint a safe spot to land.

Suddenly, the husks migrated like a flock of ravens toward the Silent Woods.

Where are they going? I asked Neve through our connection.

Soaring along the breeze, I tried to ignore the throbbing in my right wing.

Neve's *roar* shook the clouds, pulling my attention. *Look.*

At the edge of the Silent Woods, the Enchantress stood with her hand pressed against her invisible cell, lips moving, murmuring something.

She was right there.

Alone.

Vulnerable.

I licked my lips in anticipation. We'd saved the wisps. I'd feel no guilt tearing her to shreds now.

Her eyes lifted to mine, copper veins chipped through the onyx on her face. Large patches of crimson stained the ground around her. Twisting my neck, I glanced back at my wings, pierced and oozing red that smeared their span.

Then, as if an iridescent wrapper had been pinched between invisible fingers, the entire barrier surrounding the Silent Woods peeled away in one swift movement.

Gone.

My blood ran cold.

Jaw clenched.

I dove toward the evil bitch, Neve joining me, zeroing in on our prey. We needed to cut her down before she did anything with her newly spawned freedom.

When my sapphire sister began to spray ice in her direction, I joined in, sparks shooting from my throat with all the force I could manage. The husks dashed into the line of fire, absorbing the impact of our attack before it could reach their mistress. When they parted, Ox released a pointed spear at her, hurling it between two husks, headed right for the Enchantress. She caught it in her hand, a wicked grin spanning her deep-red lips.

Fuck.

Against the blackened branches jutting into Celaria's sky, naked people stumbled through the trees, drawing my attention.

Is that what he was doing? Helping them?

I didn't see him with them, though.

Where is he?

A wave of pain slammed into me, shoulder recoiling as the icy spear lodged into it. I screeched, frantically trying to keep my wing moving. It seared, the cold and pain stinging me all at once. But I didn't have time to worry about that now.

We needed to get the Enchantress. Then I needed to find Dru.

I've got her, Neve assured me, dipping in front of me while I regained control of my injured wing. Ox was balanced on her sapphire scales, another spear elongating from his fists. He pulled back his arm, sending it at the Enchantress. A husk hurtled into its path, shielding her from the blow.

You sure?

Go! Find him. With a roar, the sapphire dragon released a wave of blue and white ice shards, the husks in its path dropping and shattering as they hit the ground.

Neve could handle this.

Where was Dru?

My body staggered lower, struggling to maintain flight with my injured shoulder and shredded wings. As I faltered over the canopy, heart pounding wildly, green slowly crept in from the outer rungs of the Silent Woods.

Magic bleeding back into the barren forest.

Head whipping back and forth, I scanned for any sign of Dru. His white shirt stood out against the black trees. I dove down to reach him, noticing as I got closer that it was stained with streaks of red.

My heart plummeted.

I stopped fighting to stay adrift and pitched forward, colliding into the trees until I finally crashed to the ground. My claws scraped against the underbrush, body slamming into gnarled roots, toppling over dead trees. I staggered toward him, falling a few times onto my wounded shoulder, driving the spear deeper.

I had to get to him.

Dru was slumped over a tree trunk, deep crimson running down the length of his arm, dripping off his fingertips. My chest stuttered in pain, and I whimpered, dragging my wings across the grass to get closer. My attention shot to the glimmer of a blade coated a similar shade laying a few feet away.

What has he done?

My whole body shook, my dragon begging to retreat in order to heal me.

Not yet, I seethed, hissing and huffing through the pain. I dipped my scaled snout and grabbed his harness between my teeth, willing myself to not look at the pool of blood staining the roots, seeping into the soil.

So much blood.

The stench of iron wafted through my nostrils, and I gritted my teeth, tightening my maw around his limp form.

Everything is going to be okay.

I repeated the words over and over. Though I knew he couldn't hear them, I needed to. I needed to believe it with every aching fiber of my being. There had to be *something* I could do to help.

To *fix* this.

My shoulder gave out once again, and I fell onto it. The ice lodged in there was melting. I needed to get him help before flying was impossible.

Where could we go?

Where would *he* go?

Gripping Dru tighter, I bent my shaking legs, screeching as I launched into the sky. Every beat of my barely cooperating wing was labored, but I refused to quit. My heart's turbulent rhythm propelled me toward Renovo Falls, its steaming, shimmering waters closing in with each taxing stroke against the wind. After what felt like an eternity, the air became steeped in pine, a smell that once brought me the comfort of home. Now as iron blended into the scent, it clogged my senses, making me lightheaded.

Just a little farther.

When the crystalline waters were below me, I dove along the white waterfall, crashing into its pool. It spilled over the edge, spreading onto the rocky terrain. Wading to the edge, water continuing to slosh out of the basin, I dipped under the waterfall, ignoring how it sprayed my eyes as I set Dru on the stone ledge of its hidden cove.

Everything is going to be okay.

It had to be.

My body shook violently, the icy spear had fully melted and blood now gushed from the wound. Unable to fight any longer, my bones cracked and morphed until I returned to my human form. Dru lay in front of me, my hands quivering as I ran them along his bloodied arm. There had to have been at least three deep slices down its length.

What did you do?

"Please wake up," I pleaded, shaking his arm before moving to his torso, trying to jostle him with my one able arm. Everything around me spun, dizziness sweeping through me, threatening to pull me under.

No.

Dru needed me.

I lay my cheek on his sternum.

Listening.

Waiting.

He didn't move. There was no rise or fall to his chest.

"I've got you," I told him. "It's going to be okay."

Dragging him into the water with me, screaming through the pain, I cradled him in my arms. Blood covered my chest and seeped down my back from my wing buds.

Red spilled out from the both of us, carried away by the current of the once-crystalline waters. *So much blood.* Dru's slumped body in the Silent Woods replayed in my mind, my arms quaking as I clutched him to me. My shoulder and back tingled, the skin stitching itself back together.

The falls were healing me.

And they would heal him.

They *would.*

They fucking had to.

I leaned over, submerging his sliced arm deeper, then cupped some water to rinse off his face, tingeing the current pink.

"Come on, Dru." I pressed a kiss to his forehead. "Come on."

He lay limp in my arms.

Unresponsive.

Tears poured down my cheeks, falling onto his chest.

Slowly the bleeding stopped, and I looked at where the gashes had been, finding none remained. The magic of the falls was taking root.

My heart fluttered in hope.

"I've got you." I held him close, my body shaking as I dipped us both into the water, waiting for him to blink his gold-spun eyes.

To squish them shut.

To jolt in my grip.

To do *anything* but remain still.

The falls was a place of rebirth and healing. Where we could find a fresh start. Where he promised me more.

"Come back to me."

I wasn't struggling as much to hold him, healing more and more with each passing second. Every ounce of strength nourished belief within me. If anything could keep him with me, it was the falls.

I thought back to our first time here. Kissing under the burbling waterfall. His hands roving over my skin. Rinsing away the violence of Inverno's dungeon.

We'd come so far since then. We had so much further to go.

But he still didn't wake. His chest still didn't move.

"Please don't leave me," I whispered. "I love you."

Our story isn't over.

My mind ran at warp speed, thinking of anything else I could do to help him.

Leaning forward, I pressed a kiss to his lips, my tears falling onto his cheeks. Mouth chilled, body frozen and crushed against me, the comforting beat of his heart extinguished.

Never to reignite.

Unbearable pain seared into me, as if an invisible hand had

gripped around my heart and tore it from my chest with deft precision.

I screamed, shaking, clutching him to me. Refusing this reality in front of me. Not wanting to believe it. Knowing it was futile.

Gone.

Heat rippled in an uncontrollable wave, sparks surging through my veins. I unleashed my anguish, body igniting from the inside out. Pink and orange burst everywhere, blinding me with incandescent light.

Consuming me.

CHAPTER 62

Redmond

A violent cry came from the Silent Woods.

Gaze darting in that direction, I watched in horror as red toadstools and flowers began to spring up within its gnarled confines. Magic spreading through *her* territory.

Impossible.

That would mean... The barrier had come down.

The Enchantress.

She was *free* in Celaria.

None of us were safe.

I screeched, diving and weaving around the husks that came at me, hands and claws groping at my feathers, teeth gnashing as they tried to clamp around my neck. My phoenix fire did nothing to them, but that didn't mean I was out of options.

I raised my talons, jabbing into the first husk and ripping downward while I slashed another across its midsection. They fell like dead leaves toward the ground, crunching on impact. Speeding in the direction of the boundary, the one I'd spent weeks outlining, I prayed I made it in time to get it sealed before the Enchantress or her husks could reach Inverno.

After I'd torn apart the final husk that was after me, I

shifted, landing in the snow at the edge of my territory. Isla was there with a handful of wielders, as promised, an extra line of defense while I'd executed the first part of our plan.

She'd return to be with her people.

I'd stay here and sacrifice to protect mine.

"It looks like the worst has happened," I said to her, watching as she hastily pulled out a portal stone and dropped it onto the ground, the coordinates mapped on its copper surface ready to give her a quick exit. It sank into a layer of snow, and she kept her eyes on it, avoiding my presence, as usual.

The rest of Arafax's wielders followed suit, placing their stones in front of them.

"Took you long enough," she grumbled, crossing her arms as she rubbed them to stay warm. "How do you exist in this cold?"

"Doesn't bother me." My wings flared before fizzling out. "I always run hot."

She rolled her eyes.

"You better get going." She needed to get to the bunker beneath Arafax's fort to be with her people safely within its protection. Their Revered would be trailing the Enchantress—hopefully ending her before anyone was hurt.

"Now," she commanded her wielders. They stomped into the snow, disappearing on impact.

The Queen lifted her crimson boot—

A loud *crack* cleaved the air.

Our heads whipped in the direction of the mountains. Pink and orange sparks lit the sky, exploding into hundreds of flares that sprayed in all directions.

"Something's wrong," Isla said quietly, dropping her foot behind where the portal stone lay. The silver of her eyes glimmered a moment. Sparks continued to light the sky, streams of coral flame and smoke snaking up into the breeze.

Kyleigh.

"Go to her," I said hastily, sensing her panic.

"I won't make it in time." She took a deep breath, voice low but assured. "It has to be you."

"But I need to bring up the shield." This was the moment I'd prepared for, had contingencies set in place for. "The amount of power needed to fully seal—"

"We both have our parts to play," she swallowed hard, drawing her shoulders back, deep meaning kindling her words, "to ensure our kingdoms have a future."

"But—"

She pulled a blade from her holster, dragging it down one palm, then the other, crimson bubbling to the surface. "Her safety is all I've ever asked for, Redmond."

Kicking the snow over the portal stone, she took a step back onto the boundary line. The one that'd been set in my blood, meant to be sealed with it as well. "Go. Now."

Gulping back the acid clogging my throat, I dug my heels into the ground, taking to the sky and racing toward the rosy flares.

I only glanced back once, finding Isla lit like a red beacon, fortifying her power along the bright line, beginning to build Inverno's shield.

But I kept on flying, wings beating frantically.

I had a promise to keep.

WITHIN MINUTES, I ARRIVED AT RENOVO FALLS. Orange flames mixed with pink and coral sparks shot into the sky. This was Kyleigh's power. I'd seen it enough to know that, but I didn't see her anywhere.

Unless...

Ignoring how my wings instinctively recoiled at the idea of

getting wet, I jumped off the ledge, trying my best to hold them up as I waded closer to the fire emanating from the middle of the plunge pool.

With each step, I could make out more of her shape. Her screams. She'd cocooned herself within her burning power.

What had happened here?

I reached out, her sparks searing my skin when I grabbed her, pulling her toward me. Wrapping my wings around her, I used them to smother the flames as best I could.

"No, no, no," she mumbled, chest heaving, body tensing a moment before going completely slack. I held her upright, scanning her quickly. She was covered in ash and smears of blood, though I couldn't see any wounds. Black soot spilled from her, turning the water murky as it rippled outward.

She reached up toward the ignited orange and pink flecks that floated north.

"D-D-Dru," she sobbed, palm outstretched, quivering, her other hand drawing up to her mouth, trying and failing to stifle the cries erupting from her body.

The flecks continued to drift upward, disappearing behind the mountains.

"I-I didn't mean to." She clawed at her tarnished skin, repeating his name as if it would bring him back.

Each broken plea was like a dagger plunged through my gut.

"I know," I said, voice low, trying to calm her. We needed to fly out of here before the barrier closed. "Can you shift?"

"N-no." Her body transformed into an erratic wave of sparks, fully covered by her violent magic.

"We have to go, Kyleigh," I shouted over the crackling flames enveloping us.

She continued to ignite from within. "I can't. He's—"

"Not *here* anymore."

She collapsed, nails shredding into my chest as she clutched me. The sky darkened, white clouds shifting into streaks of black smoke. There wasn't much time. Inverno's shield would be up any moment now.

I swallowed the knot at the back of my throat.

It should've been me.

It has to be you.

Isla was right, but it felt so fucking *wrong*. Despite what I'd done in the past, my feelings about Arafax and its Queen, I could do this.

Her safety is all I've ever asked for.

I would do this. Even if Kyleigh didn't like it.

"We have to go," I said, keeping my tone firm despite the bile threatening to rise up, knowing what was happening at the boundary. Who was making the sacrifice that'd been mine to claim.

"No," Kyleigh seethed. She fought against my hold, trying to twist out of my arms as she shot sparks at me with her hands.

"I'm sorry."

Her eyes went wide at my words. Gripping under her knees I tipped her back, cradling her as I took to the sky, beating my wings harder than I ever had. If we didn't make it, we would be left out in the middle of the mountains, defenseless. The trek to get us to safety in Arafax would be too dangerous with the Enchantress free. There was nowhere else for us to go. We had to get to Inverno before the shield was sealed.

She screamed, clawed, her body barely managing to contain the flares erupting from her.

Ruby flames exploded ahead, the shield taking form, fire licking up the dome-shaped second skin. I pressed on, heading for the small gap I'd memorized on the map, just outside of Inverno's territory.

The intense heat of Isla's power, her essence, grew molten as we raced against the climbing barrier. Shooting upward, it scraped the base of my wings, the seam of the dome closing in around us. Kyleigh's fingertips were outstretched, reaching toward where we'd flown from. The shield shut tight, her mother's power kissing what it protected most one final time.

I watched in equal parts awe and horror as the barrier sealed, shield raised, keeping those on this side safe.

Knowing who it'd cost.

It should have been me.

When we landed, Kyleigh clutched my chest, curling up against me. She continued to wail, flaring in and out, the snow melting into pools around her.

I shifted, hiding in my flames, my phoenix taking her wrath.

Her fire.

A brokenness all too familiar to me.

Too fucking familiar.

But staying like this, burning with her, it was easier than burdening her with the second blow I'd have to deliver soon enough.

CHAPTER 63
Sloan

I didn't even bother to brush away the leftover pebbles of the portal stone.

After getting the last few folks into Arafax's underground bunkers, red flared in the sky, and I watched Inverno's shield begin to close up, knowing I only had moments to get back to *her*.

There was no fucking way I'd miss that.

Like a gift from the stars, there was a split second to throw down the portal stone once I'd slain the husks, securing Arafax's civilians in the bunkers.

I'd never been more grateful that I'd kept this stone from Redmond since he'd left it in my room, the first of many gifts since I'd gone to Arafax. A silent invitation.

Come home.

At first, it was tempting. My whole life in Inverno had been one path laid out for me, built upon battles and honor. Inverno's Commander was a title I'd been born to claim, but I'd earned it regardless. When that had been stripped away and I'd left with Neve for Arafax, it was like my identity had been stripped as well.

Where would I fit into this new life if I wasn't spending my days training Inverno's army and my nights drinking smoky whiskey, talking strategy with Red?

I resented my initial attraction to Aislin—someone meant to kill my friend, my king. The one I'd been sworn to protect. But I could tell from the moment we placed our pawns on the Gambit board that there was so much more to her. And when I'd touched those scars on her wrist...all I wanted to do was protect her.

Even when protecting her meant hurting the person I'd dedicated my life to keep safe.

By some miracle, she'd listened to me. I'd kept my oath, Redmond lived, but I'd broken it at the same time by handing over the gem. I thought that was it. I'd never see her again. It'd be better that way.

But then she came back into my life. A woman with striking emerald eyes and snark to match. A challenge from the stars themselves.

Once Aislin finally stopped fighting her feelings and claimed me as her champion, I had tossed the portal stone in a drawer, never planning to use it. I had everything I needed. The definition of who I was had shifted. I was hers. Her champion. And it was us against the world.

Until she was ripped away from me.

After I'd returned from the Silent Woods that day, I'd fumbled through the drawer, finding the stone tucked away in its corner, discarded. I didn't think I'd use it, but somehow keeping it in my back pocket was the comforting weight I'd needed. Besides, the only thing that made sense to me after leaving Inverno had been taken.

And now I was only steps away from her.

My heart thudded impatiently, but I held my arms stiffly at my side. She was here, but what state was she in?

Mox came into view, sitting outside my door. I gave him a

hug, running my palm along his fur before kneeling down to check his shaved hind leg and torso. Brighid's magic had worked, only a thick rope of scar was left behind that would be covered when his fur grew back.

I pressed a kiss between his pointed ears, giving his chin some scratches. Mox hummed appreciatively at the attention. Stepping backward a few paces, he made room for me to enter.

My hand hovered over the doorknob.

Fear streaked through the faint bond, so I pulled my fingers away and mustered all the warmth I could, saturating the delicate strand, sending it back until I felt her side ease. Then I steeled my spine, gripped the metal, and twisted.

I found Aislin just as I'd seen her last. Naked. Covered in dirt and blood. Her jacket draped over her shoulders.

Taking a few tentative steps into the room, I spotted the parcel laying at the edge of the bed. The sight of it churned my gut, but I picked it up, taking in its weight a second before setting it back down.

That could wait.

I knelt, crawling across the floor until I could press my back against the wall next to Aislin's.

For a few minutes, I didn't say anything. I didn't know *what* to say. But watching the rise and fall of her chest mere inches from mine gave me more comfort than any words could.

She was here.

Safe.

Mine.

Whatever she needed, I'd give her.

Aislin leaned away from the wall, reaching out and placing a hand on my knee. I straightened them as she came around, straddling me, cradling my face in her hands. My breath caught, and I looped my arms around her waist, stroking her spine, watching to see if she'd flinch when I did.

She didn't.

"I'm so fucking sorry." Her green eyes didn't leave mine, bolting me in place. "I should have told you what I—"

I shushed her before she could finish, craning my neck up just enough for her to decide what to do with the last few inches between us. "I know why you did it, and I love you all the more."

A tear streaked down her cheek, but I didn't dare acknowledge it. Her lips traced mine a moment, lingering to the point where my self-restraint nearly snapped. Her nakedness, our proximity, it wasn't lost on me.

She captured me in a kiss, tentative at first before she slid her arms around my neck, delving into my mouth with her tongue, pressing her body into mine. Her nipples dragged over my shirt, begging to be touched.

But I willed my hands down at my sides. Uncertainty keeping my fists clenched tight, stabbing divots into my palms. As much as I loved taking the reins, the need for her to be in control right now was paramount.

Her body shifted against me, her skin pebbled, warmth radiating into my thighs from where she straddled me.

Knock, knock, knock.

"Commander?" Cormac's voice filtered through the door, making us both still.

"What is it, Cormac? Do you have word from the King?" A lump caught in my throat, my eyes darting to the parcel on the edge of the bed.

"I have, Commander." He cleared his throat. "He's en route to the castle as we speak... The woman he's escorting is in rough shape."

Relief washed through me as I slumped back against the wall. "Thank you, Cormac. We'll be out shortly to meet them."

"What happened?" Aislin asked, concern etched across her face, eyes narrowing at the parcel on the bed.

The contingency I wouldn't need. *Thank the stars.* "I'm not sure, but why don't I help you get cleaned up and we can find out together?"

She nodded, but then her attention shifted back to the door.

"Cormac?" Aislin called.

Boots shuffled closer. "Yes?"

"What woman?"

There was a long pause. An awkwardness I didn't quite understand—until he spoke again.

"Arafax's new Queen."

CHAPTER 64
Kyleigh

The door groaned open, King Redmond stepping into the bedchamber.

"Leave me alone."

I huddled under the quilt I'd ripped from the bed, tucking it around me while I sat staring over the balcony, refusing to turn my head to look at him. Streams of black smoke crooked their fingers, beckoning me from across the once purple sky. The view was distorted by Inverno's shield, making me feel like I was living in a snow globe.

None of the childhood joy attached.

If only a giant hand could reach out and rattle it. Shake away this nightmare.

Gone.

Our love seemed like something out of a fairy tale, like it could conquer anything.

But this was no fairy tale, and true love's kiss wasn't magic.

It was simply tragic.

"I can't." He moved in front of me, blocking the view with his massive wings. He was back in his charcoal regalia, down to the circlet set on his head, though it wasn't ignited like it had been the last time I'd seen him wear it. "Not until—"

"It's not that hard," I tried to seethe, to unleash some emotion with my words, but all that came out was a monotone whisper. "One step after another, move your ass out the door. Or turn into your little blue bird and fly the fuck away."

"I know it's hard. And I don't want to deliver this news...but you need to know." He hesitated, eyes searching for something on the ground before meeting mine, their midnight hue pulling something inkier into the mix. "Kyleigh, you're Arafax's Queen now."

"No," I rasped out, involuntarily. *That wasn't possible.* That would mean—

"She saw the sparks flare into the sky and knew she couldn't get to you in time. That I could." His gaze softened, and he took a deep breath.

"What?" My eyes stung, but no tears came. I didn't know if I had any more left.

"A sacrifice, a powerful one, is needed to seal a shielding enchantment of that magnitude." His wings hunched forward, curling around him as his hands wrung together, their knuckles white. "She took my place and ordered me to go to you."

My voice shook, chest igniting with heat. "You're a king. You don't take orders."

Especially not from Arafax's Queen.

"I take the ones that matter."

I dropped my chin, expecting sparks to cover me again, but nothing happened. It was as if the grief had sucked away all my power.

I didn't know if I even cared.

They're gone.

"I want to be alone."

Always alone.

Always left.

"Yes, Your Majesty." He bowed his head slowly, peering up at me a moment before stalking toward the door.

"Don't call me that."

That title didn't belong to me. It belonged to someone else.

Someone who'd traded her life for my safety.

I should have been grateful. But I wasn't.

Couldn't be.

The anger I'd aimed at her for so long was suddenly heavy, smothering out any light that once ignited my veins in hope.

So much unspoken that would stay that way.

Forever.

He twisted the knob, the guard opening the door the rest of the way and holding it for him. When he looked back at me, I kept my face forward, only seeing him through my peripheral vision.

"We can talk more about it—"

"Get out."

"Kyl—"

"I hate you." It was the most vitriol I could infuse into the words, but they came out bland. Flat.

"I'll gladly claim it," he muttered, as if to himself, shutting the door behind him.

Tucking the quilt over me, I closed my eyes, imagining a snow globe and a giant hand rattling it violently.

Shaking away this nightmare.

CHAPTER 65

Ox

I threw another spear at the Enchantress, her copper claws absorbing the weapon before shooting it back in our direction. *Again.* We'd been playing this game for ages, every tactic either absorbed or deflected by our opponent. At least most of the husks had been taken care of, fewer fuckers flying at me as I tried to take her down.

I sent some encouragement through the bond, both of us feeling depleted after facing off with the Enchantress sans backup. What had happened to Kyleigh after we'd seen her briefly tear off toward the falls?

Flinging out icy discs one after another in her direction, one finally snagged the Enchantress's dress, drawing a gash. Black oozed down, barely noticeable. It was one of the few areas of her that seemed to still be flesh instead of the onyx creeping along her skin, only broken up by coppery streaks.

She smiled, as if appreciative of my ability to draw blood from her. Then the edges of her lips crumpled a moment, gaze shooting toward the mountains. Fiery orange specks floated in the distance.

I took the distraction as an opportunity to send more discs.

She did nothing to stop them, the edges slicing into her arms, torso, one even lodging into her thigh.

That got her attention.

Tearing the disc from her thigh, she served it back to me, husks following the path, surging toward me. Neve tipped sideways to avoid them, and I lost my balance, toppling off her back.

Oxygen ripped from my lungs as I plummeted toward the ground, watching an icy blast roar from the sapphire dragon above me. The husks froze, then dropped, cracking beneath me.

Atta girl.

I closed my eyes, bracing myself for the end. At least it was an honorable way to go, a warrior fulfilling his duty, fighting for his kingdom. I only wish we'd had more time...

Mó ven—

My stomach jolted, the impact of claws gripping around me, squeezing me tight.

Surely I've just pissed myself.

Neve's sapphire snout huffed a mix of smoke and frosted flecks into my face. Gasping, I opened one eye, keeping the other clenched shut. I twisted my head, realizing I was hanging about two feet off the ground before I sighed with relief.

Neve's syrupy voice stroked through our bond with reassurance. *Think you can be rid of me that easily, champion?*

I looked around us, not seeing the Enchantress. "Shit. We lost—"

Screams erupted from the direction of the fort.

We need to get to them.

Not even enough time to agree, I scrambled onto Neve's back before she took to the sky, heading toward the blares.

MERMAIDS SHRIEKED FROM THE STREAM AHEAD, hauling bodies to the water's edge. Black, white, and silver-soaked tresses clung to their faces. The weavers who'd been sent to aid us. Some of their chests heaved as they coughed out water. Others weren't so lucky.

We dipped low, coming in to land at the fort. The massacre was over by the time we'd arrived. All that remained was the brutal aftermath.

Red spilled from the throats of Arafax's guards, blending into their crimson capes. They were all dead, lining the stony walls of the fort and its outer maze. Had any of my former brothers-in-arms survived?

Nausea churned in my gut.

Dreggs, one of the men I'd squired with once upon a time, a fellow Blaze survivor, was propped against a wall. His arm was braced around his side, crimson sputtering from his lips. I staggered over to him, dropping to my knees. "What happened?"

"Th-th-there were s-so many." His eyes went to the thin ashen totem swaying a bit in the breeze.

A moment later, I realized it wasn't a totem at all. It was a tower of husks. Their bodies roped together, arms reaching out to guide the Enchantress up their length, heading straight toward Arafax's golden castle.

I swallowed hard as Dreggs slid sideways down the wall. *Dead.*

A loud suctioning sound reverberated around me, sending me on my ass. *Whoosh.* The bodies of my brothers-in-arms flew, as if sucked up by an invisible straw, toward Arafax's castle. They hung down from unseen strings, a macabre chandelier, limp and suspended in the sky.

I glanced back at Neve who'd shifted into her human form. Her dark complexion was too pale, and I could feel that her magic was nearly depleted. Taking a few wobbly steps forward, she stumbled, crashing toward the ground. The icy wall capturing her end of the bond shattered as she slammed into my arms.

It was as if all the emotions she'd dammed within now flooded into me, stealing the breath from my lungs for the second time today. I could barely exhale with the heaviness.

So much that she kept behind that frosty wall.

"Neve." I shook her, cradling her close, giving her a few smacks to her cheeks. I held her to me, whispering truths I knew she'd refuse to hear, to believe, but I whispered them all the same, pouring everything I had into the bond. "Come on, mó venéro."

She'd have to drag me through every infernal realm to be rid of me, and even then, she wouldn't be. We were bound by something we didn't even understand. Something I desperately wanted to.

I wanted it all.

Gripping my chest, I scoured my insides for the wilted tether of our bond, still there but so fragile.

Like her.

I'd never tell her I saw it. Her vulnerable side. She'd freeze off my balls before admitting it, and I preferred to keep them attached.

Small puffs of white slipped between her lips. Picking her up, I ran as fast as my feet could carry me, finding the hidden entrance to Arafax's bunker. Frantically, I slit my palm, watching the entrance appear.

Frightened faces lined the halls, some familiar, many not.

Neve still lay limp in my arms.

We didn't have much time. I knew what we'd have to do.

Craig and Leigh ran up, and I passed Neve to them.

"I need all able wielders," I shouted along the narrow hallway. Men and women pulled away from the walls to rush forward, Sweeney and Ever among them.

Sweeney looked at me, concern etching his features. "What do you need?"

"We have to seal it."

Dozens of hands pressed against the walls as we took turns reinforcing the enchantment. Locking ourselves in.

Locking everyone else out.

I prayed to the stars that we'd find a way, unsure if I'd ever see them again.

But there was no other choice.

Tonight, Arafax would *fall*.

Aislin

I stared at the blue satin sheets on the imposing four-poster bed in King Redmond's room. Sloan had offered me the chair opposite his, a velvet tufted one with silver embellishments, but I'd shaken my head, unable to do anything but stand there and listen.

The King walked over to the bar cart and poured a few glasses of whiskey.

"Want one?" he asked from over his shoulder.

"No, thanks." I couldn't stomach anything right now. Which was probably strange since I didn't know the last time I'd eaten...

I pressed my pointer finger to my opposite wrist, shooting a tiny bolt over my skin. The quick sting of pain reminded me this was *real*. This wasn't a dream or illusion concocted by the Enchantress.

When I looked up, Sloan's eyes were on me, frozen.

Did she see?

A shaky sort of warmth slithered down the strand of our bond. She had. But there wasn't anger in her stare, nor pity either.

There was so much I needed to say to her, but too much clouded my still-hazy mind. So much I couldn't even articulate.

King Redmond handed a glass to Sloan, who took a long sip.

She sighed, voice low as she asked the question we both had since we'd been told the news. "How is she?"

Kyleigh.

Arafax's new Queen.

"What happened?" I rasped, unable to contain myself.

"When I went to solidify Inverno's shield after realizing the Enchantress had escaped her banishment, the Queen—Isla —she..."

His eyes steadied on the inside of his drink as he swirled it in his palm. "We heard a cracking sound and saw sparks floating in the distance. Isla knew Kyleigh wasn't safe. Knew she wouldn't be able to get to her in time. She sent me while she closed the shield." He took a deep breath. "The power to create a barrier like that, enough to keep the Enchantress and her magic out... takes everything from the one who casts it. I'd spent months preparing..."

He took a sip of whiskey, wiping away an errant drop with his thumb. "I only just delivered the news about her mother. She's in shock. That loss compounded with Dru's... I don't know how much time she'll need, but I know that level of grief is near impossible to sift through."

It was like someone had punched me in the chest with my own dagger. Then twisted.

"Dru? He's—"

"Dead." King Redmond's voice was calm, but his hand twitched a few times before he brought the glass back to his lips. "We're still waiting for reports on Arafax's current status. From here"—his eyes darted to the window—"it doesn't look good."

Sloan lifted the corner of her tunic and wiped the tears from her eyes, making them sparkle a paler shade than their usual icy blue. "I saw him go back toward the Silent Woods. Told Kyleigh about it right before everything went to shit by the fort."

"I'm not sure what happened. She won't speak to me." His eyes glazed over a moment, then his chin drifted toward the mountains outside his window, the eerie iridescent coating of Inverno's shield blotting out the distance.

My voice shook. "I need to go see her."

If I stood here another moment, my mind would just spin into a deeper, cloudier haze. I walked to the door, opening it, sending some reassurance down the bond so Sloan wouldn't worry. The murky remnants still floating in me blotted any clarity over the last...I hadn't even asked yet how long it'd been...

But knowing that wouldn't make a difference right now. I couldn't remember anything I'd done since I was last human. I hadn't even been able to fight. Dru had, though. A fucking null —the best person I'd ever known in this miserable realm—had gone into the Silent Woods and fought.

Now he was dead.

I didn't need to know the details to know that much.

One step after another, I charged over to the room past Sloan's, Mox trailing behind me.

"Fine, you can tag along," I said to *them*, knowing she was watching.

I opened the door, finding the bed empty and a quilt-covered heap draped over the chaise. Kyleigh's muffled voice filtered through its layers. "I said go away, you feathered fuck."

The curtains on the balcony were drawn shut, only a sliver of light illuminating a strip of the space. This darkness that clung to the room was all too familiar, like the smoke-filled corners of my mind I wasn't ready to see clearly yet.

But as the walls started to close in and smother me, I realized I could siphon my grief, my pain. I could pour it into something. *Someone.*

I'd pour it into *her.*

"Wow. Sounding more like me every day." I threw some forced swagger into my tone.

The quilt drew down a few inches, revealing silver eyes that shone brighter than the moon we could no longer see clearly. I walked over as she sat upright, making room for me. Sitting down, I put my arm around her, her head falling to my shoulder. She was sniffling, covered in ash that was streaked down her cheeks. "I'm so glad you're okay."

"I don't know about okay, but I'm here." I gave her a squeeze. "So are you. And that's something."

"He's gone, Ais," she sobbed into me, my shirt soaking up her tears. Her chin lifted up, wobbling as she spoke, eyes bloodshot around her silver irises. "I found him in the woods. There was so much blood. T-took him to the falls. I tried to save him. N-n-nothing happened...my powers, they took him away."

"Your powers gave his soul a safe place to land."

"I tried to bring him back." Her voice cracked, body shaking violently against me with the force of her cries.

"Of course you did. But there's nothing you could have done."

"I have nothing," she said, lip quivering, but the tears slowed. The pain behind her eyes dug into me like silvery blades. Her hand clutched around whatever hung from the golden chain around her neck. "What am I supposed to do? How am I supposed to just...go on?"

"I don't know," I said, standing up and reaching a hand out to her. "But we'll figure it out. Together."

She gripped the quilt, as if about to pull it right back over her head. To disappear.

I couldn't blame her for wanting that.

"Why don't we get you washed up?" I offered, watching as she stared down at herself, covered in soot and blood.

She merely nodded.

I escorted her to the bathroom, keeping the quilt tucked around her. Turning the valve on the shower, I put my hands under, waiting for it to get warm before pivoting back to Kyleigh, who stood there, dazed, staring at the water as if it was the most terrifying thing in the world. I unbuttoned my pants, stepping out of them so I was just in a black tank and much too indiscreet underwear, thanks to having to borrow a pair of Sloan's until I had some clothes of my own.

Poking my head out of the bathroom, I called over Mox, figuring Sloan was still sharing sight with her familiar. "Can you bring us some more clothes?"

The snow fox padded out of the room. When I turned back around, Kyleigh was moving slow and stiff, like a wind-up doll, toward the shower. The quilt was heaped where she'd been standing, leaving her naked aside from a soot-covered heart that hung at the center of her chest. She paused just outside the rings of water pelting down, frozen in place.

Quickly, I stepped into the spray in front of her.

"I've got you," I reminded, helping her take that last step in to join me. Her eyes stared past my shoulder, glued to whatever she saw beyond the tiling. I grabbed the showerhead, holding her arm out, and began to rinse the ash off of her, the water turning murky before swirling down the drain.

The creaking of the door told me Sloan had come in. She quickly set the clean clothes in the corner of the vanity, then stripped off her tunic and trousers to help me. I handed Sloan the shampoo while Kyleigh stood like a ghost between us. Vacant and hollow. Sloan swept aside her clumped strands of soot-streaked hair as she began to lather.

Her icy eyes jolted a moment, fear bolting through our bond. She shook her head, not wanting me to say anything, but the unease didn't leave her expression. Using her head to direct me to come around next to her, I obeyed, my feet dragging through the dirty pool of water beneath us.

As she finished rinsing Kyleigh's locks, she combed through the cleaned hair with her fingers, pulling it to the side.

Clear as day sat a scar, as if a heart had been etched into her skin.

A scar that I recognized all too well.

My hand trailed to the nape of my own neck.

If Kyleigh noticed us gawking at her, she said nothing. I had a feeling she was too lost in her grief to ask. To care.

And it was probably better that way. For now.

Because I didn't know how she'd react when she learned the truth.

Not only had her mother's crown and title been passed to her...

So had her bond mark.

Epilogue

ENCHANTRESS

I rolled the parchment, holding it up to the edge of the emerald powder trailing along my forearm. Inhaling the potent dust, I wiped at my nose, enjoying the heady strength when its magic took hold. Twisting the jar shut, my mind was elsewhere as my hands worked, before handing the dust off and watching it float away.

A series of crackles came from below, the remnants of my *scáth* lifting off the ground, combining into a heap of mangled pieces that floated toward the mountains.

Pulling down the hood of his black robes, the demolier gave me a long nod, all features stripped from his face. *I've done my part.*

I nodded back to him. *Yes, you have.*

Our deal was done—at least for now. They'd come through, providing me what I needed to get here. Finally making use of the army I'd been amassing with Flynt's help all these years. I knew better than to believe that was it for our alliance. He'd be back soon enough, when they needed me.

The moon's ripples beamed down on me, and I held my

arms out to it, embracing how its light radiated on my glittering skin.

Freedom.

I thought I'd be able to indulge in this moment. To savor it. It'd taken me decades to get here, after all. Justice for my people. For *us*. Even if they'd turned him against me, twisted him to fit their narrative.

My own sapling, nourished by their toxic hands.

How had he learned the truth? I'd spent years after King Reynard had ruined our plans waiting for my wisps to bring him to me once he'd come of age. To find his magic. It'd been hidden too well, even from him.

I'd been too late.

Too late to have a life with him. Now too late to save him.

Druce.

He'd managed to crack my obsidian armor, weakening me enough to take control of the last few wisps I'd had at my disposal.

To *save* them. At what cost?

Now that he was gone, my resolve was only strengthened, and my sapling couldn't be used against me or to hinder my plans. Once I had the book back, I could re-establish my full connection to it. They were already hunting it down. It was only a matter of time until it found its way back to me, where it belonged.

A few scáth swarmed into the Great Hall, carrying the jar in. The one piece of me I'd held onto for so long. I waved them away, not wanting *that* anywhere near me.

There was much to do. I would reshape this world as I'd always planned.

I'd do it for him.

For the memories I never got to claim part of, the only keepsake, a tiny dragon dangling by a crimson cord. The first clue of many in years of puzzling and plotting to discover what'd been taken from me.

Walking inside the golden castle, I released my power, black shadows curling to replace every metallic-touched surface, washing it away as if it never existed.

The scáth kept flying in, bringing items from the cabin. Ones I'd hidden beneath the floorboards, underground, while we slowly dug our way out of the Silent Woods. They *whirred* around me, but I paid no attention to them. They weren't as intelligent or as valuable as my wisps. They brought me no power. But they'd still prove useful for now, at least until I could regain my strength.

First thing's first, though, I had a message to send.

Taking a copper talon, I sliced along my palm, smearing the blackened ichor across the charcoal stone, which scratched against my scarred obsidian armor. I clapped my hands. A jar of ruby flame, embers crackling sporadically within, floated toward me, gripped by a pair of scáth. I lifted the lid and threw in the rolled-up enchanted parchment.

Taking the pile of leaves and twigs my scáth had gathered, I scraped off the crimson remnants of the heir's blood with the tip of my claw, then swirled it along the lines of mine until it mixed together. Then I placed the jar on top and watched in awe as it slipped slowly into the stone, sucked through the tiny grains of gray sand.

Turning on my heels, I clapped my hands again, directing my scáth to continue their work. A tap on my shoulder had me spinning around to find one, mangled arms outstretched, a dusty rag in one hand and a polished crown in the other.

Hundreds of tiny diamond leaves flourished on its rim, billowing up into leaning spires, two of them twisting at its center. Five teardrop crystals set within its luster, dazzling and brilliant.

Powerful.

I walked outside, leaving my scáth to finish setting up my palace.

Moving to the ledge of the floating grounds, I looked down at Arafax, its fallen warriors dangling above them from beneath my new domain, smelling of rich earth and decay.

Many hated the smell, but I knew better.

Death signaled a new beginning.

I placed the crown atop my head, staring at the iridescent swell of the moon in front of me.

Mine.

It was only time until the rest of the realm would be as well.

The Journey Continues...

Thank you so much for reading Ascend. The fact that you've taken time to escape to Celaria means the absolute world to me.

I won't lie—writing this book was hard. While there were so many beautiful relationship moments, cool worlds to explore, and secrets to uncover, there were also a lot of painful bits.

These characters have so much healing to do and so much to overcome. I cannot wait for them to blow you away, and for you to see how the last two books unfold for *The Blaze Legacy* series.

The final two installments will release in 2024 so make sure you're signed up for my newsletter to get updates about books, giveaways, goodies, live events, and more!

If you have a moment to leave some stars and a review on Amazon & Goodreads, they are such a help for fellow readers to find indie authors and their work. Even just a few words makes a big difference!

Also by L.R. Friedman

The Blaze Legacy

Dark Portal Romantasy

Descend

Scale

Pitch: A Blaze Legacy Origin Story Novella

Ascend

Coming Soon!

Celestial Haven

Paranormal Romance series of interconnected duets and standalones set in the hidden supernatural suburbs of the Pacific Northwest.

Acknowledgments

A huge thank you to my beta and alphas for bolstering me when I needed it through all the highs and lows of bringing Ascend to the page. Angelique, Brittani, Isabel, Jennifer, Jo, Sydney, Thea, and Vanessa—you each brought such unique perspectives that were invaluable to making this story the best it could be. Thank you for reading through my words, making me smile, and being such incredible sounding boards.

To my *Initiates* who helped fuel me on the toughest of days, you will never know how much I needed it while I wrote Ascend (well maybe you do now that you've read!). You're all amazing humans and I'm honored to have you in my corner.

My parents—thank you Mom for reading my messiest words, talking all things books and characters, and for all the hours you've spent with me on this series. I'm so grateful to share it with you. And Dad, thank you for always cheering me on and for reading.

Chinah—This book couldn't have been written without your support. Thank you for always being there, making me twist the knife even when I grumble about it, and for your friendship. Your editing is top-notch, but that barely scratches the surface at how wonderful you are.

Thea—I'm so grateful that you came into my life when you did. Being your friend is a beautiful thing, and your empathy and intuition when it comes to this story and its characters is unmatched. You *see* these characters and brilliantly bring them to life in your cosplays—it's pure magic.

Sam—goodness, I honestly don't know what I would do

without you. You and your Bound By Mischief team have breathed so much belief into me and this series. I'll never be able to thank you enough for everything.

Sarah—thank you for your friendship, guidance, and beautiful words. Watching you continue to bloom has been an absolute joy and I am so grateful to know you and your heart.

Vanessa, Emmaline, Tati, & Ann—you guys continue to inspire me daily. Writing and publishing can feel like you're in a strange bubble sometimes, but I'm so grateful to walk this road with you ladies.

Thank you to my husband, Aaron, and our three incredible kiddos. I wouldn't be able to do any of this without your support and love.

And of course a huge thank you to all my readers. The fact that you take your time to read these stories and love these characters is *everything*.

About the Author

Author L.R. Friedman loves curling up with a cup of coffee while diving into fantasy and paranormal romance worlds. A Virginia native, she currently lives in Texas with her husband and three children.

When she's not writing, you'll find her enjoying tacos, dark chocolate, and the occasional glass of whiskey.

As the girl that grew up trying to find a magical realm hidden in her closet, she hopes to transport readers to beautiful, sexy, dark, and enchanted places through her stories.

For updates about upcoming releases, please visit http://www.lrfriedman.com, and sign up for her newsletter or join her group on Facebook at Books & Brews with L.R. Friedman.

Content Warnings

Explicit, on page sexual content

Graphic violence

Death

Mental health themes

Mention of child abduction

Magical Drug use & Alcohol use

Made in United States
Troutdale, OR
07/24/2023

11522088R00268